RORY

IN THE COMPANY OF SNIPERS

Book 6

IRISH WINTERS

COPYRIGHT

RORY; In the Company of Snipers, 6

Edited by Cas Peace, http://portablemagicediting.com

Cover design and author photo by Kelli Ann Morgan,
http://www.inspirecreativeservices.com

Interior book design by Bob Houston eBook Formatting

First American Paperback Edition

ISBN Paperback: 978-0-9910693-9-2
Library of Congress Control Number: 2015931440

Irish Winters can be contacted at:
http://www.irishwinters.com or http://irishwinters.blogspot.com.

In the Company of Snipers

You can find Irish Winters on Facebook:
https://www.facebook.com/author.irishwinters

On Twitter: https://twitter.com/irishwinters1

For news on upcoming releases, sign up for Irish Winters' Newsletter at IrishWinters.com.

For more information about all my books, visit IrishWinters.com.

IN THE COMPANY OF SNIPERS

This series revolves around ex-Marine scout sniper, Alex Stewart, and his covert surveillance company, The TEAM, home-based out of Alexandria, Virginia. An obsessive patriot and workaholic, he created the company to give ex-military snipers like him a chance at returning to civilian life with a decent job.

This is not a serial with each book ending at a cliffhanger. I wouldn't do that to you. *In the Company of Snipers* is a collection of passionate love stories involving women and men who are tough enough to take on the world alone. Each is a stand-alone read, where in the course of an active TEAM operation, one agent comes face to face with his or her demons. The men and women I write about are all patriots and warriors, dealing with what they've lived through or the mistakes they've made

Spoiler alert: Every novel contains adult scenes including sexual situations (some explicit), language, and violence. I don't write sweet romance, so be forewarned.

At the end of each story, it's my hope that you, along with my heroes, will come to realize...

Love changes everything.

Prologue

"One!" A little boy's cheerful voice rang out across the gym floor.

Ember watched intently from her workout on one of the gym's newest elliptical trainers. She thought the man with the boy had looked familiar, but now she was certain. There was no mistaking the Hollywood handsome guy she worked with at the best East Coast surveillance company out of Alexandria, Virginia—The TEAM.

Even sweaty and hard at work, Junior Agent Rory Dennison was eye candy. Lean muscles rippled beneath a sleeveless T-shirt while he completed crunch after crunch. He made it look simple. Smooth and easy. Steady and sure. The trademark of one of America's elite snipers.

She didn't know he had a son—if that's who the little boy was. He had to be. The resemblance was unmistakable—black hair that might be curly if it were allowed to grow longer, deep blue eyes, and the hint of a cleft in both their very masculine chins.

They had the same straight and elegant nose. Rory's jaw was more squared off, but the boy's gently arched brows were exact copies of his father's. He had the same handsome smile. He was a mini-Rory. A clone. Only a lot smaller. Never having been around kids, she guesstimated maybe five or six years of age.

"Two!" Mini-Rory couldn't seem to sit still for long. He wiggled his backside on the basketball he was sitting on and waved his hands as if shaking water off.

His father performed another sit-up as easily as his other reps, not missing a beat. Sweat glistened on his forehead, neck, and arms from the earlier sets of push-ups he'd finished. His gray T-shirt darkened in a line down his back and across his chest. And still he pumped. The boy had helped with the push-ups, too—by sitting on his father's back and counting with as much gusto.

Rory smiled through another crunch, barely grunting as he lifted upward, his arms folded over his chest. "How am I doing?"

"You doing great." Tyler beamed. "Go, Daddy, go!"

A seemingly perpetual smile tugged at the corner of Rory's lips—a most endearing sight from a man as tough and steadfast as he was. He truly seemed to be enjoying his son. *Wow. What a picture.*

"Then which crunch are we on now?"

"Six!"

"You mean eleven," Rory said, barely panting between repetitions.

The cute little guy shook his head, bounced three times on his basketball, and said very seriously, "No, I mean four."

"Okay then, four it is."

"Now is thirteen!" Tyler crowed. "I is your best counter, huh Daddy?"

"Always have been, always will be." Rory continued crunch after crunch with his son shouting random numbers in glee to urge him on.

"Eleven!" Tyler called out, but he spotted something funny. "Look. That lady gots pink in her hair."

Ember cringed. She'd been caught. She waved across the gym with a cheerful, "Hey, Rory."

He returned the wave, but his brows scowled to an unhappy V. He turned and said something quietly to Tyler.

She dismounted the trainer and checked her heart rate. A steady exercise routine made for the perfect end to the day, but it also made her sweaty, not that she usually cared about that. All the guys she worked with had seen her working out before at the onsite gym at TEAM headquarters. They knew what a mess she could be. All except Rory. He'd never used The TEAM's gym. *Interesting.*

The only reason she hadn't was the new elliptical trainers her boss, Alex Stewart, was slow to buy. He needed to be persuaded with facts and statistics, so here she was, trying out the latest equipment and fact-finding. And there was Rory— with a child who was obviously his son. *Very interesting.*

Despite his less than enthusiastic greeting, she draped her towel over the back of her neck and ambled over to chat. "Wow, it's a small world, isn't it? If I'd known you worked out here, I could've asked your opinion on these new ellipticals. I'm trying to convince Alex to upgrade some of the gym equipment. Who's this cute little guy? Your trainer?"

Tyler jumped up off his ball and wrapped both arms around Rory's thigh, proudly and loudly proclaiming, "I Tyler Den-ni-son. My number is—"

"Shh. That's enough." Rory offered an uncharacteristically tight-lipped smile that didn't even hint at reaching his eyes. "You'll have to excuse Tyler. We're learning our phone number and address. He's excited to share."

"Wow. Kids are brighter than most people give them credit for, huh?" She grinned, a thousand questions pinging in her mind for answers. Rory and she had worked together for the last year or so. Why had he kept this darling child a secret?

Rory nodded, his eyes guarded and his voice the same. "Yes, they are."

"How old is he?"

"Four."

"He speaks quite well for a little guy." She opted for small conversation.

"Yes."

"Wow." Ember couldn't think of anything else to say without coming across like a busybody. Rory seemed perturbed, his one-word answers revealing little so she didn't press. There was a time when he'd seemed friendly, when she'd almost asked him to go out for coffee or a drink after work. Somewhere in the past few months, the easygoing feeling between them had changed. She didn't know why.

He rolled his neck, ruffling his fingers through his son's hair. "Tyler, I work with this lady. Her name is Miss Davis. What do you say when you meet an adult?"

Tyler stuck out his arm for a gentleman's handshake, a big grin on his face. "I say I glad to meetcha."

Ember shook his hand, impressed with his diction. "Wow. Aren't you the polite one? It's very nice to meet you, too, Mr. Tyler Dennison. Is that your ball?"

"Uh huh," he replied, jumping out of his father's reach to scoop the basketball into both arms.

"Tyler," Rory said sternly. "How do we act in public?"

His son beamed a thousand-watt smile, dropped the ball and hugged Rory's leg again. "I did good, huh Daddy?"

"You always do." He winked down at his son, and Ember couldn't miss the bond between them. The instant Rory's eyes made contact with Tyler's, they changed from the icy cool stare he'd given her to one of genuine warmth.

She knelt at Tyler's level to take the pressure off his father. Rory needed to loosen up. "So, Mr. Tyler Dennison, do you come to the gym often?"

"Yep!" he said with gusto. "I Daddy's bestest counter. Wanna hear me? I know my twos and frees and tens."

Rory tapped the top of his son's head. "Another time. Get your ball. Let's go."

Tyler scrambled after the basketball.

"He's adorable." She stood, her hands on her hips and her eyes full of unanswered questions. "I didn't know you had a son. Where have you been hiding him?"

"It's none of your business, is it?"

She blinked, totally speechless. *Excuse me?*

Without another word, he corralled Tyler and didn't look back as they headed toward the exit. But Tyler did. Turning with a little wave before his father hurried him through the double glass doors, he shouted in a big outside voice, "Bye, Miss Davis. See ya later alligator!"

She waved at the precocious youngster. "Bye, Tyler. It was very nice to meet you. Bye, Rory. See you at work tomorrow."

He didn't even turn around.

One

A tear?

Junior Agent Rory Dennison's sixth sense jolted to life as the tear fell in slow motion, an iridescent crystal drop he couldn't stop watching—or keep from falling. It tracked over Nima Dawa's pudgy cheek, reddened from the chill of late October. The liquid pearl bounced when it hit the black velvet gathers on the four-year-old's dress, then twice more until it cleared the tucks and folds and dropped to the concrete at her feet.

Even then, he watched its impact, a soundless splash of saline that should not have caught his eye the way it did and meant absolutely nothing. Or did it?

Nima offered one short little sniff and a nod to her father, Mr. Sonam Lobsang, a Tibetan dignitary with no particular political clout or power. All he wanted was to place a wreath at the Tomb of the Unknown in Arlington National Cemetery.

In an unusual request, he'd asked the FBI to provide protection for himself on this visit to the States. But for Nima, he'd gone straight to his friend, Alex Stewart, owner of the elite covert surveillance company, The TEAM, and Rory's boss. It seemed the Tibetan dignitary did not trust the Bureau with his most dear treasure. Only with him.

Nima's lower lip puckered. Quivered. Sadness shifted over her face. For an incredible instant, all innocence was gone. She was not just a little girl dressed up for her father's special day. She appeared older. Infinitely wiser. Frighteningly un-child-like. She was—something else.

Rory's heart jumped to his throat, choking him. He shook his head, blinking hard to chase the apparition away. In that short half-second it took to do that, she transformed again. The person or entity—or whatever he'd seen, was gone. The somber child was back.

Like heck. His heart wasn't thundering for no reason at all. He'd seen something. But what?

The proper answer failed to materialize, but hyper-vigilance sure did. Fear constricted the calm right out of him. It hadn't been that long since he'd come home from the Middle East battle theater, less since he'd nearly died during a horrendously tough operation in Sonora, Mexico. His fingers turned to ice. The sickening sensation of impending doom crept up his throat, suffocating him.

Suddenly the world was not a safe place to be any longer. Danger was too near. Death, too imminent. But from where? A quick scan of the docile crowd gathered around the Arlington Amphitheater revealed no reason for the spike of adrenaline pouring into his gut. No abnormally nervous twitch amongst the onlookers disguised a hidden agenda. No darting eyes. No hands in pockets holding concealed weapons, either. No suspicious predator lurked in the midst of that flock of sheep. He would know. He'd hunted predators before.

The National Cemetery had never looked so—normal.

Or felt so—not.

Ember caught his eye, her brows furrowed as well. Leaning toward him, she whispered, "What's wrong with you?"

"Nothing. Stay sharp," he ordered out of the side of his mouth. "Keep an eye on her father, too." But something had happened. He just couldn't quantify it. Yet.

Their assignment to provide one day of escort service for the child no longer felt like a simple operation. Rory studied the crowd gathered on the white marble stairs of the Memorial Amphitheater facing the Tomb. How could there be danger here?

Mr. Lobsang was not there with a political agenda or to garner favor from the current United States administration. His request was simple. He wanted to offer a prayer for peace and to lay a wreath. The ceremony was a non-event. Both the FBI and The TEAM had certainly escorted more famous and infamous foreign diplomats.

After the inconsequential ceremony, Lobsang planned to speak to a small gathering of faithful followers at a local Buddhist temple, after which he and his daughter would return home to India on a late flight. As lead agent for the routine day, Rory planned to be home in time for dinner. He had a son and a life. Working for Alex was just a job.

So why am I on edge?

Stifling the unfounded acid build up in his gut, he watched while the joint service honor guard moved with fluid precision. Five honor guards of one Armed Service after another climbed the stairs to the white marble tomb. While the Air Force band played *The National Anthem*, the joint color guard presented all military service colors along with the American flag. Army. Navy. Marines. Coast Guard. Air Force.

Rory usually loved the sight. The red, white, and blue stirred his heart no matter where it waved—football games, Mom and Pop diners, or battlefields. It was something to be proud of. But today he couldn't wait for the show to be done, the field cleared, and his Tibetan dignitaries out of public view.

When Mr. Lobsang rose, Rory stifled the urge to escort him. He'd have been out of line. That was FBI duty, not TEAM. Two of the Bureau's finest followed Lobsang: Thomas Drake and Gilbert Sachs. Dressed in their typical black business suits, dark glasses and ear buds, they maintained a close watch across the audience.

He'd worked with Drake and Sachs before. They were thorough professionals and prone to be overly cautious, a trait he appreciated. With them on duty, dinner on time with Tyler was all but guaranteed. But the real question was, could they protect Lobsang from the unseen danger Rory sensed? Loosening his tie a notch, his hackles lifted. Instinct subsumed logic, urging him to flight or fight.

But what danger? Where might it come from? Surely not from the quiet, manicured and finely groomed Lobsang. He looked the part of any other typical businessman. Dark-skinned with a precise part to his thinning black hair, Rory noticed the man's intelligence and Western upbringing when they were introduced to each other at the airport.

Mr. Lobsang approached the honored monument to heroes unknown and bowed his head to the east, then to the west before facing the Tomb again. Reverently, he whispered into his long steepled fingers pressed against his lips. The audience stilled to hear. Rory only caught his final remark. "Bless those who guard my daughter to see farther, to hear clearly, and to know in advance from whence danger will stab at them. Shield them from my adversaries as they strive to protect my Nima."

An irksome twinge shivered up Rory's neck, ending at his still too tight shirt collar. *What adversaries? See what? Hear what?*

As if in answer to his unspoken questions, Mr. Lobsang pivoted slowly until, out of the crowd of hundreds, his eyes pinned Rory. Lobsang bowed. The crowd faded away. There were only two men in that very private dimension caught between time and space. Two fathers. No words were spoken, but Rory clearly heard the beseeching message pour into his mind: *I beg of you. Please. Save my daughter.*

Ember's sharp intake of breath from the other side of Nima Dawa caught Rory's ear. She had to have also heard, or rather felt that same shift in reality when premonition whispers imminent danger to a well-trained sniper's psyche. The national FBI Director stepped forward and asked the audience to stay in place until the dignitaries were escorted to the waiting motorcade. Again there was no indication of anything out of order. The audience was reverent and accommodating.

But Rory couldn't get his clients into the safety of the limousine and out of sight fast enough. Mr. Lobsang appeared calm, motioning for his daughter to join him. Obediently, she did, and like a dutiful little preschooler, took his hand. Dressed in the black velvet dress and patent leather Mary Janes, she'd become a child once more.

The FBI agents were swivel-necked and anxious, too. In a stifling formation of black suits and broad shoulders, they escorted the Tibetan dignitary around the back of the amphitheater to the limousine at the curb out front. Rory and Ember were as glued to the child as Drake and Sachs were to her father. If anything, there was more danger of Mr. Lobsang tripping over one of his overzealous bodyguards than anything else.

Scanning the audience one last time over the top of the limo, Rory couldn't fathom where the sensation of being watched came from. It was sniper rule number one. *If you feel like you're being watched, you probably are. Pay attention. Think. Stay sharp. Stay alive.*

The crowd had nearly all dispersed. Dress whites, dress blues, and honor guards were at ease and disassembling. Chatting. Logic whispered there was no threat, but instinct told him different. It was real. It was waiting. He slipped into the vehicle, closing the door tightly behind him.

Nima Dawa sat next to her father on the back seat. Rory sat with the FBI agents on the bench seat opposite, while Ember sat beside Nima. Again he was struck with how self-possessed the child was for her age.

With long brown hair and a pudgy build, she sat sedate and calm, gazing down at her hands serenely folded on her lap. Most children would've been petulant, spoiled, or excited. Not her. She displayed none of the typical toddler attributes Rory expected. Were all Tibetan children so docile? So disciplined? And she did not speak, another odd trait for a child her age. Tyler would've been all over the limo by now, pointing out every sight he'd never seen before. Heck. Tyler would've been jabbering a mile a minute, asking questions, but not waiting for the answers, just basically being his overexcited self. So what was up with this girl?

Her mother had died too young from a heart attack. Could that be the reason for her peculiar adult behavior?

Only when they arrived at the Buddhist Temple did another fleeting look pass between father and daughter. Again a single tear dropped from Nima's eye, glistening like a diamond as it fell to the floor. Her lower lip quivered. Mr. Lobsang gave her a tender look Rory recognized for what it was. The purest love. Rory'd seen this look before on one of the hardest days of his life. On the tarmac before he'd shipped out to Afghanistan. On the faces of his mother and father when they were afraid they might never see him alive again.

The kind Tibetan patted his daughter's hand. In the darnedest display of adult compassion, she placed her other hand over his, comforting him as if he were the child.

Rory stared, daring her to pull that mind trick one more time and turn into some kind of a shaman, or whatever it was she'd done last time, but she didn't. And yet, some silent communication had passed between father and daughter. It was as real as his mother's love that day. Anxiety spiked higher. Rolling his shoulders to push it away made no difference. His companion agent seemed affected as well. Ember's jaw was tight, her eyes sharp, intense.

The limo passed beneath an arched iron gate on its way inside the temple grounds. A three-tiered, pagoda-styled building with ground level red colonnades sat back from the street, shaded by tall oaks in brilliant reddish oranges. In front of the temple, a fifteen-foot tall white marble statue of Buddha drew everyone's attention.

A very modest crowd already waited at the entry of the temple where Mr. Lobsang's speech would be given. Rory scanned the crowd for Senior Agent David Tao. He was supposed to have been here. Given the spooky sensation creeping across Rory's shoulders, one more agent on the job certainly wouldn't hurt, but David, a devout Buddhist, was nowhere to be seen.

The limo braked to an easy stop on the circular drive. Mr. Lobsang's hand rested on his knee, his focus on his daughter when the car stopped moving. She gave another small nod. Rory watched the silent exchange, wondering what he was witnessing—and missing.

Exiting the vehicle ahead of Mr. Lobsang, Rory scanned the grounds and the crowd, searching for any sign of a threat. When nothing revealed itself, he motioned Mr. Lobsang to follow. Nima Dawa scooted off the car seat and stepped solemnly to the ground, her head held high as if she were the center of attention instead of her father. She looked—regal. There was no other word for it. The four-year-old acted as if she'd been prepared for this day all of her short life. Like she was queen.

The FBI agents flanked Lobsang. Ember followed Nima, again hovering as close as possible without picking the child up and carrying her. Rory stepped in closer than usual, the odd sensation tainting every step. His pulse quickened.

Show time.

Several monks welcomed Mr. Lobsang with bowing and soft voices. The temple grounds were definitely a place of peaceful meditation. Flowers filled the circle around the Buddha. Birds flitted across the lawn and from bush to flowerbeds. A gray squirrel bounced along the temple veranda as if it were invited to listen, too.

Senior Agent David Tao arrived. An elegant Chinese American, no one could tell he also carried a holstered revolver beneath his suit jacket, nor that he was an ex-Marine scout sniper. Five good agents ought to be able to protect one man and a little girl. Right?

Mr. Lobsang stepped to the small podium and began to speak, his words calm and assuring in the morning sun. There was no raised platform, nothing fancy at all. Nima Dawa stood with Rory and Ember to the left of Lobsang. The agents had positioned themselves between the child and the street. Drake and Sachs had done the same, both to Lobsang's immediate right.

But nothing appeared out of place here, either. If anything, these well-wishers were more reverent than the crowd at Arlington. Rory could see it on their faces. They loved this gentle Tibetan and his tiny daughter. No threat. Hyper-vigilance was becoming very annoying.

Whatever Mr. Lobsang said to his fans in Tibetan must have been humorous. The crowd chuckled, and the speech was over. Rory sighed, ready to dismiss the anxious feeling in his throat once and for all, but Mr. Lobsang waved for his daughter to join him at the podium. Rory and Ember glanced at each other.

Center stage. Not good.

The gesture put the child out of their protection and in full view of the public. Mr. Lobsang made it worse, picking Nima Dawa up like the child she was, he showed her off to the audience.

Definitely not good.

The audience bowed from their waists in one simultaneous wave of respect or adoration or whatever. Rory didn't much care. His client was center stage and vulnerable. If everyone present loved this gentle father and his daughter, then why was his gut screaming?

He moved to at least block the view from the street. Out of the corner of his eye, he saw Ember's hand reaching out to the girl.

Nima waved her hands, a happy child again. And all hell broke loose. A single shot rang out. With a soft grunt, Lobsang crumpled to the ground with Nima.

"Get the girl," Rory barked to Ember, but there was no need. Both he and Ember reached Nima at the same moment, colliding as they buried the child and her father beneath them in the ensuing chaos. The two FBI agents instantly joined the protective huddle. The crowd screamed and scattered. The monks at the temple converged on the pile of bodyguards. They circled the prone group, providing yet another wall of bodies to protect the honored guests from the assassin's bullets.

"Shit," Ember swore, somewhere within the pack of bodies beneath him. Her elbow stabbed Rory's ribs while she writhed to extricate herself. The smallest hand reached up into the light. He took hold of it. Thank God.

Nima Dawa was still alive.

Two

"Let me have her. Get out of my way."

Ember grasped the child's blood-spattered body through the closely packed males in her way. She had to get to Nima. Now.

The men eased away enough so Ember could reach her. She pulled Nima into the security of her shaky arms. The little girl appeared calm considering what had just happened. The shot seemed to have come from directly across the street. Rory crouched protectively between them and the street, his hand on Ember's thigh holding her to ground level. "Stay down."

"Are you hurt, baby?" Ember smoothed both hands over the child's arms, back, and head in one long, motherly sweep. Blood covered the side of Nima's face and her arm. Only Mr. Lobsang remained down. Ember shielded Nima from the view of her father's prostrate body. A puddle of bright red expanded onto the concrete beneath his head. Sirens screamed as D.C. Metro flooded the courtyard with cruisers, noise, and an army of armed officers.

"Get us out of here, Dennison," Ember demanded, clutching the girl to her chest.

Rory pulled them both off the ground under his arm. For one brief moment, Ember wanted to stay there, tucked into the wall of muscle and heart that stood ready to die for Nima and her. He had them inside the stone temple in no time, pressing her to the floor with his hand on her shoulder and a terse, "Sit. Stay."

She did, huddled to the floor with Nima on her lap. "Are you okay?" she asked again, still examining the child for signs of injury. Other than a scraped knee and torn tights, which she most likely received when she fell, Nima appeared uninjured. Ember expected hysterical crying, kicking, and tears. A runny nose. Anything but the unusual calm the girl exuded.

She didn't have time to worry about that now. David had joined Rory at the temple door, their weapons drawn. Ember tried to control her own shaking. The fear of losing the precious toddler to what sounded like a thirty-five millimeter rattled her to the core. Dying in the line of duty was part of the job. She'd been trained. It could happen. Hell, she'd seen it happen to the man she loved. But a baby? A sweet little girl with pudgy cheeks and stubby legs? Shot down in cold blood like her daddy had just been? The oddest sensation swept up from the soles of Ember's feet to the top of her skull. No little girl was going to die on her watch.

Nima's silence bothered her the most. Was she in shock? Had she struck her head when she'd fallen? Over the little one's head and down her neck and shoulders went Ember's probing fingers and hands again. "Tell me, baby girl. Are you hurt?"

Nima didn't answer. Ember followed the direction of her stare. The child seemed keenly interested in Rory and David at the temple entrance.

"The FBI's in transit," David said calmly. "The boss, too."

"The shooter was not in the crowd. I'm sure of it," Rory said tersely. He scanned the area beyond the temple grounds through his rangefinder. "The shot came from up above."

"Maybe from one of those buildings?" David nodded across the street. "We should've cleared them before we allowed him to speak."

"Why? He wasn't a high profile target," Rory insisted, his voice grim. "I heard one shot. You?"

"Yes. One. Given the distance, the shooter knew everyone would bow the second Nima's father presented her. The paramedics are waiting around the corner for the all-clear signal to enter the crime scene."

Rory glared over his shoulder at Ember. "She hurt?"

"No. It's her father's blood, not her's." Ember spoke in a whisper while holding her palm over Nima's ear, the girl's other ear pressed to Ember's shoulder to keep her from hearing. "But I think she's in shock or something. She's awful quiet. You guys see anything yet? Anyone?"

"Nothing."

"Who would do this? Who would—"

Rory's sardonic glare cut her short. Ember leaned against the wall behind her to steady her nerves. It had been a long time since she'd been in the middle of a battle. Even then, it had been aboard a Navy vessel and miles away from the action. A sailor didn't need to worry about incoming when the U.S. Navy lobbed Tomahawk Land Attack Missiles miles onto enemy soil.

But here in the reverent temple, her noisy heart sounded as loud and out of place as her breathing. She pressed Nima against her to comfort the child. It seemed to work the other way around. Nima's little hand patted Ember's arm while Ember patted Nima's back. For a moment, Ember calmed.

"Let's get out of here," Rory said, his hand extended to pull her up from the floor. The words were no more than out of his mouth when a louder explosion tore through the building, blasting the wall just feet from where Ember had been sitting. Shards of concrete, tile, and wood zipped through the air, transformed into shrapnel.

She yelped and rolled to her side, shielding Nima. Scooping the girl into her arms, Ember scrambled around the corner.

"Where are they?" Rory growled angrily, pointing to the twelve-story building across the street. "I'm not seeing— Wait. David. Top floor. Third window from the right. You see him?"

Ember paused to listen. The hallway to her left led into the inner room of the temple. Straight ahead, a rear exit sign beckoned. Either way would be safer than staying here.

Should I run? Without Rory?

"Sniper. Top floor. Got him. Contacting FBI to—" David's update was interrupted as another cannon shot pulverized the same front wall of the temple, hitting near Ember's previous location.

"They're probing," Rory shouted. "Where's your car?"

David tossed him the keys. "Out back. Blue Taurus. It's, umm, new."

Ember heard the consternation in her senior agent's voice, but it didn't slow Rory down. He snagged the keys in midair without apology. "Move," he ordered, grabbing Ember's elbow as he pushed her to the rear exit.

Another mortar shell blasted the front wall. Debris imploded into the inner hallway. Sheltering Nima from the cloud of flying sheetrock and dirt, she glanced behind to make sure David was safe. Rory didn't give her the chance. "Keep moving," he commanded, his hand between her shoulder blades and his jaw set.

She hesitated. There was no way to know who waited beyond the rear exit. Hell could be out there, the same assassins who had murdered Nima's father. Rory's flat palm brooked no time to second-guess his command decision, but still. What if—

"Don't you dare quit now," he growled.

The soldier within snapped to. Ember obeyed with Nima held tightly to her chest. Quitting was not on her mind. The fear of dying—maybe. Saving Nima from danger— absolutely.

"You ready?" he asked, his other hand on the exit handle.

"Yes," she answered, but her heart felt ready to climb out of her throat. One more close call like the last one and she'd turn to mush.

"I'm right behind you. Go. Now." Rory pushed her as they bolted out the exit and into the shrubbery that ran along the temple fence. A third blast hit the front of the building. She cringed, biting her lip hard enough to make it bleed. Together, they bee-lined through the brush to the parking lot beyond. A chain link fence hidden within the shrubbery blocked them momentarily, but Rory scrambled over it in no time at all. Once on the other side, he snapped enough branches to clear a large enough place for them both to stand.

"Come on over," he muttered, his eyes on the temple grounds behind her. "I'll catch you."

"Don't catch me." Ember handed Nima over the fence. "Catch her."

He tucked the girl into his side. "I've got her. You next."

Ember barely made it over the fence when another blast sounded around front. She fell to her hands and knees. Both breathing hard, they crouched as return gunfire finally sounded. Half of her wanted to run, the other half to scream.

"Damn," she muttered. "They're blowing the temple apart."

"Keep moving." Rory passed the child back to Ember, pointing out David's shiny new car. "You ready to make a break for it?"

"Yes, but the minute you hit the remote unlock, we're made."

"Nothing I can do about that," he muttered. "Get in. Stay out of sight. Keep her on the floorboards. Got it?"

"Got it," she answered, thankful he was with her on this disastrous op. What if she'd been alone? Yes, she was a trained sniper, but this was real world. Rory's world. He was the one renowned for record-breaking long shots. He was the sniper who'd taken out terrorists and insurgents in the Corps. Not her.

She cringed. *God, what was Alex thinking to send me out in the field like this?*

Rory's fingers dug into her bicep as he pulled them both to their feet. "Go. Run!"

David's car unlocked without a sound. Ember all but threw Nima to the floor and scrambled in to cover her. Rory slammed the back door and jumped behind the wheel. The second he turned the ignition over the car lurched forward. Tires squealed.

Ember steadied herself on elbows and knees over the child. Horns honked. The vehicle rocked from side to side, tires squealing again, while Rory drove like a madman from the parking lot. That alone might get some unwanted attention, but they were moving swiftly and surely away from danger. She closed her eyes and pressed her forehead to the floor, her fingers in Nima's hair.

"How you two doing back there?" he asked after a few more sharp turns, his voice serious but calm.

"Just loving the new car smell," she answered as casually as her full-blown anxiety would allow.

"Crossing the Fourteenth Street Bridge."

"Anyone following?" Ember peeked out the rear window.

"Haven't seen anyone yet."

"Wow." She let out a big sigh as she straightened.

Dark blue eyes pierced hers in the rearview mirror. "Yeah. Wow."

Pulling Nima off the floor, she snuggled the child beside her and fastened both of their seat belts. "What just happened? I kept having this creepy feeling, and hell, the next minute, shit was raining down on us like—"

His frown in the mirror cut her off. "Watch your mouth. She's only four."

"Oh. Sorry." It had been a long time since she'd been so close to dying. "You're right. I guess it's just my, umm, my..."

"Terror?" he offered blandly when she couldn't come up with a better word.

"Terror's a good word," she mumbled. "Sorry, baby girl. I'll try not to swear anymore." But that was the least of the child's problems. Her only living parent was dead. His smeared blood congealed on her clothing, some splattered on her arms and hands. Even her face.

"How is she?"

"She's, umm, real quiet." Ember tipped the girl's chin up to get a better look at her. Overall, Nima was unhurt, not shaking, not even a little bit. "How can you be calm when I'm—"

She blinked, startled at who stared back. Nima was the daughter of Tibetan exiles; both dark-skinned, dark-haired, and brown-eyed. Not Nima. The palest cornflower blue eyes drank Ember in. Perfect gold flecks ringed the black pupils like the spokes of an open umbrella, pulling her into another dimension of time and space. Nima patted Ember's cheek as if she were there to offer comfort instead of the other way around.

"She, umm... Wow, she's umm...." Ember couldn't form a coherent thought for her agent in charge. *Why didn't I notice this kid's eye color before?*

More startling was the wave of serenity washing through Ember. Her erratic breathing calmed. A normal sinus rhythm replaced her adrenaline-stoked heartbeat. The most peaceful sensation blanketed the panic of combat, numbing it into oblivion. She could have sworn she smelled the salty ocean air. Damp sand and seaweed. No hint of adrenaline lingered. No hand tremors. Only safety and quiet. And peace.

"Well? Is she okay or not?" Rory snapped from the front seat.

Ember smiled into the child's serene face. Nothing else mattered but the connection between her and Nima, not even Rory's wrath. "She's definitely good."

Before he could ask anything else, her cell phone vibrated on her belt holster. She checked the caller ID. "Yes, Alex."

"Where the hell are you?" he asked curtly.

"Just crossed the Fourteenth Street Bridge." She flipped the phone on speaker. "Coming to you in twenty if traffic holds."

"Negative," Alex ordered. "We've got trouble at TEAM headquarters. Murphy and Roy located several pipe bombs outside our building, one in the lobby. FBI called to warn us after they received a bomb threat. They're under attack. I'm with David at the temple. FBI SWAT is sweeping the immediate area to apprehend the assailants. Do not proceed to Alexandria. Turn around and get Nima Dawa to the safe house up in Maryland. Stay put."

"Why? What else is going on?" Rory asked.

"Something the sonofabitchin' FBI neglected to inform me." Alex's nasty tone filled the car. Everyone on The TEAM knew he detested working with the Federal Bureau of Investigation and with good reason. Too many times their bureaucracy had cost lives. "The ass—"

Rory cut Alex off before he could hurl another foul word through the air. "Boss. We've got a four-year-old in the car with us and—"

"Of course you do," Alex shot back. "Where the hell else would she—"

"And she doesn't need to learn any new words," Rory countered as quickly.

Ember very nearly grinned despite their predicament. Rory had just stood up to Alex, and he'd backed off. Wow. That didn't happen very often.

Alex paused. He exhaled one deep breath through the phone before his voice came back more controlled. "Point well taken. That little girl must be protected at all cost. According to the FBI, her safety is of paramount importance to Tibetans throughout the world."

Rory shrugged. He seemed to know how to get around Alex. *Interesting.* "All children are important. What's really going on?"

"All we know is we are to keep her hidden and safe, especially now that her father's been murdered. Mother is investigating."

"Tell her to be careful," Ember added. "She'll get caught one of these days if she keeps it up."

Mother's real name was Sasha Kennedy, but it should have been more along the lines of Master Hacker, Mistress Mayhem, or something similar. Everyone suspected her investigations included some serious hacking. She'd bent the law plenty in the past. Never confirmed, but always suspected.

"Call the minute you touch down." Alex returned to his usual abrupt and ornery self.

"Will do." Ember signed off. "Wow."

She caught Rory's spiked brow in the rearview mirror when he turned onto the George Washington Memorial Parkway and headed west along the south bank of the Potomac. The pleasant scenery outside their car windows did nothing to alleviate her nerves or the precariousness of their predicament. Only when she had her hands on Nima did she feel relief.

Rory carried his stress in his neck, the cords still tight from jaw to collarbone. Even the back view of his broad shoulders seemed harder than usual. He was still on high alert.

"Are you going to be all right?"

"Why?" he answered, his eyes on the road behind them.

"You don't usually handle overnight assignments, but now, you're kind of, umm, on one." Ember didn't look in the rearview mirror when she answered. He'd know what she meant. *Why don't you handle overnight assignments or overseas ops like everyone else?*

The interior of David's family sedan chilled. There was the Dennison wall again. Since she'd spotted him in the gym with Tyler, he'd erected quite the barrier between them.

"I'm fine," he replied icily. "Don't worry about me."

She turned to the scenery flying by. Rory was by far the handsomest man in the office. Tall and athletic, he had a definite knack for leadership, although he never stepped up to more than the role of humble advisor and obedient agent. From Nebraska, he was probably a farmer's son. Deeply patriotic and a topnotch marksman, Alex seemed to rely on him from the get-go, but didn't utilize him for the most difficult operations. *Interesting.*

There was a time when Alex intimidated Rory. Alex had an uncanny skill for demonstrating exactly who was alpha dog on The TEAM by ignoring the men who hadn't proved themselves yet. Being hired was one hurdle; proving yourself another. Yet Rory had gotten closer to the boss than most other agents and in a shorter amount of time.

One more thing—Ember was sure he didn't care for her, although he might have at one time. Whereas most agents came to her and Mother for assistance with their computer-related research, he tended to work on his own. About the only thing he needed them for was ordering new equipment or office supplies.

She hugged Nima tighter, not able to remember when the Dennison walls went up. Was it after he'd gotten shot in Mexico? Had the wall always been there and she'd not noticed because she was immersed in her own problems? She couldn't pinpoint a precise time, which only validated she didn't know much about him.

Mother would have read and shared his complete personnel file by now and asked enough prying questions to fill in the blanks. Since she hadn't, his file must be as lacking in personal information as the man himself. Was Rory simply a master at hiding in plain sight? Like a good sniper?

"Have you been to this safe house before?" she asked to get her mind back on task. They'd barely passed the exit for Turkey Run State Park. The bridge over the Potomac to Maryland was coming up fast.

"Nope. Why? Is that important?"

"I was just wondering if there will be food once we get there."

"Don't worry. I'll stop for groceries once we cross the river. The turn for I-495's coming up fast. Why? You hungry, Agent Davis?" The way he asked made it sound like she only cared about feeding her face.

"No." She stared back at him. "Just wondering if there'll be anything Nima likes to eat, Agent Dennison. She's not an American. She might be used to different foods than us. That's all."

He pulled the dark glasses from his inside jacket pocket and slid them over his nose. Ember sighed. There. He'd done it again. The Dennison walls were up again. She was locked out.

The rest of the drive went by uneventfully, even the quick stop for a few groceries. When he pulled into the winding driveway of a residential home, she cringed. A simple tract home built in the middle of a stand of pines in Carderock Springs, Maryland? That was Alex's idea of a safe house? Wow. She'd pictured barred windows and a steel front door with keyless entry, maybe even a retinal scanner for good measure. Instead, the brick home looked plain. Ordinary. Hardly safe at all.

The shooting back at the temple was still fresh in her mind. A wall around the house would've been nice; a moat with alligators better. Nima must have felt safe enough, though. She sagged against Ember in a warm hug, sound asleep from the excitement of the day and the drive. Ember cradled the child in her arms when Rory turned the ignition off and glanced over the front seat.

"You want me to take her?" he offered quietly.

"No." Ember scooted across the seat and opened her door. "I've got her." But when she attempted to get on her feet, she couldn't get out of David's family car. Rory came to her rescue, easily scooping Nima into his arms while he pulled Ember to her feet.

"Thanks," she said softly. "This baby's heavier than I expected."

"She's not a baby," he corrected her. "She's a little girl."

"She looks like a baby to me."

Without another word, he ushered Ember up the narrow concrete walk to the back door, his hand firmly at the small of her back. A metal mailbox beside the doorjamb unlatched upward to reveal a keyless entry pad.

Okay. This house has a security system. I feel a little safer. Rory's hand doesn't hurt, either.

He entered a five-digit code, and together they stepped inside. The double-paned kitchen windows were framed with the telltale strips of aluminum conductive foil.

Good. That will detect any attempt at forced entry. It will give us advance notice. We'll be okay. I'm feeling better now.

When they proceeded to the front room, Rory pressed his fingers to another keypad next to the only closet door in the hallway. Ember relaxed even more. What seemed to be an ordinary hollow-core door was actually a heavy steel door to a more than adequate gun safe complete with extra ammunition of various calibers, holstered sidearms, and a rack of rifles and shotguns. The deceptively lax appearance of the home was just that. Deceptive. *Whew.*

"Make yourself familiar with everything in the safe the first chance you get," he ordered.

"Yes, sir," she replied automatically. Her answer elicited a sharp look from him, which forced her to correct herself. "Umm, sure. Will do," she whispered, not sure how he wanted to be addressed. Some ex-military guys were jerks about rank. Maybe he was, too.

Rory took three steps into the small living room and laid the sleeping child on the couch. Nima didn't stir in the slightest when he covered her with the burgundy flowered throw that had draped the couch. He stood over the child for a moment, tenderly tracing the back of his finger along her pudgy, pink cheek. The tenderest expression shifted across his face.

Wow. One minute cranky, the next gentle. He was a hard guy to figure.

Ember turned away, not wanting to be caught watching. "I, umm, I'm going to check the place out," she declared to the hallway so he'd never know she'd observed his private moment.

When he didn't answer, she gave herself a quick solo tour. The kitchen emptied into the hallway and from there into the living room. The hall led to two bedrooms facing each other at the far end of the house, a bathroom in between. Windows in both bedrooms were barred and locked from the inside with an easy to release metal latch. There was no window in the bathroom, but the panel over the counter led Ember to suspect there might be an emergency exit through the attic.

She double-checked the linen closet next to the glassed-in shower. Sure enough, it was not what it appeared to be, either. Another steel door led into a vault, a safe room, complete with an amply stocked pantry, satellite phone, emergency first-aid, and other essentials for surviving a hostile takeover. Her apprehension evaporated. Nima would definitely be safe here.

She wandered back to the kitchen. Someone had carefully stocked it with all the culinary tools a real cook might need. *Good thing I'm not a real cook.*

Rory walked past her on his way out the back door. "Wait here with Nima. I'll get the groceries."

Within a minute, he was back with the two paper bags of whatever he'd bought. Ember left him to his work. He seemed preoccupied, so once more she walked the rooms of the little house. Other security measures were now obvious.

Motion sensor floodlights hung from the eaves over each window, and, now that she had time to examine the windows, she was sure the extra thick panes were bulletproof. Sturdy dead bolts secured both front and back doors.

Besides, she and Rory were well-armed and very capable snipers. She herself carried a Glock 27, and Rory his trusty SIG Sauer P290, a small but deadly .9mm. It didn't hurt he held The TEAM's sharpshooter record at the moment. It seemed to bounce back and forth between him and Connor Maher.

She rolled the last knot of stress out of her neck. Back at the kitchen door, Rory had his back to her and his cell phone to his ear. He stood at the rear window looking out, his voice low and guarded. She didn't mean to eavesdrop.

"I'll let you know when the operation is done, and again, Mrs. Godfrey, I'm sorry I couldn't tell you sooner. It was supposed to be a one-day assignment." He stilled as he listened. "Give him a hug for me when he wakes up. Yes, ma'am, I will. Thanks. I'll be in touch."

Ember turned into the front room before Rory noticed her indiscretion. The man perplexed her. Why would anyone feel the need to hide the fact they had a child? Why did he not share that incredibly great side of himself, that he was a father and a good one if the light in Tyler's eyes was any indication?

Her reality intruded. Rory was a different kind of man than what she'd grown up with. She took a seat near Nima where she could remain in shadow while she watched her agent in charge busy at the kitchen sink. Even preoccupied with domestic duties like he was, Rory was a study in masculinity. Or maybe it was because of the efficient way he moved, as if the kitchen were familiar territory. As if he'd fixed dinner a million times before.

The oddest sensation prickled her insides. What was it about a man in the kitchen that turned on every single one of her female receptors? Was it the way he washed his hands thoroughly and dried them on the towel tucked at his waist? Even the way he curled his fingernails in his left hand to meet the blade in his right while he chopped cabbage looked like he knew what he was doing.

The man was efficient and skilled. That alone spoke volumes. Not once had he hesitated, expecting her to turn all domestic or something equally un-Ember-like just because they needed to eat. That would have been a long wait. He looked at ease in the kitchen. Competent. And he'd bought bean sprouts. Onions. Real food instead of take-out. *Wow.*

But he also seemed like a closed book. There had to have been a Mrs. Dennison in his past. Why had no one at the office ever met his significant other? Was she ill? Crazy? Dead? The notion he might have buried a young wife sent a shiver across Ember's shoulders.

Or—he might be gay. Her eyes swept over him from head to toe. There was an understated elegance to his kind of handsome, more Pierce Brosnan in a tux than Hugh Jackman as *Wolverine*; not that Mr. Brosnan was inclined toward his own gender. But still. It was a definite possibility with Rory. He was, after all, pretty darned gorgeous.

Her tongue slid over her bottom lip. *Hmm. Rory in a tux. Killer. Lover. Ready to take on the world. Shaken not stirred. He's that kind of deadly. Dangerously beautiful. Seductive. Panty-combusting sexy.*

She shook the ridiculous notion out of her head, leaned back into the shadows and let the stress of the day go, her wild imaginations with it.

Let him keep his secrets. She certainly had hers.

Three

Time to eat.

Rory pulled out a large saucepan and filled it with water. In no time at all, he had rice noodles boiling, vegetables sliced and cabbage chopped for dinner. Tossing a cup full of slivered almonds into a sauté pan, he let them toast while he mixed a simple rice-vinegar dressing.

Most of the plates and dinnerware had been left in the dishwasher from the last time the safe house was used. Removing just what he intended to use, he set the table and took two plastic bottles of water from the refrigerator. When everything was ready, he went to find Ember. She hadn't been back to the kitchen since he'd started dinner, but he didn't expect to find her sitting upright with Nima. Sound asleep.

He nudged her shoulder. "Hey. Are you hungry?"

She came awake instantly and jumped up off the couch, shaking her head.

"Damn. I'm sorry." Brushing one hand through her hair, she blinked herself awake. Soft, blonde layers fell around her flushed and embarrassed face. Even in the darkened room, a blush blossomed up her neck and over her cheeks.

Those green eyes of hers, all dreamy and full of sleep, caught his attention. An arc of energy sizzled between them, knotting his gut as tight as a bowstring. Or maybe it wasn't his gut....

"I didn't mean to fall asleep with her. Honest. I'm sorry," she murmured. "It's just that, umm—"

"Don't worry about it," he whispered, not willing to believe what he'd glimpsed in his annoying sidekick. He had to be wrong. There was no way Ember could look like—her. Maybe he was better off when she'd worn all those piercings and dyed her hair black. When she looked like a freak.

Ember still shook her head, trying to clear the sleep. With her hand at the back of her neck and stretching like she was, all those adorable little girl qualities were too close to the surface. The qualified weapons expert was gone. She scrunched her nose, her eyes soft and sleepy in the pale evening light. *Green eyes, huh. Just like.... No. Not like hers. Not. Never. No.*

He turned toward the kitchen, ignoring the stupid direction his mind had taken. His automatic pilot seemed to have malfunctioned, sending him on another wild goose chase. He adjusted course. "Dinner's ready. Are you hungry?"

Ember stood unmoving at Nima's side. The little girl was out for the count and snoring softly into her clenched fist. "Do you think she wears diapers?"

With a glance over his shoulder, Rory focused on his number one responsibility, and it wasn't Ember. "I doubt it. She's four. I don't know how they handle potty training in northern India or Tibet, but she's old enough to tell us when she has to go."

"I don't want her to, you know, get embarrassed if she... if she...." Ember seemed tongue-tied.

"If she has an accident?" Rory supplied the proper toddler jargon his companion had valiantly failed to come up with. "Let's eat. She'll wake up when she's ready."

"But she's been asleep for so long."

"Probably jetlag. Trust me. She'll be fine."

"Wow," Ember whispered when she saw the table ready with dinner. "You cook?"

"And I do windows." He aimed for sincerity but ended with sarcasm. Ember had a way of making the simplest thing seem like a big deal. Her overuse of the word 'wow' annoyed him more than most days.

Mental note to self: cut the poor-me act. She's smart enough to put two and two together, and you don't need the BS.

Pulling a chair out for Ember, he seated her before he settled into his. He'd already moved the table where they could keep an eye on Nima while they ate. All the lights in the home were off except for the dim light from the range hood. Dishing a plateful of Chinese chicken salad for Ember, he handed her the oriental dressing he'd made to go along with the main course.

The salad was one thing he could always count on Tyler to eat. It was easy, healthy, and a surefire way to get vegetables into his spunky son without a battle. The already hot, rotisserie chicken from the grocer's deli-counter made the decision easy. When pressed for time, something quick and filling was the only way to go. Besides, Tyler loved the noodles.

"There's carrot sticks and cucumber slices if you want any." He pointed out the relish tray and dished himself a helping of salad.

"Wow," Ember said again, her mouth full of food. "It's good."

Well, of course it's good. Do you think I feed my son garbage? "It will do."

Before she took another bite, Ember complimented him again. "No, I mean it. It's delicious. Where'd you learn to cook?"

Rory sighed, his dismay clear. The answer was obvious. She'd seen him with Tyler, but still she insisted on asking why he had domestic skills. How dumb was she? He paused, his fork of salad halfway to his mouth. "Where do you think?" Again he hoped his tone didn't sound as sharp to her as it did to him.

She stopped chewing, her voice subdued. "Geez, I'm sorry already."

Great. Now I've hurt her feelings. Hoping to divert her attention, he glanced past Ember to the sleeping child on the couch. "She's had a rough day. Poor little thing."

"Wow, has she ever. I wonder what she'll do when she wakes up."

And that was the last straw. Enough with the dumb blonde routine. "She'll be afraid. What do you think?"

Ember dropped her fork. "What is the problem with you? I can't open my mouth without you jumping down my throat."

"Think about it, Davis. You saw me at the gym with Tyler. You know darned well where I learned to cook. And how's a kid supposed to feel after she's seen her father gunned down?" he hissed. "Why don't you think before you open your big mouth once in awhile?"

His words stung; he could tell. Her face blanched white. She certainly hadn't expected a tirade from a colleague. Rory shook his head and focused on his food. Anger at his own big mouth filled him. As good as the meal was a minute ago, it tasted more like cardboard now. Darn. Sometimes he put his foot in it, right up to his knee. And why? Ember was just asking questions. God help him the day the entire team found out he had a son, which would no doubt happen the minute Ember opened her big mouth back at the office, if she hadn't already. He couldn't win.

"Listen." He pursed his lips and did what he did best. Staring at his plate, he apologized to get her off his back. "That was uncalled for. I shouldn't have talked to you like that. I'm sorry."

"You call that an apology? You say all the right words, but you don't even look at me when you do it?"

So Rory looked at her. Extra dark green shimmered back at him. The flush rising up her neck and blossoming over her cheeks made her a surprising force to be reckoned with. Or maybe it was the fire in her eyes. His breath hitched. He'd never seen her angry before. Or this beautiful. His whole damned body tingled. This kind of attraction had to stop.

"I said I'm sorry. Don't make a big deal out of it."

"First of all." She leaned closer, her voice low. "I'm not the one making a big deal. You opened that door, buddy. So what if I saw you and Tyler at the gym? What's so bad about admitting you have a son? He's a great—"

"Drop it, Davis. You're the last person I'm discussing him with." Rory returned to his salad, the conversation ended. He hoped.

She ignored the barb and speared a slice of cucumber with her fork. "I don't get it." She nibbled the crunchy vegetable and waited for him to ask.

Fine. Let's get it out in the open and done with. "Spit it out. What don't you get?"

Setting her fork on her plate, she rested her chin on interlocked fingers that culminated in trimmed fingernails instead of the thick artificial ones Mother fussed with. Ember's hands were delicate, slender and clean in comparison. Feminine. In their way, they quietly proclaimed they served an elegant woman. They didn't fit with her usual bizarre office attire. It irritated him he'd never noticed this detail before. On her Goth days, she should paint them black. Red on her clown days, and for those rare Marilyn Monroe days....

Gah! His brain hopped, skipped, and jumped over those days when it was all he could do to NOT look at her every chance he could. No sense going there.

Dang. I forgot the almonds. Leaning back on his chair to retrieve the small fry pan he'd left cooling on the wooden chopping block, he muttered, "Here. Throw some of these on your salad. They'll add a nice crunch."

"See what I mean?" She grinned. "You've made a very nice dinner. It's healthy, it's crunchy, and it's—"

"It's food. Eat." Rory concentrated on drizzling dressing over his salad. Those darn emerald greens were studying him like he hadn't been studied in a long time. Ember had sneaked inside his radar. Her next words seemed extra soft, but he could feel those probing lasers.

"It's like you have a veil of secrecy around you, like you're this mystery man no one at work really knows."

He shot her a quick look of annoyance hoping to distract her, but her face lit with mischief. He knew better. There was nothing mysterious about him, just private. She needed to back off.

"I do, huh," he said while avoiding her stare. Thankfully, her mouth was full of food again. "What do you think they were using back there? Fifty cals? Armor piercing?" he asked, trying to distract her. "Cop killers?"

She scrunched her nose and took a sip of water before she answered. "Oh no, you don't. I know what you're doing. You think you can change the subject like you do back at the office, and I'll forget what we're talking about."

"I just think you have an opinion about what happened back there, and I'd like to hear it. You are the weapons proficiency expert, aren't you?"

"And you're a father, only no one on The TEAM knows about Tyler, do they?" she countered.

"I'm sure you'll take care of that, won't you?" Sarcasm dripped off his lips.

She blinked at that hard truth, digesting what he had and hadn't said. Her lips formed a perfect O. "Now I get it. You think I told everyone I saw you with Tyler at the gym, don't you? You think I talked about you behind your back."

"Let it go, Davis. Drop it. I don't want to discuss—"

"For your information, I didn't say a word." She aimed the tines of her fork at him. "But I'm right. You don't want anyone to know about Tyler, do you?"

"Like you and Mother don't sit up there with your heads together and rake everyone over the coals every day? I've already caught her going through my personnel files. My son is off limits, do you hear me?" He looked past her to the sleeping child on the couch. He hadn't intended to raise his voice. Thankfully, Nima didn't stir.

Ember's gentle hand on his wrist caught him unprepared. "Geez, Rory. Trust me. I didn't tell Mother I saw you. I knew you didn't want anyone to know. I don't get it, but it's not my story to tell. And you're right. I know how she is. She's a busybody. Alex had a talk with her about the absolute confidentiality of personnel files."

Rory jerked away, trying to decide if he could believe her. Women could be so damned deceitful and men could be so damned blind. And dumb. It all came down to blood supply. All a good-looking woman had to do was bat her baby greens, blow a kiss, and a guy turned into a blithering idiot. Like he had. Five years ago.

"Since you made dinner, I'll do dishes," she said quietly.

He set his plate and fork in the sink with the pans already soaking there. "I need to call Alex. Can you stay awake long enough to watch our little girl out there?"

"Go. Call Alex. I'm sure he's waiting to hear from you."

Rory brushed his hand through his hair, frustrated with himself as much as her. The last thing he needed was someone like Ember in his life. She was the key investigative techie on The TEAM and hands down the best in D.C., zany but analytical in her own bizarre way.

Rory recognized her genius, and that's what concerned him. She'd start asking questions, and he didn't need a couple of busybodies interfering with his son. Ever. Tyler had already dealt with enough drama and trauma in his short life.

Retreating to one of the back bedrooms, Rory closed the door behind him and dialed his boss's office number.

Leave it to Alex to be working late. "Stewart."

"Hey, Boss." Rory sat at the edge of the bed, his cell phone to his ear. "We're secure for the night."

"How is she?"

"She's fine. She's been asleep since we got here. Must be because of the time change. What did Mother find out?"

Alex sighed. "Nima Dawa is more than special. Do you know who the Dalai Lama is?"

"Yes. He's the spiritual leader of the Tibetan people. So?"

"His name is Tenzin Gyatso. He's the fourteenth Dalai Lama. Some of his followers believe the little girl you're protecting is his successor."

"She's only four, Boss. That's kind of young, don't you think?"

"Another reason she needs our protection. Every newspaper in the country is running her story. Her picture is everywhere. Keep her undercover and out of sight."

"Those guys at the temple weren't trying to kill her father then, were they?"

"No. Lobsang was nothing but collateral damage."

Rory blew out a sigh. "Wow." *Darn. I sound like Ember.* "Who killed him?"

"Not positive. FBI intel points to a radical group out of China called the Yushu Sangha. They're vehemently against the notion of a female Dalai Lama. Interpol suspects they're behind her mother's early death, but they have no concrete evidence."

"China took over Tibet in what, the 1950s?" Rory asked.

"Yes, 1951 to be exact. The current Dalai Lama's government was formally abolished in '59. He's been living in exile since."

"But would a group out of China really assassinate a little girl?"

"You bet. They're hell bent on their ideals. You know the type. The world's full of 'em. I'll let you know what David finds out."

"He's still at the temple?"

Alex chuckled. "You know how he is."

Rory had to smile. David was a devout Buddhist. No doubt he'd chat well into the night with the monks if he could.

"Do you need me to contact your Mrs. Godfrey and tell her what's happened?" Alex asked quietly.

"Already did. Thanks, though."

"Hopefully, we can find the people behind this before Tyler's bedtime tomorrow."

"It's okay, Boss. Mrs. Godfrey will stay with him until I get back. She knows the drill. Just glad I can help."

"How's Ember?"

"Umm, she's fine, I guess. Why?"

"Just wondering how she handled her first assignment under fire. It's been awhile since she's been on the front line, much less in the middle of a warzone."

"She did good, Boss. She was right on the ball. Yeah, she did real good." Rory had to admit. She might be irritating, but she had done well under pressure.

"Okay, then. Sit tight. I'll be in touch."

"Will do." Rory hung up, still thinking how well Ember had responded during the shootout. She'd taken orders without the slightest hesitation. The memory of her climbing over the fence in the middle of all those bushes made him smile. A woman straddling a fence was always worth watching, but especially one with her build and curves. She was no tiny little thing. Ember had a body a man could appreciate, and for all her weird hairdos and ridiculous get-ups, she was tougher than he'd expected. Agile, too.

All those very proper buttons on her white shirt tightened across her bosom, but when she dropped to her knees, well, heck. He could see right down her shirt. It wasn't silicone jiggling in those triple C pure white cups with light rose-colored trim, a dark mauve rosebud stuck between. Despite the danger they were in, his all-male brain demanded a peek at her nipples. They'd be mauve, too, peaked and pebbled like that rosebud. Had to be. No doubt about it.

Why the heck am I thinking about her nipples? He stowed his phone and went back to the kitchen. Everything had been wiped clean, the dishes washed, and Ember knelt at the open gun safe in the hall, stuffing a backpack. He peered over her shoulder. "What's up?"

She went on with her packing without looking up. "I found some stuff we'll need. Burn phones. Extra mags that fit your pistol and mine. Things like that."

"Good. Bring 'em. Is there another spare backpack in there?"

Ember replied by handing a bag over her shoulder.

"Thanks." He went back to the kitchen and loaded it with necessities before he returned to the hallway. Ember was still on her knees, her head and arms inside the closet. He paused to take in the very attractive curve of her derrière. Dress slacks on a woman, especially one bent over and preoccupied like she was, were always worth looking at. He cocked his head for a better view.

The good thing about her was she was all woman; not the skin and bones version Hollywood portrayed as desirable. The bad thing about Ember was—she was all woman.

Her backside swelled to a nice round bubble, gorgeously balancing her full breasts. Coming or going, she was a sight to behold. His hands filled with the need to reach out and touch. When she pushed back a strand of tangled blonde that had escaped her clip, desire he'd not expected hit his groin—hard. He jerked his eyes away from her. Dessert. Ember was flaming, sexed-up dessert, and he'd been starving for a long time.

He coughed politely to announce his presence, needing to clear out before things got any—harder. "I'm going out to the car. Be right back." *And then I need a cold shower.*

She didn't look up. "Whatever."

Slipping out the back door, he entered the quiet night of an upscale residential neighborhood in Maryland, where homes stood on one-acre plots and most people probably never knew their neighbors. Nothing stirred. He stood at the back door surveying the quiet yard before he took one step toward the car. Night came early in late October. And cold. The chill in the air tonight spelled frost on the pumpkins in the morning. The windshields, too.

David's Taurus was parked where he'd left it. He didn't want to store it in the heated two-car garage connected to the house. Yes, it housed another arms cache and a steel-reinforced safe room, but it took time to get from point A, the house, to point B, the garage. If things turned bad, he opted for a fast getaway instead of retreating to another bunker. Sitting around and waiting to be rescued was never a good option. Bad could always get worse.

He disengaged the interior dome lights and the door alarm of David's sedan, then stowed the full backpack directly behind the passenger seat within easy reach. After one more trip back inside for a blanket and pillow, he breathed easier. Draping a bath towel over the windshield to keep the frost at bay, he glanced over his shoulder at the house. Ember better be up off her knees by now.

Rory ventured inside, locking the back door securely behind him. She was still on the floor, but cross-legged and turned toward him. He gulped and kept his eyes on her face. Not her crotch. Darn. The girl had no inhibitions.

"We'll need to stock the car with a couple more weapons and plenty of ammo," he whispered. "Bring the sawed-off for sure. We can't be too prepared."

"Already did. I was just straightening up." She rolled to her knees and stood, nodding at the softly snoring child on the couch. "That fancy dress she's wearing is still covered in blood. I didn't want to disturb her, so I left her in it for now, but we need to buy new clothes the first chance we get."

"Good idea," he agreed. "For us, too."

Ember pulled at her slacks. "I hate this outfit. I look like a man."

He smiled at her innocent comment. He and she might dress like FBI agents—starched, stuffy, and extremely institutionalized. That alone was very un-Ember-like, but there was no way she looked like a man. It didn't matter what she wore, she made it look good. Darn good. Voluptuous and well-endowed, she was the gold standard for her gender, even if she camouflaged it behind Goth, hippie, and weird getups.

"You're definitely not a man." His big mouth answered before his brain could throw up a filter.

She grunted indifferently and walked down the hall to the bathroom. "Whatever."

Four

I need a shower.

Ember went into the bathroom to wash her face. She deliberated one second before turning on the shower as to whether she should let Rory know her plans or not, but he'd been such an ass. Let him figure it out.

In a second, she'd stripped out of her ugly menswear and folded it neatly on the counter. The hot water soothed the knots out of her neck and shoulders. She let it run over her head and face while the body wash swept the cares of the world down the drain. Coconut and honey, it filled her nose with calm and clean. The shampoo was as fragrant and soothing. Wow. She should've done this earlier.

Today had definitely overwhelmed her. As if the shootout at the Buddhist temple wasn't enough, she found herself stuck in the middle of nowhere with a man who didn't trust her, and a child with spooky, blue eyes. Despite the hot shower, she shivered. There was definitely something unusual about Nima, but not in a bad way. Simply thinking about her brought an otherworldly calmness into the bathroom. How did a sleeping child do that?

After a long, luxurious moment without stress, Ember stepped out of the shower a new woman and toweled herself dry. The hair drier purred in her hand while she finger-combed her long, layered tresses. When this operation was over, all those colorless locks were turning red. Yes, a pleasant raspberry red would definitely erase this disastrous operation from memory. Taking one last look at herself in the mirror, she liked what she saw. Refreshed and energized, she could handle anything, even what's-his-name.

Ugh. Easing back into her work clothes spoiled the upbeat mood. Day old underwear—Ewww. There had to be a decent boutique in the neighborhood. She needed to shop. Dampening a washcloth with warm water, she folded it into quarters, planning to wipe the blood off that sleeping baby's face, arms, and hands. Maybe the dress, too.

All the lights in the house were turned off when she opened the door. She stood stock still, letting her eyes adjust to the absence of light, her instincts on high alert. Where the hell was Rory? Why did he—

"I'm over here by the couch," he whispered, instantly diffusing her panic.

She didn't answer until she could make out his dark shape sitting on the floor in front of the couch. "Which bedroom do you want?" she asked hoarsely, not wanting him to know he'd frightened her.

"Neither. I'm staying right here."

"You're sleeping on the floor?"

"Yes. I don't want Nima to wake up scared during the night."

Ember went back to the bathroom and turned the light switch on, closing the door until the light barely showed in the hall. "There. That will make it easier for her to see in case she does."

"Thanks."

Wow. A sincere thank you. Rory sounded more like himself right now. Sitting opposite him on the edge of the easy chair, she kept her voice low. "What's the plan for tomorrow?"

"Fix breakfast. Maybe run into town for new clothes. More food. Stuff like that. We don't want to take any chances, though. We'll stick close to the safe house most of the time."

"I could run into town alone. That way you and Nima—"

"No. We stay together. Both of us with Nima. At all times."

"You're right." She acquiesced, although agents often separated to make food runs during covert ops and stakeouts. "Do you want to at least take a shower? It's been a long day."

"You're not sleepy anymore, are you?"

She couldn't tell if he was still being sarcastic or not, but she didn't care. He'd been rude one too many times. "I'm sure I can manage without you," she replied tartly.

He stood. "Listen. I'm sorry if I hurt your feelings before. I was out of line. You've done real good."

"Forget it. I'm not losing any sleep over it."

He crossed the living room but paused in the pale bathroom light, his hand on the knob. "It's just that—"

She didn't give him a chance to explain. "I said forget it. I have."

Rory ran a hand through his hair. Always shiny clean, he had the blackest hair she'd ever seen. Not one strand of silver showed at his temples, and he kept it neatly trimmed. She liked the shaved skull look Zack Lennox and David Tao wore better, but Rory's head of hair added to his movie star quality. He should've been a male model. He'd be one hot hunk in underwear commercials. In the deepening darkness, she could just make out the confused look on his face.

"Tyler's been through enough," he muttered. "I'm overly protective where he's concerned."

Ember didn't respond to his quiet revelation. Tyler was not the rude one in the Dennison family.

"And I don't want Mother in my business. She's a gossip. I'll not have Tyler discussed by people who've never met him. That's all." He seemed to be waiting for Ember to say something. When she didn't, he ran a hand over his head again. "I won't be long."

Only after he shut the bathroom door did Ember move to the couch with Nima. Rory could apologize all he wanted. She was not ready to cozy up to him just because he decided to be nice for a change. The shower faucet turned on. Good. Maybe once he was clean, he'd feel better.

Resting her hand in the middle of Nima's back, she stilled to listen to the little girl's breathing. "Wow, you're one tired little one," Ember whispered as she began washing Nima's hands, arms, and face as gently as she could.

If he intended to sleep in the living room, she would, too. It made sense to stick close together. The home seemed sturdy enough, and now that she was fed and clean, her nerves had calmed down. The night was peaceful, and the neighborhood Alex had chosen for this particular safe house seemed quiet.

The only problem was tomorrow. The boring bodyguard detail she'd accepted had certainly turned out to be something else. With any luck, Alex would call them to come back into Alexandria. Or maybe David would find out what was happening. Whatever, there had to be a better way to protect this little girl from the men who had assassinated her father than sticking her in a safe house with two agents who didn't care for each other.

Ember relaxed into the comfy couch cushions. They were safe. For now. But Rory's words tickled her mind. *Tyler's been through enough.* Enough what? He looked like every other healthy, happy little guy when she'd seen him at the gym. In fact, he was an exact replica of his father, only shorter. And nicer. What could the cute little guy have experienced at his young age that made Rory rabidly overprotective?

And yes, Mother was a busybody and a gossip, but that was just the way she was. The minute she'd shown up to work for Alex, he and his employees had become her family. That was part of her extraordinary genius. She tended to drive away the people she loved the most.

In a way, Rory's need to shield his son confirmed he might be gay. The whole gender orientation thing was a big non-issue in Ember's freethinking mind. People were people. Get over it.

The shower door shut. That meant uppity Rory Dennison was taking a shower. Ember forgot about Tyler when a quick image of his father standing naked under the shower spray flashed through her tired brain. Gay or not, he was now in the buff. Tanned from head to toe—she suspected. Strong enough to be gentle—she wished. And not too far away. At this very minute hot water would be sluicing over his broad shoulders and down the finely chiseled six-pack of his abdomen all the way to his—

Her cell phone vibrated at her waist. "Hey, Mother. What's up?" she answered in a hushed voice, her ears still trained on the water dripping off Rory.

"You've got two vehicles approaching your twenty," Mother barked.

Ember jumped to her feet. "What? Where?"

"Just turned onto your road. They're running dark and silent. Get out of that house. Now."

Ember hit the bathroom door without thinking. She pushed it open. Gasped. She closed the door. And opened it again. *Oh, my. Oh, wowza. Oh, my.*

A deep voice rumbled through the steamy spray. "Did you need something?"

She couldn't answer with her mouth hanging open. He was everything she'd imagined, only so much hotter in person. Drenched and steaming from the hot water, he stood with both hands against the wall directly under the showerhead. All she could see was the perfect profile of— everything. His tan ended at his belt line, his butt perfectly white. No way could this guy be gay, not with a manly butt like that. Could he? The only thing marring his perfect physique was the ragged red scar left from his near death experience in Mexico last year.

Argh! Ember jerked her entire body backward into the hall, slamming the door behind her. She shouldn't have looked. Her heart pounded up high in her throat where it only climbed when she was scared. Or excited. Or totally amazed. Wow. How could she go back in there and face him now? How could she not?

Assassins are on the way. For heaven's sake. Move it.

Gulping past her embarrassment, she pushed the door open and focused on what she needed to say instead of the glorious view. "We've got to move," she croaked, her stern voice gone along with her good sense. "Now."

"What?" He wiped one quick hand across the fogged-up shower door. "Why?"

She averted her eyes like she should have done in the first place. "Someone's coming. We've got to run."

The glass door banged open and out he came, all six feet three of an angry guy in the nude, jerking the nearest towel off the rack. She couldn't help it. She gulped and looked again. The man was ripped, his chest dusted with dark hairs that led downward to, wow, more than enough to make any woman—

"Don't just stand there!" Stormy blues clashed with hers. He stabbed his index finger toward the living room while he brushed the towel in one long swipe down his chest and abdomen. "Grab Nima. Go get her! Now!"

Her brain kicked in, and her libido dropped to manageable. Almost. She hurried back to the couch and pulled the still sleeping child into her arms. Instinctively, she wrapped the burgundy blanket around Nima. "Sorry, baby girl. Hang on tight," she soothed.

Rory had his shoes in his hands by then. His shirt was open, but at least his zipper was up. Ember grabbed the bag she'd left by the back door, mentally reprimanding herself for noticing those very personal and attractive features about her agent in charge. Her favorite gay boy was right behind her, his wet hand hard between her shoulder blades.

When he reached around her to open the door, a shiver skated up her arm and over her shoulders. Tendrils of steam still rose from the back of his hand and his fingers on the knob. There was no way this hot hunk could be gay, not with the equipment he had. Another shiver danced up her spine and—

"What is wrong with you, Davis?" he hissed, his breath moist and hot in her ear. Damn, she didn't know his lips were so close. "Don't look back. Get in the car and stay on the floor."

"Got it." She tried really hard to focus on the very urgent need at hand instead of the feel of all that muscle at her back, but the sensation wouldn't go away. He kept bumping her backside with his hip, hurrying her along. His palm flattened in the middle of her back created an uncanny reaction all the way to her stomach. And beyond.

It was difficult to run with rubbery legs, never mind what he was doing to the rest of her body. Their very dangerous predicament seemed to enhance her sensual response to this angry alpha male. Everything about this guy was panty-dropping hot. Wow. Now she knew why crazy people had sex in weird places like warzones and jetliners cruising at thirty-five thousand feet. She didn't even like this guy and she was ready to take him on. Or under.

That image didn't help. *Focus, damn it!*

At last at the car, Rory opened the back door and firmly pushed her inside and to the floor with Nima. "Hang onto that little girl," he ordered as he slammed the door behind her.

Sheesh. What did he think she'd do? Toss Nima out the window? He seriously needed to climb off the boss-of-the-world bandwagon he seemed to be on. With a quiet purr and no headlights, the Taurus moved smoothly across the back lawn and to the road below. The ride got bumpy while he maneuvered through and around the pine trees. A big bump and he'd gone over a curb. Another big bump.

Ember held the little girl's face against her shoulder, her heart pounding as she soothed, "There, there. It's all right."

A tiny hand patted her cheek while Rory's much larger and warmer hand was suddenly on her backside, groping for what, she didn't know. "Get your hands off my butt, Dennison," she growled so he wouldn't know how much she appreciated it.

"Where's my backpack? I put it behind the passenger seat where I could reach it. What did you do with it?"

"I had to make room for Nima and me. It's on the back seat. What do you need?"

"My SIG. It's on top, and it's loaded. Be careful."

His warning irked her. As weapons certification officer for The TEAM, she of all people knew how to handle a loaded weapon. Opening the bag, she handed him the pistol with expert care. "Here. Wow. You've got everything in here but the kitchen sink."

"Did you bring the extra ammo I told you to?" he asked brusquely.

"It's in my backpack." Sheesh. He was starting to make her mad. Who did he think he was talking to? A civilian?

"Hand me a couple mags."

Ember opened the ammo backpack and placed two .9mm mags that fit his specific weapon on his open palm. "Do you want more?"

"Not now."

She resumed her crouched position, listening while he chambered a round and set the gun on the seat beside him. By the sound of the tires, they were back on pavement and moving fast.

"Who called?"

"Mother," Ember replied quietly, nose to nose with Nima. The little girl seemed to be studying her, those soft baby blues taking in the geography of her face. The arch of her brows. Her nose. Her lips. Everything.

"And?"

"And she said two cars were on the road to our safe house. They were running silent. No headlights." She nuzzled Nima's cheek to break her calm scrutiny. Wow. Did nothing upset this kid?

Rory grunted.

"And she said to get out of the house right away." Ember felt like she needed to explain further, but he didn't ask more questions. At last, bright streetlights flickered through the car windows. They were traveling through well-lighted residential streets.

"Can we get off the floor yet?"

"No. The interstate's up ahead. I'll tell you when—"

WHOOSH! CRACK!

Damn it to hell!

An earth-shattering explosion split the night behind them. The sedan shuddered with the ensuing shockwave. Ember hunkered down around Nima, but curiosity got the best of her. She squinted out the back window at the hellish scene where the safe house had once stood. The entire neighborhood turned bright as day. Billowing orange clouds of fire launched upward with spiraling licks of black smoke. Shredded glowing debris plummeted down upon the black silhouette of tall pines while the cloud lifted higher, filling the night sky. Burning fireflies scattered on the updraft. Hell had come to Maryland.

"Wow." She couldn't keep the awe out of her voice. Or the fear. They'd been inside that structure only minutes ago. What if Mother hadn't called? What if Rory hadn't been prepared to flee as quickly as they had? Her throat closed at all the worst-case scenarios while the tires of the Taurus squealed eastward onto the I-495 on-ramp. They were running for their lives. Again.

She gulped, her throat dry and tight. "They... they... blew up the safe house."

"Ya think?" he snapped, instantly reminding her how much emotional support he was NOT. Dead silence continued for a good twenty minutes more. Finally, he turned, glancing behind her. "Sit up so we can both talk with Alex."

Ember placed the child on the seat and fastened the seat belt and harness around her. Nima peered up, her pale eyes glowing under the fluorescent freeway lights. She didn't smile or speak. Ember patted her chubby little cheek and kissed her forehead. "Not a very nice way to wake up, is it?"

"Mama?" Nima asked in a small voice. "Mama?"

"No, baby. I'm not your mama," Ember replied. *No way am I ever going to be anybody's mother.*

By then Rory had a rabid boss on his cell phone. "Where the hell are you?" Alex demanded.

"Back on four-ninety-five, headed north. The safe house is blown, as in blown up."

"I'm watching what's left of it now." Alex's voice softened. That he had eyes on the house was good thinking. "Half a dozen men in black approached it from the south. They never intended for you and the girls to survive. Damned glad you didn't stay in the secure rooms. The whole place is a smoking crater. Garage, too."

"What'd they use, Boss? LAWs? RPGs?"

"Don't think so. Didn't see a smoke trail. Might have been SEMTEX or C-4. Maybe dynamite. They've pulled back now. I can't see them." It was a bad day when the boss was rattled. "You guys still have your cell phones?"

Silently, Rory motioned for Ember to give hers up. "Not for long. We'll ditch them the first chance we get."

"Call me when you do," Alex ordered.

"Copy that," Rory said as he signed off.

At the next off-ramp, he exited the freeway and pulled into the parking lot of an all-night convenience store. Three vehicles were parked there: an old farm truck with a flatbed trailer full of firewood, a local police cruiser, and a milk delivery truck. He lifted an eyebrow. "Any preference?"

"Police cruiser. Definitely. They can shoot back if the assassins catch up with them." Ember relinquished her phone with a sigh. "Darn. Just when I beat Mother's score on Froggy Pond."

"That must be heartbreaking." The heavy sarcasm in his voice spiked her ire, but he was out the door before she could retaliate. Nonchalantly, he dropped their cells into the cruiser's open rear window before proceeding into the store. He returned with what she needed most.

"Two cream. No sugar," he said as he handed an extra large Styrofoam drink cup through the open passenger window for her and a carton of chocolate milk for Nima.

"Wow. How'd you know?" She clutched it greedily to her lips. Ah. Coffee—the nectar of the gods.

He stared at her like she was dumber than dirt.

"What?" she asked, the coffee cup between her knees while she opened the carton of milk. "Oh. Never mind. I guess it's the way you're trained, all that observation and surveillance stuff, huh? And you've probably heard me and Mother talking in the office, haven't you?"

Wordlessly, he tossed a new burner phone to the seat beside her. It might have been the cheapest on the market, but it was perfect for their needs. After giving Nima a sip of milk, she unsealed hers from the plastic packaging while he did the same. Finally back on the grid but anonymous, he pulled into traffic and headed north while their personal phones went in the opposite direction. She hoped. It would be an awful coincidence if the police cruisers ended up on the freeway behind them with the cell phones they'd just discarded.

"So what was on your phone? NFL scores? The World series?" she asked, her nerves getting the best of her and her mouth out of control.

"What do you think?"

"I don't know," she said honestly. She'd never noticed his subtle nuances before. "I'm only trying to make conversation. It's not like it's national security or—"

"Pictures, all right? I had pictures on my phone. Now drop it."

"What kind of pictures?" For some reason, her mouth couldn't shut up. His glance in the rearview couldn't have stabbed sharper if it had been a razorblade. And just as quickly she understood. *Oh. Pictures. Of Tyler. Wow. I really did ask a lot of dumb questions.*

He ended further discussion by thumb-dialing Alex while he drove. "Where do you want us to go now, Boss?"

"I just got off the phone with Jed McCormack," Alex replied. "He's got a summer home near Gettysburg. Take I-270 north, then Highway 15 out of Frederick, Maryland."

"You sure you want us in one of his mansions? That's asking for trouble," Rory argued. "Why not TEAM headquarters? Are you guys safe yet or not?"

"Are you telling me you'd rather pass this op to the FBI and let them run with it? Is that what you're telling me, Junior Agent? Jesus H. Christ, Dennison! They planted bombs in my damned lobby!"

Ember cringed. Wow. Last name and title all in one breath. And swearing a blue streak. Alex was either pissed or backed into a corner. Probably both tonight. The FBI had to be leaning on him extra hard since they'd screwed up and got Nima's father killed at the temple.

Rory didn't argue. "No. Understood. We can keep her alive a lot longer than they can. You know that as well as I do."

"Exactly." Alex sighed loud and clear, his weariness meter obviously pegged for the day. "They're climbing all over me as it is, the bastards. Mother's backtracking the vehicles that approached the safe house to see where they came from, but we've only got traffic cams to go by. She's getting close to figuring out who's behind this, but we do not have specific details yet. Once you get to Gettysburg, lay low. You'll be safe there. The code to his front door is 1776. And Rory."

"Yes, Boss?"

"It's all up to you now. Keep our girls safe."

"Will do." Rory hung up and slipped his new phone into his shirt pocket.

"He's such a male chauvinist," Ember muttered from the back seat.

He glanced at her through the rearview mirror, his brow raised in that imperious way he had. Like he knew better than she did. Like she'd better jump when he told her to. "Why do you say that?"

"You know, his little *'keep our girls safe'* comment. He forgets I'm perfectly capable of taking care of myself." She rolled her eyes at the archaic thought. "I've been doing it for years. Long before I ever came to work for him."

"He's old school. For some stupid reason, us dumb guys think it's our job to protect our women. Go figure."

Our women? Rory made her sound like property.

"We aren't all defenseless little girls, you know," she reminded him.

"Believe me," he snapped. "I know."

Her coffee slipped from her fingers. *Sheesh!*

Five

"Ember. Wake up."

Rory reached over the seat and tapped her knee once with the tip of his index finger. After a couple quiet hours on the road without being followed, he'd pulled off the interstate and into a shopping center. It was early morning, but something had to be open by now. They were in luck. The megastore he'd pulled into carried everything from groceries to sporting goods.

She arched her back and stretched, blinking her eyes open in surprise. "Dang. Sorry. I did it again. I fell asleep."

He forced his eyes to quit scrolling over her body. With every blink of those sleepy greens, his resolve weakened. The way she pushed her chest forward when she yawned didn't help. Men's clothing did nothing to disguise the goods that made her noticeable and mouth-wateringly delectable. He wanted nothing more than to climb over the seat and enfold that gorgeous body in his hands and arms, but it wasn't really her he wanted, was it?

A face from the past messed with his thinking. The line between Ember and the other woman who'd been part of his life blurred at moments like this. Was it their startling similarities or was he a sucker and falling for—

Hell, no. He pushed that stupid idea out of his mind for good. He didn't date coworkers. The day for fun and frivolity was over. Finished. Never to be seen again.

"You were tired," he said quietly. "It's been a tough night. Besides, you've got a snuggly little baby doll keeping you extra warm." He nodded at Nima, her little mouth open and a trail of drool trickling down her chin.

"Are you okay?" Ember asked cautiously.

"Sure. Why wouldn't I be?"

"You're, umm, nice." She didn't look at him when she answered.

He ignored the implication and determined to be a better agent in charge instead of the snarky ass he'd been. "Come on. Let's go in and get some new duds."

"Don't you think it's odd Nima sleeps as much as she does?" Ember asked. "I don't have any kids, but it seems funny she's sleeping so much. Does Tyler do that?"

Rory hesitated discussing anything related to his son, but it was an innocent question. "Not unless he's sick, but kids go through different stages. I don't think she's sick. It could be jetlag. She and her father flew in from India the night before last. What worries me more is she hasn't used a restroom since she's been in our custody. Let's get her up and moving. That's kind of important."

"Ah, sure," Ember murmured as she smoothed her hand gently over Nima's rosy cheek, wiping the drool away with her thumb. "Hey, little one, it's time to rise and shine." She blew gently across Nima's face.

Rory couldn't help but smile at the motherly scene, not at all what he'd expected. Ember was gentle with the little girl and concerned about hurting her feelings. It was an entirely different side to the woman who could show up in the office dressed like a zombie one day and Dorothy from the Wizard of Oz the next. Who would have guessed she'd have a knack for children buried beneath the bizarre?

Nima yawned, her lips scrunched together in a pout. She rubbed her eyes with both fists and blinked up with a dazed smile. "Mama?" she asked drowsily.

Ember glanced up at Rory. "That's another thing. She keeps calling me 'mama.' You don't think she's got a concussion or something?"

Rory got out of the car and came around to open Ember's door. Leaning in, he took Nima's little round skull gently in his hands, feeling for a knot or a bump, anything that would spell trouble. "I should've thought of that yesterday. A concussion might explain why she's been sleeping so much, too. I'm not feeling any bumps, and I don't see any bruises. How's she been breathing?"

"Fine." Ember shrugged. "She snores a little, but that's all."

He performed a quiet examination of the girl's neck and shoulders next. When Nima giggled and arched her back, he relaxed. She was ticklish. There was nothing wrong with her that breakfast and clean clothes couldn't fix. "She's fine. Let's go," he said, not liking that he was out in the open and exposed. A quick scan of the mostly empty parking lot revealed a few early morning shoppers, but the need to get inside and out of sight prevailed.

"I'm sorry," Ember said softly to the child on her lap, "but we've got to go shopping with Uncle Rory."

"Uncle Rory?" That caught him by surprise.

"Well, for goodness sake, you can't be Auntie Rory, now can you?" Ember still had a lot of sleep in her eyes, but mischief tugged the corners of her full lips. He forced his eyes to look at something else. Like the pavement. The blue sky. Anything else.

"Unless this is one of those *don't ask, don't tell* situations you don't want to talk about," she teased.

"What? Who? Me?" How did that stupid notion get into her ditsy blonde head? "I'm not gay. No way," he declared. Instinctively, his gut sucked in, his chin stuck out and every muscle in his body flexed to prove his masculinity like the big dumb jock he usually was not.

She giggled, her face full of the golden morning light. "I'm not judging. Sheesh, Rory. Climb down. Lots of guys are coming out of the closet these days. Lots of girls, too. It's no big deal."

"I'm. Not. Gay," he repeated extra clearly.

"Honest. I don't mind." She wouldn't let it go. "Don't worry. I won't tell anyone about this, either."

"Move," he growled. There was no sense arguing. Let her think he was bi-sexual for all he cared. "Do you want me to carry her?"

"I've got her." Ember had no trouble getting out of the car this time. She had Nima balanced on her hip with the sleepy little girl's arms wrapped tightly around her neck. "Us girls have to stick together."

Nima didn't smile or answer, her too serious eyes taking in the sights of early morning shoppers in a land far different than her homeland of India.

Rory walked alertly beside Ember, his hand on her shoulder to add authenticity in case anyone cared. He doubted it. There were very few shoppers out and about, but the innocent gesture unleashed a familiar feeling he couldn't place. For sure he'd never shopped with a woman and little girl like this before, much less a woman as tall as Ember. Heck, he was six-three. She had to be pushing five-ten. The pleasant feeling of a happy family persisted.

He sized her up out of the corner of his eye. Her honey-blonde hair bounced when she walked, each layer fluffy and alive in the hardly noticeable early morning breeze. When she tipped her head to nuzzle the top of Nima's head, his hand moved automatically to the back of her neck just to feel how soft her hair was. He was right. Soft and silky. She shivered and scrunched her shoulders, but he didn't remove his hand. Not only did it make them look like a real couple, it felt— right.

One word kept bubbling to the surface. *Elegant.* Beneath her oftentimes eclectic appearance, Ember was an elegant woman. He just hadn't seen this side of her in a long time. It was a nice change.

By the time they were inside, Nima was wriggling on Ember's hip. "That little one is trying to tell you something," he whispered.

"Oh, yeah? What do you want to tell me? Go on. You can tell me anything." She was nose to nose with Nima and still didn't get it. Nima wiggled faster in obvious discomfort.

"For heaven's sake, she needs a restroom. Hurry."

"Are you sure?"

Her astonishment made him smile. He pointed sternly toward the restrooms at the front of the store. "Let's not have an accident this early in the day."

She balked at the entrance to the women's room. "You can't go in there with us. Gay or not, you'll scare the ladies if there's anyone in here."

"I'm not gay, darn it," he growled. With his hand more firmly at the small of her back, he ushered them through the door and up to the extra-large stall with the diaper changing shelf inside. "Be sure to use a sanitizer seat cover."

"Man, you're bossy."

He arched his brows impatiently. "Keep it up and you'll be sorry."

She rushed into the stall and closed the door. Shortly, the appropriate sounds of a healthy young lady and the toilet flushing filled the empty restroom. Ember's indulgent mother hen sounds were interesting, too. She was so gentle with the child. At last she opened the stall and handed Nima to him. "Here. My turn. Please make sure she washes her hands."

"Come on, little one." Rory took Nima with a smile. "Do you want to play in some suds?" He balanced her between the sink counter and his body, squirted soap on his hands and hers. Soon she was splashing and clapping in the water. He didn't notice Ember at his side until she bumped him with her hip.

"We're covert agents, for Pete's sake. Have some dignity."

Nima squealed and clapped when she caught sight of Ember in the mirror. "Mama!"

"See?" Ember asked. "There she goes again."

"Maybe you look like her mother," he offered, but there was no way that could be it. Nima's mother was not blonde, tall, or sexy. It didn't make sense, but it didn't matter, either. "Let's get this done," he said to hurry things along.

Ember clapped her hands and Nima reached for her, snuggling into her shoulder. "My Mama," she murmured, her nose in Ember's neck.

That happy family sensation shivered across his shoulders again. He ignored it, determined to stick to the standard operating procedure of two covert agents on duty. Grabbing a handful of paper towels off the dispenser, he shook the image off. He had a job to do. That was all. *Ember and me? Never.*

It was a good plan until his knuckles accidentally brushed Ember's breast when he reached for Nima's hands. An arc of feminine energy leapt from her body to his, shocking the living hell out of his dormant male receptors. Every last masculine nerve stood up and took notice. All of them. Even—that one.

He tossed the paper towel into the trash and shivered like a damned high school kid with a testosterone spike and acne. Shit. It was time to get to work and get out of the women's restroom. A little distance from Ember wouldn't hurt, either.

They set a quick path through the department store. Since the men's department was closest, he shopped, quickly selecting a pair of denim jeans and a gray flannel shirt, a package of socks and men's boxers. Ember was as quick to choose black denim jeans with a black hoody, a package of socks and a few intimates in the women's department. But when it came to the little girl's department, she lost control.

"Oh, my gosh," she exclaimed, holding up a matching purple toddler set of top and pants while Nima yawned from the child seat of the shopping cart. "Little girls have the most amazing outfits. Look at these."

"Let's move," he urged. It had been less than thirty minutes, but they couldn't take chances. He jerked his head toward the cash registers at the front of the store. "We're supposed to be keeping a low profile, remember?"

Her head ducked into her shoulders. "Sorry. I got carried away. You're right."

While he loaded the cashier's counter with their purchases, she snagged a pre-packaged bag of bagels, two bottles of iced-coffee, and a small carton of orange juice from the refrigerator case at the check stand. "We'll need a quick breakfast," she explained.

"Is there anything else? A kitchen sink, maybe?"

"Yes, but I can wait," she replied haughtily.

"Well, halleluiah."

After a quick stop at a nearby service station to refuel, he turned David's trusty vehicle onto the interstate once more. Ember still sat in the backseat, singing some insane little ditty to Nima, who munched quietly on a blueberry bagel. There was that family feeling again. Rory ignored the pinch in his heart. He missed Tyler.

Nima burped an extra healthy burp. Ember's brows arched at the very adult sound, her mouth open in surprise. Rory caught it all in the rearview mirror. For the first time since the operation began, he laughed. Ember grinned back at him. The miles flew by.

By the time they arrived at Jed McCormack's Pennsylvania home, Ember had checked in with the office and Alex knew where they were. For once, her word of choice was spot on.

"Wow," she exclaimed as they pulled up the long drive toward a spacious plantation-style home with ten white columns spread majestically across the front entry.

Tucked beyond a privacy shield of pine and oak, it was nothing less than breathtaking. A red barn and other outbuildings completed the idyllic setting. Closer to the house, the gravel drive gave way to massive stretches of artistically laid red brick wrapped around the north side to the rear of the home.

They climbed the three steps to the wide front porch in awe. After keying in the security code Alex had given him, Rory opened the front door. It swung into an enormous entry hung with stained-glass cathedral windows. The gold-toned glass with contrasting white doves caught in upward flight cast a gentle glow across the black marble floor. From the high peaked ceiling, an enormous crystal chandelier rained down glints of glittering sparkles. Wooden beams enhanced the arched cathedral ceiling.

"Wow," Ember murmured at the extravagant display. A wide stairway circled the entrance leading upstairs, its polished wooden banister glowing from the chandelier dangling in the center. "This is Jed's summer place?"

"I take it you've never been to his home in Georgetown?" Rory asked quietly.

"Uh, no. Have you?" She craned her neck as she turned around in a full circle in the middle of the room. A carved wooden eagle gleamed from a sturdy table set to the right of the entrance. The gold plaque beneath it was inscribed with eloquent scrolled handwriting, thanking Jed McCormack for his service to his country. The etched signature on the plaque belonged to the previous President of the United States.

She couldn't shut her mouth in amazement. "Wow," she said, for the third time.

"I've never been invited to any of Jed's homes, but I think Alex, Murphy, and Roy have. You can put Nima down now," Rory said with a smirk. "She's a big girl. She can walk."

Ember set the toddler gingerly on the polished floor. "Wow," she repeated as she made another circle around the room. "I feel like I'm in a castle. Did you wipe your feet?"

Rory knelt to the child's level, ignoring Ember's barb. "Nima. Are you okay?"

He finally looked into the special little girl's ghostly blue eyes. The person behind them seemed eons older. She reached for him. Obediently, he took her tiny fingers in his hand. It was as if she'd told him to, as if he had no choice but to accept her kind gesture. His breath hitched. The world shuddered to a startlingly abrupt halt.

He gulped. Nima was not looking at him within the boundaries of time and space that he understood. For an unsettling moment, the planet shifted in a tectonic plate kind of a shift that left him off balance and dizzy. Vulnerable. It was as if she was looking at the moments of his life at once, all of them spread like a roll of carpet unfurled through the years before and the years ahead. Somehow he sensed she could see his birth twenty-eight years ago, his childhood and school years, every football game he'd ever quarterbacked, all of his graduations, military assignments and deployments.

The oddest smile tugged at the right side of her mouth. The memories of his winnings and losses, his fears, accomplishments, and failures shimmied through his mind in the twinkling of an eye. He was nothing more than a book she had instantly read from cover to cover. The sheer magnitude of her power clamped his windpipe closed.

She whispered, her fingers tightly clutching his, "If you keep hiding, no one can find you."

Ember's raucous voice broke the magnetic spell. "She talks? In English?"

Rory blinked, his eyes still riveted to Nima's. An image of Tyler's bright, smiling face resonated in his mind. A sweet feeling of truth spoken and received burned in his heart. As if in a dream, he sensed Ember kneeling at his side—like she'd always belonged there—with him. For him.

His heart stopped beating. The oddest sensation of stepping out of his body settled upon Rory. Now was the defining moment when he could leave the mayhem of mortality behind, when he could drift away to a higher sphere. If not for Tyler....

Ember's fingers on his arm pulled him out of the amazing child's eyes and back to the hard marble floor. Drawing in a long gasping breath, air filled his lungs. He sat back onto his butt with a thump, not realizing he'd been holding his breath. Nima climbed onto his lap as if nothing extraordinary had just happened.

"What's wrong with you?" Ember asked from somewhere very far away.

He couldn't speak. Spiraling dizziness swirled up from the floor. When it seemed the mini-cyclone would lift him off the floor and fling him upward, Ember cupped his chin and made him face her. "Talk to me, Rory Dennison. You're scaring the hell out of me."

"Language," he muttered weakly. "Please. Don't swear." Coughing and trying to understand what had just happened, he blinked into Ember's worried gaze. She felt his forehead with the back of her fingers, like a mother checking a feverish child. He pushed her hand away. "I said I'm fine."

The dizzy feeling left. Ember's worried face came into clearer focus. "You looked into her eyes, didn't you?" she asked intently, her gaze still fixed on his.

There was no word to describe what he'd experienced. Fortunately, Ember knew one. "Wow, huh?"

Nima closed her eyes and began rocking while she hummed that crazy tune Ember had taught her in the car. Once more, Rory was a covert operator, not a stark raving lunatic who'd seen a benevolent sorceress in a four-year-old's eyes. And yet he had seen something. The world had changed. The magnificent McCormack mansion now appeared sterile, crude and coarse. Mortal. Full of decay.

"Alex is right," he whispered in the silence of the great hall.

"Why? What did he say?"

"Sorry, I forgot to tell you what he said last night. Some Tibetans believe Nima is destined to be the next Dalai Lama."

"I can see why."

"Me, too," he whispered.

Ember was back to her usual animated self. "I know what you mean, Rory. Wow, when she looked at me in the car yesterday, I had this peaceful feeling, like all of a sudden I was totally calm when we'd just left the scariest shootout I've ever been in. Weird, huh?"

"No. Yes. No. Umm, I don't know," he murmured as he got to his feet, still processing what he'd felt and seen. The words of Nima's message had clicked deep inside of him, as if the combination lock to his failures had been breached and the doors flung open wide.

Ember stood next to him. "We can't stay here. There's no way the two of us can defend a place this big."

"Umm, no. I mean, right," he muttered, his legs feeling like jelly.

She bumped him with her hip. "Come on. I'll take Nima. You lead the way. Find us a safe place, Boss."

He couldn't release Nima. Her words left a feeling of peace he didn't want to relinquish. Not yet. He pressed her to his hip where she straddled comfortably like a baby orangutan.

"Hey, Dennison, are you with me?" Ember asked kindly. "You're kinda spooky-looking right now."

"I've, umm, got her. I'll carry her," he said, more to himself than to Ember. He felt spooky all right, like he had one foot in Jed's mansion and the other in the *Twilight Zone*. He took a few steps down the hall next to the grand staircase, glancing behind to make sure Ember followed. By the time they entered the next room, he'd caught his equilibrium again.

This room was as huge as the last, only circular and lined with sheer gold curtains along the entire outside wall. A dining table stood solidly in the center of the room with a stone fireplace at the opposite end. Three golden candelabra divided the linen tablecloth into four equal sections. The formal place settings divided the table into another twenty seats on each side. Rose-colored silk flowers decorated the center section. Oddly, they reminded him of the rose on Ember's bra. And of course that thought led him to think of her nipples. Again.

"I'm tempted to call Alex and tell him thanks, but no thanks," Ember whispered in awe.

"No kidding."

"But wow. Wouldn't you love to live here?" Her reverent whisper changed to gushing.

He didn't answer. She was obviously enamored with the wealth she saw displayed on every side. He was not. He'd learned a tough lesson about wealth and all its glory a long time ago. Five years to be exact.

At last they were at the rear of the home, in an extravagant sitting room. Between the extra-long leather couches and numerous easy chairs, a crowd could comfortably sit and chat the night away. Everything in the home spoke hugely and eloquently of their wealthy host's love of entertaining friends and family.

"Look out there." Ember stood at the back window. Across from the elaborately bricked driveway and courtyard stood a smaller home. "That's more our style."

"Let's find out." He opened the back door and together they ventured forth.

"How does one man get this rich?" she asked, bewildered.

"You need to Google Jed McCormack sometime. The man's a genius, no two ways about it. He's made millions, maybe billions. He bankrolled Alex when he started his business. Did you know that?"

"Mother told me," she answered, "but it's different when you see it person."

Rory handed Nima off to Ember while he keyed in the same security code and opened the door with a small flourish. "Shall we, ladies?"

The home was definitely more their style. Most likely built to accommodate guests, the front entry displayed a second story loft built toward the back of the home. Built in an A-frame style, the stairs to the loft were covered in hunter green carpet, while the entire lower level was gray stone tile. A low wall enclosed the loft.

The open floor plan included a full kitchen, separated by a butcher-block island from the rest of the room. A leather couch lined the wall opposite two easy chairs and a spacious coffee table, while the gas fireplace at the far end of the room completed the cozy ambience.

"This is better," he said.

"I could stay here for awhile." Ember settled Nima onto one of the easy chairs.

"I'll move the car. Let's fix something to eat."

"You got it," she replied.

He made sure the larger home was locked and secure before he took a quick tour of the grounds. The brick driveway extended around the back of the bungalow, ending in a comfortable two-car garage, which he chose not to use. The freedom to move quickly should the need arise had saved their lives before. He pulled David's car alongside the back door of the bungalow instead—just in case.

A large barn stood behind the two homes, but no farm animals came into view. He tried the barn door latch but found it locked. Peering in the grimy windows, he saw why. Old Jed McCormack had a sizeable collection of antique farm implements and vehicles. Several old tractors occupied the center floor. Machinery Rory recognized from back home surrounded the outside walls: a horse-drawn sickle mower, a hay rake, various iron tractor wheels and plows, plus several of the old-time milking machines. A rusted harrow stood at the far end. The turn of the century threshing machine in the corner made him smile. His grandfather in Nebraska had one just like it.

He turned to the peaceful panorama of the countryside. No wonder Jed liked the country. Beyond the barn lay nothing but fields and trees. The air smelled of earth and life, a breath of Nebraska in the middle of an extremely hectic workday. Tyler would love it. But not today. Precautions had to be taken. Rory meant to strike a defensive position instead of running away like they had last night. He might not win the war, but whoever had attacked them back at the safe house would know they had a fight on their hands if they showed here. He pulled the backpack from the Taurus. It held more than food items.

He was on his way back to the bungalow when his phone rang. Alex.

"You sure Jed doesn't mind us staying on his home?"

Alex chuckled. "Don't worry about it."

"I take it you've been here?"

"Once or twice. He's invited me and Kelsey to spend a few weekends."

"Man, you'd have to spend more than a few weekends. This place is huge." Rory scrubbed a hand over his head, hating the situation. "Anyway, we're in safe and sound."

"Let's hope you stay that way. Mother and David are working on the latest satellite images, but she's having trouble with the digital feed. She's gotten nothing but static and interference since last night."

"You don't think you're being scrambled?"

"That's exactly what I think," Alex growled. "I'm sending Maxwell and Fred for support."

"Thanks," Rory replied. Two more TEAM agents on scene would be a welcome addition. "What do you want us to do? Hide out here until the coast is clear?"

"Yes. I'll have David call you later to share what he learned at the temple last night. Settle in for the night. Jed keeps his place well stocked. Use what you need. Expect Maxwell and Fred in four hours."

"Copy that." Rory hung up, allowing a measure of relief. Both new to The TEAM, Maxwell and Fred came as highly qualified snipers, both Army Rangers and ready to rock and roll. He held no bias against Ember, but he and she needed help against whoever the assassins were.

She was standing at the open refrigerator when he unlocked and re-entered the front door to their new digs. Her nose twitched. "Hmm. Do I smell C-4? What have you been up to, Agent Dennison? Are you planning a surprise party for anyone in particular?"

"Only if they show up like they did last night. Hope McCormack knew what he was getting into when he said we should come here."

"Cool, company. I'll fix a big lunch. Do you have anything particular in mind?"

"Surprise me." He passed through the home to double-check the rear exit and make sure it was bolted and secure. Nima still sat where Ember had set her. She watched solemnly as Rory climbed the stairs to check out the loft. He gave her a small wave from the landing overhead. She waved back.

The loft was smaller, but as nicely furnished. A queen-size bed stood off to the left, a luxurious bathroom on the right. The bathroom was as big as the bedroom area. It included an oversized sunken tub, glassed-in shower, and two elegant crystal bowl-sinks on the black granite counter. The cabinets were gloss white; the floor tiles ebony with white grout.

Plush black towels sat folded and ready at the edge of the sunken black tub. A brass ice bucket with a bottle of champagne completed the setting. The only thing missing was the ice—and a happy couple to enjoy the rendezvous. The place said *ROMANCE* with a very loud outside-voice. *Me and Ember? Not going to happen.*

He leaned over the wall of the loft to view the scene below. Ember stood busy at the kitchen sink. Something smelled good. A wok warmed on the stove. Nima still watched him. He winked at the little girl like he would with Tyler. Only Tyler couldn't wink back yet. He'd try, but just end up squeezing both eyes shut. Rory winked again. She winked back.

"What do you want?" he asked softly from his lofty position. She patted the chair cushion next to her. He came down the stairs and scooped her up into his lap and sat with her. "You are an amazing little girl," he whispered.

By then she'd wiggled around to face him and patted his cheek. "'Kay?" she whispered in the softest baby voice, not at all the adult voice she'd used to bestow those words of wisdom earlier. He smoothed his hand over her head and placed a kiss in her hair. The fact that she'd witnessed her father's death pained him. She had already lost her mother to a suspicious heart attack, yet here she sat orphaned and asking if he was okay?

He peered into her pale eyes. "You do know I will keep you safe at all cost, don't you?"

She snuggled into him then, but it seemed she snuggled because he needed it, not her. She patted his arm, soothing him while he'd thought he was soothing her.

Ember hollered from the kitchen sink. "Hey, Rory."

"I'm right here," he answered quietly.

She turned to him and Nima. "Oh, there you are. You guys are so quiet. I thought you were still upstairs."

He didn't respond. When Nima relaxed against him, that familiar fatherhood habit kicked in. He began to rock the orphaned little waif in his arms.

"I had an idea." Ember said, running water over the colander of raw shrimp while she munched a carrot stick. "How about we eat like royalty tonight? The refrigerator is stocked with some yummy food. I thought we'd start with a Szechuan stir-fry. Would you like that?"

For a fraction of a second, the sensation where a child lived happily-ever-after with both a mother and father intruded again. He shook his head to chase it away.

"What? You don't like Szechuan?" Ember frowned at his headshake, her eyes full of energy and sparkles and— ARGH! How could she be annoying, charming, and sexy at the same time?

"That's not what I meant. Whatever you fix, I'll eat."

"Cool. Then get your butt in here and chop some cabbage for me."

"No."

She glanced up from her work. "But there are vegetables to chop and shrimp to clean and—"

"No, I'm rocking."

"You're rocking?"

"Yes. When my mom rocks Tyler to sleep, she sings him a song about how cobwebs and dust needed to take a number and wait for more important things like little boys and girls. It's a good song."

Ember cocked an eyebrow, a question in her puzzled greens. She had no husband, no children and no clue what was important in life. But he did. Not very long ago he'd been no smarter than she was now, but life had brought him Tyler, and now Nima. The world needed to step back and give him and Nima some quiet time.

She'd cuddled in under his chin, her little hand splayed over his heart and patting him like he needed it. He might look like a sap, but he didn't care. If only Ember would quiet down along with the dust and cobwebs of his mother's wise lullaby.

As if on cue, she lowered her voice. "Okay. I can fix lunch myself." Ember looked content standing there at the sink, chopping vegetables while the wok warmed on the stove. The fleeting sensation of a happy family taunted.

No way. Not with her. Never.

Six

"Let's add some more bubble bath, okay?" Ember added the amber liquid to the stream beneath the running faucet. After a delicious lunch, she'd taken Nima upstairs for a bath in the oversized tub. Ember wanted to make sure every last bit of blood evidence was washed off the girl's pudgy body. But mostly, she wanted to get that ugly, old-fashioned velvet dress out of sight. Ugh. What an awful thing to put on a sweet little girl.

Maxwell Farr and Fred Middleton had yet to show, but it was a decent drive from Alexandria, so she wasn't worried. Both new to The TEAM, they were ex-Army rangers who knew about good defensive tactical strategy. Fred hailed from the bayous of southern Louisiana, while Maxwell was Montana born and raised. They'd be there soon enough.

But the tub was so big, and naked little Nima looked lost sitting in the middle of it. The more it filled with water and bubbles, the smaller she seemed. There was only one solution. Ember undressed and joined her.

Nima clapped when the water level rose with Ember's arrival, and the bubbles flew. Her eyes wide with surprise, she clapped again and sputtered. Ember giggled at the unexpected playful side to the usually somber child. She clapped and played pat-a-cake. More bubbles flew.

"Mama!" Nima squealed, another surprising foray into no-kidding, childish behavior.

"No, sweetheart," Ember explained. "Me Ember. You Nima."

"Mama Ember!" Nima chortled, her face full of mischief.

"But I'm not really…" Ember paused. What did it hurt? If Nima wanted to call her Mama, then so be it. It was puzzling that Nima spoke so seldom, though. Maybe it was the language barrier, but Ember doubted it. Nima didn't seem to have much trouble speaking in perfect English when she wanted to. Interesting. No, make that spooky, but kind of cute. Nima already had some serious feminine mystique going for her.

"Okay. If I'm Mama Ember, you're Princess Nima, okay?"

Nima clapped, her face filled with delight. Ember couldn't hold back a full-blown giggle. Playing in the tub with this delightful little girl almost made the disasters of the operation fade away. Before long, they had bubbles in their hair, on the walls, and all over the floor.

"You are such a doll," Ember said as she snagged the washcloth and pulled Nima toward her. "But we've got to get you clean. Let me check those ears."

Nima cocked her head while Ember cleaned gently. She washed the little girl's hair, then her own until they both looked like drowned but happy divas.

"Hang on, baby," she said as she lowered underwater to rinse her head. "Don't let go of my fingers."

Nima grinned and gripped Ember's fingers. The kid was nearly floating on top of the water, her little pink backside peeking up through the bubbles. Ember leaned backward until her hair submersed, and then, oh, why not? She ducked entirely underwater, shook the shampoo out, and came up quickly, much to Nima's delighted squeal. Sudsy water shifted from one end of the tub and back again. Ember smoothed the water off her face with one hand, the other still gripping Nima. She blinked, her eyes still full of bath water.

And oh, my hell.

Rory stood at the door, his mouth gaping like a goldfish. If he'd been underwater with her, he could have made bubbles with all the lip-smacking he was doing.

"Umm, hi," she said, because she was as surprised as he was.

He took a quick step backward and slammed the door.

Nima's eyes widened at his abrupt departure, but Ember grinned. "Oh, oh. I think Uncle Rory saw something he wasn't supposed to see. He's been a naughty boy."

Nima splashed and more bubbles flew, only there weren't many left. The shampoo had decimated the suds, leaving Ember and Nima exposed. Ember's, umm, other *girls* were exposed, too. She scooped a handful of the remaining suds to cover her breasts, which didn't really cover much. The bubbles were mostly gone. Her *girls* were—not.

"Did you need to see me?" she called out after Rory, chuckling at the innuendo she'd tossed in his direction. Ha! Hadn't Alex told him to take care of his *girls?* Had Rory already seen enough of his *girls*? Maybe not. Oh, if Alex only knew how many ways she could twist his innocent, male chauvinist comment. Men. Flash a little skin and they all turned into little boys with a hard-on.

Aggravation emanated from the other side of the door. "You were supposed to be giving her a bath."

"I am."

"You never said you were taking one with her."

She was right. He was angry. "I didn't plan to." She used her most patient voice. He was, after all, the guy in charge. She owed him a polite explanation. Kind of. "We're both girls, in case you haven't noticed. Besides, it's not like I'm doing a striptease in here. Sheesh. We're just taking a bath together. Give it a rest."

"But you're... you're...." He sputtered. "You're not dressed, and she's just a little girl."

"So what? Don't you ever shower or bathe with Tyler? Not even at the swimming pool?" Ember put a dollop of the remaining suds on Nima's head. "There. That will keep him quiet."

Nima ducked her head into her shoulders, peeking out from under the drippy suds with a big smile.

"Yeah, b-b-but...."

"But what, Dennison?" She egged him on. "You want to join us? Come on in. There's plenty of room in this big ole tub. The water's fine and so are your *girls*."

"No. David's on the phone. Thought you'd want to hear what he has to say. That's all."

"I'd love to. What's keeping you?" Ember grinned wickedly at Nima and whispered, "How much do you want to bet he says no?"

"No!"

Wow. That answer was quicker than she'd expected. Nima giggled at the fun game like she knew what Ember was doing.

"Gee whiz. I guess you'll have to tell David I'm indisposed at the moment. Could you, like, take a message for me and my *girls*?" She wrinkled her nose and instantly Nima did the same. "He's so grumpy, isn't he?"

Nima scrunched her shoulders, her cute little nose, too

Ember giggled harder. She could picture him at the other side of the door, his hands on the frame, his head lowered, maybe shaking it as he tried to figure her out.

"I guess." His grumbly voice receded down the stairs. Apparently he was taking the call from the safety of the couch. The big chicken.

She stepped out of the tub and wrapped herself in one of the huge bath sheets before she pulled Nima out of the water and dried her. Then the real fun began. Ember dressed the little girl in comfortable, chocolate brown leggings with a pink ruffled top. To finish it off, she dried Nima's hair, pulled it up into a topknot and tied it off with a pink ribbon. By the time she was through, Nima looked more like the all-American little girl next door instead of the future Dalai Lama. She looked cute.

"You're beautiful," Ember exclaimed.

Nima scrunched her nose. "Me boo-di-foo."

And then, simply because it would irritate Rory, Ember walked downstairs with nothing on but the towel. He was on the phone with David when she plopped Nima onto his lap, but wow. If only he could've seen the look on his face. Those dark blues all but popped out of his head. Ten shades of scarlet slithered up his neck and right on into the roots of all that gorgeous dark hair. For once, nothing sarcastic poured out of his lips because his smirky mouth had dropped open. Wide open.

"And for your information," she announced with her nose lifted high, "my name is Mama Ember and this is Princess Nima. You will treat us accordingly."

"Mama!" Nima bounced on Rory's lap. "Yep! Mama Ember!"

He winced. The big jerk probably needed to make a major adjustment in his, umm, major guy department. She sashayed back upstairs, making sure to put a little more jiggle into her swinging hips than normal. Not until she was out of his sight did she drop the towel. *Yes! Take that, Dennison. Mission accomplished!* Fist pumping her right arm, she grinned at the one-sided conversation coming from below.

"Umm, what? What'd you say, David?" Rory didn't sound so smart now. "I'm sorry. Say again."

She grinned in triumph. He might be the grumpy one in the house. He might be rude and bossy and grouchy most of the time, but her agent in charge had just gotten the comeuppance he deserved.

She dressed in the new black jeans and hoody she'd just bought, and took extra time drying and brushing her hair. Before she left the bathroom, she leaned over and shook her head to give those blonde tresses a windblown effect. Hopefully, it would rattle him even more. It might not be her usual feisty look for the day, but he'd get the message. *The gloves are off, buddy. There are two women in the house, and you are so outnumbered.*

Rory was off the phone by the time she walked downstairs. Instead of joining him and Nima, though, she busied herself in the kitchen doing dishes. He stayed quiet on the couch. But there were only so many dishes. It didn't take long to tidy the small kitchen.

She turned to face him, fully expecting a stern rebuke from her agent in charge. The sight that met her eyes melted her heart. Rory had Nima snuggled in his arms, the two of them sound asleep in the corner of the couch. With one boot on the floor, his other leg bent to cradle Nima, she was tucked under his chin, one tiny hand fisted against her lips.

Ember's heart stuttered. *Aww. What a sweet picture.*

Sitting in the chair opposite them, she just watched. It did her heart good. A handsome man with a kid was the most adorable and sexy combination in her playbook. And he could cook, too. Despite their antagonism toward each other, she had no doubt he was a good man and a great father. His good looks had always been her downfall, which was why his sudden disapproval had hurt her feelings. But here he was, the one to fall asleep instead of her this time. He had to be exhausted.

But why was it important not to share the domestic side of his life with his friends at work? The TEAM was comprised of nothing but old soldiers, herself, and Mother. And yes, she got why he might not want Mother in his business. No one did. Mother could be intrusive, nosy, and controlling. She even tried the patience of Alex, not like that was hard to do. She seemed to forget who was the boss, but for the most part, she was just lonely. Mother didn't even have a cat like Ember did, just her online gaming buddies who built video games and played hacking scenarios with her when she wasn't in the office. That was the lonely genius called Mother.

Nima wiggled on Rory's stomach. Instantly, he patted her back to soothe her, even in his sleep. Ember smiled. She made the rounds to the little bungalow, checked the locks and tidied the bathroom in case Rory might want to shower later.

And then, because he hadn't stirred, she opened the front door very carefully and sat on the brick step outside the door. Maxwell and Fred would arrive soon. That alone brought added comfort. Reinforcements always made a difference.

The crisp autumn air smelled earthy and fresh. Dark clouds along the west horizon pushed a light breeze over the brick driveway. From her vantage point, green fields wrapped around the McCormack summer home and barn. Deciduous trees in various shades of reds, yellows, and oranges lined the fields. When the door opened quietly behind her, Ember held her breath. *Here it comes. I'm in trouble.*

Rory joined her on the step, but he didn't say a word about her sensational act with the towel. "I thought I heard the door," he said quietly.

"I needed some air. It's pretty out here." She glanced sideways at him. He didn't look mad. "Is Nima still asleep?"

"Yes. Sorry about that. I didn't mean to fall asleep with her."

"I've done it enough. Something about Nima makes us relax."

"She likes to snuggle," he said simply. "And she's warm. Maxwell and Fred should be here any minute."

"That will be good. What did David have to say?"

"Not much. He explained the process of how the High Lamas select the next Dalai Lama. That's about all. David gets into all that stuff. I was only half listening."

Of course he was only half listening. What red-blooded man wouldn't be half listening with a naked woman traipsing around the place in nothing but a towel?

"So you're Mama Ember now?" he asked, without a trace of sarcasm.

"I am according to Nima. What else did David have to say?" she asked, hoping to divert him away from her towel routine. She still couldn't believe she'd acted like that. What the heck came over her?

Rory yawned. "He mentioned something about the Living Buddhas of the three great monasteries and a series of tests and the direction of the smoke when the current Dalai Lama is cremated. It sounds like a lot of mumbo-jumbo to me."

"I think all religions sound like a lot of mumbo-jumbo."

"That's because you don't believe."

"You're right, and I don't want to. I mean, look at all the religions in the world. They all want you to think they're the right church, whatever that is. They all want your money. And they're the reason for most of the world's problems. I don't need any of them."

"You've got to believe in something, Ember."

"So what religion are you?" she asked defensively.

"Catholic."

"Why?" That surprised her. A lot of the guys coming home from the Mideast returned disillusioned with God in general.

"It's how I was raised."

"Wow." She rolled her eyes. "Now there's a good reason to believe in something."

"Actually, it is." He turned to face her. "I follow in the footsteps of some very brave and smart men and women who've sweat blood and tears to give me what I have today. They taught me right from wrong. My family is why I'm a Marine. It's a proud tradition. Who else would I want to follow, some idiot in Hollywood who tells me what to wear, eat, and drink? Think about it."

"Whatever." She brushed his very logical answer away, like cobwebs that might get into her head if she listened too long. He did make sense in his annoying, smug way.

"Let's not talk religion, okay?" He turned away, the subject closed like everything else in his life. Annoyance edged back into his voice.

"Good. Religion is stupid anyway." Ember turned away from him too, toward the trees. For a moment, they sat in silence. She changed the subject. "Fall is my favorite time of year," she said wistfully.

"I give. Why?"

She answered despite the perturbed tone to his voice. "All the colors, I guess. Spring is all pinks and soft colors, but fall is bright and vivid. It's like it takes Mother Nature all summer long to come up with the most awesome colors. They're like fireworks. They make the rest of the world pop and zing before everything turns gray and cold."

"I did notice you like vivid colors. Why all the crazy get-ups?" For once, he'd asked a personal question without the sting of sarcasm.

She shrugged. "They make me feel good."

"Hmm. Colors and crazy clothes make you feel good. Why?"

He didn't understand. Men usually didn't. "It's like this. Say I'm feeling sad and need a boost, you know, like a pick me up for my inner soul. I change the way I look outside, and it affects the way I feel inside. It's like a new hairdo. It works every time."

"Go on."

"Okay, like I had a close friend who died a while ago. You remember him, Todd Chandler. At first I wore nothing but black because I was sad. I missed him, but one day I was putting on my kohl black eyeliner, and I decided I was only making myself sadder. So I changed my hair to blue, then bright orange. By the time I got to green, I felt a whole lot better."

"I do recall the green hair." He sounded so analytical, like he was working a puzzle. "Why all the piercings and tattoos? Same reason?"

"Sure. Look at this one." Ember pulled the side of her shirt up and the top of her pants down enough to reveal her slender waist and hip. An artfully inked, small green frog tattoo sat at the top of her hip, its long back leg hanging to one side as if it had barely landed.

Rory glanced and quickly looked away.

"For Pete's sake. Did you even see it?"

"I saw it. It's a frog." He scanned the brickwork to the big house, obviously flustered at her display.

She twisted around to help him see it better. "Come on, Dennison. Look again. It's cute."

At her insistence, he eyeballed her exposed skin one more time. The inked green frog licked its lips. It had bright orange eyes, and it was the cutest thing ever, but Rory blushed, blinked, and averted his eyes too quickly to have really seen the fantastic artwork.

She smacked his shoulder with her open palm. "I can't believe it. I'm embarrassing you, aren't I?"

"No," he answered a little too quickly. "Okay. Maybe a little."

That made her grin. "Wow. A big old Marine like you and you're shy? What? You don't like looking at a lady's bare hip?"

He pursed his lips thoughtfully. "I just don't think women should be ogled."

Wow. He's uptight with women's bodies. Maybe he's gay after all.

"What about you? What do you do when you're feeling sad?" she asked.

Again he raked his fingers through his hair. Waves of ebony ruffled and stood straight only to fall against his scalp where they belonged. The image of her fingers combing over that hard head tantalized. What would his hair feel like between her fingers? Some guys shaved their heads to varying lengths for the sake of fashion, all of it prickly or spiked, but his? Two or three inches and trimmed at the neckline, nothing like the jarhead cut of a USMC grunt. More like....

Stop thinking about his hair already. But soft. Yeah. His hair would feel soft. And clean.

"I play with Tyler. We go to baseball games and the gym. Guy stuff."

The wistful tone in his answer struck a chord. She held her breath.

"Can I ask you a personal question?"

"Go ahead."

"Where's Tyler's mother?"

Seven

Rolling his neck, he stared over the top of Jed McCormack's huge house like he was a thousand miles away all of a sudden. When she thought he wouldn't answer, he did. "New York, I guess." He didn't meet her eyes.

"Is she a model or something? A stock broker?"

He grunted. "Hardly. She's a pro, Ember. She works the streets to support her drug habit. Meth, the last I heard."

Meth? So not good. Just as quickly, another enlightenment came. *Damn. His wife's a prostitute. That's why he doesn't objectify women's bodies. That's why he protects Tyler. Wow. He might not be gay after all.*

"I'm sorry," was all she could come up with.

"Me, too." He stretched his long legs down the steps in front of him. "We got married during my last tour. She seemed full of life and energy, and me? I was stupid in love— or lust—or whatever the heck was going on in my head. It sure wasn't brains. I missed all the signs. One day the Red Cross contacted me. I'd just come in from a two-month field assignment. They said I had a family emergency; that my wife was in premature labor with complications. I flew home on compassionate leave. It wasn't until she delivered that I wised up to how bad things really were. Her doctor let me have it."

"What complications?"

"Tyler was addicted when he was born. Poor little guy screamed for months. God, he suffered."

A picture of sweet little Tyler waving to her at the gym and telling her *'See you later, alligator,'* flashed to her mind. She wanted to cry at the thought of him suffering for the stupid decisions of his mother. "That had to be awful."

"It was. That's why he talks like he does. We live a very structured life at home. I work with him every night on his numbers. Speech. Letters. Everything. I enrolled him in preschool, but they wanted him on medication before they'd let him attend. Said they couldn't handle him because he wouldn't sit still. He's got Attention Deficit Disorder and hyperactivity as a result of his addiction. That's all. He could've been a lot worse."

"Me, too," she admitted. "It's not as bad as when I was younger, but there are ways to deal with it."

"I won't medicate my son, so I tutor him myself." Dark blues scrutinized McCormack's lavish brick design. "That's why I'm protective of Tyler. No one will ever hurt him again."

"That's why you don't take overseas assignments, isn't it?"

"Right. Alex has been real good to work with me. He knows I'll pinch hit when necessary, like the op into Mexico last year, but mostly I handle day jobs, bodyguard or escort assignments. I'm his least valuable asset."

Ember couldn't believe the change in her companion agent. "You are not. I've heard him. You got shot in Mexico. You kept shooting even though you'd taken three hits. You saved Mark's life. Alex thinks the world of you. Everyone does." *And I knew there was a reason I liked you.*

"If you say so."

"It's true."

He didn't answer.

"So I'm the only one who knows?" she asked quietly.

"Connor and Izza do. They're good friends. And Alex." Rory looked directly at her. "Sorry. It's not something fun like belonging to a party-all-night club."

"It's nice you're telling me all this, though," she said thoughtfully. "Your private eye guy located your wife in New York, then?"

Rory blew out a weary sigh, his tongue stuck in his cheek. "The first time she was in Detroit. She said she had family there, if that's what you want to call her customers, you know, all her johns. Then Cleveland, New Jersey, New York. Last I heard she had a pimp. I quit looking."

"So, umm, you're divorced?" Ember cringed when she asked. She'd always been attracted to Rory. His single status had a lot to do with that attraction. If he was still married, even in what sounded like a really bad marriage, she didn't want to entertain the notion. Married men were hands off. Trouble.

"I had to divorce her. She was killing me. She racked up more debt in a couple of months than I'd had in my whole life. I had to cut her off to save Tyler. He's the one who needs me. Not her. All she needs is a fix and a cheap place to sleep it off."

"But you still love her."

No answer. Dumb question. Of course he still loved her. Ember backpedaled, afraid she'd passed the limit of covert agent propriety, whatever that was. "You have a son to be proud of."

"I do. I am. He's the best part in my life."

"If you don't mind me asking, what was her name?"

"Elizabeth Winchester Calhoun Dennison." He grunted like the memory didn't hurt. "Everyone called her Ellie."

Hmm. That meant he called her Ellie. And he loved Ellie once upon a time, enough to make a baby with her.

"That's a beautiful name. What did she look like?" Ember cringed again, not sure why she needed to know what his ex-wife looked like. It wasn't important, but if he was willing to share....

"It doesn't matter. She's gone."

The Dennison wall was back up, but Ember heard the real reason. He didn't *want* to tell her. Ellie must've been beautiful. Ember couldn't imagine him with anything less. "I'm sorry. I'll shut up. It's none of my business anyway."

The silence between them lasted only as long as his next sigh. "No, you're good. It's just that she never saw Tyler, not even once. He wasn't breathing when he was born. The nurses grabbed him and rushed him away. Scared the hell out of me. She was in the birthing room getting cleaned up. He was in the NICU, the neonatal intensive care unit, while I was getting my butt reamed for *letting* her do drugs. Like I had anything to say about the crap she did while I was deployed. By the time I got back to her room, she'd taken off. Left a note on her pillow. Said she never really wanted to get married in the first place; the kid was my fault. My problem. She was out of there. Here she'd given birth to the most perfect little guy in the universe, and she threw him away like trash."

A tear slipped out of her eye. What a stupid trade-off, leaving a guy the likes of Rory and a son as sweet as Tyler for drugs. Gold for chaff. Ellie was just plain stupid.

All at once, Rory's hand was on her shoulder. "Sorry. You don't need to hear my problems."

She stifled a sob, wanting to rush back to the gym and snuggle sweet little Tyler. He and his father both needed a hug. She did, too. If only.

"Come on, don't cry," he persisted, his hand gently massaging her shoulder. "Guess I need to learn when to shut up, don't I?"

And I need to stop jumping to conclusions.

"Give me a minute," she said through her sniffles. "I'm sorry I gave you such a bad time before. I never knew."

"There was no way you could've. I run a pretty tight ship. Mark and Zack don't even know. Harley might. He's more intuitive than most guys."

She wiped her nose on the sleeve of her hoody. "Sheesh. I wish tear ducts were on the bottom of our feet, don't you?"

Unexpectedly, he put his arm around her. With a gentle swipe of his fingertip, he wiped the moisture from her cheek. "But think of all the soggy socks you'd have."

Her breath hitched. For once, she couldn't meet his handsome gaze. Time stopped ticking. She couldn't have heard it anyway the way her heart was hammering like it needed to get out of her chest. Sheesh. His breath on her cheek sent shivers down to her toes. She blinked. He didn't. *Wow. He has really thick lashes.*

"If I still had my phone, I'd show you the pictures from Yellowstone. They'd make you smile again."

"Oh?" Right now everything out of this man's mouth made her lips want to smile and do a couple other things, too. Like kiss him. Taste him.

"Yes. I got a real cute shot of Tyler sitting with his Sizzly Bear at Fishing Bridge. I was going to frame it and hang it in his bedroom. Guess I missed my chance."

"His what?" She wiped her face with her hoody sleeve one last time.

"I bought him a stuffed bear at Yellowstone. He couldn't say Grizzly Bear, so it became Mr. Sizzly Bear, only he says it kind of like Sizz-wee Bear."

"I didn't know you went to Yellowstone," she said, still enjoying the feel of his arm around her. *Wow. He's so strong. And solid. And warm.* Her nose twitched. She couldn't remember him buying men's cologne when they'd stopped for new clothes, but damn. He smelled good. Kind of like soap. Body wash. Him.

"Alex gave everyone involved in the Mexico operation quite a bit of time off when we got home. While I was recuperating, Tyler and me headed west. We camped out, did some fly-fishing in Montana, about everything two guys could think of. Went through the east gate of Yellowstone and had a ball seeing the sights."

"How'd you do all that with your leg injury? Weren't you shot in the leg?"

"Guess it's the Marine in me. I'm never too banged up I can't make my son happy. 'Sides, I used a cane for awhile."

"Why are you telling me this?" she asked, his lips close enough she could taste them if she wanted to. Her tongue involuntarily responded to the thought, moistening her bottom lip. Just in case he was thinking the same thing. His eyes were extra blue right now. Extra deep. Dark. Sexy. Her heart fluttered. He licked his bottom lip. Wow. He just might be thinking the same thing.

"Maybe it's because I can finally see you instead of all your make-up." Playfully, he tapped the end of her nose, breaking the spell.

She was speechless, but he wasn't done.

"Nima said something before. She told me that if I keep hiding, no one would ever find me. I got the oddest sensation I should tell you about Tyler, that I didn't have to hide him from you anymore. I usually keep him to myself."

Wow. Rory trusted her? She'd just become part of a very private club.

She heard a light knock on the door behind them. Rory reached back and turned the knob. Out walked a sleepy Nima straight for Ember's lap. Thankful for the interruption to his heady revelations, Ember leaned away from him and snuggled the girl into her arms. "Are you feeling better?"

Nima stared straight through her with those spooky eyes of hers. Ember's breath caught. She had to clutch Rory's elbow for support. The oddest sensation of being violated swept through her, but at the same time, she was infused with peace.

Nima's calmer than calm voice radiated all the way to her unorthodox, free-spirited toes. "If you seek to heal your own tears, seek first to heal the sadness of another."

Ember reeled. The words pierced her heart. That's what she'd felt for Rory and Tyler—like she'd wanted to ease their sadness, but how could Nima know? How could a tiny little person even form that kind of a sentence when she hardly spoke any other time in any language? Why now? Ember shivered, feeling suddenly stripped bare and exposed.

"What did you say?" Rory turned the child to face him. Nima only smiled while her countenance returned to normal. Her lips sealed again, she snuggled into Ember's arms like an embarrassed little girl.

Ember's heart beat like a full brass band in her ribcage. She glanced over at Rory, sure he could hear it, too. "This kid is too much. Wow."

"What did she tell you?"

Right on cue, the wind came up. Leaves blew across the driveway in a swirling bluster of dust. Dark clouds closed in from the west.

"Looks like it might storm." He picked Nima up and helped Ember to her feet. "Let's go in, ladies, then we'll talk."

Ember glanced skyward. The air was charged with electricity that made the hair on the back of her neck stand up. A sharp crack of lightning hit somewhere close by, too close for comfort. Most children would have been scared to death at the display Mother Nature unleashed, but not Nima. She smiled that same mysterious smile again and peered up at the sky as if she'd been looking for the rain, and it was late.

Was the little girl somehow in tune with Mother Nature? Did Nima anticipate the storm? As quickly as Ember shook the foolish notion from her head, another materialized. Had Nima simply requested the storm and Mother Nature obeyed?

It feels true, but wow. Who is this little girl?

Rory shut the door behind them as the fury of the storm unleashed. Lightning stabbed the green field and woods. Trees bent to the earth as a wild wind raged, pillaged, and thunder roared. Pounding sheets of driven rain hammered the house.

"Whew! Just in time." He stomped his feet at the door, shaking the rain out of his hair. "That came up in a hurry. Hope Maxwell and Fred don't get lost. They should've been here by now. So what'd she say?"

Ember didn't answer. She couldn't. Still speechless from what she thought she'd witnessed, she went straight to the couch, needing to sit before she fell down.

He came to sit beside her with Nima. "You okay?"

Maybe. Maybe not. Seek first to heal my own tears? Wow. Where to begin?

Todd Chandler's handsome smiling face came to mind. Losing him had literally pushed her into the deep end. She'd gone dark. Darker than dark. Immersed her body in the blackest clothes and her hair in the deepest, blackest dyes, her heart in soulless music and unholy thinking. She'd sought for an end to the pain gnawing from the inside out, but settled for lesser ways to vent the anguish.

In the end only work kept her sane. The guys on The TEAM kept her returning to the job she loved; her real family. Not her mother. Never her father. Only the ones who valued her when she didn't value herself. Alex. Harley. Mother. Zack. That real family. It dawned on her that Rory was part of that same good family. Aloof maybe, but present even when she was not there for herself.

Wow.

Her nose detected the men's body wash from the safe house, mingled with that other smell—that all American, he-should-have-been, could-have-been a model smell. It was in the wind they'd run in from. Fresh. Clean. Full of life. And power. *Wow.* Ember gulped without enough saliva in her throat to actually swallow. In one fell swoop, Nima had tied Ember's heart to another. To Rory. To Tyler. Why now? Why him?

Yet he sat oblivious to the revelation, waiting for an answer. Just like a man. A good man.

When she could speak, her voice sounded far away, as if someone else was speaking for her. "If you seek to heal your own tears, seek first to heal the sadness of another."

Nima scooted from his arms to hers. "Yep," she said quietly.

"It's like she knows us inside out," he said, his voice full of gentleness. "But what tears could you possibly need to heal?"

"I, umm, guess everyone's got some sad days in their past. I'm no different than you," she said quietly, wondering why the deep connection with him all of a sudden. She'd thoroughly enjoyed her relationship with Todd. It was easy. Uncomplicated. They'd loved and played together, but Rory? Nothing about him seemed easy, not from the start. A connection with him would bring pain. There'd be no easing of sadness. There might even be—love. And that's what scared her the most. She'd been down that road with Todd Chandler. Love meant pain. The greater the love, the harder the hit when it ended, and it always ended. In the front yard. In foster homes. At Arlington.

"How about if I start a fire?" he asked softly. "You look cold."

Ember shivered. She was definitely cold all right, but Mother Nature had nothing to do with the change in temperature. Ember wasn't on her safe, comfortable path anymore. Her paradigms had changed, and she knew it. She wanted her cat. Maple Syrup was huggable. Comfortable. Safe.

Rory knelt at the fireplace. When the gas flame sprang to life, he was caught in the silhouette of the orange-gold glow. He turned back to her with a grin and a wink. "That was hard. You gotta love a gas fireplace, huh? Just flick a switch and bam, instant cozy."

She couldn't make her eyes move off of him. The spotlight of gold behind him rattled another paradigm. Just when her life was predictable, the universe opened wide and out dropped—Rory Dennison. And Tyler. And Nima. A ready made family. *Wow....*

He came back to sit with her and Nima, and with one fluid motion, rested his arm along the back of the couch. It felt completely natural behind her and Nima's shoulders. Like a father's arm around his child and his—

Ember jumped to her feet. "Anyone want a bowl of ice cream? I think I spotted some in the freezer."

"Sure. I'll help." He was agreeable all of a sudden. What happened to the rude guy who'd snapped her head off every time she opened her mouth yesterday? She wanted him back, and she wanted him now. And why did the glow from the fireplace stick to him?

He pulled three bowls from the cupboard and three spoons from the drawer while she'd gone from eight fingers to ten thumbs. Her trembling fingers would not lift the lid off the carton of chocolate almond ice cream. *What is wrong with me?*

"Do you think Nima has ever tasted ice cream before?" he asked. "Do they have ice cream in India?"

Whoa. Even his voice had changed. It was somehow deeper and stronger and—

No! No! No! This was so not happening! It had to stop, but when she glanced sideways at him, prepared to snap his head off for being so—nice, her stupid heart got stuck in her throat, suffocating any denial from squeaking forth. Her resolve melted like the chocolate almond ice cream in the rain.

"Hope so," she said, as sweetly as if she meant it.

Eight

"Shit!" Rory growled. "Grab Nima. Now!"

Ember blinked at him like he'd suddenly spoken Greek.

"We've got company. Move it!"

She got the message. With a mad dash, she grabbed Nima off the couch. Ember looped her arm through the plastic bags of clothing they'd bought. "Hold tight, baby girl. Don't let go."

"There's a couple of men outside McCormack's back door," Rory growled. "Not Maxwell and Fred. Damn it. Where are they?"

Lightning detonated outside, the bright flash followed swiftly by booming thunder. Rory had his SIG drawn, his back flat to the wall beside the front door. He motioned Ember to his side. She looked plenty scared, and for the first time, so was he. How were these guys tracking them?

"Wait until they go inside the big house. When I say go, run for the car. Same drill as last time. Shit!" he cursed under his breath, but immediately apologized. "Sorry, Nima."

She didn't say a word.

"Let's give these guys something to think about." He pulled a remote detonator from his pocket, glaring at Ember. "You ready?"

"Yes, sir," she answered meekly.

"Go!" He pressed the detonator and immediately, several explosions shook the ground between the big house and the little house. Obediently, she bolted through the door.

He pressed his hand hard in the middle of her back, pushing her all the way to the Taurus. He all but shoved her and Nima to the backseat floor. How had these guys found them so fast? His mind going a thousand miles a minute, he was at a loss. Another troubling development—Mother hadn't given them advance notice. Why not? What the hell was going on?

Shots rang out. Too damn close! Rory ducked as he turned the ignition. He slammed his door shut. Tires squealed off the brick pavement and the car slid sideways for a minute over the wet grass. Rory growled, jerked the steering wheel into the slide and back again before the tires grabbed hold. More shots sounded and the back window shattered. The car shot forward. Glass sprayed from the back window to the front dash.

He gunned the engine. The Taurus responded nicely, fishtailing through the green field all the way to the rear of the barn. But the rain had left the hard-packed soil muddy with a slick top layer of no traction. The rear of the car whipped back and forth, the mud transformed to black ice on a green highway. Another shot reduced his driver's side mirror to dust. The bombs he'd set had offered nothing but temporary confusion, not death like he'd wanted. He had company coming up close and fast behind him.

Headlights shot bright daggers through the rearview mirror into his line of vision. He growled and gave the accelerator another demanding stab. The car groaned, lifted out of the mud, and its tires caught on what he didn't know. It sped forward as if he'd salted the ground beneath it. Around the edge of the field he flew, turned abruptly right when the trees gave him an opening, and gunned the car alongside the square patch of trees. No cars followed. Yet.

The more adrenaline pumped into him, the harder he pressed the accelerator. Now would be a damned good time for Maxwell and Fred to show up and rain hellfire on these bastards. The engine screamed for all it was worth. He rounded the long stand of trees and caught the flash of a bright light in the rearview mirror. *What? RPG? No freaking way!*

"Hang on!" he ordered his precious cargo as he swerved hard to the right. Trees buckled to the left behind him, torn apart by the assassins' determination that meant one thing and one thing only. Death. Huge splinters and sheered-off branches flew through the air. The car lifted two wheels from the ground—two left wheels. For a second, he expected they'd roll, but no. The car righted as if it knew better. Thudding mightily back to all four tires, it bounced, and dug into solid traction one more time. He watched desperately for a road but saw only trees on the right, fields to the left.

Shit! Shit! Shit! He should've scouted the perimeter better, made damn sure they had a rock solid escape plan. Obviously, the few C-4 charges he'd planted weren't enough deterrent. He pushed the car for all it was worth. Rain blurred the windshield, but even the wipers seemed determined. They flopped, flailed, but kept clearing the rain, mud, and leaves off the glass in front of him.

Finally, a dirt road appeared alongside another field of tall brown corn. He turned left sharply, the rear end of the car taking out more than a few rows of corn before it decided to follow. But the road was exactly what he needed. It ran straight and true—and north, away from the McCormack estate and hopefully from whoever was trying to kill them.

He reached around to pat Ember's back. "How are you doing back there?"

"Good," she said, but her voice was shaky. She was scared. Well, so was he.

"Stay down. Things may get bumpy." He wanted to pat her back again but didn't. Instead, he pulled out his cell phone. No bars. "You got a signal on your phone?"

"No. Do you?"

"I don't. The storm might have taken out the nearest cell tower." That explained why there was no advance notice from Mother. No one knew the trouble they were in. But where were Maxwell and Fred? Had the assassins engaged them prior to the attack on McCormack's? A sickening sensation gripped his gut. There could only be one reason his buddies hadn't shown. The assassins had struck again. Help wasn't coming.

"How are these killers finding us?"

"Let's think about that. What do we know?" He heard the fear in her voice, so he forced calmness into his reply. Leadership training took over. *Think better. Analyze what you know. Understand the enemy. Then react.*

"They aren't tracking us by GPS anymore because we tossed our cell phones. There's no way they could have a tracking device on David's car. We didn't even know we'd be driving it. Neither could they know we've gotten new phones."

"Right. What else do we know?" He forced her to dig deeper. *And above all, keep calm. Hysterical leaders do not inspire troops to follow.*

"What's left? What do we still have with us that we had back at the temple?"

She sounded a whole lot more vulnerable than he'd ever imagined Ember could sound. He pressed the accelerator for more. The car surged ahead, corn whipping past them for miles. *Damn, this is a huge field of corn.*

Logic got lost when headlights flashed in the rearview. Out of nowhere, a black car plowed sideways into their vehicle, pushing it several rows to the right and back into the corn. Another car appeared on their right, pushing them back to the dirt road and into the first. A third car rammed the rear bumper. They were trapped.

I need the damned highway patrol. NOW!

"Hang on!" He slammed the steering wheel first left then hard to the right. It was all he could do to hold it steady and not send the car rolling. The slippery conditions made for an unpredictable racetrack. For a moment both assailant cars at his sides backed off, but too soon they lurched back against David's family car. Side to side. Metal ground upon metal. Plastic trim flew through the air. The vehicles pitched back and forth as the assailants pushed in for the kill.

BLAM!

Ember's gunshot rang out directly behind him. "You want to try that again, you bastard!" she screamed, firing again. The tremendous heaving groan from a metal body digging into the soft earth from somewhere to his left sounded loud and clear. He caught a glimpse of the car before it flipped end over end into the forest of crushed brown cornstalks.

Ember changed positions, aimed out the opposite window and fired again, screaming all the way, "I'm sick and tired of you assholes trying to kill us!"

Tires blew. The car at his right rolled off in another cloud of corn and mud. Rory glanced at his companion. Ember was mad. Her teeth were clenched. Those baby greens looked fierce and deadly. She took another careful aim out the shattered rear window. "There's no freaking way you're gonna kill this baby, you hear me! Over my dead body!"

She missed the shot. The car behind them swerved to the right and sped up until it was alongside Rory. With a slam, it pushed the Taurus farther out of the corn and toward the trees and fence lining the field.

Rory braked hard. Unprepared for that defensive maneuver, the other car swerved ahead of them. Now Rory pursued his assailant. The minute the other car braked, he punched the Taurus into high gear and roared to the right.

The other car fell behind, but not for long. In minutes, it closed in alongside the Taurus. With a jerk, it ground against the passenger door. Both cars seemed locked together in equal battle, neither able to dissuade the other from its path. The driver's window rolled down. A man with a black balaclava covering his entire head sat behind the wheel. He pointed his index finger at Rory like a gun. And that pissed Ember off.

"You wanna play?" she shouted, scrambling to that side of the car. "Suck on this!"

Rory winced. She'd traded her Glock for the short-barreled, pump action shotgun. Too late the guy ramming them glimpsed his new reality. He swerved, but not before Ember's blast blew out every window in his car and possibly the guy's face. Rory couldn't take his eyes off the road long enough to see what happened. Whatever, the car disappeared into the cornfield and the rain, taking the assassin with it.

Rory glanced in the rearview. Ember checked Nima's seatbelt like any dutiful mother after a shoot out with a bunch of murderers. Rain pelted her back through the broken window while she hunched over the child. A mix of tenderness and rage still shifted over her face. Raking her rain-soaked hair out of her eyes, she met his gaze. Instead of the zany techie from the office, a warrior goddess glared back. Righteous fire sparked from those emerald greens, daring him to challenge her.

"You good?" he asked, trying hard not to smile at the transformation in his partner.

"I am now. Why?"

"Just asking." His lip twitched to smile even as his stupid heart flipped backward somersaults. *Why haven't I seen this side of you before?*

They traveled for more than a half hour before he ventured onto solid pavement. By then the adrenaline rush was over. He pulled the battered Taurus off the freeway at the first service station he found and quickly gassed up. Despite the downpour, Ember was out the car and back before he knew it. She'd bought two coffees, a small carton of chocolate milk and four hot dogs. The entire stop took less than five minutes. When she came back, she sat in the front seat with Nima on her lap and the seatbelt across both of them.

"It's raining," she snapped. "Nima doesn't need to catch cold on top of everything else."

She sounded like an old drill sergeant. He kept his mouth shut. *Yes, ma'am,* was the only thing that came to mind anyway. Urging the Taurus onto the rain-flooded highway, he floored the accelerator and pressed onward.

"I called Mother on the payphone back there," Ember said curtly while she opened Nima's milk. Authority dominated her voice. "Told her where we were and asked if she knew what happened. You were right. The storm knocked out the power. Police are at McCormack's, and the highway patrol is looking for David's car. She said to expect an escort soon. Alex wants the police to bring us in. He's got someone at his office who can help Nima. I don't believe it. I vote we keep running. I don't trust anyone but you."

"The drive through the cornfield sure woke you up."

The hard glint in her eye faded with a sniffle and a tightening hold on Nima, who wanted nothing more than to eat her hot dog. "They made me mad. I can't figure how they're tracking us. I mean, we just left the other safe house this morning—or last night anyway. It's like they've got us on radar. I'm tired of running scared all the time."

"How's Nima?"

At the mention of her name, little Nima reached up and patted Ember's cheek with sticky, catsup-covered fingers.

"She's fine. What do you want to do?"

"First, let's see what happens with the highway patrol. Second, I'm never getting on your bad side."

Ember stuck her tongue out at him.

Rory stayed on the highway for a fifty-mile stretch. No highway patrol appeared. No more assassins, either. Only rain. The fall thunderstorm turned into a torrential downpour, transforming the highway into a slippery water-covered river in some areas. This was tornado weather plain and simple. The car's wheels hydroplaned, causing Rory to drive slower. Other travelers on the freeway were fewer and farther between. Cold seeped into everything. It didn't help that the Taurus was without most of its windows. No matter how high he cranked the heater, the chill blowing through the vehicle added to their desperate dilemma.

Ember huddled protectively with Nima tucked inside her arms, the little one thankfully sound asleep again despite the cold. He shot a sideways glance at the cherubic light on the baby's face, but she was snuggled against Ember's lush curves and bosom. He had no doubt he'd have the same look on his face if he were in Nima's shoes. Lucky little girl.

Still, it was a toss up, death by automobile or assassin. Rory called it. "How about we find a motel and dig in for the night?"

She shook her head. "No. Keep driving. We're not safe anywhere."

"The roads aren't safe, either." He didn't argue; just calmly stated the obvious, wanting her to come to the same conclusion. A tremendous stab of lightning flashed ahead of them, adding emphasis. Thunder boomed in less time than he could say, *'One-one thousand, two-one thousand.'*

Ember was outnumbered. She bit her lip. "It is kinda scary out here. So where, then?"

What they found in the next town was a broken down motel that offered see-through towels as *luxury accommodations* and a rickety standard-sized mattress on a repainted metal bed-frame for *heavenly comfort*. Good enough. A railroad track ran within feet of the narrow parking lot. Perfect. Rory insisted on the room at the far end of the motel because it had two windows, one facing the tracks as well as the one facing the parking lot. Even better.

He parked the Taurus on the far side where it couldn't be seen from the street. Cold, wet, and shivering, he ushered his little family into the security of the euphemistically named *Over the Rainbow Inn.* Ember snuggled the sleeping child against the flat bed pillows, pulling the shabby blanket around her into a nest for extra warmth.

"Are you going to be okay, Mrs. Dillon?" he asked gently while closing the drapes and turning the window heater to high. At least it worked. A wave of dry heat drifted into the room and across the bed.

She turned away, wringing her hands. "I could use a cup of coffee."

He filled the miniature glass pot with tap water, dumped it into the coffeemaker, and crossed his fingers. "One cup of coffee coming up. How about some leftover chicken salad in the meantime?"

"Sure. Thanks."

"Stay close. I need to check in with Alex. He may want to talk with you."

That got her attention. "Why call him? Did you ever stop to think that maybe that's how they keep finding us? Maybe they've tapped The TEAM's phone lines. Maybe they've tapped Alex's cell. Maybe he's the problem, not us."

Her voice rapped up higher with every logical explanation. She made good sense. As quick as these assassins had been at locating them, maybe contacting The TEAM wasn't the smartest move. Rory compromised. "Then I'll call the Highway Patrol directly. There's no way their phones could be bugged."

Ember stared at him, her nostrils flared and breathing hard. She pursed her lips long and hard before she finally agreed. "Okay. That should work."

Rory placed a quick call, keeping it on speaker for Ember's benefit. Apparently he and she were big news, local and national. The sheriff agreed to send an armored car and plenty of backup. He told Rory to sit tight. Help was on the way, and no, he would not notify Alex on the slim possibility Ember was right and the assassins were intercepting TEAM communications.

She visibly relaxed at the news. "Slim possibility, huh?"

Rory shrugged. "Hey, he's a guy. You know how us male chauvinists are. We think we're the only ones who know anything."

She didn't crack even a glimmer of a smile.

Rory dished two paper plates of the leftover salad. He offered the dressing, but she refused it. "Come on," he coaxed. "We'll both feel better after we eat. A quick hot shower will warm you up. I'll keep watch."

She nodded, close to tears. "My clothes are wet."

And that was the problem with all the adrenaline that floods your head and body during the battle. It leaves you high and dry once the fight's done, tired as heck and sometimes a little emotional. An odd sensation rippled at the back of his mind. This was the first real crack in her composure he'd seen.

"Mind if I try something?" he asked, taking the paper plate out of her hands and setting it on the nearest nightstand.

"What?"

"Tyler gets a little crazy at the end of the day sometimes. I think it's because he was addicted when he was born.

Anyway, I used to get frustrated. Nothing I did worked. It was tough listening to a baby scream for hours on end. Drugs would've shut him up, but I refused to medicate him. He didn't need more crap in his little head. Anyway, one night I closed the door to his bedroom and walked out of the apartment. I called my mother because I'm not kidding. I was losing it. She told me sometimes the world is too big for the littlest guys. She said they're still nothing more than downy little chicks that need someone to keep them from blowing away in the wind. They need someone to hold them together."

Ember shot him a questioning glance out of the corner of her eye.

Rory shrugged one shoulder, darned if this didn't sound like a big cheesy come on to him, too. But it was true, and best of all, Mom was right. "She told me to wrap him up tight in a receiving blanket like a papoose. It worked, Ember. He's bigger now, but Tyler still gets spun up at the end of the day. Sometimes it's all he can do to sit still. I wrap him up tight and snug. We talk about dinosaurs and robots, and the next thing we know, he's himself again."

She licked her lower lip and came to sit beside him. "Now what?" she whispered, her voice trembling as much as her fingers. The poor woman was shivering, but not just from the cold.

Rory put one arm around her and pulled her in tight. "Now I do this."

She leaned into him. "Why aren't you falling apart? What is wrong with me?"

He pulled her into his shoulder, his fingers beneath her damp hair softly massaging the nape of her neck. "It's been a long time since you've been in battle. That's all."

"For hell's sake, Rory. I was an IT tech on a Navy ship. I coordinated datalinks, network diagnostics and corrective system maintenance. I've never been in a real battle until today. I've never shot..." She pressed her knuckles against her lips when a hiccup blurted out instead of words. "I've never shot anyone before."

"It's okay. I know," he said, "and it wasn't supposed to be a battle today, either, remember? This was supposed to be a babysitting job, not dodging assassins and bombs. Certainly not forced to defend our retreat." He circled her with both arms and held her a little tighter.

"It's just that one minute they're shooting at us. I thought they might hit Nima, and then I didn't care if they hit me or not, but I shouldn't have done that in front of a baby. I mean, she's sitting right next to me watching me shoot and listening to me swear and... and..." Ember turned her face into his shirt. "And kill."

"You surprised me," he muttered into the top of her head. "I turned around to see who was in the car with me. Thought maybe you turned into Mark or Harley. Heck, Ember, you sounded just like Alex." He meant it humorously. Alex did have a potty mouth. He tended to turn into the fiend from hell when pushed.

"But I killed someone today," she whined, wetting his shirt with tears.

He squeezed her tighter, his heart hammering with the need to pull her onto his lap and kiss those tears away. "And I'm glad you did. You saved Nima. Think of it that way. There was nothing else you could've done."

She nodded and sniffed. Bleary, red-rimmed emeralds peered up at him. "I know, but—"

"But nothing. You'd do it again. As hard as it was, you'd save Nima and me every time. I know you would."

Her head bobbed with another shiver and a gulp. "You're right. I would."

He cupped her chin with his fingers, fighting for willpower not to seal those sad puckered lips with his. "You done good out there, Agent Davis. I had my hands full driving the car, but Nima's alive because of your fast thinking and guts. I'm damned proud to serve with you."

She gulped and wiped her face. "Thanks. I think."

"Don't overthink it. You did what you had to do. That's all. Move on."

"I'm a mess, huh?"

He gave her a handful of tissues. Yes, she was a mess. A beautiful, disheveled needing to be loved mess, and maybe his lap was no longer the safest place for her. He strove for more self-control than he'd needed in a long time. "Nah, you just look like most guys after battle. You're not the first to feel this way. You won't be the last." He pushed a loose blonde curl away from the lip she kept chewing.

"I bet you didn't hug many Marines like this back in Iraq."

He focused on tucking the strand of hair behind her ear, his boys alive with the need to do more than hug her. "You'd be surprised. Sometimes even the toughest guys need a hug."

The words were no more than out of his mouth when she threw her arms around his neck, quivering with what sure felt like fear mixed with something else. The need for forgiveness, maybe? Security? Intimacy? His heart lurched. He squeezed his eyes shut and held her, soaking in the warmth and tenderness of a good woman.

"Thanks," she whispered into his neck. "Your mom was right."

Protectiveness demolished his last shred of sound judgment. He couldn't speak, the feel of her in his arms so right. This was definitely who and what was missing from his life. The urge to hold her in a more intimate embrace flooded him with heat. The long denied masculine response of a man who'd lived alone and apart for too long sprang to life, filled with blood and heavy with desire. She wasn't the only one with needs. Their world had changed. The mission, too. He had to keep her as safe as Nima.

Sheepishly, she turned sideways and into his chest, looking at the sleeping child on the bed and pushing away. He let her go, but only because he had to.

"This little girl of ours doesn't seem to eat much, does she?"

She probably didn't even realize what she'd said, but he did. *This little girl of ours....*

If only....

"I've noticed. Let's wake her up when you're done with your shower. At least get her on the same schedule we're on, whatever that is." He arched his brows at that ridiculous statement, needing to create distance between him and his co-agent. She was right to pull away. Neither of them needed the trouble. "Sound like a plan?"

"And then we'll run for our lives again?"

It took all of his restraint to not taste the quivering shells of her pink lips. "Maybe, but I'll bet the storm slowed down whoever's after us, too. Let's do what we can for now. Let's rest up and get some food. Who knows? Maybe we can find another car in this one horse town and drive all night. How does California sound?"

"Good," Ember agreed quickly. "Poor David, huh?"

"His car doesn't look like a family car anymore, does it?"

"It is missing a few things."

"Like the back window," Rory quipped, still trying to lighten the moment.

"And a lot of paint."

"Go take your shower."

"I'll be done in a minute."

Rory listened until she'd closed the bathroom door and turned the shower on. Nima snored softly on the motel bed. The place was a dive, no ifs, ands or buts about it, but tonight, it served its purpose. Thunder still boomed and lightning popped outside. Tonight was definitely a good night to stay off the roads.

Whoever these people were who'd tracked him and Ember to the safe house and as quickly to McCormack's summer home, they were fast and determined. He counted their time spent in the safe house between arrival and departure: less than ten hours. Their time at McCormack's was even less. The shopping spree had been a stupid decision. No doubt these assassins could've finished the fight at the department store while he and Ember foolishly picked out new clothes like they had all the time in the world.

Another stab of lightning flashed. Rory worried. As much as he'd tried to calm Ember, his gut still needled him. Rain wouldn't stop these assassins any more than it would've stopped him. It might have slowed him down, but not for long. The assassins were still coming. The shabby motel would not stand in their way.

Tendrils of worry kept pushing him to the edge of an enlightenment that wouldn't materialize. He was missing something else. He just didn't know what.

Nine

Ember didn't linger in the shower, only enough to rinse off and get warm. Or try to. Within minutes, she eased her legs back in her damp jeans. She shivered into her wet hoody. The bathroom, with its cracked floor tiles and dingy grout along the tub, matched the dark day. Whoever owned the *Over the Rainbow Dive* certainly didn't understand the concept of re-investing in their own business.

Too edgy to take the time to blow dry her hair, she wrapped her hair in a quick braid and twisted it into a knot at the back of her head. One glance in the mirror only added to her dark mood. Puffy red eyes stared back at her. Could she possibly embarrass herself any worse? Falling apart in front of her senior agent in charge? Just the thought of her indiscretion sent a shudder up her spine. She'd actually hugged him like a snot-nosed little girl who needed her daddy. Eww. This was not one of her better days.

Man, she wanted a cup of coffee. Two cream, no sugar, just like Rory had handed her this morning. He'd certainly turned out to be a surprise. Hell, the whole damned operation had.

When she opened the bathroom door, he was sprawled on the bed beside Nima, humming rock-a-bye baby. Ember watched for a minute, content to take in the view of his shoulders, wide, strong and sure. He wore the new jeans and the comfortable gray flannel shirt. Had he tossed bales of hay as a young man? He sure looked like he had. Strength seemed to sit as comfortably on him as flannel and denim.

Ember looked down over his back at Nima. The little girl stared up with drowsy, half-open eyes. Rory stroked her cheek enough to keep her waking up.

"Aww, she's tired. Maybe we should let her sleep."

"Can't. The sheriff's escort should be here soon and she needs to eat."

Ember leaned over his back to Nima. Wow. She might as well have been leaning over a rock wall. This guy was solid.

"Hey, baby girl. Are you ready to get up?" she asked, trying real hard not to notice the warmth of Rory's back against her thighs. Or her stomach. Or the temptation to climb into bed next to him and feel his arms around her again.

Nima yawned and stretched, arching her back off the mattress. A tiny red handprint showed on her cheek from where she'd lain on it. She stuck her lips out in a cute pout, her nose scrunched up. Everything about this little gal was just plain adorable.

"Come on. Up you go," Ember coaxed, pulling the little one up and over Rory while she got her head on straight. The domestic feeling between him and her had to stop. Teasing him in a black towel was one thing. Listening to him open up and share the feelings of his heart quite another. There had to be a way to get back to the professional standoff they'd started this operation with.

But picking up Nima came with the warm whiff of—him. Ember's throat tightened. It was hard to talk when she wanted to breathe deeply. "How about you shower while I feed Nima? That way we can get out of here faster."

"Okay, Boss, whatever you say." He rolled off the bed and headed to the bathroom, seemingly oblivious to the encounter she'd felt right down to her toes.

She pulled open his backpack, looking for more food. The pack was so—Rory. Yogurt on top of blue ice packs where it wouldn't spoil. He'd also packed two plastic bags, one full of sliced vegetables, the other chocolate bars. His thoughtfulness and foresight stirred an inner restlessness. Why did everything about him tug at her?

"Let's eat." Ember opened the carton of vanilla yogurt before it dawned on her they had no spoons. Or did they? She checked the backpack. Sure enough. Safely tucked in an inside pocket, she found a kitchen towel with utensils. Further rummaging revealed another plastic bag with several paper plates.

Nima gobbled the yogurt. With a lip-smacking pop, she was done and ready for more.

"Are you still hungry?"

Nima smacked her lips enthusiastically, so Ember dished a small helping of the salad. "Look what else I found? Uncle Rory's been holding out on us." She held up one of the chocolate bars. "When you finish eating, we'll have dessert."

Nima froze and pivoted her head from her paper plate of salad to the treat under her nose.

"Oh, no you don't. Food first. Dessert second."

The cutest mischief sparkled in the little girl's eyes. "Me chock-it?"

"You like chocolate?"

Soft blue eyes lit up. The con was on. Nima leaned forward, her fingers outstretched and nodding. "Me. Chock-it." She wasn't asking. The tip of her tiny pink tongue stuck out between her lips. The glint in her eye was Ember's undoing. How could anyone resist? By the time Rory was done showering, Ember had Nima on her lap sharing the chocolate treat.

A warm smile split his face. "You two look comfy."

"We found the chocolate."

"How'd she eat?" Rory sat on the edge of the bed to lace up his boots.

"Good. You pack a mighty fine backpack, Agent Dennison."

"Looks like dessert hit the spot."

Nima licked her index finger with another satisfied pop. "Yep."

He smirked. "Women."

"Hey, what's that supposed to mean?" Ember feigned offense.

"Oh, just that women and chocolate go together like salt and pepper. Let's call Alex."

Her expression darkened. "I don't care what he says. I'm not taking her back. It's not safe in Virginia. The TEAM might be there, but so were the assassins. That's where everything started. Why doesn't Alex come to us?"

"Sometimes what you want is not what you need."

Nima had just blurted another one of her soul-searing revelations. Without batting an eye, she helped herself to the uneaten chocolate in Ember's limp fingers and smiled while chocolate dribbled at the corners of her lips.

Ember froze. Nima's words struck a chord all the way to her soul. *What do you want, Ember? Rory needs Tyler. Tyler needs his dad. What is it you need to be truly happy, Ember?*

She could have answered the question clearly the day before the operation began. Now, not so much.

"I don't know."

Rory's brows arched.

Damn. Did I just say that out loud?

He'd already dialed Alex, disturbing her reverie with, "Hey, Boss—"

And a different kind of lightning struck inside their shabby hotel room. Rory couldn't get a complete sentence out of his mouth. "Well, yeah, but we've been kind of busy—"

"I know, but—"

"Okay, but—"

Alex must be his usual, ornery and ignorant self, a welcome distraction from the confusing sensations bubbling inside what used to be her logical brain. As much as she loved the man, there were times he needed a good smack upside his hard head. Listening was not his forte.

Rory stood, his shoulders back, his breath coming in short bursts through his nostrils. He seemed taller all of a sudden, his back ramrod straight. He listened for a final second of what sounded like abuse before he spoke, but when he did, his voice carried a definite tone of, *'Shut the hell up and listen.'* From what Ember could hear coming through the receiver, Rory talked right over Alex.

"And I fully understand, but if you'd think for one second instead of biting my head off, you'd understand we were under extreme duress. We had no way to contact you until we stopped for gas. And for your information, Ember contacted Mother at that point. Where were you?" His voice strong and low, he didn't sound accusatory as very much no-nonsense. "And there you have it. You were in a meeting with I don't damned care who. I have a child to think of. She and Ember get top billing. Not you!"

Nima and I get top billing? A very pleasant warmth replaced the emptiness in Ember's core at his words, but they wouldn't go over too well with Alex, the absolute alpha male of bosses. Everything was always about him. Rory's voice mellowed. *Hmm.* Was Alex actually listening? Wow. A definite first.

"No. Ember and I both agree we are not bringing Nima back to Virginia." He was silent as he listened again. "Yes. Understood. We're at a motel called the *Over the Rainbow Inn*. When the storm lets up, we're buying another car and getting back on the road." He was quiet. "Did Mother find out who's after us yet?" Rory pursed his lips. "Sure. We'll sit tight, but they said they'd provide an escort earlier. No one showed."

He was quiet again. "Where are Maxwell and Fred?"

She held her breath. It seemed obvious.

"Goodnight," Rory said. He shot her a somber glance.

"They're...?" She let her question hang. The word itself was not necessary. What could he say? Once again the assassins had the upper hand. Rory pushed both hands through his damp hair. It was not fear in his eyes. More like do or die.

"The highway patrol will be here in twenty minutes. They're giving us an armored escort. Alex wants us home where The TEAM can protect us. He's got the FBI on-site. He thinks we can draw the assassins out in the open. What do you think?"

"He thought Maxwell and Fred could help us, too," she said quietly. "That didn't happen."

He nodded, the light in his eyes subdued. "Right."

"Nima won't be safe no matter where we go."

"No, Ember. It only seems that way because you've gotten attached to her. No one can keep her as safe as you and me. Let's go with the highway patrol. Give them a chance. At least we'll have a couple more shotguns along for the ride. It couldn't hurt."

"They'd better be driving an MRAP then," she growled.

He cocked his head, listening to something outside. The rumble of a slow moving train shook the walls of their motel room next to the tracks. "I'm glad we won't have to sleep with that racket tonight. Anything else you want to take with you?"

"Just this little one and you." Damn. Her heart had spoken out loud for the first time in a long time. Needing to change the subject, she said, "It will be nice to sleep in my own bed tonight."

"Uh, huh."

"Maybe I'll have you and Tyler over for dinner sometime. Would you like that?"

He was glued to the window, obviously not listening.

"I might dance naked on the table while I'm at it," she murmured, testing his lack of focus.

"Dance naked later. They're here." He winked as he hoisted the backpacks over one shoulder. "That, I've got to see. Come on. They're in the parking lot. Let's not keep 'em waiting."

Sheesh. That was definitely not the smartest wisecrack she could've made, especially after her escapade with the towel. His wink didn't help, neither did the gentle hand on her back when he opened the door.

Three Pennsylvania state patrol cruisers filled the motel's weedy asphalt parking lot, their powerful engines growling. Santa and eight tiny reindeer couldn't have looked any better. Rory seemed pleased, too. He winked. She snuggled Nima on her hip and took another step. The nightmare was nearly—

BLAM! WHOOSH! BANG!

She bounced backward to her butt. Oomph! Nima was plastered against her, punching the breath out of her. Motel windows shattered. Flaming debris ricocheted through the air and fell from the sky. A car wheel landed not two feet in front of her with a dull thud. Wicked flames devoured what was left of the vehicles. Nima squealed, her tiny hands now a suffocating grip on Ember's neck.

Salvation was come and gone. Clutching Nima tightly to her chest, Ember crab-scrambled backward to the safety of their open motel room. Instantly, she met a wall named Rory. He pushed his knee into her back as quickly as her butt hit the threshold and her hand gripped the doorjamb.

She elbowed him hard. "Get outta my way!"

"Knock it off, Davis." The steel vise of his hand pulled her backside off the ground. "Get up. Run, damn it."

She had no choice, not with his palm in the middle of her back pushing her toward the end of the motel. There sat David's battered Taurus, still ready for flight. She grabbed the back door handle, ready to climb in and cover Nima again. A human shield. That's all she was and she was good with it. *Get us outta here!*

The handle didn't budge when she pulled on it. "Open it!" she screamed, not wanting to climb through the broken windows.

He grabbed her elbow and shoved her past the car toward the track. What the hell? The damned train still lumbered westward with boxcars full of who the hell cared what. Fear paralyzed her feet and legs. They were trapped. No way forward and no way back. The crappy motel had an eight-foot concrete wall on this side, the only thing on the property not decrepit and worn.

"Don't just stand there! Move it!" He pushed her relentlessly toward the track. The next boxcar's side doors were wide open. *Hell, no. Is he crazy? He means to board a slow moving train?*

"I can't!" she shouted. What a stupid solution, especially with a child.

"You will!" he shouted back, fierce and angry. "There's no choice."

"No way! I—"

"Do it!" By then he'd tossed both backpacks through the open doors of a boxcar and pulled Nima out of her arms. He was going. With or without her. In one easy leap, he was in the car with Nima. They were safe. Ember was not. A hard knot of fear choked her. *He's leaving me!*

Running alongside the train, she guesstimated the distance to the swiftly approaching stone wall. It would intercept her within forty, maybe fifty feet. To make matters worse, a semi-truck had parked on the other side of the wall. Its trailer nearly butted against the edge of the track. Holy shit! One sway of the train and the trailer would be reduced to wreckage. What was that truck driver thinking when he'd parked so close to the tracks? Better question—what was Rory thinking now?

"Run!" he commanded.

"I am!" Her shrill reply was lost between the roar of iron wheels on iron tracks, the crack of thunder overhead, and still exploding carnage in the parking lot. Gunfire strafed the pavement behind her. She ran, scared she couldn't make the jump, just as scared she could.

What if I fall under the wheels? What if I can't run fast enough? What if the assassins kill me before I can get on board?

Rory must have pushed Nima into the dark confines of the boxcar. He leaned out of the boxcar, one arm stretched out. "Give me your hand," he urged.

Her feet pounded fast and hard. She was almost close enough to reach him.

I'm too close! It's a huge piece of moving metal! Metal wheels! I'll be sliced into ribbons!

He reached farther. If he leaned any farther out of the car, he might fall. She ran faster.

Don't leave me!

Just when she thought she could run no more, his arm seemed to extend another few inches. With one fell swoop, it snaked out and clutched her wrist, pulling her up and forward. She grabbed the edge of the doorway.

The wall! The wheels! They're sharp.

She was off the ground now but not any safer. Her feet swung beneath the train car. Terror climbed on board instead of her. Lifting her butt, she willed herself inside.

Up! Pull me the hell up!

His fingertips raced over her shoulder blades, down her spine, quickly digging into her ass with one determined handful. She squeezed her eyes tight, urging her weight up and off the ground. More gunshots splattered the steel walls of the boxcar. Reason kicked in.

"Let me go. Save Nima!"

"Shut the hell up." His fingernails dug into her back and butt. With a tremendous roar, he yanked her in by belt loops and backside. One split second too late. She'd reached the end of the line. Her dangling leg hit the wall. Even through the denim jeans, she felt layers of skin being torn away. The impact flung her into the boxcar to land on Rory. He fell backward and took the hit, his arms turned into steel bands that held her fast and kept her from falling. The damned train kept rolling. Good. She was safe. And dying.

Pure shock stormed her. She'd hit a wall—not just hit it, but slammed into it like a freaking freight train! She willed herself not to scream, not to frighten Nima. The pain roared out of her mouth anyway. "Ow-w-w-w! Damn you, Dennison!"

"I'm sorry. I know." He rolled to his knees, grabbed her wrist to elbow and dragged her out of sight. The train lumbered westward. Nima huddled into Ember's arm, but for once, Ember didn't hold her. She couldn't. She was too busy writhing as fire climbed up her leg and filled her body. Her eyes watered. She didn't want to look like a completely helpless woman, but damn. This was a first—a painful first.

Rory fumbled with his damned backpack and suddenly there was light. Great! He had a flashlight when she needed an emergency room. Did he have one of those in his handy dandy backpack, too?

"You're hurt pretty bad," he said grimly, the light flickering over what was left of her thigh. "I need to stop the bleeding."

No shit, Sherlock!

It didn't look as bad as it felt. She'd expected to find her leg hanging by a thread, but it was only scraped. A lot. And her pants weren't gone, just kind of embedded into the bloody meat of one damned raw thigh. She pulled the fabric away from her skin, but just as fast quit that stupid idea. It hurt!

He leaned over her leg, his face deadly serious in the dim light of the rumbling boxcar while he tore the rest of her pant leg away. Great. By now he also knew she hadn't shaved when she'd bathed with Nima. *My hell, the stupid thoughts that run through your mind when you're dying. Who cares about shaved legs? I don't!*

The pain in her thigh felt alive. "You did this to me," she hissed.

He winced. "Yeah. It's my fault."

"Bullshit! It's not like we had much choice!" she snarled. He needed to shut up and stop being so damned responsible for a change. Tears ran down her face, making her even angrier. Now was the time to prove her superior resilience, not fall apart. Yeah. Right.

She turned away, the desolation in his eyes stabbing her as much as the pain climbing up her leg. Adrenaline hit hard. Pushing her palms to the floor to stop the shaking didn't work. If anything, resisting made it worse. "I'm hurt," she ground out between clenched teeth, like he didn't already know that.

He eased his hand and forearm under her head and pushed several tablets between her teeth. "Here, swallow."

"What is it?"

"Advil."

She gulped them down with the bottle of water he offered. "You got any morphine in that bag?"

"No, but I've got this." He held up a couple plastic-wrapped towels and a prescription pill bottle. "Pain we can live with. Infection is another thing altogether."

She glared at the stupidity pouring out of his mouth. "You learn that line of BS in the Corps? Maybe watching TV?"

"Sorry." He held her so she could swallow two more tablets. Another gulp of water and he turned his attention to her wound. "This might hurt." He clutched her knee and barely touched one finger to pull something out of her wounded thigh. It stung—a lot.

"Stop touching me. Damn it!" Instantly, she felt bad she'd hollered at him, but not bad enough.

"You want something to hold onto?" he asked.

"Why?" she snapped.

"I'll be as careful as I can, but I need to wash the dirt out before I bandage it." He sounded so steady she wanted to smack him, and then he smoothed something over the scrape. It wasn't so bad—at first. But by the time he was through, it was all she could do to grit her teeth and not kick him through the boxcar doors and off the train. The gentle scrubbing wrenched the living daylights out of her. Moisture trickled out of her eyes and nose in a steady stream she couldn't stop. Poor Nima stood nearby, whimpering in sympathy.

"There. You did real good," he outright lied, but he made it sound comforting. A little. "Hang on. We're almost done. Now I'm covering it with a wet towel."

"Whatever." Like he would listen if she told him no? The cool wet towel made gentle contact with her shredded thigh. It felt good. She took a deep breath. She might live.

"Let's get you sitting up and more comfortable." Rory dragged her gently by her armpits to lean against a wooden box in the center of the train car. All she could do was shake and pant and try not to cry any harder than she already was. Sheesh. She was sweaty, blubbering like a baby, and she'd sworn in front of Nima. Damn.

The little girl snuggled into Ember's uninjured side like a sad little puppy.

"Wow. You sure know how to show a girl a good time, Dennison."

"I kinda saw it going a little differently," he admitted softly. Guilt darkened his expression. "It could've been a lot worse, but it's a good-sized scrape. I'm sorry."

"Me, too." She was tired. The drama and trauma of the day had taken its toll. Rory positioned her where she could watch the countryside pass by. She stared out the door, determined not to cry anymore. Most of her view was nothing but dark fields, herds of dark cattle, or shadowy trees. Lightning still flashed and thunder still boomed. Rain poured in steady sheets, adding to the gloom.

The noisy train rocked back and forth. He stood at the open boxcar door looking both directions before he came back and crouched at her side.

"What's up?"

"I was looking for something to bandage your leg with when I found this." He pulled Nima's dress from the bag. "Here. Hold the flashlight for a minute. Shine it on my hands."

She did. Three oversized buttons graced the bodice of the dress. Rory peeled the cap off one of them with his pocketknife. What looked like a watch battery lay nestled inside the hollow shell. A thin silvery wire threaded back inside the lining of the bodice, then connected the other two up through the buttonholes before it disappeared back inside the lining. Rory pulled more than a dozen feet of the shiny filament from the dress.

"Wow," Ember whispered. "Antenna wire and transmitter. That's how they've been tracking us."

"We should've changed her clothes while we were shopping. If we'd dropped them in the garbage then, we'd still be safe at Jed's."

Ember bit her lip. "My fault. That dress is all she had left of her father. I couldn't throw it away. God, Rory. What have I done?"

"Don't worry. Now we know that somebody close to Nima's father planted these bugs. Someone he trusted." Rory folded the wire back into the dress and wrapped it around Nima's pretty patent leather dress shoes.

Ember hugged Nima closer to her. "Maybe someone she knows?"

"Whoever it was, they knew she'd be wearing that dress yesterday."

Ember turned Nima's sad face toward hers. "Nima? See your pretty dress?"

"Mine," she said softly, reaching for the familiar item.

"Yes, it's yours. Who gave it to you?"

"Mine Poppa." She fingered the dress, her eyes keeping careful track of her only familiar possession.

Ember kissed the girl's grimy forehead. "She's just a baby. Why can't they leave her alone?"

"I'll toss it into the nearest river. Let it float east while we go west or wherever."

She nodded. All she wanted was to disappear where no one could hurt Nima anymore. A wave of protectiveness coursed through her, so tangible she shivered. She pulled Nima closer.

Rory stood at the open doorway for the longest time. The train car rocked back and forth, its swaying motion a lullaby all in itself. The night was dark and she was beyond tired. Her eyes drooped. He cocked his arm, looking like a handsome baseball legend in the moonlight, strong, sure, and—

She fell asleep mid-pitch.

Ten

Clickety-clack. Clickety-clack.

Times that by a couple million and before long it equates to nothing more than a lot of white noise. Rory covered Ember and Nima with the two suit jackets he and Ember had worn the day before. His mind going a thousand miles a minute, he couldn't sleep. He'd searched through the two backpacks for the burn phones and didn't find them. Somehow they'd been left behind at the motel. Maybe Ember had taken them out to charge them. He didn't know. Whatever. The detail added more frustration to their predicament.

He'd just gotten his butt reamed for not contacting his boss, but here he was again, no way to let Alex know where they were or where they were headed. That was the least of their problems. Because they were safe now didn't translate to safety in the morning. And Ember was pretty banged up. Even though he'd given her a couple of antibiotic tablets, she might still get an infection. The scrape was too large to treat lightly. Yet he'd treated it in a dirty old boxcar that could have previously hauled any number of things, maybe even animals. She whimpered in her sleep while he cursed quietly to the full moon rising behind the storm clouds.

Plus their food was nearly gone, the bottled water, too. Until they stopped in whatever town the train was headed to, there was no way to replenish anything. By now, their room back at the motel was undoubtedly ransacked. Whoever bombed the patrol cars most likely had the burn phones and might have already tracked their last calls back to Alex and The TEAM headquarters.

That was another problem. There was no way to alert Alex.

In the dark exhaustion of the hopeless night, Rory thought of Tyler, home safe and sound, asleep in his bed by now. That much was a blessing and he recognized it as such. Mrs. Godfrey would have read Tyler his bedtime story and tucked him in. She'd have hugged him and kissed him and told him that hug and kiss were from his daddy. And Tyler would have asked, *'But where is Daddy?'* And Mrs. Godfrey would've patiently explained his daddy had to go out of town and maybe he'd be home tomorrow.

Rory sighed. Tyler was the perfect son, his dark blue eyes forever happy and always loving. Pure sunlight, that's what poured out of his little boy's eyes. It was like being loved simply for waking up every morning. Tyler was light and life and all things good in Rory's life. And he missed him now.

His eyes turned back to Ember and Nima snuggled together by the empty wooden freight box. *His girls.* The phrase came to him as easy as butter to pancakes. Nima lay on Ember under her chin, her hand across Ember's neck and resting on her cheek. They looked like mother and daughter.

Ember held the little girl against her good hip, the one with the little green frog with orange eyes. Rory smiled. Leave it to Ember to decorate her body like construction paper in grade school. He wanted to strip all the crap away from her. She was beautiful without embellishment. Why didn't she see that? Heck, for that matter, how come it took him so long to notice?

What was behind the façade that was Ember? She'd told him the line about how color improved her mood and a bunch of other psychobabble he'd listened to and heard, but didn't believe. Maybe Ember believed it, but he'd detected something else in the depths of those emerald greens. As much as the adult demanded to be seen and heard, the little girl side of her still peeked around the mask. There was more to her than met the eye.

He grunted to himself. He was a great one to talk. He'd been in the exact same boat only twenty-four hours ago. Uptight. Overprotective of his son. Hiding. Heck, he was no better than Ember. The real reason? Pride. His force field was more about his stupid pride than it ever was about protecting Tyler. Until Nima came along.

Wow. That was definitely an unsettling moment. How had he not peered into those pale blue eyes until that moment at the McCormack summer home? It wasn't that he hadn't. It was more that she hadn't looked directly at him—yet. It wasn't his time.

But when she did, it all but turned him inside out and upside down. His carefully maintained force field disintegrated. And for the first time since Tyler was born, Rory wanted to share his son with another woman. Oddly, the moment he opened up to Ember, she pulled back. One minute she was asking questions like she wanted to know him better, the next minute her own force field was fully charged and activated. She'd all but jumped off the couch to get away from him on the pretense of needing ice cream.

Ember and Nima had fallen asleep. Ember clutched his jacket like she was cold. He went to her side and smoothed his hand along her bare arm. When she shivered, he lay down beside her and wrapped his arms around her shoulders. She still shivered. He pulled the makeshift cover of suit jackets over her and Nima. There. Now both his girls were warm.

The noisy banging of metal on metal woke him from a light sleep. It was zero dark thirty and the train still creaked slowly along. As careful as possible, he scooted away from Ember and went back to the door. The storm had dissipated and the moon shone brightly to the south, casting a silvery light over the small town they were passing through. It was a one-stoplight kind of a town. A milk delivery truck rolled slowly along the road parallel to the track. The driver waved. Rory raised his hand in quiet salute. A train ride would be fun with Tyler at his side.

When he lay down again, Ember nuzzled his neck, still very much asleep and dreaming. What did she nuzzle at home, a childhood teddy bear maybe? Her cat? A man? That annoyed him. He'd heard a lot of chit chat between Mother and Ember back at the office. His own workspace was adjacent to theirs', but he didn't recall discussions about late night dates, wild parties or other men. It made sense. Both Mother and Ember spent an inordinate amount of time at Alex's beck and call. It was unlikely Ember had a man in her life.

And that friend of hers who had died years ago? Junior Agent Todd Chandler, the new kid in the office and scared to death of Alex like most new recruits were. Todd was killed in the line of duty shortly after he'd joined The TEAM. Alex made sure he was buried with honor at Arlington. But Ember and Todd hadn't dated very long before it happened. And that was interesting, too. She'd fallen hard for a guy she barely knew.

Ember's breath at his neck felt warm. Comforting. So did his hand at her hip. The fragrance of shampoo in her blonde braid smelled good. He closed his eyes and drifted between sleep and wakefulness. She stirred. Stiffened. Relaxed again. And then she really snuggled under his chin. He pulled her closer, his hand in the middle of her back. She came easily. Willingly. He smiled in his in-between-dream state, at last falling into a deeper sleep.

When he awoke, Ember and Nima sat opposite him in the boxcar, chatting quietly. By the looks of it, they'd been awake for a while. Ember was playing pat-a-cake with Nima, but Nima didn't look to be enjoying it as much as Ember. A bottle of water stood in front of them and an empty yogurt cup. Light streamed through the open door. He lay there watching the happy scene.

It took a few minutes before it dawned on him. The boxcar had turned north. Jumping to his feet, he went straight to the door. Residential neighborhoods whizzed by now instead of fields and trees. Horns sounded beyond concrete walls marked with bold, boxy colors of graffiti. Another train roared past, headed in the opposite direction.

"Good morning," Ember said calmly when the noise diminished.

He brushed a hand through his hair for the umpteenth time, wondering where they were. "Morning."

"You have your choice: yogurt or the last of the salad. I saved some of each." She held up a bottle of water, which he promptly took. She seemed shy, maybe a little embarrassed, probably because she'd woken up in his arms.

"Thanks. This will do." He sat with them.

"You should eat. You need to keep your strength up."

"How's the leg?"

"Not bad. Whatever you gave me did the trick."

"Ibuprofen and amoxicillin. Let me get you some more." He reached for his backpack.

"Do you always carry antibiotics with you?"

"It's an old habit. I always pack the basic things a soldier needs to treat his own wounds. Stuff like a good antibiotic, gauze, bandages, things like that." He shrugged. "It's a soldier thing. Learned it in the Corps."

She smiled. "I always carry a thumb drive. It's a techie thing. Learned it in the Navy."

He stared out the door. "When the train stops, we need to hightail it out of the rail yard. Do you think you can walk?"

"You bet. I've been thinking. If you've still got our old clothes, we could use our dress shirts for new bandages, and maybe I could get my dress slacks back on. I mean, these ratty old jeans kind of stand out." She tugged at the ripped denim.

"You want to do that now?"

"The sooner the better."

Rory rummaged through the backpack until he found both of their dress shirts and her slacks. Before they started, he gave Ember four more Advil. He took a deep breath. "Here we go."

The first problem was the damp towel he'd covered her wound with the night before. He expected it to have stuck to the damaged skin beneath it. It wasn't. "Good thinking. You've already dampened the bandage, haven't you?"

"I thought if I soaked it, it would loosen right up."

She scrunched her nose the minute he touched her leg. He pulled the towel gently off and winced. Her leg was scary red.

"Wow," she exclaimed as she took in the sight of her massive injury. "Now it hurts."

"Don't look at it then. Let's get it re-wrapped and get you to the nearest hospital the first chance we get."

Her eyes fixed on his face. "I used to have a dragon tattoo there. He had black wings and green eyes. Like mine."

Rory grimaced at the raw patch of thigh muscle. If there was any ink left, it was more troll than magic.

"I used up all the ointment last night. I also carry a small can of antiseptic spray, but it won't work on a wound this size. Besides, it would sting like crazy." He ripped her dress shirt neatly into four long pieces of cloth. After he soaked them with a bottle of water, he laid them gently over the wound and used the remaining strips as ties. He tied it as snug as he dared. "Better?"

"I guess."

He could see it in her eyes. It wasn't better. The pain was back. "Are you sure you want to change pants now?"

She smiled weakly. "Might as well get it over with. I can't go train-hopping looking like this. What will people say?" Her attempt at humor fell flat. Neither of them could laugh at what she was going through.

"Let's get you on your feet." Rory helped her up, his arm firmly around her waist, her arm tight around his neck. For as tall as she was, she was an easy armful. He balanced her backside against the wooden freight box. It didn't have a lid, but it made a handy if narrow seat.

"Hand me my pants. And now..." She waved him off. "Go play with Nima. I can do this next part by myself. And don't turn around. No fair peeking."

He did, but he was afraid to release her. She was shaking so hard. He kept an ear tuned to the grunting and fumbling behind him just in case she needed him. She whined. That meant she was either pulling her jeans down over her wounded thigh or trying to.

"Ow. Ow. Ow," she muttered. Some bumps and another groan.

He wanted to help. It would go easier with two people, but he stayed with Nima like he was told. Not once did he turn around to look. The little girl watched him with such serious eyes, but he was too focused on the noise behind him to pay attention to her.

A sad voice reached out to him. She sounded exhausted. "Uh, Rory?"

He didn't look. "Yes?"

"I, umm, need some help."

"May I turn around now?"

"Uh, huh." There she stood with her jeans off and the black slacks draped modestly over her bare legs. Trembling and out of breath, her hair hung in a crimped fluff over her eyes. She blew it off her face as she panted. "These are too tight now. I can't get my fat leg into them."

He scrambled for the backpack and pulled his dress slacks out. "These might be a little big, but they'll go over your leg easier. I'll loan you my belt to hold them up."

"This is just great."

"May I help?"

"Uh, huh." She dropped her too small slacks to the floor, and as quickly as he could, Rory pulled his slacks up and over her bandaged leg. She whined when the fabric moved over the makeshift bandage, but she didn't let go of his shoulders. He secured his belt through the loops and buckled it. "Good?"

She smoothed her hair out of her eyes again. "Yes. I need to sit down."

He scooped her off her feet. Her breath hitched. His own heart flip-flopped at the feel of her in his arms. Fragile. Never in a hundred years would he have used that adjective until now. He set her gently beside Nima. The little girl instantly snuggled into Ember's side.

Ember's teeth chattered. "Whew. First I'm hot. Then I'm cold. Not good."

He knew the minute he'd touched her. She had a fever. He located the Advil and amoxicillin and doubled the dose of both. After she downed the pills, he went to the door, both hands in his hair in total frustration at the helplessness of their situation. They had to get off the train, but there was nothing to be done. He came back to sit by Ember. The moment he put his arm around her, she leaned into his shoulder.

"We're getting you to a doctor the minute we stop," he whispered into her hair.

"Good idea. I'm tired."

"Then sleep. I'll take care of Nima while you rest."

Two sad blue eyes skewered him from Ember's other side.

"Come here, Nima. Mama Ember's not feeling real good right now. Come sit with me."

She stepped carefully around Ember and climbed onto his lap. "Everything will be fine. We'll take Mama Ember to a doctor, and pretty soon she'll be dancing on tables again."

He could feel Ember smile against his neck.

"That will be the day," she whispered.

"I intend to collect," he teased.

"Sure. Sure. You don't like naked ladies, remember?"

"I'll make an exception."

Ember didn't respond, but Nima patted his cheek for attention. He was almost afraid to look into her eyes, but he did. "Whatcha need, Nima?"

"Drink?" she asked innocently.

"You need some water? Here." He reached for the bag with the last few water bottles in it. But Nima got up and pulled it closer. She handed him a bottle of water.

"You. Water," she said calmly.

"Thank you." He pulled the youngster back onto his lap.

She patted his chest again, still watching with wide eyes. "'Kay?"

"Yes, Nima. Everything is going to be all right."

I hope.

Eleven

Ember lay heavy in Rory's arms, definitely not her finest hour. Sick, ugly, and to top it off, her co-worker had helped her change her pants. *Ugh*. Just what every girl wants. Not. And it had been darned hard getting those tight jeans down over her big butt and injured thigh, too.

Waking up in his arms earlier was bad enough. Yes, she'd been nicely covered, but she'd also felt much more sensually comfortable than a wounded woman should. And wiggling out from under his arms without waking him took every last one of her feminine resources, never mind the fact that he'd clutched her right breast in his sleep. Or that his breath felt deliciously warm in her ear. Or that one specific body part of his had a mind of its own.

When he'd growled, she thought she'd disturbed him, but he'd only rearranged that handsome body of his and huffed back to sleep. Could this operation get anymore bizarre? One minute they were biting each other's heads off, the next they're cuddled like lovers?

And now they were all but cuddled again. Gradually, the raw feeling in her leg subsided. She didn't move away from Rory this time, though. No. She needed all the comfort she could find, and lying in his arms was her happy place. Besides, he smelled good. Without thinking, she sniffed a tear back. He noticed.

"How're you feeling?" He smoothed a very gentle hand over her cheek. He'd pulled her almost entirely on top of his body, trying to keep her leg off the dirty floor.

"Almost ready to buff ceilings," she chuckled weakly. "How about you?"

"I've had better days."

"Like when?" She needed positive reinforcement right now. One of his stories about Tyler would fit the bill.

He obliged. "Like the first time I saw you at the office. But you only had eyes for Todd back then."

Wow. Double zing.

"Remember when Harley put salt in Mother's sugar bowl?" he asked.

She smiled. Junior Agent Harley Mortimer. Fake Texas drawl. Outrageous hair that looked uncombed no matter what product he tried. And a heart as big as the New York state he hailed from. The man lived to tease and Mother made an easy target.

"And I've never seen a better Santa Claus than Mark."

Another good memory. Junior Agent Mark Houston had made the fatal mistake of calling Alex *sir.* The next thing he knew, he was volunteered for the big red suit. But Mark was a good sport and ended up being the best Santa. The look on David's youngest son's face when Santa promised him a new bike for Christmas was precious, but the surprise on David's face? Priceless.

"Your turn." Rory smoothed a hand gently over her hair. "Let's hear some of your good memories for a change."

"I'd rather listen to you."

"Aw, come on. Just one?" He still had a tease in his voice.

"I told you my favorite memory."

"You did?"

"Yeah. Tyler."

"Oh, right." She stalled.

Rory didn't ask again, but he had opened up with her. Guilt prodded. Since he'd taken a risk, she did, too. "You already know about Todd Chandler. He and I were close, I guess you could say. Anyway, I kind of fell off the deep end after he died. Got most of my tattoos then."

The silence stretched. Maybe talking about Todd wasn't such a good idea. It certainly didn't qualify as a good memory, not the way it ended. She gulped. "But my best day was when my dad left my mom."

"What?"

"Umm. Yeah. The house was quiet all of a sudden. It was—nice."

"How old were you?" His question was filled with disbelief.

"Ten." *Oh, the memories this story dragged up.*

"You want to talk about it?"

That was definitely one thing she didn't want to talk about, but apparently her mouth did because all of a sudden it developed loose lips. "I can still hear them fighting. A lot. I never figured why they got married in the first place. Maybe that was my fault, because my mother got pregnant with me. I don't know, but they were awful mean to each other. They used to say the nastiest things."

"Did they hurt you?"

"Not physically." She shivered, maybe from the fever, maybe from the memories. It felt like yesterday. "One time my dad came home early and mom was drinking and he was screaming. Called her a lot of filthy names. She called him just as many."

Rory's hand gently massaged the nape of her neck while her crazy mouth kept on spilling the beans. "He said he couldn't stand looking at her ugly face anymore, so he got in his car to go back to work. It was May. The lilacs were in blossom...." She stopped talking. Lilacs stopped being beautiful that day. Everything did.

Rory didn't make a sound, the only reason she continued. "He ran over my dog when he backed out of the driveway." *Yeah. Childhood sucked.*

The strong heartbeat beneath her ear kept her talking. "He got out of his car screaming at my mom because the dumb dog got in his way, and he was going to be late. Taffy was flopping all over. I couldn't make him hold still. He kept looking at me like he was begging me to, *'Please make it stop hurting. Please save me.'* But I couldn't."

All of a sudden she was ten years old again and holding that poor Cocker Spaniel in her arms, him bleeding all over her. Taffy whined and panted right up to the end, and all she'd wanted was for someone to please come save him, but she couldn't leave him to run and ask for help. He didn't last long, just long enough to—leave.

Dad screamed away in his ugly car. Mom never even came out of the house to see what had happened. Not that she was in any condition to help anyway. But Ember sat alone on her front lawn crying until the light left Taffy's sweet brown eyes. She'd never seen anything die before. *Poor Taffy.* He was her only friend, her only buddy, the one she snuggled with when the fighting and name-calling got bad. He'd lived simply to follow her around with his sappy smile. The things and people she'd loved had been leaving her ever since.

Rory's arms tightened around her. "You poor little girl."

She wanted to push away, but the tears started in earnest, so she buried her face in his shirt instead, hoping he wouldn't see. That's the last thing she was, a poor little girl. She was a brat. A slut. An ugly freak! She wasn't born; she was hatched. Only a blind man could want her, and then only after he got rip-roaring drunk.

How fast her mother's mean words flooded back, the scab of a lifetime ripped off again. She was too tall, her boobs were too big, and she had zits from here to eternity. Her mother was right. No one could possibly love her. Loving Todd was a mistake. All it did was get him killed.

Rory rummaged through the backpack and soon she felt tissues against her nose. "Here. Blow."

So she did. He held another tissue for her. "One more time."

She did as she was told. And then she heard the sweetest words she'd never heard before. "You're beautiful the way you are. Don't ever change." He rocked her, his hand in her hair as he held her head under his chin. "And some day you will see yourself the way I see you. Because all I see is a beautiful woman who'll make the best mother in the world some day. You're a good girl, Ember."

Obviously, he needed glasses.

She could barely see by then. Her hateful wish leaked out along with the tears. "No. You're wrong. I won't be a mother. Not if I have to be like my mother."

"Then don't. Be you. You're strong. Heck, you've already proved that. You just jumped onboard a moving train."

"Yeah, well that didn't work out too good, did it?"

"And you saved me and Nima back in the cornfield," he persisted.

Well, okay. Maybe she was a little stronger than she felt right now.

He tipped her face up, his eyes the deepest blue. A girl could get lost in there. Or drown. His lips were so close she could almost taste them. That was never going to happen. What she had with Todd was a rare surprise she'd not seen coming. Lightning didn't strike twice in the same place.

Rory leaned in. She closed her eyes and—

"Go to sleep," he murmured against her forehead. "You'll feel better once you've had some rest."

She swallowed her pride, the foolish notion he might have kissed her along with it. She tried to push out of his arms, but he easily held her. Too weak to resist, Ember gave up and wallowed, feeling ten-year-old sorry for herself. Not her usual forte. She was tougher than this, just not today.

Memories swirled like autumn leaves in the wind. One minute she was on fire in the desert, the next freezing in the chill of winter. Rory wiped her face gently and rocked her to the rhythm of the train. She listened to him tell Nima the story of the three little pigs. Nima laughed and clapped her hands like she always did.

That little girl was just plain odd. Sweet, but way different than other kids. Too quiet. When she did speak, she said the darndest things. Maybe it was the language barrier. Maybe not. She didn't even babble in Chinese or Tibetan or whatever language she should be speaking in. Shouldn't all little kids be jabberboxes like Tyler? If he had Attention

Deficit Disorder, what did Nima have? What was the opposite of ADD?

Ember stared, too tired to think and make sense at the same time. Nima looked like any other four-year-old, her plump little apple cheeks rosy, her eyes bright with childish glee. But then she turned to Ember as if she knew she was being watched. Her brows furrowed. Her countenance changed. The little girl was gone. A soothing command spoken in a very adult voice that sounded, no, felt, like it was centuries old, pierced Ember's feverish mind. *Sleep. Heal. Now.*

"Who are you?" Ember muttered thickly.

A gentle smile tweaked Nima's mouth. "I am come."

Whatever that meant. The darned little girl or old woman or whoever she was—winked. And in Ember's delirium, because she had to be really sick to be seeing what she thought she was seeing, she lifted off the ground. Rory didn't seem to notice. He kept telling Nima stories, and Nima kept watching Ember while the wind blew around her and through her. A flighty, floaty feeling enveloped Ember. She was blowing away.

Caught on the breeze, her arms and legs separated from her body in a bizarre cartoon-like scene of discombobulated body parts. Colors turned to a thousand shades of gray before they burst into bright lights that flashed and zigged and zagged. And she didn't care anymore because the pain dissipated. And pain-free was a very good thing.

But Rory was still there. Somewhere. She could smell the body wash on his flannel shirt, and one thing was for sure. He was her companion agent. He'd never let her go, if only because Alex would kill him if he did.

"Ma'am? Ma'am?" An annoying voice shattered the rambling sensation in her mind. "Can you hear me?"

Go. Away. She turned her face into a pillow, nuzzling after the smell of a certain guy in a certain cotton shirt. Voices talked around her in steady professional tones. She drifted back to—

"Ma'am. I need you to wake up. Can you do that for me?" That damned voice again. Strong hands gave her shoulders a gentle but firm squeeze.

"Mmm, sure," she mumbled. *Where am I?*

"There you go. Can you hear me?" That annoying voice belonged to a white-masked face with bushy gray eyebrows leaning too close to her nose for comfort. His breath smelled like tuna fish. And then she knew why the bright lights.

"Do you know where you are?" Bushy Brows asked.

"Umm." She squinted into his annoying face. "Hospital?"

"Yes, ma'am. You're at Saint John's Hospital in Chicago. Do you know how you got here?"

She shook her head, trying to recall anything after she'd fallen asleep in Rory's arms. "Umm, what?"

"Just think for a few minutes. You were pretty out of it when you first got here. Take your time."

Someone wrapped a blood pressure cuff around her left bicep. Ember faded between the glare of hospital lights and the enticement of heavy slumber, beyond the point of exhaustion. Only the continual squeeze of the cuff kept her half awake.

"Mrs. Swift. You're cleaned up and bandaged. We've given you a strong antibiotic drip. We need to move you into another room now."

What? Wait. Mrs. who?

It was a short ride. Gentle hands transferred her to another bed and she was extremely tired, but she knew enough to ask the most important question. "Where is he?"

A nurse leaned in close. Bushy Brows was apparently busy bugging someone else. "What did you say, Mrs. Swift? Do you need something?"

Yeah. To get the hell out of here. She wanted to sit up, to get her bearings, but weakness weighed her down. "Where is he?"

"Where is who?"

"Him. The guy who brought me in here. Where—"

"A transient found you by the railroad tracks. He took off the minute he dropped you off at the ER door. Now get some rest." The efficient nurse set the IV line, dimmed the lights and left.

Reality stabbed hard and sharp. Where were Rory and Nima? What had he done? Had the assassins attacked again? Ember choked. She should've expected nothing less, but still. Wow. He'd really done it. Rory had sacrificed her to save Nima.

Pulling herself into a sitting position, she dangled both legs over the edge of the bed until her head cleared. Her injured leg had been bandaged in sterile cotton and tape. It felt light years better. For the most part she was simply dizzy and a little disoriented. Nothing a junior agent couldn't deal with all by herself.

Stripped the IV line out of her wrist, she shuffled like an old woman to the closet in her hospital room. Her clothes might be dirty, but they meant freedom. Good enough.

The in-suite bathroom beckoned. She hesitated. A shower would feel good, but her thigh was wrapped in pristine white gauze and tape, a definite deal breaker for a woman who could barely stand on her feet.

Think about it later. Get out of here. Find a way to contact Alex, and hang out until he sends someone from The TEAM.

But where were her shoes? She sank against the bed, too tired to think. A woman on the run couldn't get far in bare feet. Her resolve faded at that seemingly insurmountable roadblock.

The door cracked open slowly. A man's hand, sheathed in the sleeve of a black trench coat, clenched the wooden doorjamb, and—

They're here! I've been found! The assassins are here!

Ember dropped to the floor, looking for cover. The metal tray banged to the floor with her. The water bottle spilled. But hospital beds were not made to hide under. There was no escape this time.

Twelve

"That will be seventy-seven dollars and forty-two cents."

Rory rifled through the few bills left in his wallet and handed over four twenties. The clerk promptly made change and bagged his purchase of women's wear. Within minutes, he and his pudgy accomplice were back on the street. He scooped Nima into his arms to make better time. She tended to want to people-watch, and they just did not have the time.

Everything was more difficult with no wheels or usable credit cards. And the shortage of cash wasn't his only problem. To stay undercover and protect Ember's identity, he'd traded clothes with an old man bumming the rail yard after the train stopped. That made his transient story plausible when he showed up in the emergency room with a ragged woman in urgent need of medical treatment. He'd all but run out the door after making sure Ember was in good hands. He had to. He couldn't risk the authorities taking Nima.

Now, he was ready to assume the identity of Mr. Swift, a concerned husband and father searching for his ex-Navy wife with Post-Traumatic Stress Disorder. It was a thin cover story at best. He planned not to have to use it.

He'd bought decent clothes for himself and Nima, her sweet face obscured behind children's sunglasses and a low-brimmed winter hat. With the final purchase for Ember, he was ready. He still hadn't called Alex. Too risky. The people behind Nima's father's assassination were savvy enough to be tracking incoming calls to The TEAM.

"Mama Ember?" Nima asked for the umpteenth time, her eyes wide with her two-word question. She'd loudly resisted leaving Ember behind at the hospital. Like a child with separation anxiety, she'd pitched a normal four-year-old temper tantrum.

It surprised him to see that different side of the normally sedate, otherworldly child. She hadn't reacted that strongly after her father was killed.

"Yes, Nima. We are going to see Mama Ember right now." Crossing the busy intersection, he scanned the twelve-story brick building, pointing to the seventh floor of the east wing. "Mama Ember is all the way up there. See?"

"Yep," Nima answered instantly. Rory smiled. For all of her otherworldly traits, she was still a little girl at heart. Yep had become her one-word-fits-all.

They crossed the street and entered the hospital through the front doors. Without stopping at the information desk, he and Nima boarded the elevator and proceeded to the seventh floor. He turned left when they exited the elevator and walked confidently to Ember's room.

A Chinese man in a black suit passed him in the hall. Tall. Pencil thin mustache and goatee. He glanced at Rory and Nima as they passed. Rory nodded in silent acknowledgement, taking in the hooded eyes and masked expression of the man. Fear hurried his feet. The stranger fit an assassin's profile to a T.

"Almost there, Nima."

She didn't answer, too preoccupied with the man who'd passed them in the hall, craning her neck to see him better.

Rory glanced over his shoulder while he opened Ember's room. The strange man stood at the elevator doors, still watching. Rory didn't have time to challenge him. The sight inside Ember's room tore his heart out.

He dropped to his knees with Nima. "What happened? Who did this to you?" He cradled her on his lap, searching frantically for gunshot holes he couldn't seem to find. It hit him hard. The man in the hall had eyes as cold as ice. An assassin's eyes. "Where'd he shoot you?"

She stared at him, blood on the front of her hospital gown and her wringing hands. "I thought... I mean.... Wow. You came back."

"I thought you'd be safe here." Anguish choked him. His hands moved surely and quickly over her abdomen and breasts, searching for the wound to apply pressure. It had to be here somewhere.

"Stop, Rory. I thought you were them."

"Them? Who?" He couldn't connect the dots that quickly. "Wait here with Nima. I'll go get help."

"No." Ember stilled his hands against her cheek. "Just cut my finger when I tried to hide under the bed because… because I thought you were them. I panicked. I thought...."

"You what?" Logic penetrated his panic. It made sense. She hadn't been shot. She was bleeding from a cut finger. That's all. Relief stormed over him. He grabbed both his girls and buried his face in their hair. But time was at a premium.

"We've got to move," he whispered urgently.

She nestled into his neck. "Give me a minute."

"When you're safe." He scooped both his girls off the floor and onto their feet. "We're moving."

"I can't find my shoes," she complained.

"I'll buy new ones. Here. Put these on." He tossed her the hospital footies from the counter. Fortunately there was a wheelchair outside her room. With Ember safely tucked beneath a hospital blanket and Nima holding tightly to her hand, he strolled past the nurses' station flashing a grin. It usually worked. "Just taking my wife out for a little air. We'll be right back."

The pretty nurse on the phone smiled, smitten with what she probably thought was a husband's attention to his poor, injured wife.

His plan fell apart at the elevator.

"You have something I need," the Chinese man said hoarsely, his eyes pinned to Nima.

"Get out of my way," Rory ordered, every muscle tensed. He could fire the SIG hidden beneath his coat before the man drew his weapon, if he had one—until Nima dropped Ember's hand and walked right up to the stranger, raising her hands to be picked up.

"Nima! Get back here!" Rory ordered. "Now!"

"Nima!" Ember cried. "Don't!"

The stranger sank to the floor and bowed. He was sobbing.

"'Kay," she whispered, grabbing the stranger's elbow to pull him up. He resisted, sobbing into the linoleum. She pulled harder. At last he lifted his head, tears streaming over his cheeks. She plopped her little self onto his lap. He had no choice but to hold her.

"Gyalwa Rinpoche," he whispered reverently, holding her like a piece of delicate china.

"I knew it was you. The minute I saw you, I knew who you were. I've been waiting. We all have. I knew you would come."

Taking his face between her palms, she whispered with that other voice again. "Remember not what you could not do, but what you did do. You did not leave."

Rory clutched his chest. Her words stabbed his heart with actual pain this time. In a crushing wave, the self-doubt and self-loathing he always carried dropped him to his knees, jerking him back to that pivotal moment in the hospital. That point in time—that day—that first ragged gasp in the delivery room. Only it wasn't Tyler's. It was his. His baby was born blue and underweight. Not breathing. Not fighting to live.

The whole world changed in that second. Only Dr. Brown's kind hand in the middle of his back turned the tragedy around. Only four blessed words: *He's going to live.*

But there were other regrets. The stupidity of marrying a drug addict in the first place. His lost career with the Corps. The knowledge that he'd never be one of the sharpshooters Alex sent to far-off lands on dangerous operations. Compound those failures with the twenty-four-seven challenge of caring for a sickly newborn, and for months, life held very little hope or relief.

It was during one of those bleak nights when the miracle happened in the middle of a preemie diaper change. Tyler stopped crying. The tiny little guy latched onto his father's pinkie finger, and Rory could've sworn he smiled. It might have been gas. Heck, it might have been his imagination, but it was enough. Father and son had turned a corner.

You did not leave.

Standing, Rory composed himself. False pride evaporated. He was already on the most perfect mission of his life—to raise his son. He took in a lungful and finally let go. The Corps would go on without him. So would The TEAM. He let *her* go, too.

You had your chance, Ellie Dennison. I've taken back my name. Now I take back my heart. You have no hold on me. Tyler, either. You made your choice. Live with it.

Like a brother, Rory offered his hand to the distraught man on the floor. Embarrassed, his story choked out. "I was just with my wife when she died of cancer. I blamed myself. But this precious child has healed my heart. I understand now. My wife is free, as am I." He bowed reverently to Nima. "You are the one. You have finally come."

"Yep," she said quietly, returning to Ember's side.

"Come with me," the man said as he held the elevator door open, still not able to keep his eyes off Nima while Rory wheeled Ember and Nima onboard. "You are strangers to this town."

"No. We're not," Rory lied, pressing the ground floor button, still keeping his eyes on the stranger.

"Forgive me, but yes, you are. Please let me introduce myself. I am Dr. Choden. I will make a way for you." He spoke matter-of-factly as he pressed the button to the basement parking-garage and pulled a roll of one hundred dollar bills from his jacket pocket. "I offer you this. I don't know your circumstances, but you have a greater need than I. It shows in your eyes."

"No, sir, we couldn't—"

He shoved the cash into Rory's chest. "Please, yes. Wealth hinders my enlightenment. You need it. I do not. Take it." Then he made it worse by stuffing a key fob into Rory's trench coat pocket. "The tank is full. It is yours. Keep her safe." He nodded at Nima. "She is the salvation of many. Maybe even the world."

The elevator doors opened. Rory called to the retreating figure. "But wait. You called her something. What did it mean?"

Dr. Choden turned back, his face no longer showing his previous sadness. "I called her Gyalwa Rinpoche. It means Precious Victor." Without another word, he walked away.

"Wow. Do you do anything the simple way?" Ember asked softly.

He hit the parking level button again. "I guess not."

The shiny black Cadillac parked in stall number eight, reserved for *Physicians Only*, purred like the precision automobile it was. Before long, Rory and Ember were on the outskirts of Chicago at a strip mall. He made a fast purchase at a kid's store to buy a booster seat for Nima, then onto a nearby computer store for two more burn phones and the laptop Ember requested.

Soon, they were registered under the names of Mr. and Mrs. Douglas Chance at a high-priced hotel chain. The new clothes he'd purchased hung in their closet, while a hot bath ran in the tub. After Rory bathed Nima and dressed her in new pajamas, it was Ember's turn.

He swept her off the bed and placed her on a shower stool in the middle of the lavish tub, clothes and all, her feet dangling outside the tub, her bandaged leg protected in a layer of plastic. Handing her the handheld shower attachment, he showed her how it worked. He placed the shampoo and body wash within reach.

She eyed him coyly. "Are you trying to tell me something, Dennison?"

"Yes. You stink, Agent Davis." He pulled the wastebasket over to the tub. "Peel your clothes off and drop them into this can. I'll dump everything when we leave town. Your new pajamas are on the counter along with some other things you might need. Tomorrow's clothes are hanging in the closet. Do you need help?" He paused at the door.

"No. I'll be fine. It's just that I thought for a minute you, umm, you...." Those pretty greens drifted down to her feet.

"You thought I'd left you behind, didn't you?" He came back to the side of the tub. "Look at me, Ember."

She did as he asked. Looking down on her hopeful face, feelings he hadn't allowed in years flashed hot and ready. Every urge in his male heart said, '*Kiss her.*' But two agents on a mission must never get romantically involved. They had to stay focused on the little girl snuggled under the covers in the other room. Besides, one kiss on Ember's sweet lips would lead to another. And another.

Standing over her in the tub with his hand against the tiled wall, he leaned in close enough to whisper, "You should know by now that I never leave a man or woman behind. Enjoy your shower."

Thirteen

You're driving me crazy, Dennison. You get close enough to kiss me, but then you leave?

Ember sat on the shower stool while the tub filled, feeling ten kinds of sorry for herself and confused as hell. She'd survive, but she couldn't take much more of this one step closer, two steps back dance routine with Rory. *Touching but never really making contact. Lean in. Lean out. Hold me in your arms and listen to me cry and then you leave? You're nothing but a tease.*

Nima's earlier message to her didn't help. *What do I want?*

"Hell, I don't know," Ember muttered to herself. "Him? Yes. No. Maybe. Does he want me? I think so. Maybe not. ARGH!"

Determined to get her head back in the game, she showered and washed her hair, being careful not to get her bandage wet. The handheld attachment made everything easier, but it looked brand new. Had he bought it just for her? He'd do something like that, but he was just an agent in charge. Wasn't he?

Sliding carefully out of the tub, she dried off with the luxurious hotel towel, one she couldn't see through like the towels in the *Over the Rainbow Inn*. Tucking it under her arms, she wrapped herself in plush Egyptian cotton. It took a little bit longer than usual to get her hair dried, but she managed. Using the small cosmetic bag Rory had left by the sink, she brushed her teeth, used every bit of the tiny bottle of minty mouthwash, and shaved what she could reach. Finished, she gave herself an appraising look in the mirror.

With one last shake of her head and a flounce of her hair, Ember Davis smiled back at her again. About damned time she showed up. Being clean and smelling like lavender instead of grime and sweat worked wonders. She felt better. She didn't look so bad, either.

This operation had proved tough, but she was tougher. A little thing like a scraped thigh was not going to get her down. Dennison, either. She opened the department store bag he'd left on the counter. And then she didn't know what to think.

The unmentionables he'd bought for her were exquisitely feminine without being raunchy. Her cheeks burned. Wow. He'd sized her up quite accurately. The man had a good eye, and the pajamas were just as—nice. And that was the problem. Rory hadn't always been so damned nice. Why now? Did he or did he not have feelings for her? Maybe he was waiting for her to take the first step? Stowing her rant, she dressed and limped out of the bathroom with a real no-kidding smile.

Nima squealed to see her, jumping up and down on the bed like a miniature cheerleader. "Mama Ember!"

Ember did a slow pirouette. She and Nima were wearing identical snowflake-covered, blue flannel tops and bottoms. "These are the cutest pajamas I've ever seen. And the other things, too. Thank you." *And if we were alone, I'd show you those other things, too.*

A rosy glow warmed his tanned and rugged features. "It's a mother and daughter set. I thought you might like it."

She limped over to the chair where he sat so smug and sure of himself, but just that fast, the Dennison wall came back up. She couldn't decipher the feelings she saw shifting through his eyes. Hope, maybe? Tenderness, yes. Too damned much honor and discipline? Absolutely.

If this were another place and time she'd have taken the chance and kissed him, but he'd leaned back in the chair. When those dark eyes didn't invite her in, disappointment crushed her. And he was right. The mission was Nima. She alone mattered. Ember had just hoped....

Oh, hell, she didn't know what she hoped for. There was no sense hoping for what could never be. There couldn't be a connection. Not with him. Never. He was just being nice. And she was a fool to think his careful attention was anything else. That's who he was. Just a nice guy.

"Thanks for the clothes," she said brusquely, needing to put more space between him and her. "You're not as bad as I first thought."

And there it was again, that look in his eyes she didn't understand. Ember pivoted as quickly as her wounded leg would allow. She was too tired to care.

Nima threw herself into Ember's arms, giggling. Catching her in one quick armful, Ember sank down onto the bed, her back to Rory. The one thing she could handle was rejection. "I know it's early, baby girl, but I'm tired. Do you want to go to bed?"

Nima's favorite word came without hesitation. "Yep!"

Instantly, Rory was out of his chair and at her side, helping get Nima under the covers and situated. She pushed his hand away. "I've got this, thanks."

"Are you sure?"

He stood there perplexed, his hand in his hair again. The man was as confused as she was, so she decided for the both of them. "I'm tired. Leave me alone."

She climbed into bed with her favorite little girl and pulled the blanket up. Rory dimmed the lights, and she was warm and comfortable. It didn't take long before Nima snored quietly in her arms. Ember refused to feel bad anymore. She had better things to think about than her aggravating agent in charge. Like her one and only true friend.

Did I leave enough cat food out for Maple Syrup? Enough water? I hope so. Never thought I'd be gone this long. Poor kitty might have to lose a little weight before I get back. I'll have to make it up to him. I'll buy him a pound of salmon. He'll like that.

When she woke hours later, Nima was gone. Ember pulled the covers back to see Rory's serious face staring at the happy child seated in front of the television. He must miss Tyler.

Not my problem. I have one mission and one mission only—Nima. When I'm done she'll be out of my life and it will be hard, but I'll get used to it. And everything will go back to normal and Alex better never send me on an op like this again.

Ember shoved the blankets aside and set her feet on the carpeted floor. Without a word to Rory she limped to the closet, pulled out the hanger with her new outfit and walked into the bathroom. Bed head is not a pretty sight any time of day.

You look awful.

Behind the privacy of the closed bathroom door, she had to give Rory credit. The man had good taste. The light tan jeans he'd bought were the perfect size and very soft. Comfortable. She pulled them easily up and over her bandaged thigh. The cotton ramie top made her look sporty. Dark brown definitely brought out the green in her eyes and it wasn't too tight across her bust either, always a problem area to shop for. She stared at her reflection, fluffed her hair with her hand and went out the door to face another day in the life of a fugitive on the run.

"What's the plan?" she asked when she lowered to the bed.

Rory met her with the same sad stare. Black eyes, black hair, and drop dead gorgeous, he was nothing but a nice companion agent on a mission. They had a job to do. That's all.

She stifled her feelings for him because they were obviously a product of her imagination. When they got this child back to safety, he'd go back to the workspace next to hers, eavesdropping on her and Mother's conversations like he'd done before. Ember would never tell anyone about Tyler because she'd never give Rory the satisfaction of being right about her.

"Well?"

"It's only five a.m. Your thoughts?"

"Didn't you sleep at all?"

He glanced at the adjoining queen-sized bed, its blankets tucked under the pillows but obviously ruffled and used. "I did until Nima decided it was time to get up."

She got the message. He'd gotten up with Nima so she could sleep in. Nice. For the first time she noticed he was in pajamas, too. Navy blue and black plaid bottoms with a black T-shirt. Her foolish mind wandered. The reality of two adults in pajamas at the same time in the same hotel room messed with her head. Heat crept up her neck and over her cheeks at the too fast detour her mind had just taken. Damn. Why'd he have to look so good?

"We haven't been attacked in what, two whole days now?"

He raised his pinkie finger along with the next two, his eyes hooded and probably dissecting her again. They were back to square one, guarded with each other and both wanting to be somewhere else; him with Tyler, her with her one true love. Maple Syrup. Good enough.

"We were on the train for three days?" That was a surprise. She could only recall the first night and part of the next day.

"No. Two days on the train, one at the hospital. Makes three," he corrected.

She didn't care to play games. "Fine. Whatever. Are we staying or going?"

"I'm tempted to hang out here while you heal and get a little more rest. How does another day of downtime sound? No sense rushing it." His dark eyes drilled hers.

She turned away, filled with the need to get away from this particular alpha male. "I'm going for a walk."

"No." His one word answer was instant and filled with calm authority.

"Why not? You said it yourself. We'll hang out here for a couple days. That means you think we're fairly safe. And I need some air."

He shook his head. "No. What I said is that we'd hang out here another day, not a couple days. And you don't need to go for a walk to get some air. Open the window."

Who do you think you are?

She limped toward the door and unlocked it, intending defiance. His arm blocked her exit before she had a chance to pull the door open any wider than a crack. He forced it shut and locked the dead bolt. And that pissed her off.

"It's five in the morning, Dennison. Give me a break. No one—"

"That little girl glued to the television over there depends on us to act in tandem, Junior Agent. You stay. I stay. You go. I go."

He stood breathing in her face and calling her Junior Agent like he needed to remind her who was in charge?

"Fine." Sitting at the desk, she pulled out the new laptop he'd bought the day before. If she couldn't escape physically, she could mentally. Her fingers itched to escape. Once she went online, the possibilities were endless. Firing up the device, she set up the few programs it came with, enabled the hotel's Wi-Fi, and forgot he existed.

Rory quietly closed the laptop with one big hand splayed over the lid. He leaned over her, one hand on the laptop, the other on the back of her chair, his voice rumbling all the way to her toes. "Think about what you're doing, Junior Agent."

There it was again, the reminder that he was the boss.

"And what would that be, Senior Agent?" she spat back at him, still not sure why she couldn't be nice to him. He hadn't deserted her. He'd done nothing but treat her with kindness—well, once the first safe house blew up, anyway. So why was he bugging the hell out of her this morning?

He gazed at her. "If we access any of our established social network sites, we might jeopardize our location. Is there another way?"

Ember couldn't let him have the last word. "I'll set up an alias, then."

"A what?"

"Another account. Another email address."

"You can do that?"

She rolled her eyes. *Duh.*

"And who would you contact? Mother?" Furrowed brows betrayed his doubt.

"Kelsey. Do you mind? You're breathing on me." *And I really like it, damn it.*

That raised those smug eyebrows. "Alex's wife? Why?"

"Because she's savvy enough to recognize a hidden message when she sees one. Think about it. I'll send her a rambling email from her long lost sister in Chicago, only her real sister lives in Oregon."

He shifted his weight to his other foot. "Keep talking."

And oh, my hell, she wanted to, but those deep blues were directly above her and she was caught in their beam like one of those UFO kooks in an alien force field. Trapped. Willingly trapped. And melting.

Is it even possible to fall into someone's eyes when you're looking up at them? Did he have a clue what he was doing to her right now, that with just his little finger he could command her? She swallowed hard, willing her heart to stop lying. *No one commands me. Absolutely freaking no one.*

Ember dropped her chin to break the connection.

"Kelsey would go straight to Alex with the email I'm going to send her," she explained, her voice tighter than she expected, her fingers tapping the closed laptop lid because he was still looking down at her. She could feel him. Sense him. Wow, could she.

Her nose betrayed her. Like it or not, her nostrils flared to pull in more of that beguiling male fragrance. Had to be aftershave. He smelled so—clean. Showered. Him.

For hell's sake! He. Does. Not. Want. You!

I know, but....

She squeezed her eyes tight to shake the connection. Let him think she was mad enough not to want to look at him. "We could communicate with Alex without making direct contact through The TEAM. At least he'd know we're still alive."

"Are you sure?"

She gulped before she opened her eyes. The man exuded enough raw male energy to curl her toes, but damn it, she couldn't think. *Am I sure of what?*

"Listen, Dennison." She opted for his last name to prove she was still strong-willed and capable despite the fact she'd forgotten what she was talking about. *Oh, yeah. A message to Kelsey.* "Alex isn't tech savvy, but Kelsey is. Plus she's a woman. She'll read between the lines."

"You're relying on feminine intuition?" he asked, a smile tugging the corner of his mouth.

No, I'm relying on you getting out of my face so my brain will work. Sheesh!

Rory deliberated a minute too long. She inhaled a deep breath and opened the laptop, fighting for balance.

He didn't push it closed. "What will you say?"

"I don't know," she replied honestly, the delectable odor of tall, dark and handsome filling her addled head again. After all, a woman still has to breathe. Deeply. "I have to work that out. What, umm, message do you think we should send?"

"Something succinct."

"Well, duh." Ember couldn't help the sarcasm. It helped get her mind off the way his lips and chin probably tasted. His neck. *Just a hint of tangy spice. Maybe a little salty. Hmm.*

His fingers raked through his hair. "Is there a way to send GPS coordinates?"

She rolled her eyes. This man could be so dense. "Are you serious? Why not just open the door and invite the bad guys in for coffee?"

"No need to be rude, Ember. It was the first thing that came to my mind. You're right. I'm not as smart at these things as you are." His lip lifted. He smirked that amused, devil-may-care smirk of his. As angry as he seemed a moment ago, he was relaxed now. Almost playful.

Her heart swelled with warmth like the fool she was. It was easy to believe he cared for her more that just as Agent in charge, just as easy to be swept up by his confidence in himself and his physical prowess. His hand on the back of her chair and the way he leaned around to see her eyes made her body want to do things she wasn't proud of. He could pin her in less than a split second—if he wanted to. And like the man he was, he probably didn't know the effect he had on her.

She had to concentrate on something else just to breathe. *My mother was right. I'm nothing but a slut.* That derogatory slur worked. She could breathe just fine.

Ember concentrated on the keyboard under her sweaty fingertips. "Leave me alone. Let me see what I can come up with."

He stepped over to the television where Nima still sat enthralled watching some cartoon.

Ember's fingers flew. Within minutes, she'd crafted a gossipy sounding email from Louise Timpson, Kelsey's sister. Instead of including all the news from Pendleton, Oregon, Louise's real hometown, Ember filled it with trivia from the Midwest; how her husband, Phil, had to stop in Chicago to see the U.S. Cellular Ballpark where the Chicago White Sox played. *My, my, what a train ride. Next time we're taking the bus. Can't wait to see you and Alex in Sonora, Mexico. Hope Tyler doesn't mind the surprise visit. Do you think we should tell him we're coming?*

"What do you think?" Ember asked, her composure back in place and the letter done.

He returned, peering over her shoulder, his arm on the back of her chair, his fingers on her shoulder. Just that fast, logic jumped ship. Why did his touch make her tingle like it did? She'd been hugged by the best. Alex. Harley. Zack. Certainly Todd. But with Rory it was different. His touch was—electric. Not shocking, but—magic. Like fireworks kind of—wow.

"Add one more thing," he murmured, pointing to the screen, like he needed to get any closer. His bicep bumping hers had already short-circuited her brain. The man was made of steel. Hot sexy steel that she wanted to touch. Rub. Oh, hell. Who was she kidding? She wanted to manhandle every last inch of this guy.

"Tell Kelsey to watch out for bark scorpions in Mexico," he instructed.

"Why? Did you get bit by one?"

"No, but that's how Alejandra Ramirez killed her husband on that op last year. I think we've peppered this note with enough clues. What do you think?"

I think I'm an idiot. I could sit here and look at you all day.

"Well?" He peered into her face when she didn't respond like she should have.

"Works for me," she murmured, tamping down her libido. *Damn. What was in that IV at the hospital?*

And just like that they were friends again. She set up her new account and sent the puzzling message. "What's next?"

He laid his hand on her shoulder, still standing too close and peering intently down into her eyes. "Do you still want to go for a walk?"

Ember looked up and her breath got stuck. Every last speck of blood fled her brain, pooling in the nether regions now clothed in the silky panties Rory had bought. *Now tell me, does a boring, this-is-just-a-job Agent in charge really buy women's underwear like those?*

I'm a slut. I'm a slut!

The memory of her mother's cruel taunts didn't work this time. Not one bit. Ember knew better. Taffy had proved it long ago. She wasn't all bad. She had skills. She just couldn't think of any at the moment.

Speak, Ember. Speak!

He waited for an answer, his fingers gently squeezing her shoulder in the sweetest caress. He probably though he was being encouraging. Not loving. How could he touch her like that and not understand what he was doing to her? Worse, how could she let him? Worst, she couldn't deny the tenderness welling up in those dark blues. Her heart climbed up her throat and every last muscle in her body clenched to hug and hold this guy.

Damn him. Damn me! I'm so dumb!

It's your shoulder, girlfriend. Only your shoulder. Hell, he's not even near your bra strap. He thinks of you as a guy. You're just another agent. Forget him and focus.

"Sure, why not?" she mumbled because she had to say something.

"Then grab that little girl over there who can't take her eyes off Cinderella, and let's go some place nice for breakfast. I think we're safe enough." He pulled her chair out, and like a silly Disney princess, she did as she was told.

You, Ember Davis, are an idiot.

"Come on, Nima. Let's go for a walk." She held out her hand to the little girl, but the scary blue eyes were back.

"Remember to use tragedy as a source of strength," Nima whispered.

Ember dropped to the floor, her injured leg stretched awkwardly in front of her and the breath knocked out of her. "What?"

But there was no further explanation. Nima climbed onto Ember's lap, still holding onto her fingers.

"I can't take much more of this, Rory. I mean it. Every time I turn around she comes up with some amazingly bizarre stuff that rips my heart out and—"

The premonition swept through her with a blast of fire and smoke so real she could smell the acrid stench of fuel burning, the sting of smoke in her eyes. And through the cloud of destruction came—Death. Alex cried. Harley smiled, but Rory lay belly to the earth, his face covered in blood and sweat. He would die.

She choked, the scene more than she could absorb or understand. A kaleidoscope of oranges, reds, and thick dark blacks defined and redefined the strongest prison ever. Hers. The vision ended with the peaceful flutter of white doves that in no way eased the prickly terror climbing up her throat.

Rory clutched her elbow, asking for the words Nima wouldn't share. "Ember, talk to me. Look at me."

The world passed in such slow motion she could've counted his incredibly long eyelashes if she'd wanted to. The deep blues beneath them were fierce. Angry. And scared. But for what? A smile blossomed slowly across her face. It tugged the corner of her lips first, then her cheeks as she came back to reality in the blast of his anger.

"Ember! For the love of—"

"Rory."

He calmed the second she cupped his cheek. "Ember. Honey. Tell me what she told you."

Honey. Hmm. Not Junior Agent?

She sat dazed and disconnected from reality. "Death. And Alex. And life, I think." The words dripping off her tongue sounded distant in her ears, as if someone else was speaking from far away.

"What do you mean?" he asked earnestly, his fingers feeling gently over her cheeks and through her hair as if she'd been injured.

Reality shifted again. Truth glistening in his eyes, Rory was just a man trying to hold this insane operation together. And he did care; he just could not speak it. And that scared her as much as the vision. Unrequited love never brought peace. Only pain to last for years.

"What did she tell you?" he asked again.

Ember leaned into the luxurious feel of his touch, her eyes closed as she soaked up the comforting strength of this tender warrior. "She told me to use tragedy as a source of strength. That's all."

"But what does that mean? You saw something else, didn't you?" He traced his fingertips over her cheek. "What did you see? Come on, Ember. You can tell me."

"I saw these things. I saw Alex crying, but then I saw Harley smiling. Then...." She stopped cold. How could she tell him she'd seen the day Tyler would become an orphan like Nima? "And then I saw smoke and fire. That's all."

Suspicion shifted over his face. She should have known better than to deceive a covert operator. These guys were good at their jobs. Rory was no exception.

"What aren't you telling me?"

There was no way she'd ever tell. Never. "That's all there was, right, Nima? You saw it, too, didn't you?" she asked.

The wise little girl only smiled and continued to hold Ember's hand as calmly as if she were an eighty-year-old monk.

Rory gathered them both against him and they sat for the longest time on the floor. He didn't seem able to get close enough, continually running his hands up her arms and over her shoulder to cup her cheek. His breath came in short hard pants. He was close enough to kiss again, but he was scared.

And so was she. She closed her eyes to block it out, but the vision came back with crystal clarity, the details crisp enough to touch. Rory lay belly to the ground, his SIG clutched in his outstretched right hand. Blood and dirt obscured his features, but his eyes were wide open. Orange flame reflected back from the black of his lifeless gaze. No tender look of love radiated within.

An icy fingertip slithered across her shoulder, its nail tapping the message home. Death meant to visit her again. It would come to rob. To crush. She bit her lip and shivered. *Why me? Why can't one person, please, just stay in my life? Is that too much to ask of the universe? Why—me?*

He held her tighter. "You're as cold as ice. Are you sure that's all you saw?"

She turned her tearful face away from him, exposing the back of her neck to his heated breath, the feel of it too exquisite to bear—or to lose. He leaned in, his chin warm at the back of her neck. Ripples of wanton desire coursed through her from this simple contact, desire that would never find release. She bowed her head at the injustice of fate, willing to accept that this might be as close as she'd ever get to the man she was fairly sure loved her.

"Yes," she whispered softly. "It's all I saw."

He planted the lightest kiss beneath her ear lobe, his arms and legs all but encompassing hers. "I believe you."

She held her breath, wanting so much more, but letting all of her foolish hopes go at the same time. This single stolen moment needed to last as long as possible. She didn't even hint at turning in his arms to offer her heart or body. More was never meant to be. Not with this man. Not for her. She should've known.

Life was cruel. Death more so.

Fourteen

Rory eyed Ember suspiciously. For a woman who'd wanted to go for a walk bad enough to risk insubordination earlier, she was determined to stay indoors now. They didn't go to breakfast or lunch. Instead, they ordered room service and clung to the seclusion of their room.

She made paper dolls out of the daily newspaper delivered to their door, and together she and Nima dressed them in cut-out tissues. Rory disappeared for two minutes to dump their old clothes in the hotel garbage bins. When he came back, he brought a handful of orange and red autumn leaves, which they promptly cut up into designer shoes and purses for their dolls with fingernail scissors from the front desk. The floor was a mess, but he didn't care. As long as his girls were happy, he was, too.

Only he was pretty sure Ember wasn't happy. She'd changed since her vision. Her bright smile had faded. She was holding something back.

"What are you two giggling about?" he asked.

"We made a Rory doll," Ember replied while Nima held up a paper doll with curly black inked hair. For a prognosticating, eighty-year-old child, her eyes held the cutest sparkle of mischief.

Rory shook his head in mock dismay. "You girls always stick together. You'll make a great mother someday, Ember."

She shook her head. "No. I won't."

The way she said it stabbed his heart. She was so sure and so sad at the same time, but the scene he watched now betrayed her. She and Nima acted like mother and daughter. There were no other words for it. Maybe she couldn't see it, but he could.

Rory went back to reading what was left of the newspaper, but his mind was zeroed in on the woman on the floor. Invisible strings pulsated between them with every movement she made and every whispered word to Nima. The tension quivered like a spider's web when she bit her lip or smoothed her hair out of her face. Every breath of hers resonated with his. Even the air transmitted her essence to him. Whether she knew it or not, he still held her in his arms, close and warm—and his.

The distance between them right now seemed too far. He ached for her. The laugh bubbling out of her throat as she played with Nima felt like tinkling bells on the stretched tight cords of his heart. How had it happened? How had this woman gotten under his skin in less than a week?

He forced his mind back to the dilemma at hand. The other dilemma. They couldn't remain incommunicado forever. He needed to know what The TEAM was doing to help them as much as Alex needed to hear from him. But how could they do that without raising the attention of the assassins? And who could they trust? Until he was certain who'd rigged the dress with transmitters, he couldn't trust anyone, not even the FBI. Even the gentle Buddhist monks at the temple were suspect.

Ember's email to Kelsey might ease Alex's mind for about two seconds, but Alex was a man of action. It wasn't enough. Plus, Ember was holding back. Nima's latest words didn't speak to Rory the way they had to Ember. He was missing part of the picture and he didn't like it.

Remember to use tragedy as a source of strength? What did that mean?

He'd been doing that all his life; Ember, too, by the sounds of it. He watched them play with their paper dolls for a while longer. "When you girls are finished playing, would you help me with something on your computer?"

"You? On the computer? Sure." She ruffled Nima's hair and stood up. "Be back in a jiffy, baby girl." She turned to Rory. "What do you need?"

"I'd like to record Nima's words before I forget them."

Ember sat at the desk with the laptop and opened a new document. "Fire away."

He sat cross-legged on the floor beside Ember. Nima instantly tired of the paper dolls and climbed up on his lap. "You said you got a calming feeling from Nima in David's car, right? Did she say anything?"

Ember typed the first encounter into the computer. "No. She didn't say anything, but it was the first time I really looked into her eyes. We were making our getaway and all of a sudden I'm looking into light blue eyes. It kind of spooked me, but I also felt like everything would turn out fine, like we were already safe. Weird, huh?"

"Not now that we've gotten more messages. The next time she spoke was at Jed McCormack's place. She told me, *'If you keep hiding, no one can find you.'*"

Ember typed the second event. "How'd you feel when you heard it?"

"My knee-jerk reaction was hell, yeah, it's the only way we'll be safe, but that's not what she meant. She was telling me personally to stop hiding my son. And for the first time in a long time, I felt like I wanted to tell someone about Tyler. And that person should be you."

"Why?"

"Because I trust you. What did our little girl say next?"

"It happened at Jed McCormack's. You'd just told me everything you went through with Tyler and.... Anyway, Nima said, *'If you seek to heal your own sadness, seek first to heal the sadness of another.'*"

"How did that make you feel?" Rory watched her tough girl façade crumble. He couldn't look away.

She gulped, her attention on the keyboard, the pads of her fingers barely making a sound as she translated feelings into words. "It made me feel like I wanted to help you and Tyler somehow, maybe by just understanding what you guys were going through because I didn't know any of this until you told me. I didn't want you to think I didn't care, umm, about you."

Every muscle yearned to pull her into his arms, but he didn't. "Nima gave you another one of her pearls of wisdom at the motel, didn't she?"

"Yes." She scrutinized the words at her fingertips. "Her exact words were, *'Sometimes what you want is not what you need.'*"

"Wow." He hijacked Ember's usual comeback. "What is it you need, Ember?"

"I need... I need to get this operation over and this baby girl safely home." Her words tumbled out too fast. "Then I need to feed my cat and make sure I get the debrief done and ready for Alex. You know how he is."

"I'll help with your report," he said calmly. Somehow he had to let her know he cared without igniting the world between them on fire. "The next message was for Dr. Choden, but it was also meant for me. *'Remember not what you could not do, but what you did do. You did not leave.'"*

"What was that all about?"

"I don't know what it meant to Dr. Choden, but it told me loud and clear that my worries about not being a good enough father and agent were groundless. Alex has never complained, but I've beaten myself up for months. Guess it's that old be-all-you-can-be mindset drilled into us Marines. I wasn't measuring up to my own standards. And that little piece of paper called a divorce decree doesn't end the ugly feelings that go with it. But enough of me. Are we missing anything?" *Of course we are.*

"Only what she said today."

"You mean when she told you to use tragedy as a source of strength?"

Now is the moment. Either she'll tell me the truth or she'll lie. Again.

Ember turned away from the keyboard, but still wouldn't face him. "At first I was mad because she says these incredibly gut wrenching things, then she smiles with those scary blue eyes of hers, and I'm always off balance when she's around. Like at Arlington the first day. Didn't you feel it? It was like the earth stopped spinning or something."

"I did," he stated calmly.

She stopped talking, her clenched knuckles to her mouth. "Only this time...."

He held his breath while she crumbled. It took all of his will power not to pull her onto his lap. "Life is scary sometimes, but we will get through this," he said gently.

She wouldn't answer, but her eyes shouted what her mouth wouldn't whisper. *No! We're not going to be okay!* Up off her chair she came and into the bathroom. The door locked. The sink faucets turned on. Then the shower.

"I think I hurt Mama Ember's feelings," he whispered to Nima. "I don't know how, but we are going to be fine. I promise. You'll see. When she comes out of the bathroom, she'll be herself again."

Nima wiggled off his lap and went to the closed door. With hands too small to be heard over the running water from the other side, she smacked it a couple times before turning back to him with tears in her eyes. "Want Mama."

"I don't think she wants to talk to us right now, little girl, but sure. I'll help." He joined Nima and rapped three times. No answer. He knocked again.

Still no answer.

"She doesn't want to talk to us right now. I'm sorry."

The little girl's lip turned into a pout and she started to wail. Rory smiled, she was so cute about it with her eyes squinted closed and her mouth wide open. He chuckled as he picked her up. "It's okay. It's going to be—"

Ember jerked the door open. If looks could kill, he'd have been skewered at first sight. She held a handful of shredded tissues to her nose. And she was radioactive mad.

"You're wrong. It's not okay. You didn't see it, and I can't bear what I saw, so stop telling Nima we're going to be okay." She reached for Nima and instantly the little girl switched places. There it was, that mother/daughter thing again.

"Tell me then. What didn't I see?"

"And that was a dirty trick, getting me to record all Nima's brilliant sayings, Dennison. I'm done helping you on the computer." Sparks flashed from her eyes, and he stood directly in the blast zone. Rory couldn't hold back another smile. He'd learned so much about Ember these past few days, even which buttons to push to rile her up.

"Wipe the smug look off your face while you're at it!" She strode from the bathroom doorway like a woman on a mission. "I'll tell you what we're going to do. We're not going back to Alexandria, and we are not putting this baby of mine in harm's way! Do you hear me?"

Baby of mine? Ember definitely had that mad mother bear thing going on again. He shook his head, bemused at the fierce dynamics of pure motherhood. As much as he wanted to laugh at the lovely scene, he also wanted to cry. This was exactly what was missing from his marriage—a real, no kidding mother who'd fight for her child.

He tucked his sentiment back where it belonged and pulled rank on the sweet woman sitting with her arms wrapped defensively around Nima. "Then you need to tell me what's going on, Agent Davis. We've been in hostile territory since this op started. I can't form solid strategy until I know everything I'm dealing with. And I can't have my companion agent running around with a tissue stuffed up her nose every time something doesn't go her way." He hoped he came across tougher than he felt, because all he heard was, *Gosh, I think I'm falling in love.*

Ember blinked. "I...." She snapped her mouth shut.

"Spill it, Davis. I can pull you off this assignment anytime I think you're jeopardizing the mission. Do you get that? And you've screwed up big time."

"I saw you die!" she spat, but then her demeanor crumbled. "There! Are you happy now? I saw you die. Is that what you wanted to hear?"

He caught her in his arms before her first teardrop fell. She didn't resist as they sank to the floor together, and he couldn't hold back if he wanted to. "It's okay. Don't cry," he whispered into her hair.

"But it's not!"

Nima wailed with her. This mother/daughter tag team was hard on his tender heart. "Shush now. We'll be fine. I'm not going to die, and neither are you."

"And you can't fire me, because I won't leave. Knock off the drill sergeant crap. That's just plain mean."

He smiled, thankful she couldn't see the effect she had on him. Ember was herself again, and he was a smitten man. "Are you better now?"

She wiped Nima's face and her own with her sleeve before she looked him in the eye. "No. I'm not."

"Tell me everything you saw. Please?"

"I saw you die. I saw smoke and fire like I told you. And I saw Alex cry, which he would if you were dead, but then I saw Harley smiling one of his goofy smiles. You know the ones I mean. And then I saw you lying there like you were—"

He placed a finger to her lips. "I'm not going to die. I haven't felt this good in years."

Desolation stared back at him. "But it looked so real, like I was watching a television commercial. Right after Nima said those words, I saw it and... and...."

"And Nima is bound for certain destiny, but you and me," his words come out of his mouth like he and Ember belonged together. "We're two of the toughest agents on The TEAM. The only thing we're destined for is to keep Nima safe and sound."

Her eyes still sparked. She wasn't convinced, but at least she was talking to him.

Nima patted Ember's cheek and asked in her patient way, "'Kay?"

Ember shook her head and gave Nima another squeeze. "No. I don't think I'll ever be okay again. But I'm glad I told you, Rory. Now you know."

"Well, I know a couple of things. For instance, how about we go to a nice place for dinner? I might even buy you a bottle of champagne and we'll celebrate our last night in Chicago together. Would you like that?"

"I don't want to go anywhere."

"Come on. Get dressed. I'll take you gals to one of Tyler's favorite places on the planet. They've got cheeseburgers, nuggets and fries," he rambled, coaxing her mind off her vision or whatever it was.

"I didn't know they had champagne at Burger King."

"That's another thing I know. It comes in those little boxes with those skinny little straws." He winked at Nima like it was a secret between the two of them. Nima winked back. A tiny smile cracked Ember's face.

And just like that they were friends again.

Fifteen

"Are you sleeping?" Ember whispered, her brain going a mile a minute.

"No," came Rory's answer from the other queen-sized bed.

Good. She suspected he was as wide-awake as she was. Nima snored lightly by her side.

"I have an idea."

"So do I."

He was already padding toward the bathroom in his bare feet. Wow. She'd never noticed before how lazily he walked or the way those flannels PJs hung suggestively off his hips. The man was a study in contrasts. Wide-shoulders, narrow hips, and ripped abs. He scratched his belly in typical guy, I-got-an-itch fashion. Closing the bathroom door, he left just enough room to reach inside and turn on the light. "Let's talk."

And so they sat cross-legged in their flannel pajamas at the end of Nima's bed and strategized in the dim light seeping through the cracked bathroom door. Rory's plan was simple. Sometimes hiding in plain sight was the right thing to do.

Halloween was two days away. If they could make it all the way to Alexandria without the assassins finding them, they could walk right up to Kelsey's front door disguised as trick-or-treaters. The TEAM office was nearby. Alex could have all available agents on his front doorstep in less than five minutes the way he drove.

"This is where we might run into trouble," he said. "We can't stay there very long or we'll endanger Kelsey."

"Wow, Rory. It's like we're sharing the same brain. Your plan fits perfectly with mine. You can be a big fat caveman."

His hand went to his flat stomach. "Excuse me? I'm not fat."

And Ember could've kissed him. He could be so darned endearing. Despite the less than cheery premonition she'd received from Nima, it felt good to strategize with her agent in charge. They were back on the same page.

"You will be by the time I'm through with you. You'll be concealing not only your handgun in your big belly, but another Nima, too. We'll name her Nima Two. Won't Kelsey be surprised? You'll show up pregnant at her front door. We'll drop off the real Nima by sleight of hand and leave with your four-year-old latex daughter in tow."

His face crinkled with the first smirk of the day. "Slow down. What are you talking about?"

Ember took a deep breath to calm her excitement. Finally, they could be one step ahead of the assassins, but she needed to explain better. "I make dolls, Rory. Didn't you know? And if we stay here another day or two, and if you go shopping for me first thing in the morning and get everything I need, I can make a doll that looks just like Nima. And now that I think of it...."

Her brain pinged. A flood of inspiration took over. Enthusiasm struck. She knew precisely how to bait the assassins. They wanted Nima? They could have her. This would work!

Without thinking for once, Ember launched herself at Rory and planted one on his very surprised lips. Only he didn't seem as surprised as she'd expected.

He rolled to his back on the carpet with his arms around her, not letting go. And there she was, her hands and breasts on his chest, her heart suddenly in her throat. She'd broken the fraternization rule, big time.

He no longer seemed to be the uptight agent in charge. His right hand brushed her hair away from her face while his other found purchase at the back of her neck, his fingers gently pulling her in.

She wanted this. Needed this, but— "No," squeaked out in a heated rush.

"Yes," he growled softly, closing the distance, his tongue moistening his lips in anticipation. She shut her eyes, daring to hope. He brushed his nose against her cheek, pressing his lips to the seam of hers. Just his lips. No tongue. No pressure for more. Just the minty toothpaste flavor of his mouth. The brush of his whiskered chin against hers. The feel of his hard body beneath hers.

Her heart melted. This gentle warrior had hold of her now. This was what she'd wanted, just one kiss that didn't feel stolen or forced, one that he actually wanted to share. Everything would be okay. Only—it wouldn't.

He deepened the kiss and she let him, parting her lips. Fraternization rules be damned. With her palms to his cheeks, her heart took over. She poured all her hopes and fears into that kiss. Only....

He mumbled into her mouth, "Easy, Mrs. Dillon. We're not alone."

He probably meant Nima, but Ember knew better. The vision flooded back and spoiled everything. She stood to lose everything she'd just found. The moment his death had been revealed, the magic was ruined, her hopes with it.

Reality set in. The vision was scary real. She eased away from his chest and back to her haunches where she belonged. Where she couldn't get hurt.

"Hey, you." He sat up with her, pulling her hand back to his chest. "I'm sorry."

"No, I'm sorry," she whispered. Her fingers didn't want to leave the warmth where he held her. Any other time, she would've pulled him back for more by the color of his T-shirt. "I shouldn't have done that. We have to plan this Halloween routine down to the last detail. Sit up and listen."

He already was sitting cross-legged, his brows knitted with more than just worry. He'd clasped her hand to his chest, holding it in place. "So talk. I'm listening."

Tamping down her impulsive heart, she focused on the most important strategy of her lifetime. "Like I said. I make dolls."

He nodded, his thumb tucked inside her hand and rubbing a small circle of encouragement on her palm.

Her heart seemed to have taken up residence where her brain should be. "And, umm, I make dolls," she repeated, "and if you'll get me the supplies I need, I have a plan to give the assassins Nima. At least to make them think that's who they're getting."

"How?" He flattened her palm over his heart, like that helped her brain work any better. His heart. The one that would cease to beat if the vision was true. If Alex cried. If Harley—

Ember took a deep breath and took her hand back. The only way to change his future was to implement her plan. Rory was going to live. "Think about it, Dennison. We're officially off the grid. Mother can't even find us, and all Alex knows is we were in Chicago and safe at the time we sent the email. Right now we could place Nima just about anywhere and she'd be safe."

"If he understood the message you sent," Rory cautioned. He leaned in, his elbows on his crossed knees, his chin on his interlocked fingers.

"He did," Ember replied confidently, her traitorous eyes scrolling over Rory's lean frame. The slightest brush of chest hair peeked up from his T-shirt, teasing her. "We gave him enough clues, but here's the thing. We have to assume the assassins are watching everyone even remotely associated with The TEAM, so we can't just walk in and drop Nima off with Kelsey. We'll have to look like everyone else when we show up at her front door. I'm thinking you'd make a good caveman. That way we can hide the Nima doll inside your big belly. I'll be a cavewoman. Nima can be the cute cavebaby."

"I'm listening."

"Right, so we need to look like we still have Nima with us when we leave. We get back in our car. We place a call to Alex, only he already knows what's going on. The TEAM is already set to move in. The assassins intercept the call. We lure them into the open."

"And blam. They go up in smoke this time. This just might work. Alex has a fairly decent gun collection at his home," Rory murmured. "By the time we left Kelsey's, we could also be armed to the teeth."

"And if I know Alex like I'm pretty sure I do, the guys on The TEAM are already on twenty-four-seven alert. He might even have the FBI standing by to go after these assassins."

He nodded. "We'll still need to give him advance warning so he can get all the players in place. While you're making your Nima doll, I'll put the plan in writing for Alex. Kelsey will know how to get it to him. If the assassins are intercepting TEAM communications, that one call should trigger them."

"Right," she murmured. Here she was planning what very well could be her and Rory's deaths. There seemed no way around it.

"You do realize we're taking a huge risk leaving Nima with Kelsey, don't you? That's my biggest concern. Kelsey might be tough, but she's still just one woman. Plus, we'll have abdicated our responsibilities to Alex's wife, not something I'm thrilled about doing." Rory tapped her knee. "Hey. Are you still with me?"

Ember jolted out of her daze. "Yes, just thinking is all. I know leaving Nima alone with Kelsey is a risk, but like I said. We're off the grid. Even if the assassins are watching her place, we'll look like the rest of the goblins and spooks roaming the streets. Alexandria always puts on a good Halloween extravaganza. It's a big deal. There will be tons of tourists and families with little kids going from business to business and door to door. We'll blend right in. What else can we do?"

His fist went to his chin. "It just might work."

Rory looked convinced, but honestly? She didn't know if she wanted it to work or not. Killing the assassins, yes. Losing him, Nima, or Kelsey? No way.

"Suppose we do make it safely to Kelsey's, where's a good place to lure the assassins to?" he asked. "You got any bright ideas?"

"There's a new subdivision going up west of the Masonic temple. It's still vacant."

"Good deal." He placed both palms to his kneecaps. "Listen. About before—"

She rolled to her feet. "Forget it. All this planning's made me tired. I'm going back to sleep."

Ember left him sitting there. She had to. Her plan seemed fraught with too much risk. And death. Climbing in next to Nima, she snuggled the sleeping child to calm her nerves.

"Are you sleeping?" he asked after a few minutes from his bed.

"Trying to," she answered.

"Goodnight, Ember."

It took all her strength to answer calmly. "Goodnight, Rory."

Sleep never came, only a continual rerun of the premonition. Exhausted with worry, she rolled out of bed before the sun was up, showered and dressed for the new day. She had a doll to make. Nima Two had to be perfect.

It took one day to fashion the doll's body out of pre-formed molded plastic face, arms and hands. Rory was a faithful servant, running to the nearest hobby store for fabric and sewing supplies for the doll's body and their caveman costumes. Ember used all of her artistic skills to paint the perfect Nima face, light blue eyes and all. And Rory, God bless him, also bought a small USB recording device and a Bluetooth speaker. By the end of the second day, not only did they have a set of realistic costumes, they had a moving, talking Nima doll puppet.

"Watch this," Rory whispered, the remote control for Nima Two in the palm of his hand. "I've been playing with Nima and recording her voice. How's it sound?"

Nima sat on the floor facing Rory and Nima Two, her twin.

"Mama Ember," the doll said while he made its head turn to the side and back again.

Nima's eyes widened.

"Me want down," Nima Two said.

Ember smiled at the look of wonder on Nima's face. If she believed, maybe the assassins would, too.

The next morning found them on the road again, Nima Two stowed in the trunk along with their costumes. The fields and towns of Indiana flew by. Before long, Rory pulled over at a Mom and Pop's diner across the Indiana/Ohio state line for lunch. The sunny autumn weather couldn't have made a nicer day. Farming implements, pumpkins, and garlands of autumn leaves decorated the little diner. Lunch was a hundred times better than their fast food meal of the night before: grilled chicken salad, homemade cinnamon applesauce, and hot cornbread dripping with honey butter.

In the middle of eating, Nima's little head plunked to her outstretched arm on the table. "I think that's our signal to go." Rory scooped her out of her booster seat and into his arms. "You ready?"

Ember pushed her chair back and turned away. Her heart had been tenderized to the point of mush. Rory's skillful handling of that little girl didn't make it easier. Despite his attempts to cheer her, the dark mood of the vision lingered.

Her worst day was still ahead. They could laugh and joke all they wanted today, but too soon Rory would fall in the line of duty just like Todd.

"Oh, look." Rory pulled an extra long black and orange striped scarf off the counter display rack and draped it around her neck, a big cheesy smile on his face. He was relaxed and handsome, his smile full of mischief. "This is so-o-o you."

Focusing on exact change at the check out counter, she tried to sound stern. "I'm not buying it. Put it back."

"Oh, come on, Mama Ember," he begged in his best imitation of a little boy. "Puh-leezz?"

Darn him. A woman could fall into those deep blue pools and never be seen again.

"Come on. Can I have it?" It was so charming when he did that!

One more look into those teasing, mischievous little boy eyes and she turned into the biggest sucker on earth. Ember paid for the goofy scarf.

"You sound like a real mother."

"You're a brat. I do not."

"See? You've got the vocabulary down. You're mom material through and through." He stooped to pick up something off the ground. "Hold out your hand and close your eyes."

When she complied, he placed something light in her open palm. Ember looked down at a golf ball-sized pinecone. "I'm glad it's not a bug. What's this about?"

"Simple. Mom sent one with every care package while I was deployed. They were from the tree in our front yard. You don't have to keep it," he said as he pulled the car out of the parking lot and into traffic. "But you'd be surprised how a little thing from home can turn a dark day around."

She tucked the pinecone under the flap to one of the backpacks. Mrs. Dennison sounded like a neat mom. "How many pinecones did she send?"

He grinned. "You'll see."

Before long, they stopped for the night at another nice but out of the way motel. Rory secured the car and got Ember and Nima situated. Then he took a walk around the premises to ensure he knew where all the exits were. By then, Ember had Nima bathed and in her pajamas for the night. It was late. They'd driven all day and Nima fell asleep quickly. Dinner was oriental take-out, which they ordered from the café in the lobby and ate in their room. Entertainment was whatever was on the television. Rory and Ember lounged around the room like they had nothing better to do.

Oh, yeah. Sure.

More and more she had to look away to keep from throwing herself at him. He was an industrial-sized magnet; she was molten, pliable steel ready to fly across the room into his arms. All he had to do was say the word. Or not. One smoldering look would do. Heck, all he had to do was breathe hard.

Separate queen-sized beds placed only feet apart from each other declared the problem louder. She was supposed to sleep with Nima in the one while he slept alone in the other? Yeah, right. Like she didn't hear every sound he made during the night, every rustle of the blankets, every moan and grumbling groan? Like she couldn't picture lying next to him, feeling his arms and legs wrapped around her? She bit her lip hard to shift her feelings off him. It didn't work.

Stop it already. Think, Ember. Think. You know better. Marriage, motherhood and all that stuff are not in the cards for you. No way. You're not Mom material. You don't want to be.

She took a cold shower and wore her clothes to bed. Somehow the blue flannel with snowflakes had taken a turn toward sexy, a slippery slope since their midnight strategy meeting.

His brow arched when she pulled the bedcovers over her jeans, but he didn't say anything. He had to have felt it, too. He sat against the headboard of his bed, still fully dressed except for his boots, still watching television, and still as irresistible as ever.

When he turned the TV off, the room darkened enough that she took the chance. Opening her eyes, she sought his profile across the room. Only he wasn't there. He was sitting on the edge of his bed, his hands on his knees, watching her.

"Hi," he said softly. "I figured you wouldn't be able to sleep, either."

She gulped down her foolish, feminine hopes and dreams. "You were right."

"You're one heck of an operator, Ember Davis. I couldn't have done this operation without you."

With her heart climbing up her throat, she didn't dare lift the covers to sit up for the conversation. That would be too much like daring fate. No meant no. Remember?

"When everything settles down, I'd like you to come over to my place for dinner. I grill a mean T-bone. Tyler would get a kick out of you, and I know you already like him. We could knock back a bottle of wine and, you know. Chill."

"That would be nice," she whispered. *How does a woman on fire even begin to chill?*

"I'd like another kiss now," he whispered, "but I'll understand if you say no."

She was off her bed and in his arms before he knew what hit him. But he didn't kiss her. The groan that swelled out of him sounded pain-filled. Anguished. Maybe even heartbroken. Cupping her head to his chest, he pressed her under his chin. His heart thundered beneath his black T-shirt almost as much as hers pounded back.

Despite the dire premonition, contentment flooded the motel room. Wanted was a very good place to be. It was enough just to be in this man's very capable hands, just to be held against the only heart that beat in sync with hers. He pressed his mouth to her forehead, branding her with an intimate, yet chaste kiss. So much strength and love radiated from him. So much confidence. She closed her eyes and let herself believe. The vision had to be wrong. Maybe there was hope.

Rory pulled her onto the bed with him, snuggling on top of the covers with his nose in her hair, his arms circled around her. Nima snored softly from the other bed, but for this one moment in time, Ember had everything.

Tomorrow would have to take care of itself.

Sixteen

The next morning began the same as the first, with breakfast at a fast food joint once they were back on the road. Finally in the home stretch, Rory parked at a motel in Crystal City, Virginia, in late afternoon. Shadows were already low, the sun sinking fast. After scouting the hotel grounds to get the lay of the land, he brought their few bags up to the room, bolted and locked the door.

This was where the rubber would hit the road, and as usual, he had pre-combat jitters. Tonight would be hard. His girls' lives were on the line.

"We've got to hurry," Ember said urgently. "All the trick-or-treaters will be out pretty soon."

"I'm hurrying. Where's the stuff?"

"In the bathroom. I'll get Nima ready while you shower and dress."

He went straight to work. By the time he'd transformed into a dumpy caveman, Ember and Nima were ready to go. And darn. This cavewoman stopped him cold. Yes, the flesh-colored elastic material covered her real skin, but that faux-fur bikini top did a number on her already-full bosom. And that brown-colored furry skirt thingee? She might as well have been wearing flannel pajamas again. Nothing hid those splendid hips or the taunting sway when she walked.

She'd pulled her hair into a topknot ponytail and sprayed some red coloring into it. A plastic bone completed both her and Nima's ensemble. Nima looked cute, but Ember? Gorgeously sexy and downright steamy. He tugged at his collar, hoping his costume hid what his body was thinking.

"Cute costume. I always did like saber-tooth tiger furs. What are you looking at?" she asked, amusement shifting over her face.

"Yabba-dabba-do?" he offered weakly.

"Ha! I told you that you'd make a good Neanderthal." She patted his belly. "Is Nima Two in there?"

"Of course. And my pistol. And the last of my magazines." *And the most painful hard-on I've had in a long time.*

They stood there, her hand on his padded belly, Nima on her hip, and the darnedest sensation of a happy family taking over the last of his good senses.

"You can't go looking like that. Where's your hair?"

He pulled the scruffy wig out of his caveman pocket. "Got it."

Only Nima's light blue eyes would give her away, but he was supposed to put both of these girls in danger? His girls? The whole plan seemed utterly ridiculous. It wouldn't work and even if it might, he couldn't take the chance.

"Rory," Ember said sternly. "Knock it off. I know what you're thinking because I'm thinking the same thing. It's a big risk we're taking, but we have to do something. Trust me. Let's get to Alexandria. The sooner the better."

He'd lost his ability to swallow. She might be right, but wow. She might be wrong.

Ember nodded toward the door. "We're off the grid, remember? Let's move it, soldier."

That much was true. They were off the grid. This might be their only opportunity. Okay. As preposterous as he looked, it seemed the only way. Hide Nima. Bait the assassins. Finish the job.

He took hold of Ember's outstretched hand. The curtain was rising. It was time to blend in and surprise the heck out of Kelsey Stewart.

Only it didn't work that way. They parked their car at the end of the block and made their way to the Stewart home along with a crowd of happy trick-or-treaters. Nima got to collect way too many sugary treats in her little plastic jack-o-lantern. He kept his eyes peeled and his girls safe, but the minute the Stewart's front door swung open to their boisterous, "Trick-or-treat!" everything changed.

"It's about damned time," Alex hissed, waving them inside in his usual brusque way. "What took you so long?"

"Boss? How'd you even know we were coming?" Rory had to ask. Was this guy omniscient?

Alex shut the door behind them, scowling at his wife. "I didn't. Kelsey did. She hasn't slept a wink since you sent that damned message. And she's been looking everywhere for you. I can't get her to come to bed at night."

"I just knew you'd come here," Kelsey said. A slender woman with long brown hair pulled into a clip at the back of her head, she took their coats and ushered them into an inviting living room. "You couldn't go to The TEAM, so they had to come to you. It's the only thing that made sense."

And then the crazy plan changed again. Not only was Alex there, but Harley, too. Alex's guard dogs, Whisper and

Smoke, were settled alongside the fireplace. Zack Lennox offered a high-five from the couch. Gabe Cartwright dropped the magazine in his hands to the coffee table with a sarcastic, "Don't you look sweet?"

Rory jerked his fake hair off his head. Relief flooded the knots out of his shoulders. His guys were there. Alex and his team had never looked so good. "How'd you guys get here? Were you followed?"

Gabe held up a plastic yellow helmet. "I'm TV repair. I've been here since late Monday. No sign of a tail."

"The rest of us came undercover of night," Zack said. "I'm still not sure anyone's watching this place, though. I've been patrolling the neighborhood. Nothing's out of place. No strange cars lurking in the neighbors' driveways, either. I don't think the assassins are as good as we think."

"You wouldn't say that if you'd had everything blown up around you," Ember disagreed.

Alex offered no time for further discussion. "How were you thinking of ending this op?"

"We're leaving Nima here while we meet with the assassins and finish them off," Ember said. "Only we're not really. Turn around, Dennison."

Rory complied. She had her mojo back, as bossy as ever. Ember unzipped the back of his costume. He dropped the sleeves over his arms and out popped his latest child, Nima Two, where he'd belted her to his abdomen.

Kelsey grinned. By now, she was on the couch with Nima on her lap. "Oh, my, it looks just like Nima."

Harley snickered. "You're the first pregnant guy I've ever met."

"Don't even start with me, Mortimer." Rory offered his fist. "We're leaving the real Nima here with Kelsey and you two baboons while we run the ambush scenario. Boss, I'm going to place a call to you when we're in place. I figure the assassins are still monitoring TEAM phone lines, right?"

Alex shrugged. "Mother thinks so. No pipe bombs since the start of this op, but she's convinced we've got someone hacking our server."

"That will never happen," Ember said. "Mother's too good."

"That's what she says," Alex grumbled.

"Ember and I need time to change, Boss. After we leave here, we'll go back to our motel, change our clothes, and get Nima Two ready. Can you get an ambush set up at this location?"

"Tonight?"

Rory looked to Ember for her input. "Sure. Are we ready to rock and roll or not?"

"I am," she replied evenly. "Nima's safe. Let's get this done before those guys know what hit 'em."

Alex tapped his ear, and Rory would've hugged him if they'd been alone. The boss was wearing a wire. That meant he was already in league with the FBI, maybe Homeland Defense, too. He held his hand out, his fingers snapping. "Give me the location."

Rory placed the sticky note with the address in his boss's very capable hands.

"Why don't you two stay here with Nima? Catch your breath. I can task two other agents to finish this op."

"And exactly who would you get to fill my thirty-eight Cs, huh Alex?" Ember asked with a jiggle of her very lovely and extremely sexy cavewoman accessories. "These guys who've been chasing us know exactly who's got Nima. They've seen us up close and personal. And they're smart. Do you think Harley or Mark could even pretend to walk like me, much less work it so they'll look like a real woman? I'd like to see 'em try." She wiggled everything she had, top and bottom, working it all while poor Alex turned crimson with embarrassment. He shot a pointed glare at Rory, probably needed interference

"Hey. Don't look at me." Rory grinned, palms forward to deflect the obvious call for help. It wasn't often his boss got caught in the sticky web of feminine logic. "We do need to finish what we started, though, if you'll promise to take good care of our little girl over there."

"Consider it done. When can you two be there?" Alex recovered quickly, offering Rory a new cell phone. "Here. You'll need this."

"The motel's not far. Give us two hours," Ember said, crouching at Kelsey's knee. "Will you be okay?" she asked Nima.

Nima mumbled something that sounded like Chinese, the first time she'd drifted into her native tongue during the entire operation.

"She'll be fine," Kelsey assured her. "Now go. Make the world a safer place for this little girl."

Rory donned his wig while Ember zipped up the back of his costume. He snagged the adorable Nima doll, stuck his hand up her back and converted her into an animated hand puppet.

"Bye-bye," Nima Two said in a husky voice. "Don't go anywhere, little girl. We'll be right back."

Real Nima squealed.

Rory turned to the door before he changed his mind. It was happening.

Halloween had come and gone, but not the ghosts.

Ember shivered. The evening turned chilly, but it wasn't the only reason for the goose flesh creeping up the back of her neck. This place was downright spooky. The wooden framework of half-finished homes cast silvery shadows in the dark October evening. Others, still unsold and uninhabited, gazed with empty stares from windows cold and dark. Lifeless. Like skeletons. Like Death was watching.

Rory had parked Dr. Choden's vehicle at the curb. He'd dressed in comfortable jeans and a light shirt, his only protection the trench coat that hid his weapon securely installed in a shoulder holster hanging down his right side. She was dressed the same, but wore a light windbreaker. Nima Two was now concealed beneath the baby blanket in her arms, along with the same type of closed bolt mini-submachine gun Rory carried.

The meet was just doors down the block, but Rory and Ember opted to walk the distance instead of parking any closer. It gave them time to draw the assassins out. To make sure Nima's would-be murders had a good view of Nima Two. To make sure they'd believe the doll was the child.

"Are you ready?" Rory asked. He'd placed the call to Alex twenty minutes earlier. The clock was ticking.

She took a deep breath, fingering the weapon beneath the blanket. Her earlier confidence had fled. Before the night ended, she'd have to kill again. Or be killed. Somehow the concept of self-defense didn't calm her nerves. "Do it."

"Let's move," Rory growled. He came to her side of the car and opened her door like the dutiful agent he was. Cupping her elbow, he pulled her away from the street, sheltering her with his body. "Don't look so glum. Alex is already here."

He was right. A power and light utility truck parked near the only power poles in the tract, its cherry-picker basket hung high against the pole, its crew working overtime to satisfy some urgent need. Or else it was the FBI. Maybe Homeland Security. Or The TEAM.

Feral cats skulked in the shadows, their stealthy eyes glittering in the dim lights cast from headlights a block away. Dried leaves skittered across the sidewalk, scratching spooky whispers on the wind. Or else it was the assassins already here, come to kill Nima.

Far to the east the orange globe of a harvest moon hung low in the sky, itself a harbinger of things otherworldly and evil. Spidery shadows stretched bony webs from one black tree to the next. Planted too early, the trees moaned in spooky chorus as if wishing for a few drops of moisture. And Ember wished this ungodly night was far behind her.

Rory pulled his collar tight to his chin. "Feels like a Nor'easter's headed in."

Feels more like the breath of Hades if you ask me. She leaned into him as they walked, Nima Two wrapped snugly in the dark blue blanket as if asleep. "I don't see anyone."

"Just wait. They're here. I can feel them."

"How'd they get here so fast? It might be our guys."

"It might be."

A yowling scream wrenched her already stretched nerves.

"Just cats," he assured her in his way, always looking out for his companion agent. She loved and hated that about him. It would put him in the line of fire every damned time. When he glanced over his shoulder, the cords in his neck tightened, his jaw clenched in the pale moonlight. Any other time she would've appreciated the handsome profile. Tonight, it just made her sad. Dread seemed to match their pace, loping alongside like a lone wolf, testing for weakness or fear.

"It's the fifth house on your right." He nodded his chin toward the home he meant.

"The one with the porch?" She focused on walking. Running would only betray her fear.

"Yes."

The fifth stood as dark as the rest. Empty houses made her thoughtful. What kind of family would eventually live there? Would they be kind to each other? Or would they fight and be cruel to their children? Their pets? Would they gather at Thanksgiving to cheer each other's football teams? Or would they tear each other apart in word and deed?

Three houses to go and the vision accompanied every step. *Will Alex cry tonight? Will Harley laugh? God, I hope not.*

A black car rolled out of the shadows on the dark street ahead, startling her. No headlights and no engine sound. It slowed. Braked. Made a U-turn and shifted into drive again to match their walking speed. Rory tensed, his stride quicker and longer.

"We're almost there," he whispered. "Don't worry. Help is only a breath away."

How about a scream away? She couldn't answer, not wanting to sound as scared as she felt. Instead, she smothered Nima Two to her breast and lowered her head. The wind watered her eyes. Or maybe it was tears.

"Not so fast," he cautioned. "Give them time to make sure we've got what they came for."

She tried, but her feet itched to run in the opposite direction. The car matched their pace. Watching. Calculating. Possibly aiming. Suspense gripped her shoulder muscles, anxiety her throat. The assassins could take them out without making contact. She glanced to her left, peering around Rory, needing to see into the vehicle beside them. She should've known better. Black windows swallowed her reflection. It wasn't a car. It was a death coach.

Two houses to go. A light flickered on from somewhere inside. Just as quickly, it went out. The sign was given. Whatever happened next would determine all. Ember closed her eyes and bowed her head to the child's soft sweet hair, hoping with all her heart the vision was a lie.

"Now," Rory whispered.

Nima raised her pretty face, her sleepy light blue eyes ghostly in the pale moonlight. She turned to the car with childish curiosity.

Ember grasped for a better hold on her child even as she pulled the blanket tighter. "Please go back to sleep," she muttered loud enough for all to hear.

A tiny hand pushed out of the blanket and grasped Ember's shoulder as the child elbowed her way upright. She peered into the dark windows of the vehicle as if she could see beyond the tint. Tires screeched. The car swerved over the curb to block their path.

"Make her sit down," Rory hissed, his hand clamped tightly to Ember's shoulder as they froze in their steps. "For God's sake, cover her up!"

Four men leapt from the car, each covered in black from head to toe, balaclavas hiding their facial features. The shadows of the trees sprang to life. More wraiths surrounded Ember, Rory, and Nima, ten or twelve altogether. In full-blown panic, she lost her ability to count.

Breathe. This is what you're trained for. Smooth and easy.

Rory jerked her against him, Nima Two sandwiched between.

One man stepped forward, pulling the mask off his head. A knife glinted in his hand. Why a knife when the others displayed Uzis, some micros, some minis? All were extremely lethal. The rate of automatic fire ran between six to twelve hundred deadly rounds per minute, certainly more than adequate to annihilate two adults and a child. So why the knife?

She couldn't take her eyes off the wicked blade. Was it only for show? For cruelty's sake? For intimidation? It worked.

The man approached in silence. Like a snake. Definitely Chinese. Clean-shaven. Shaved head, too. Narrow black eyebrows over a wide forehead. Cold, mean eyes. He stopped within ten feet of them, pointing to his feet with the blade. "You will give me the child. Do it now."

"Why would I give you my child?" Rory shot back, positioning Ember under his arm, the Nima doll shielded from the assassin's view.

"Let us not play games. She is not your child, Agent Dennison," Cold Eyes spat out. "You see. I do know who you are. And your little girlfriend there is Agent Ember Davis. That thing she carries belongs to the people of Tibet. I have come to spill its blood."

Nima struggled to rise again, but Ember pulled her firmly back against her chest. Cold Eyes had to believe.

"Who the hell are you?" Rory growled. "Triad? Snakehead? Wah Ching?"

Cold Eyes grunted. "Not even close. We are not of the Han. They are weak. We are the spiritual warriors of exiled Tibet, the Yushu Sangha. Our sole purpose for living is to cleanse this disgusting aberration from the face of the earth. The line of the Goddess must be kept pure. Give me the girl."

Nima struggled again, softly murmuring against Ember's neck to be released, "Mama Ember. Me down."

"No," she whispered firmly. "Please be still."

Cold Eyes' upper left lip lifted in a sneer. "I hear her. Even she knows she must die. Put her down."

Nima's pudgy hand peeled back the blanket, once again exposing her beautiful face for all to see. Hurriedly, Ember covered her. These guys didn't deserve even one peek at this perfect child.

"No." Ember shook her head fearfully. "I can't let you kill her. I won't."

The circle closed. Panic stole her breath, like she had any to begin with. Instinctively, she scanned behind the assassins for reinforcements. She should've known better. The TEAM was made of black operators. Ghosts. Of course she couldn't see them. Not yet.

Cold Eyes stepped toward her, his knife held high in his hand. "Then I will—"

"No!" Rory raised his arm to ward off the blade. "She's just a little girl. We can work this out. Let us keep the girl. You'll never see her again. I promise."

The leader of the assassins sneered. "As long as she breathes, her evil will spread. The child must die. The bloodletting must be done tonight. I will not ask again."

"Why tonight?" Rory asked, stalling for what Ember did not know.

"For peace," Cold Eyes replied. "She is not human. She will only bring war."

Ember sobbed, "I can't. I'd rather die first. I can't—"

"Then it begins!" he roared, signaling his group of murderers to close in. They raised their weapons.

"No!" Rory shouted. "For God's sake! Just wait a minute!" He sheltered his girls in one last hug, hiding their faces and his from view.

Ember cringed, smothering the fake Nima against her. "I can't let her go. Don't make me."

She sobbed so violently that Nima's pudgy hand slipped out of the blanket and fell to the sidewalk. Her chubby-cheeked face dropped next. Soulful blue eyes blinked at the sky, her mouth still speaking in eerie mechanical repetition, "Mama. Me down. Me down. Me down."

Cold Eyes stared at the dismembered body parts twitching on the ground. He only got one good look. Rory spun behind Ember, back-to-back, his weapon ready. At the same time, she pulled hers from the folds of the blanket. In perfect tandem, they sprayed the stunned assassins, left to right and back again with deadly fire. Cold Eyes fell first.

A blinding spotlight from high overhead turned the kill zone bright as day. FBI SWAT fast-roped from their amazingly quiet stealth helicopters hovering above. By the time the first FBI boots hit the ground, the job was done. Seventeen assassins had fallen without firing a single effective round. Cold Eyes' knife lay in his dead hand where it could spill no innocent blood tonight or any other night.

Ember still stood with Rory at her six, their smoking barrels pointed skyward.

"You good?" he asked, panting frosty vapor into the cold night air.

"Yes. You?"

He turned her to face him, one arm protectively around her shoulders again. A tender smile tweaked the corners of his mouth. "Am now."

She blew out a huge sigh, glancing at the scene around them. "Wow."

He cupped her chin, pulling her gaze back to zero—to him. "Don't look. It's not a pretty sight. You've done enough for one operation, Mrs. Dillon. Clean up is not what we do."

"Again with the Mrs. Dillon stuff," she said, thankful he'd stopped her from seeing more than her stomach could handle. Despite the very capable weapon in her hand, he still sought to protect her, and he was right. Called for or not, violence always made her sick. But his thoughtfulness touched her as much as the strong hands holding her together. Her energy had fled with the last round fired, her knees right along with it.

She leaned forward to nuzzle that sweet spot under his jaw before the moment passed. All she needed was the warmth of his skin, but he was focused on something to his left.

"Are you two okay? No one hurt?" Alex asked, his gaze as probing as ever. He clapped them both on the back before she could touch her lips to Rory's neck, before she could inhale the smell and strength of him. Instead, she looked into sharp blue eyes, sure Alex had seen her illicit intentions for her companion agent.

"We're good, Boss," Rory answered quickly.

"Yeah. Good." Ember handed Alex her weapon, hoping the movement disguised her tremors along with her feelings. "I could use a good cup of coffee is all."

He took her weapon in his gloved hand, the barrel up, and nodded toward the fifth house on the right. "Mother's waiting. She's got plenty of coffee."

"Who else is here?" Rory asked as they turned to leave.

Alex shot him a quizzical look. "Hell, everyone. FBI. Alexandria PD. ICE, too. CIA is interested as hell but they're not on site. I get to brief them later."

Now that the worst was over, Ember saw Junior Agents Harley Mortimer and Mark Houston, all dressed in tactical black and assisting the Bureau. Others from The TEAM were there as well—Senior Agents Murphy Finnegan and Roy Hudson, along with rookies Taylor Armstrong and Maverick Carson. The army of FBI SWAT agents didn't look so bad, either. Who'd have thought? Alex working with the FBI? Maybe this was the night for miracles.

She knelt to pick up the doll parts. Gathering them into the blanket, she stood to see Rory watching, a bemused smirk on his face. "Well, I did say I couldn't let her go, didn't I?"

He took the bundle gently from her hands. "You can't take these with you."

"Why not? I made them."

"Because they're evidence."

Oh, yeah. I know that. I just—forgot.

The tender look in his eyes stabbed her. The operation was finally over. She gulped. Giving up these small pieces of the Nima doll was nothing compared to what she had to give up next.

Passing the remnants of the doll to Alex, Rory pulled her into his side and steered her toward the house. "Come on, Mrs. Dillon. Let's get that cup of coffee."

Seventeen

"We had you covered the whole time!" Mother blurted out the minute Rory and Ember cleared the doorway. No longer disguised as a dark, vacant house, the home was filled with lights, computer equipment, and an ecstatic lead techie. "You kids rock! Those Yushu Sangha creeps never saw you coming."

Rory went straight to the coffee machine and poured two cups, while Ember plopped tiredly on the leather couch. Adrenaline might bring an over the top rush when needed, but exhaustion always followed. Ember was beat.

He handed her a cup with his back turned so Mother couldn't see his wink. "Here you are, ma'am. Two cream. No sugar. Just the way you like it."

She accepted it with trembling fingers. He read the expression on her face. It seemed he'd known her for a lifetime. She needed a good cry as much as she needed the caffeine. The cup in her hand shook until she balanced it on her knee to keep the coffee from sloshing out. Easy day was done. The hardest part of their mission together lay ahead.

"Hey. Are you sure you're okay?" he asked tenderly.

When she opened her mouth to speak, Mother answered for her in typical busybody fashion. "Of course she's okay. What do you guys think anyway, that a gal as smart and gorgeous as Ember can't handle a real operation? Ha! She's better than all you guys put together."

His eyes were still fixed on Ember. He saw the nod Mother couldn't, the quiet signal of a woman whose heart was breaking while Mother bragged and ranted, totally oblivious of what was really going on. "My goodness, look at how clever that puppet was. All the parts were so real-looking. Bet you couldn't have done that, Rory."

"No, I couldn't," he agreed, taking a seat on the coffee table to face Ember. He'd have gladly sat beside her and pulled her into his arms, but Mother would pick up on any hint of intimacy and broadcast it to the world. That's how she worked—telegraph, telephone, tele-Mother. He stayed where he could see into Ember's green eyes. Where Mother couldn't.

"I'm fixing you another cup, Ember. I know how you like it. Don't you worry. The operation is done, and you, honey, are the star." Mother couldn't shut up to save her life.

Alex sat next to Ember with his own coffee in hand. "The FBI will be processing this scene for a week."

Ember sipped, still focused entirely on Rory.

"It's late. We'll debrief first thing tomorrow. How does 10 a.m. sound?" Alex always had way too much energy. A dyed-in-the-wool, over-the-top type-A personality, he thrived on stress and deadlines like no man Rory had ever known. But sometimes he missed the forest for the trees.

"Sure thing, Boss." Rory stood to leave, his hand extended to Ember. "Where is she?"

Ember was off the couch and at his side in a heartbeat.

"Where you left her. Why?" Alex glanced up from his coffee, his brow arched, that brusque what's-it-to-you snap to his voice.

"Because we're going to go see her."

"That's not a good idea. She's probably asleep by now and besides—"

"We're going," Rory said firmly. "I know it's late, but we need to see her."

"You've got to let this go, son," Alex countered. "It's not a good idea."

"We will, but not tonight." Rory saw the quiet command in Alex's eye, but he had his girls to think of, and they came first whether Alex liked it or not. "We'll see you at 10 a.m."

Alex pursed his lips as if considering the challenge, but said, "Fine. In the morning then."

Rory ushered Ember out the door with a nod to Alex. They didn't say a word to Mother, just left Alex to explain. Rory only drove two blocks from the prying eyes of the crime scene before pulling the Cadillac to the curb. "I figured you could use some Tyler treatment right about now."

She leaned over the console and into his arms. "I do. I was doing okay until it was over, but then I started thinking. I have to tell her goodbye now, don't I?"

There was no need to answer. He drove the rest of the way with one hand on the wheel, the other around Ember. "I could get used to this, Agent Davis," he whispered into the top of her head.

"Me, too," she murmured, her voice sadly quiet.

He turned onto a calm Alexandria street where a little brick home sat safe and protected under one hundred-year-old oak trees. The house was ordinary, nondescript, what others would call a starter home. The porch light shone like every other on the street. Only the cheery Halloween decorations on the porch were different. He parked the truck at the curb and hurried to the passenger side to help Ember.

"I never understood why Alex stays here," he said as they walked arm in arm up the front steps. "Not with the kind of money he has to be making."

"He stays here because Kelsey loves it. She won't move," Ember whispered, rubbing her arms. "To her, this place is about Alex. The house, too."

"Are you cold?"

Her teary eyes answered. She wasn't cold. She was scared of what they had to do next.

"Come in," Kelsey said quietly. "Zack will be right back. He's walking the perimeter."

"There's no need," Rory said. "It's done. I'll tell him when he gets back." He called the dogs to his side. "Hey, Whisper. Hey, Smoke. How's it going?"

Immediately, both reverted to friendly house pets instead of the guard dogs they really were. Once they made the rounds between him and Ember, Kelsey gave them a quick command to guard. They resumed their post by the front and back doors, their ears forward, their heads cocked. Kelsey turned to Ember. "Can I get you some coffee or something?"

Ember crumbled at Kelsey's kindness. Rory pulled her into his side while Kelsey handed him a box of tissues. "It's been a tough night. Coffee would be good."

While Kelsey went to the kitchen, Ember blew her nose and composed herself as much as she could. "I can do this," she said. "I just don't want to."

"I know." He just wasn't sure he could.

Kelsey returned with a tray of coffee, sugar, creamer, and three cups. "I take it things went well?"

"Yes," Ember said shakily. "No problems for a change."

"I still can't tell you how glad I was to see you at my door with all the trick-or-treaters." Kelsey's brown eyes sparkled.

"We needed some place safe to stash Nima while we confronted the assassins," Rory explained. "Sure glad you were home. We kind of took a chance, but we didn't have much choice."

Ember chuckled sadly. "You did make a great caveman."

He rolled his eyes. "I bet I never hear the end of that one."

"And your costumes were perfect, too," Kelsey said. "Too bad we can't get Alex into one."

Rory chuckled. "I did see a fire breathing dragon get-up at one of your neighbors' houses."

"Or the big bad wolf," Ember said quietly, the cup of coffee still clenched in her hands.

Kelsey grinned. "He does a lot of huffing and puffing, doesn't he?"

And just like that the atmosphere in Kelsey's home changed. The coffee tasted bitter. The cozy flame in the Stewarts' wonderful fireplace sputtered and cast a chill instead of warmth. It felt as if shadows took over.

"Would you like to see her?" Kelsey offered. "She's asleep, but I know she'll be happy to see you. She's been asking for you both all night."

"Yes," Ember said. The time had come. Her heart was breaking right in front of his eyes, and Rory couldn't do anything to stop it.

Kelsey led them down the hall to a small guest bedroom. A nightlight illuminated the bed where Nima lay sound asleep, her hands over the top of her head in complete relaxation. Dressed in her snowflake pajamas, she was an angel, her dark brown hair fluffed on the pillow. She snored. If she were his child he'd have that snoring checked. He knew the signs. Tyler snored. He had asthma. Maybe she did, too.

Ember slipped off her shoes and scooted her body around the sleeping child. Nima turned on her side, gently snoring. Ember stroked her pudgy cheek with the back of her fingers and kissed her again. Two soft blue eyes blinked open. Her back arched with a big stretch as she awakened. Nima pushed the covers off and scrambled into her arms.

"Mama," she whispered hoarsely, and then she started to cry. By then, Ember drenched Nima with tears anyway. Kelsey shoved a handful of tissues into Rory's hands and left them alone.

Ember choked. "Oh, my perfect baby girl. How can I let you go?"

He shrugged off his suit jacket, kicked his dress shoes off and joined them on the bed, gathering them both into his arms. Nima traded places for a moment and moved onto his lap.

"Hey, little one," he said, kissing her cheek. "It's been a choice blessing to have served you. I will never forget you."

Her blue eyes didn't look wise right now. It was hard to remember she was destined for notoriety and responsibility, especially sitting in pajamas with sleep in her eyes and her hair mussed.

"What's the plan for tomorrow?" Ember asked, for the moment able to speak.

"When David comes, he'll transfer her into the custody of the Tibetan High Lamas. Either that, or they'll come with him to take her. They'll keep her safe and secluded for the rest of her life."

"Oh." The one syllable word cracked in her throat.

"They'll raise her and train her in the way she should go," Rory continued softly. "When she's old enough, they'll test her to confirm she truly is the next Dalai Lama."

"What kind of tests? Will it hurt?"

"No. If I understood David correctly, they will show her several artifacts, one of which belonged to the previous Dalai Lama. If the indications are right, it will confirm their choice."

"Indications? Like what?"

"According to David, the High Lamas go to some lake in central Tibet where they'll seek guidance if she's the true reincarnation. I guess they see visions or something. David said they spend most of their time meditating. Anyway, there's supposed to be some female guardian spirit of the lake who protects the lineage of the reincarnation of the Dalai Lama. She'll send some kind of indications to prove which candidate is right. Crazy, huh?"

Ember smoothed Nima's hair as she snuggled her. "I did a computer search. Most of the things she's said are similar to things Buddha or the current Dalai Lama have already taught."

"That's weird."

"Even her name means something. Nima Dawa means *the sun—the one who gives light or removes darkness*."

Ember buried her face in Nima's hair and cried, "And that's what she's done, Rory. She's made the darkness inside me disappear."

Words failed. It didn't seem possible that a child of revelation, *the one who gave light and removed darkness,* would be snuggled contentedly in Ember's arms like she was. Nima peered up with the same look as Tyler's, filling him with warmth. It was love. Just—love.

Rory leaned back against the pillow. The future he'd always longed for seemed within reach. He didn't want the moment to end.

"Who will love our little girl?" Ember asked.

The pain in her words matched the ache in his heart. His only answer was the pitiful one David had given. "The monks. The people of Tibet. Maybe the world." He didn't have to look into Ember's sad face to know the answer sucked.

A whimper shuddered out of her. "But who'll give her chocolate when she's been a good girl? Who will dress her up in cute little girl outfits with princesses and bunnies and...." A ragged hiccup escaped Ember's lips. "And who'll snuggle her at night when I'm not there?"

The sadness in her words ripped his tender heart apart. All he could think of was Tyler, alone in some cold, stone monastery on the side of a mountain in the clouds with a bunch of old men who didn't know the first thing about the World Series or Super Bowls. How could strangers take the place of a father or a mother, much less teach a boy to catch a baseball? Who would laugh at his silly knock-knock jokes or hug him when he got overexcited at the end of a long day? Did monks even know how to laugh?

"Stop it," he whispered. "You're only hurting yourself. We'll never understand. It's just the way it is."

Her hand cupped his cheek, the pad of her thumb gentle under his eye. Yes. Now she knew. He was crying.

She pulled Nima closer and wept like any mother giving her child away. The weariness of the mission was more than he could stand. This was their last night with Nima, their last time to love her and let her be nothing more than a child who loved chocolate, Mama Ember, and him. When David came to take Nima in the morning, it wouldn't just be goodbye. It would be goodbye forever.

Rory lifted his arm and covered his eyes. The next thing he felt was Kelsey's gentle hand on his arm. "Rory?" she whispered.

With a jolt he blinked his eyes open. Slivers of sunlight streamed through the bedroom blinds. Great. He'd fallen asleep in his boss's spare bedroom with.... *My girls.* He glanced at the sleeping girls in his arms. The words came to him like the saddest lullaby. *Until the end of forever, these two will always be my girls.*

"David's here." Her voice was tight. A shadow clouded her pretty face. She'd been crying, too. Poor Kelsey looked as bad as he felt.

"Thanks. We'll be right out."

"I put her new clothes in the bathroom. Whenever you're ready." She shut the door softly.

He kissed Ember's forehead. They'd both slept the entire night in a protective huddle around their little girl. She stirred and sniffed. Handing her another tissue, he untangled himself from the nest they'd made of Nima's bed covers. She still slept soundly in Ember's arms.

"It's time."

Ember stared at him from swollen red eyes. "I didn't go to sleep, not even once. I just breathed and breathed and breathed her into my soul all night long."

Yeah. He'd done the same thing with his brand new baby boy when he was afraid Tyler wouldn't live through those first couple nights in the hospital. Even though the boy was in an isolette, he'd breathed that little boy smell into his heart and soul and any other multi-dimensional part of himself that might exist, scared to death he'd never be able to get enough of the child he stood to lose.

"Do you want to give her a bath before we get her dressed?"

Ember nodded. By now, Nima lay awake and watching. The poor little thing had to know something was up. "Come on. Let's make you beautiful one last time."

Eighteen

Ember knelt at the tub. They bathed their little girl together and played in the bubbles until the water turned cool. But nothing they did today brought joy. They were stalling. At last, Ember dried Nima in the big fluffy bath towel Kelsey had left for them. She dressed Nima in the lavender corduroy pants and purple hoody top she'd bought only days before. Ember dried Nima's thick brown hair with Kelsey's blow dryer and tied it back with a violet ribbon while Rory watched.

The somber threesome finally walked into the living room with Nima holding onto Rory and Ember's hands. David sat there with Alex, Kelsey, and three Buddhist monks. Two of the robe-clad men looked to be in their eighties, the other much younger. As soon as they spotted Nima, the monks stood and bowed. She clutched Ember's hand tighter and pressed her little backside into Rory's leg.

"Nima Gyatso," they said in unison, their wizened faces softened into smiles.

"No. She's Nima Dawa," Ember corrected them. "Not Gyatso—or whatever you guys said."

They smiled as if she were a child who amused them with her ignorance. David politely intervened. "The new name, Nima Gyatso, is given in anticipation of her becoming the next Dalai Lama. She'll keep her first name, but her second name will change. Gyatso means ocean. It is the standard naming tradition for all Dalai Lamas."

Rory stood on the other side of Nima, her hand still securely in his. The minute Nima glanced up at him, he lifted her into his arms. Ember circled Rory's waist with one arm.

"Exactly who will be raising our little girl?" he asked.

David winced at the direct question, but Ember didn't care. Someone better have a good answer.

The youngest monk bowed respectfully. "We have selected a woman to act as her governess until she is old enough to speak for herself."

Another stepped forward. "Please accept my humble apologies. We were overzealous when we first glimpsed the child. We should not have addressed her as Gyatso yet. In our culture, the Dalai Lama is the embodiment of all good things in our country. If Nima Dawa is truly the reincarnation of Chenrezig, that is, the patron deity of Tibet, then she will assume the proper name in due time. We have already received reports of her great compassion and spiritual advisements. You have done a great service to the people of Tibet by protecting her."

Rory shifted Nima to his hip, shielding her from their eager and too direct overtures. "Let's get something straight. I didn't do the mission for the people of Tibet, and you guys have not answered my question. I asked who will care for this little girl? She's four years old. I doubt she cares about all that other mumbo jumbo right now. I don't. But I do want to know who'll feed her in the morning? Who'll read her bedtime stories at night? All you've told me is some woman. Not good enough. I want a name, not more of your ancient mystical history."

The monks turned to each other in quiet whispers. The youngest spoke. "We are not permitted to share the woman's name with you right now. You must understand, the child has been the subject of death threats and—"

Rory held his palm right into the face of that gentle monk. "Give me a break. You think I don't know someone's trying to kill her?"

"Yeah, you guys," Ember sputtered. "Where do you think we've been the last week?"

David patiently intervened again. "Rory. The child belongs to the Tibetan people and—"

"No, David. No, she doesn't!" He raised his voice and Ember couldn't take her eyes off him. The man had nothing more than the welfare of Nima on his mind and she was so proud of him. "You guys act like she's property. She's not. She's a little girl who's lost everything. She has a name! Nima belongs in a safe and child-friendly environment where she'll live to the ripe old age of a hundred or more. She belongs with a mother and a father and a real family. Would you do this to one of your children, David? Would you send them to live with a bunch of old men? I don't care who these guys are. They're not taking her until I'm convinced she'll be safe. You got that, David? Or did you forget who you work for?"

Wow. You go, Rory. And wherever you're going, I am so going with you.

David stared back at Rory, his lips pursed in thoughtful deliberation. He didn't seem angry, more like he'd run out of persuasive arguments. He looked to Alex, who'd been sitting on the couch quietly observing the heated discourse between one of his senior agents and a very perturbed junior agent who had a helluva lot of nerve to speak back like he had.

Alex sat silent with his arm around Kelsey, for once, not in the middle of the power struggle. He shrugged. "I agree with Rory. Give me a name. Who is the mystery woman who will take care of Nima? Let Mother run that person through her checks and balances. Let's make damned sure first. Then we'll talk."

The three monks politely bowed to Alex before they resumed another private conversation. Again, the youngest spoke. "We must ask for the way forward from the High Lamas. You will keep her safe until we return?"

"Yes!" Ember blurted. She could've danced on Kelsey's coffee table. "I mean, yes, we'll keep her safe and—"

Rory offered a handshake. "That's exactly what we'll do, sir. Will you keep in touch with us and let us know what to expect?"

"Yes. I will continue to converse with Agent Tao. May I ask one thing before we depart? I can see you both love Nima Dawa very much. May I please have your permission to touch her? Just her fingers?"

Rory turned to Ember. She lifted her shoulders. "Sure. We've been touching her all week."

The young man cautiously approached Nima. The smile on her face couldn't have shone brighter. He hadn't even touched her yet when she launched herself at him.

He caught her easily and knelt to one knee, his eyes closed with her on his lap. She cocked her cute little head to one side then the other, like this was a fun game of hide-and-seek. With all the solemnity of a child at play, she knocked on his forehead. The young man opened his eyes, but he couldn't seem to look directly into Nima's.

The room stilled at the tender proceedings, but the tiny girl's countenance changed. Her sweet blue eyes turned darker than Ember had seen them during their time together. She squeezed Rory's bicep. "Watch. She's doing it again."

The young monk sputtered and choked, tilting backward. Nima leaned over him, nearly climbing onto his chest. For the first time, he met her gaze.

She growled, "I am come."

Ember gulped. She'd heard Nima say those exact words before. In the train car. When she thought she was hallucinating. Wow.

The monk's eyes widened with sudden understanding. David and the other monks fell to their knees. Nima knocked on the young man's shaved head once more. "'Kay?" she asked softly.

When he could only tremble and shake, she pressed her forehead to his and said it for him. "Yep. 'Kay now." Untangling herself from his robes, she returned to Rory and lifted her arms up. The playful child was back.

Rory picked her up while the young monk got shakily to his feet. He kept his eyes averted from Nima. Neither did David or the other monks look at her. They left the house, their heads bowed.

"What the hell was that all about?" Alex asked when the door closed.

"Language," Rory muttered good-naturedly. "She's four." Alex scowled, but nodded.

"I can Google the name she called herself," Kelsey said. "What was it again? Palden Lhamo? Did I hear her right?"

Already at her computer, she brought up an image and its accompanying description while everyone leaned over her shoulder. "My gosh. Look what I've found."

"What the hell?" growled Alex.

On the screen, riding sidesaddle on a white mule, was Palden Lhamo, a three-eyed, fierce-looking woman with bright blue skin and dark red hair. In one hand she held a human skull that looked like it was full of red blood. She wielded a sickle in her other hand while a cloud of bright orange flames surrounded her and the mule.

The description was even more frightening. She was the lone female goddess among the Eight Guardians of the Law in Tibetan culture, and protected all Dalai Lamas. But it also characterized her as a mother who'd killed her son when he attempted to destroy Buddhism. If that wasn't bad enough, she also drank his blood, ate his flesh, and used his skin as a saddle blanket for her mule.

"Wow. If that's who you really are, you are one tough little cookie," Ember said.

Nima peered down at the bright colors on the computer screen, clapped her hands on Ember's cheeks and giggled.

Alex stretched out of sheer boredom. He never held much with organized religions of any kind. His wife seemed to be the only gospel he lived for. "Whatcha think, Kelsey? Should we feed these kids breakfast since it looks like they're staying?"

"I'll help you fix it, Boss," Rory offered.

The men went into the kitchen to get the show on the road. Breakfast was waffles, scrambled eggs, bacon, sliced honeydew melon, coffee for the adults, and milk for Nima.

Everyone sat around the kitchen table discussing the events of the last week.

For the first time, Ember was relaxed and at ease. The assassins were dead and Nima's farewell was postponed till who knew when. She helped herself to another slice of melon.

Even Rory was slouched back in his chair, apologizing for falling asleep and not making it into work for the 10 a.m. debrief.

Alex waved it off. "It's not like I'm there, either. We'll do it tomorrow. Besides, you two still look like you need a good night's rest."

Rory agreed. "Not much sleep on this op, huh, Ember?"

"Only when I was in the hospital and that didn't last long."

"The hospital?" Alex exclaimed. "When were you two going to tell me?"

Rory smirked. "During the debrief. You want to hear about everything we've been through now?"

"Here, hold Nima so I can show you my leg." Ember handed Nima to Alex when she caught Rory cringe. "Never mind. I'd kinda have to, umm, show a little bit more than you probably want to see." She scrunched her nose at Rory and sat back down. He visibly relaxed. He could be such a prude.

But Alex was entirely focused on the child in his arms. Nima sat facing him. With a soft murmur she laid her head against his chest and closed her eyes. He coughed, pushed away from the table and rushed out the back door with Nima still cradled in his arms.

"Oh, oh. She's doing it again," Ember said softly.

"What's she doing?" Kelsey asked.

Rory shook his head. "That little girl says the darnedest things."

Kelsey stood to watch Alex through the kitchen window. "Like what kinds of things?"

"Like she told me to stop hiding so someone could find me. And so," Rory turned to Ember with a soft light in his eye, "I told Ember all about my son, Tyler."

"You have a son?" Kelsey asked. "But Alex never—"

"I asked him to keep it confidential. I didn't want…. Heck, I don't know why I didn't want anyone to know about Tyler. He's a good boy."

"And she's said a lot of different things that have been scary in a real personal way, kind of like she's reading our minds or something," Ember explained.

She and Rory joined Kelsey at the window. Alex paced the yard with Nima still hugged up against him.

"What could she have said to him?" Kelsey asked.

"All I heard her say was *'Daddy,'*" Rory said.

Kelsey flew out the door. When she drew close to Alex and Nima, he grabbed her against him.

"Now he's getting an idea of what we've been living with," Rory observed somberly.

"I've only seen him cry once, when Todd—" Ember stopped and sputtered. "Oh, my gosh! My vision! Remember? Alex is crying just like in my vision. That means—"

"It's just—"

"No. It's my vision. It's true. It's all going to—"

The linoleum floor lifted up like an ocean swell. Darkness engulfed Ember in one huge swallow. All she could hear was a distant voice calling, "Ember. Ember."

Nineteen

Down she went.

Rory tried to catch Ember. He couldn't stop her from falling, but he did manage to shield her head before she hit herself on her way down. She'd turned white as a ghost the second she recalled the vision. Alex and Kelsey came back inside to find him and Ember on the floor.

"What the hell now?" Alex asked the minute he saw them.

Kelsey soaked a cool cloth for Ember's forehead and knelt with Rory on the floor.

"She had a vision," he said calmly. "She thinks she saw life and death, and you crying, Boss. When she remembered that part, she fainted."

Alex still held Nima on his lap at the kitchen table. He looked like he needed a good night's sleep. "This little friend of yours said something I wasn't expecting."

"Now you know what we've been going through."

"What's the rest of the vision?"

"I'm not sure I should say. Ember's positive what she saw, but I'm not sure what it means."

"What?" Alex asked again.

Rory sighed. "She got this message from Nima: *Remember to use tragedy as a source of strength.* But then she also received a vision. She saw you crying, Harley smiling, and me dead. She saw some other stuff, too. It sounds crazy, but—"

"Oh, my," Kelsey murmured.

Ember groaned and stretched in Rory's arms.

"How are you doing?" he asked, patting her cheek gently.

"Awful." She scrunched her nose and blinked several times. "I'm seeing two of you. How'd you do that?"

He shook his head and smiled. Sometimes the things that came out of her mouth amazed the living heck out of him. "Lie still until you feel better."

Alex and Kelsey sat at the kitchen table with Nima, waiting until Ember could get up from the floor. When she was steady again, Rory guided her to the living room couch.

"If we weren't getting shot at or fire-bombed by assassins," he said, "we were dealing with mind-blowing prophecies and revelations from Nima. It's been an interesting week to say the least."

Alex still held a sleepy Nima on his lap when David knocked and let himself in. He took a seat and faced Rory and Ember, but he didn't look at Nima.

"We already Googled Palden Lhamo," Rory said before David had a chance to speak. "We know she's some scary Tibetan goddess. Just saying."

"Good." David sat forward on his chair. "Tell me what else you think you know."

"Just what's on the internet," Kelsey said, pointing to the fierce image still on her computer screen.

David went to the desk and closed the laptop. As soon as he sat back down, Rory wanted to know, "Why won't you look at Nima?"

David sighed, his hands to his knees. "You have to understand. Palden Lhamo is the Lady Goddess in Tibetan culture. She is the protector of all Dalai Lamas, but she is also the Queen of Armies. She is usually depicted crossing a sea of blood on a white mule. Her hair is red because it depicts her wrathful nature, not the latest fashion. Very often, she is shown with a crown of skulls and a serpent. The serpent is Wrath, which she may choose to unleash upon the world at her leisure or if she is summoned by one who is the most faithful. The most beloved."

"So?" Alex didn't sound impressed.

David blew out a deep breath. "You may think I'm overreacting, Boss, but in Buddhist temples the picture of Palden Lhamo is kept covered in the farthest corner of the temple at all times. We do not look upon her face."

"Why not?" Ember asked.

"Because we believe she has great power, the worst kind, and to look upon her is to invite her wrath."

"But Dr. Choden called her Gyalwa something," Rory said. "He didn't mind looking at Nima."

"Gyalwa Rinpoche," David enunciated the Tibetan name. "It means Precious Victor."

"I know. That's what he said. What's so bad about that?"

"Because the Precious Victor only emerges after great chaos and ruin. You know your World War Two history, Rory. War is never good."

"Give me a break. Do you really think Nima is this ancient killer goddess?" Rory asked.

"You tell me. You don't always see a child when you look at her, do you?"

"Mostly I see a little girl who says some scary things once in awhile. That's all. She hasn't said or done one mean thing while we've had her."

"But you heard her tell us who she is." David pressed his argument. "Did it sound like the voice of a four-year-old child coming out of her mouth?"

Rory shook his head. "No. She doesn't say a lot, but she knows how to get our attention."

"And she told me the same thing as the monks," Ember said. "I thought I was just delirious on the train, and—"

"Wait. You were on a train?" Alex interrupted.

"Well, sure. We had to jump into a boxcar to get away from—"

"You jumped onto a damned moving train?"

"Yes, Alex. That's when I hurt my leg. I hit a wall or something and—"

Alex sat upright, his anger palpable. "You hit a damned wall?" he growled, shooting a dark glance at Rory.

"It was the only option, Boss," Rory explained. "We had to hop the train. It was either that or—"

"Alex," Ember muttered. "Let me finish, will you? Yes, we jumped onto a moving train. We had to. The assassins bombed the Highway Patrol you sent to bring us home. That's when I hurt my leg, but it's also when Nima told me what she just told the monks. She said she was come. Not coming. Not going to come. Just—*come*."

David glanced at Ember, Rory, Alex, and Kelsey in turn. "In our culture it is called the voice of judgment. It has not been heard for hundreds of years. Those of us who believe Nima is divine also believe the goddess is speaking directly through her. She may not be the next Dalai Lama, but she must be protected at all cost."

"Am I going to live to regret accepting this contract to protect her?" Alex asked.

"No," Rory said. "She's just a little girl. Protecting innocents is what we do, remember?"

A small smile tugged the corner of Alex's mouth. "You're right. I'd just like to know when I'm signing a contract to start World War Three."

David shook his head abruptly, continuing in earnest. "There's more. Recently the presiding Dalai Lama offered a prayer to Palden Lhamo. In his prayer, he summoned the Lady Goddess to come forth to face the great oppressors. He summoned Palden Lhamo by name, Rory. Think about that in the light of what I've just told you. He also promised her that the country of Tibet, although destroyed by the enemy, still believes in her. The faithful are waiting for deliverance that only Palden Lhamo can bring."

"And the presiding Dalai Lama is the most beloved?" Rory asked, his brows furrowed. "He'd be the one to summon the Goddess, right?"

"I believe that is true. Yes."

It made no sense. The Yushu Sangha and Palden Lhamo sounded an awful lot like they were on the same page. They both wanted war. They both wanted a form of Buddhism to prevail over the world. And they were both scary bloodthirsty. What was the difference?

"Tell me about the Yushu Sangha," Rory asked. "Their leader last night seemed to believe like you do, that Nima is the Warrior Goddess reincarnated. He said it was their job to keep the line of the Goddess pure, that he had to kill her because she's not human. That she needed to die to keep peace. What's that all about?"

"The Yushu Sangha do not want world peace. They want their peace," David explained. "They're a splinter group of terrorists who've waged war against the Dalai Lama since Tibet was subsumed into the People's Republic years ago. They claim to be from Tibet, but they're not. They seek a male-dominant, perverted twist to Buddha's teachings that would eradicate what they call the parasite of freedom, democracy, and free thought. If they had their way, China would install someone they could control as the next Dalai Lama. Anyone who disagreed would be destroyed or reduced to slavery. Women would be nothing more than chattels."

"So I still don't get it. They need to kill Nima because, if she really is the Warrior Goddess they're so scared of, she'd do the exact same thing they plan to do? Kill everyone who doesn't agree with her?" Ember asked.

"It sounds like you think the Goddess's brand of peace would be better than the Yushu Sangha's brand. Am I right?" Rory asked facetiously. "What? Would she'd be more selective with who she killed or something?"

David shook his head in patient frustration. "Either way, there will be a purge, but yes. In the long run, the Goddess would bring peace to the earth. The Yushu Sangha would only bring death and chaos until the world burned itself out."

"Leaving only them?" Ember asked.

David nodded.

"But how can you be so sure?"

"Because there is relative peace now."

"And you think this era of peace is somehow linked to what Palden Lhamo did in the past?" Rory asked.

"Listen, I know you don't believe as I do, but please believe this. If nothing else, Nima is a threat to the current state of affairs in Tibet. From what I saw earlier in this very living room, she is the one faithful Tibetans have been waiting for. If her prophetic utterance is true, if she really is *come* as we all heard her say, she will deliver Tibet from its enemies. If the ancient story is true, she will do so with great wars and tremendous bloodshed, the likes of which this world has never seen. And she's sitting on your lap, Boss."

David nodded toward Nima in all seriousness, but it was hard to take him at his word. The great and terrible Warrior Goddess had fallen asleep in Alex's arms. She snored softly. And she drooled.

And Alex was totally unimpressed by David's fervent words. "What do you want us to do with her?" he snapped. "Cover her up with a veil like you guys do with her picture in your temples? Hide her in a box? Stash her in a cave on a mountaintop in the Himalayas? What?"

David leaned back in his chair. "No, Boss. With her pale eye color, she'll be hard to hide. I was thinking the WPP."

"The Witness Protection Program?" Rory growled scornfully. "You've got to be kidding. What makes you think we can trust them? Witnesses end up dead in the WPP all the time."

"Yes. You're right. There is only one other place she would be safe."

"Where's that?" Rory asked.

"Dharamsala, India. If we take her to Tsuglagkhnag, the main Tibetan temple in the free world, she would be safe."

"What makes you think she'd be safer there than here with us?" Rory asked.

"Because that is the residence and monastery of the Dalai Lama, and he is safe there." David's voice turned reverent.

It made sense. The paradox lay in the fact that one of the most influential and potentially powerful personalities in the world lay asleep in Alex's arms, oblivious to the plans being made for her future. What if they chose wrong?

Rory turned to Alex. "All I know for sure is that Nima needs someone to care for her until she comes of age. I don't care if it's on the highest mountain in the Himalayas or in a tent in the Appalachians. I want her safe."

Ember had the sappiest look on her face again. If they'd been alone, he would've kissed her and she would have known she'd been kissed. Instead, he just winked.

"Agreed," Alex said. "But we move her today and we keep moving her until we hear back from the monks. We take no chances. When will you hear back from them, David?"

"I hope today, but it could take several days before they receive word from the High Lamas."

"Make it quick. Until they can prove Nima will be safer in their keeping than ours, we stay on task. Right now the only ones who know her location are the monks who just left. I'd like to believe they're on our side, but we need to be sure." Alex stared at David expectantly.

"Yes, Boss. I will ask Mother to run background checks on them immediately," David replied.

"Good. Then it's settled. Rory and Ember, you're off the case. David and I will handle it from now on."

"What?" Rory sputtered, jumping to his feet. "But Boss—"

Alex held up his hand. "Don't *but boss* me. You and Ember are attached to this case. It's better if we—"

"No, it isn't!" Ember stood with Rory. "Nima feels safe with us. Don't do this to her. She's had enough crap to last a lifetime."

Alex passed the sleeping girl to Kelsey and stood to confront his junior agents. "I'm not asking. I'm—"

"I'm not asking, either." Rory squared off, nose to nose with his boss. "Ember's right. Nima's had enough tragedy to last a lifetime. You assigned this op to Ember and me. We've done everything you trained us to do. Let us finish what we started."

Alex downright sneered. No one argued with him. It was his company, his rules. Rory took another step forward. The testosterone level in the room ratcheted to an all time high. The energy of two headstrong males squaring off woke Nima. She yawned loudly enough she caught both men's attention. And the battle was done.

Alex sat back down with Kelsey, nodding his chin dismissively. "Fine. Finish it. Take her to the safe house in Anacostia tonight. Then Arlington the next day, and so on."

Nima scrambled back onto his lap and settled down for another nap, her arms tucked beneath her and her cheek against his chest.

The fight went out of him. "She is a special little girl, isn't she?"

Rory smirked. Once again, a woman had stopped Alex in his tracks, albeit a three-foot high woman this time. "You could say that."

This is a safe house?

Located in Anacostia, southeast of D.C., the place appeared more derelict than respectable. It raised Rory's hackles just being there. What was Alex thinking? With boarded up windows and the accompanying graffiti every other inner city building bore, rain and wind had plastered trash against the concrete foundation. The place was a dive. At first glance, it made no sense. At second glance, it was the perfect location. Who would suspect a safe house in one of the most dangerous neighborhoods on the Potomac?

He ushered his girls through the rear alley and into the house, listening for the sealing hiss as the heavy steel security door clamped shut behind them. Inside was another story, as were all of the safe homes Alex had bought and restored to his precise specifications. Major security had been taken at every turn; from the steel doors and the bars on the windows to a wealth of alarms.

The creepy sensation that he and Ember were being watched this time was well founded. Alex had enlisted the overbearing support of the FBI. Even now, the Bureau's best had the safe house covered from all directions. He kept his pistols holstered under his arms anyway. Now, at the end of the mission, was no time to relax his guard. He knew better. Anything could happen.

Guilt tainted everything. Rory had barely spoken with his son. It hadn't seemed fair to go home for a quick visit only to turn around and have to leave Tyler again. He'd sounded so sad when Rory called to say he wasn't coming home yet.

"But Daddy, I miss you. Ax Mrs. Gobfree," Tyler cried.

Talking with Mrs. *Gobfree* only made him feel worse. "No, we're fine, Mr. Dennison," she assured him. "Do what you have to do. We made sugar cookies today. It kept his mind off things. He'll be okay."

"How is he sleeping at night?"

"He had a little bit of a nightmare last night, but he's coming down with a cold. He's been a little out of sorts today, too. He misses you."

The operation needed to be over and done with. It was long past time to go home.

Ember wasn't so chipper, either. Nima's latest pronouncement had sounded very much like a threat and a promise. The young monk's reaction to her words was different than David's and the others'. He'd seemed downright frightened. Guilty. As if he'd been caught.

David might be right after all. The change in Nima's voice with her last declaration made Rory realize he might be out of his league. The little girl playing sweetly with Ember on the couch might just be more powerful than any of them had realized.

He made his customary sweep through the home to ensure all doors and windows were locked, all alarms activated, and all precautions taken. Alex had stocked the place with food before they arrived. Piping hot lasagna, garlic toast, and a cold Italian pasta salad waited for them on the kitchen counter when they arrived. Whoever stocked the safes houses, they were good.

Rory wasn't hungry. He prowled like a caged animal. There was definitely some wiggle room in what Ember thought she'd seen. Alex was supposed to have cried when Rory died, but that's not what happened. Besides, Ember only said he *looked* dead. Well, looking dead and being dead were two completely different things. He brushed the nonsense out of his mind. Worry never solved anything.

It was nearly six p.m. and the early November night was cold. Wind howled at the door. Rain was in the forecast. He tussled Nima's hair and joined them in the small living room, identical to the one that had blown up in Maryland. Now *that* was something to worry about instead of some cockamamie vision. He rolled the pinch out of his neck again. It wouldn't leave.

"I'm going to unpack dinner," Ember said. "Would you watch Nima?"

"Sure."

Nima clambered onto his lap, her pale eyes full of mischief.

"You sure turned out to be a surprise, Miss Dawa. But why don't you talk like other kids your age?" He had to know. There was so much to this child.

She winked, and that simple childlike gesture stole his breath. Wow. How had he not seen? How had he not known? It was never that she couldn't speak. She'd simply chosen not to. She'd chosen silence while the rest of the world had chosen noisy clamoring of ego, pride and opinion.

When he straightened on the couch, she leaned into his chest as if she was listening to his heartbeat. He wrapped his arms around the most puzzling person he'd ever met. It made sense. Would the world listen if she were just another talking head, another celebrity media blast?

As usual when holding her, his angst dissipated. The turmoil in his mind calmed. Nima had chosen to speak only to those who would listen. Maybe that's how she'd fight her war this time. Maybe instead of the bloodshed foretold in ancient lore, she'd come to change hearts, to set things right. To heal from the inside of every man's heart to the outside, like she'd done with him. To restore a more perfect peace than the one she'd restored the last time.

The notion messed with his Christian paradigms. Her mission, if it really was to bring peace, seemed oddly familiar. Rory dipped his chin to the top of her head. The scent of baby shampoo drifted into his nose, reminding him of another child in another time who'd come just as quietly into the world with the same message. God, it all made sense.

He held her tight, needing with all his heart to protect her from the big wide world like he protected Tyler. To hold her together, to shelter this little downy chick until she had wings to fly.

"Thank you, Nima," he whispered reverently.

"Hey. Are you guys hungry?" Ember asked.

"No. My breakfast is still stuck in my throat, but let's feed Nima." He lifted Nima into his arms and went into the kitchen. Ember sliced the lasagna while Rory settled Nima onto a chair and set the table. For some unknown reason there was a candle in the middle of it, so Rory lit it. The glow from the single flame added a faint glimmer of cheer.

Once Ember and he sat with Nima between them, the Dennison tradition of a lifetime intruded. He reached for Ember and Nima's hands, needing more than just the food on the table. "If it's all right with you, I'd like to offer grace on our last night together."

Ember balked. "You know I don't believe that stuff."

"Yes, but I do. You don't have to listen if you don't want to."

"Fine. Then let's hear it."

He bowed his head and blocked the world, aware that Ember's slender fingers still rested comfortably in his hand. The wind howling outside was the only sound. He let the prayer come forth from his heart. "Heavenly Father, I come to you tonight in humility and gratitude, seeking your wisdom for the day, your strength for the task, and your blessing on *my family*." He squeezed Ember and Nima's fingers with those words. "Amen."

"That wasn't so bad," she said playfully, one shoulder dipped in a shrug.

He dished a small serving of everything onto Nima's plate. She ate with relish, but Ember nibbled at the pasta salad and Rory pushed a serving of lasagna around with his fork, his mind too full for his empty stomach.

"Have you heard the story about Alex's daughter, Abby Stewart?" Ember asked.

"No. I saw the pictures on his mantle, though. Those are his kids?"

"Only the girl. The boys belonged to Kelsey," Ember said quietly as she twirled the pasta around her fork. "But the sad thing is none of those kids are alive today."

"Seriously?"

"Yes. Kelsey's first husband killed her boys a couple years back. I was working for Alex then. Her ex tried to kill her, too. That's when Alex found her."

A pit opened up deep inside Rory. Kelsey had lost her sons to a murderer, and yet she'd taken Nima into her home without any hesitation. A shiver raced up his neck. From the oldest to the youngest, he was surrounded by amazing women.

"I think that's why she and he still live in that little house," Ember continued. "It's kind of like they know what's really important in life, and it's not big mansions and yachts and stuff like that. They've both seen the ugliest side of mankind. They're happy just to be taking care of each other. It's sweet."

"What happened?" Rory asked, surprised he didn't know this story. But then, he worked with a group of covert operators who weren't prone to gossip or chat. Kind of like him. Go figure.

"Abby and her mother Sara were killed in an automobile accident." Ember leaned back into her chair. "It happened before I started working for Alex. He was a lot meaner than he is now."

"I wouldn't say he's mean," Rory corrected. "Intense maybe, bullheaded, stubborn, and a little rude sometimes, but never mean."

"Whatever. Trust me. He was mean when he started the business and mad all the time. It didn't matter if things went right or wrong, nothing made him happy. He yelled a lot. Kicked things. I think he was in over his head with the administrative side of The TEAM, but he was too proud to admit it. Plus, he's a Marine. He didn't want to be stuck in an office all day long. He didn't believe in himself back then. He never expected his idea would really take off and be as successful as it is."

"That's when his wife and daughter died?"

"No. That happened while he was still in the Corps. He's like you. He gave up his career for family reasons, only I think with him, it was more medical than family. He could've stayed in the Corps, but losing Sara and Abby took everything out of him. He wasn't a whole guy again until Kelsey came along."

"She's a sweetheart," Rory commented. "They make a good match."

"She loves him. That's for sure."

Rory set his fork on his plate, tired of chasing the food he wasn't going to eat. "Why are you telling me all this good gossip? Where are you going with this?"

"Because I think Nima gave Alex a message from Abby when she hugged him and said *Daddy.* Whatever she said or did, I think it helped him accept Abby's death a little bit more."

It made sense. Alex did bolt out the back door as soon as Nima said that one word. *Daddy.* It would certainly rip his heart out of his chest if he'd lost his child.

"A father never stops being a father."

"You're wishing you were home with Tyler right now, huh?"

"Of course. I miss him. He's not happy right now. It's my fault."

"No, it's not." She pointed her fork at him. "It's life. It's not like you've deserted him like what's-her-name did. The op will be over soon. You two guys will go to a baseball game and eat popcorn and burp and fart like fathers and sons are supposed to do when they hang out together. Just you wait. You'll see."

He shook his head, not able to stop the smile from lifting one corner of his mouth. There she was again, doing that mothering thing. He changed the subject. "Want to know what my ex looked like?"

She blinked at the quick shift in conversation. "Sure. I guess."

He dragged up the mental picture of Ellie, the one he kept filed away with other stuff he wanted to, but couldn't, forget. "She was blonde with green eyes. About your height. Same fair complexion. A few freckles. A lot like you."

Rory swallowed hard. He pushed his plate away and waited for the fallout. There. It was finally out in the open, the foolish other reason he'd never let himself get too close to Ember. She looked like *her.*

"Excuse me? That's why you wouldn't tell me before? Because she kinda looked like me? Well, that's just plain stupid." She pushed her plate back, too, and crossed her arms over her very lovely breasts. "Eye color doesn't make us who we are. Was she smart like me? Did she know how to dance? Did she know how to jump on slow-moving trains like I do? Well, did she?"

He chuckled. He'd built his force field for all the wrong reasons. She still sat there with her green eyes full of mischief.

"No," he said softly. "She wasn't anything like you." *Not really.*

"Course not. How could she be? I'm a covert agent. I've single-handedly fought off assassins and murderers, and I've—" Ember sucked in a deep breath. "Is that what happened? Is that why you stopped being friendly toward me at work? Just because I looked like your crazy ex?" She rolled those gorgeous emeralds, daring him to deny it.

Dang. She had him dead to right. Chagrin hit him in the face like a lip-puckering, sour lemon meringue pie. He'd judged Ember before he'd given her a chance, and why? Pride again. Stupid male pride.

"Well?" Ember's toes tapped the leg of the kitchen table. She did have a tough edge when she wanted. Her top lip lifted just enough to shoot an arc of sexy defiance straight through him. Her brow arched next. She wasn't going to let go of this.

He swallowed his pride. "It's like this. My private investigator called and said Ellie was still in New York, so I thought, why not? Maybe I could get through to her. Maybe there was something I could say to make her change her mind. Only when I caught up with her, she looked right through me like I wasn't even there. She needed to score. I wanted my wife back, Tyler's mother, only...." He gulped. Pride didn't go down easy. "When I got back into the office, you'd dyed your hair green. Just like hers. You looked exactly like her and I... I...."

What else could he say? Ember was the polar opposite of Ellie. Any fool with half a brain could see that. He interlocked his fingers, wishing he hadn't been so tough on her. So self-righteous.

"I get it. You couldn't take a chance on someone who looked like your ex," Ember said gently. "It's called displaced anger, Rory. You've been mad at me because I looked like someone I'm not. It's okay. I get it. I still like you."

She couldn't have said anything better. Or kinder. Or more forgiving. And he had to make her his. Heat cascaded up from his groin, flooding his body with desire for this elegant woman. He wanted her right then and there. On the table. Bent over the table, or flat on the floor.

A look shifted over her face, a very tender look. And right on its heels, a beautiful shade of crimson flared up from her shirt collar and blossomed over her face. Energy arced between them. Red hot energy. She had to be thinking the same thing he was.

"There's chocolate mousse in the refrigerator. Anyone interested?" he asked, more to get his mind off the demanding muscle standing damned near at attention beneath his zipper than the need for dessert. Instantly, his horny male brain kicked in with—*Hmm. The things you could do to her with chocolate mousse.*

Nima's eyes lit up at the word 'chocolate.' Ember still glowed red, but he lifted slowly out of his chair, hoping she didn't catch the adjustment he quickly made. The candle flickered. He blew it out when he brought the plates of mousse back to the table, focused on the detailed after-action report he'd have to write instead of the way Ember's lips worked around every mouthful of dessert. Darn. Women and chocolate. She made every forkful look like heaven the way she rolled it around her tongue before she swallowed. And why did she have to lick those lips—those soft luscious lips that begged to be kissed and kissed hard?

He tore his eyes off the delightful dessert of her body. Like a foolish teenage boy, he swallowed a spoonful of the mousse wrong. He choked, spitting the dessert into his hand so he didn't launch it all over the table. *Not cool, Dennison.*

"Are you okay?" She outright flirted, her head cocked to the side and blonde hair rippling over her shoulder in one soft wave, the ends of it curled and cupping her breast. Yeah. She knew exactly what that fork in her mouth was doing to him. One more come hither spark in her eye like the last and he was a goner.

Good heck, just kill me now. He turned his head and choked to the side. At last he could breathe without coughing.

Finally, the dessert plates were clean and the darned mousse was back in the refrigerator where it belonged. Ember cleared the few dishes while he wiped the chocolate off Nima's happy face. Even she was different tonight, playful and almost sassy. She chomped on the washcloth when he wiped her mouth and wouldn't let it go. She growled, twisting the cloth back and forth, giggling the whole time. In a rowdy mood, she dived headfirst off the kitchen counter and into his arms. He swung her high over his head and caught her in an upside down position that only made her giggle harder.

"You are a silly rascal," he exclaimed, turning her upside right.

Ember smiled from loading the dishwasher. "That's the most she's laughed all week."

Rory winced. Everything they were doing combined to make a happy family. Only the child was different. There should've been two. He could almost hear his son's infectious giggle within Nima's, as if he were there, also.

Their frivolity was interrupted by a breaking news bulletin from the television in the other room. A local reporter was on site in China Town, downtown D.C., where two monks had just immolated themselves to protest the ongoing Chinese occupation of Tibet.

Rory's ears perked up. "Ember. Are you seeing this?"

She was already watching. "Wow. Those are the same guys who came to see Nima this morning."

"But where's the other one? The young guy? Where's the guy who asked to touch her?"

"Let's find out." Ember dialed the office on the new cell phone Alex had given them. "Hey, Mother. Are you catching the news report on—" She cocked her head. "Wow. Yes, I'll tell him. Of course, I tell him everything. He's agent in charge, isn't he? I have to go."

Ember hung up on her chatty lead techie. "Mother is still trying to locate him, but these two guys were thrown out of a moving vehicle, Rory. A traffic cam caught the whole thing. It wasn't a political protest. It's murder."

He was on Nima in a heartbeat. "He touched Nima. Get her clothes off. Now!"

In two seconds flat, the little girl stood wide-eyed and shivering in her underwear while Rory and Ember examined her hoody and pants.

"Wait!" Ember pulled the top out of Rory's hand. "Look."

A single cloth-covered button was stuck inside the interfacing of Nima's purple hoody. Rory cut it out with his pocketknife and peeled the plastic cap off. Another transmitter.

"Shit! We're moving," he roared. "Get her dressed!"

"I should call Alex first—"

"I said now!" Slinging his backpack across his shoulder, he snagged two sawed-offs from the gun safe while Ember hurriedly dressed the little girl. With his cell phone to his ear, he called Alex while he tapped the code to unlock the rear exit. "We're moving. I'll call you when—"

"Stay put. Harley and I are on our way," Alex shot back.

"No, we're made. That bastard bugged Nima this morning. He knows where we are."

"We're only minutes away. So's the FBI."

"Then cover us!" Rory hung up on his boss, barely cracking the back door to peer at the Cadillac. He'd truly hoped they wouldn't need it to run again. Good God, how many times could they be lucky enough to stay ahead of these determined assassins?

At least he hadn't destroyed the tracking device. That might've have alerted the assassins he was on to them. Still, the assassins now knew where Nima was. Every second counted.

Holding his pistol at the ready, he crept stealthily down the steps. Dr. Choden's Cadillac looked the same, but nothing stirred. Not the wind. Not one leaf. Not good. The FBI should've been engaged with the assassins by now if they were coming. Unless they were already there....

Shit! *Are the FBI agents already dead?* Training kicked in. He waved Ember to retreat to safety. "Go back. Get her inside and—"

WHOOSH!

The car lurched up from its four wheels in a pyroclastic belch of flying death. Something hard thudded against the back of his head. Ember leaned backward, twisting in slow motion to protect Nima as they fell onto the kitchen floor. Shrapnel from the obliterated Cadillac peppered the outside brick walls of the safe house with a voracious, *Zip. Whip. Zip!*

He lost his balance. The asphalt jumped up to meet him, shifting beneath his boots even as he fell to his hands and knees. "Shut the door!" he cried.

Too late. The world turned red. Then black. It bucked him like a horse. Off.

Twenty

Just like the vision.

Nima shrieked. Ember screamed. Searing heat blew her backward into the kitchen. She choked. Fumes burned her lungs. All she saw through the open doorway was orange fire and black smoke. Ember buried Nima's face against her chest and slammed the door shut, but just as quickly opened it again. She needed to see. He was there a second ago.

"Rory!" This time she screamed in all-out panic. Choden's car had turned into a burning wreck. Training kicked in and she dropped to the floor with Nima. Visibility still sucked, but she could breathe. Squinting, she strained to catch a glimpse of her partner.

The smoke curled, seeming to point an eerie finger at her. It lifted. There he was, face down at the bottom of the steps, his forehead covered in blood. Grayish vapor lifted out of his clothes. His arm stretched out in front of him, his hand still clutching his SIG. But his eyes were wide open. He stared back at her, his face blank in death.

Just like the vision.

"No!" Terror choked her throat. "Rory! God, no!"

Every piece of her heart screamed, *Run to him. Save him!* But Nima sobbed. Reality sucked the hope out of her. She couldn't save him. The vision was right. He was already gone.

Ember kicked the door shut, scrambling backward on her butt with Nima in her arms. The damned vision suffocated the life and hope right out of her. For a moment all she could do was sit against the gun safe, trying desperately to breathe, too scared to think what she should do next. Her training faltered. *Rory! I can't do this without you!*

Angry voices at the back of the house jolted her to action. The assassins were out there, still coming for Nima. Still planning to kill her.

"Not on my watch." Grabbing an Uzi from the open safe and a spare backpack full of ammo and gear, she zeroed her soul on the job ahead. Snuggling Nima into her side, she prepared a solid strategy. *Make them come to me.*

The weapon in her hand was the same model she'd used at the ambush. It seemed like forever ago, but it would work nicely. She knew it well. At twelve hundred rounds per minute, she could hold them off until help showed. *Move it, Alex. I'm in trouble.*

Two sawed-offs bumped her hands when she reached for the ammo bag. Good. She could handle two at a time once the Uzi got too hot to handle. She'd done it before during weapons certification, just never in real life, never when her hands were shaking this much. Stuffing the pack with extra magazines and clips, she talked down the fear hammering in her chest. *I can do this. Slow and easy. Steady. Focus. Make 'em wish they'd never been born.*

Glass shattered behind her as grappling hooks shot through the kitchen windows and anchored over the sills and countertops. These guys were tearing the house apart. If they were coming for Nima, they would pay dearly. In blood.

Nima clutched her like a baby orangutan, still whining in fright. By now, she and Nima were in the living room on the floor next to the couch. "Are you hurt?" she asked as she smoothed a hurried hand across the baby's grimy face.

Two frightened eyes blinked back at her through ash and tears. There were no special words this time. No prophecy or wisdom beyond the ages, only a damned scared kid hanging on for dear life.

"Just remember. Us girls stick together no matter what comes through that door."

Right on cue, the front door was jerked off its hinges and dragged into the street. Cold wind blew in. Scrambling down the hall and into the front bedroom, she pushed Nima beneath the bed.

"Stay down. Cover your ears." Ember heard the calm in her voice. It couldn't be hers.

She held her breath, planned her only line of defense and waited, craning to listen over the racket of heavy machinery clearing debris outside the house. No one had entered the home yet. Maybe the steel door needed to be towed out of the way?

Sure enough. In seconds, heavy footsteps pounded through the house from front door to back. She cracked the bedroom door and watched the assassins search. Too soon those same footsteps turned in her direction.

She didn't think twice. Squeezing the trigger of the lethal tool in her hand, she loosed a steady stream of death down the hallway. Men cursed. Hulking bodies dropped to the floor. Another hopped away on one foot. One man screamed something in Chinese or Tibetan. If nothing else, she'd made her intentions clear. She wouldn't go easy.

"Come to Mama Ember, suckers," she hissed under her breath. "I'll show you a freaking goddess of war."

Nima whimpered behind her. Another charge of black shapes stampeded down the hall. What the hell was wrong with these guys? Were they on drugs? Had to be to think she'd do anything different than before.

Screaming in rage, she let her weapon do the talking. It spit round after round like death-seeking hornets, reducing her enemy to everything she hated about war. Death spewed from her hands, but this time she was glad of it. The smell of blood and body fluids emanating from the kill zone of the hallway only incited her more.

Bring it on! I'll kill every last one of you before I let you take her!

A wrenching mechanical shriek interrupted her outburst. A metal chain blasted through the bedroom window behind her. Damn it to hell! Another grappling hook had found purchase on the edge of the window frame, pulling it to shreds.

With one final spray of gunfire for good measure, she pulled Nima from beneath the bed, tucked her under her arm and charged into the bedroom across the hall, firing wildly down the hall at anyone dumb enough to still be there.

Slamming the door shut, she shook with as much fear as rage. This small bedroom was where she'd make her last stand. Here she would die in the line of duty, shot down by cold-blooded killers out to murder a tiny girl who'd never hurt anyone in her whole life!

Alex, get your dumb ass here right damned now!

Her fingers fumbled the .9mm pistol out of her belt holster. If she could only stop her hands from shaking, she would survive. The Uzi was fast becoming too hot to handle, so she pulled both sawed-off shotguns out of her bag. Setting the pistol on the floor, she lined up a row of cartridges beside it and hunkered down to wait, as alone as she never expected to be. Ready to kill. Ready to die. Both felt the same somehow. It didn't matter, them or her, as long as Nima lived.

Ember ran her fingers over the little girl's head. This was not exactly the image of motherhood she had in mind. "If you are Palden Lhamo, I could really use some help right now," she said softly. "Didn't you Tibetans believe in fire breathing dragons or stuff like that? Couldn't you conjure up just one to save the day? A big one? With horns?"

Nima stared, no longer crying, her blue eyes full of trust. Not magic. Not death. Just the childish belief that Mama Ember could do anything. But Ember knew better. She was outnumbered. The odds were against her the minute Rory dropped in the line of duty. There would be no strikes of lightning to waste the murderers at the door. No miracle rescue at the final hour. Only her.

Too soon the screeching sounds of the bars being pulled from other windows in the home told her plenty. She was the only thing standing between Nima and certain death. Gulping a mouthful of fear, she turned it into sheer determination. Nima would not die. Not like this. Not today.

"Go hide in the closet." She shoved the little girl toward the louvered doors. Nima hid and for a second, the house was deadly quiet, the eerie kind of stillness that precedes an F5 in the middle of flat-as-hell Kansas.

Ember steadied her mind and took a deep breath. *I can do this for Nima. For Rory. I know I can.* Another deep breath and more footsteps tramped through the hall. *I can do this for me.*

Automatic fire pierced the bedroom walls, spraying bits of sheetrock and plaster everywhere. The house rocked as another explosion roared. They'd chosen grenades for their final assault. Or did they? Was it C-4? She couldn't tell. There was so much noise. Heavy boots thundered toward the bedroom door. She crouched in front of the closet where Nima hid.

Ember conjured her own fierce dragon, the one with blue eyes. *Alex! Get here! Save us! Right damned now!*

But it didn't matter where he was anymore. He was not there. She was. The bed between her and Nima's wannabe killers would provide no cover once they breached the door. Every shot from her hand had to count. Men had to die and if she had her way, die they would.

"I love you," she muttered to the child she'd sworn to die for. *I love you, too, Rory.*

She took aim, leveling her shotgun as the door blew inward off its hinges and bounced onto the bed. Blinding white light lit the room as an explosive charge roared. Flashbangs. The lights flickered and went out. No electricity remained in the home. No hope, either. She fired blindly, screaming defiance to the overwhelming odds against her.

A hard blow from behind sent her sprawling to the floor. The house had been breached, its walls torn down to get at Nima. Some bastard stepped between her shoulder blades, pinning her to the debris-littered floor. Another tore the weapon from her fingers. At least they'd stopped shooting, but it took a minute to see through the smoke and darkness.

Blinking through stinging tears, she could just make out the arrogant prick who led this pack of wolves. It was him, that lying bastard who'd bugged Nima's dress. Was he the same guy who'd bugged her black velvet dress, too? Who killed her father? It no longer mattered. The Bastard Monk had Nima. The Creep Monk had Ember. Death had arrived in all its heartless glory.

He held Nima by the scruff of her neck in one hand and raised her high for his buddies to see. "We have her now. Our task is nearly done," he declared, his eyes glittering despite the dark. Someone ran in with a spotlight, filling the room with stark light and starker shadows. More assassins crowded through the door even as the distinct odor of their dead companions in the hall filled Ember's nose.

"Let her down," she growled, her hands pressed to the floor near her shoulders, arching her back against the creep stepping on her, holding her down. Her empty-handed fingers clenched for her missing gun. Her soul longed to kill every last one of them!

Another blunt hit to the back of her head laid her flat again. She stopped fighting, wishing she could instill confidence into her frightened girl. Tears washed Nima's face. Twisting back and forth in the bastard's grip, her sad blue eyes searched frantically for Ember.

"I'm here," Ember called to her. "I'm down here, Nima. Look at me, not them."

"Not for long," Bastard Monk hissed, his wicked mouth twisted into a sneer.

A roar went up among the men in the room. The Creep Monk holding Ember in place on the floor stepped harder, compressing the air right out of her. It didn't mater. God, they smelled of body odor, blood, and the horrible stench that accompanied gut-shot bodies. None of them seemed to care for their wounded buddies in the hallway, if there were any. Ember certainly didn't. She hadn't intended survivors.

Bastard Monk swung Nima to the floor like a rug. She landed on her stomach only inches from Ember's face, staring with shock from the body slam, the wind knocked out of her.

"It's okay. Mama Ember is here," Ember soothed, her fingers clenched out for Nima in futility. *But I am going to kill that sonofabitch if he hurts you one more time!* Too many men's boots and legs blocked her from reaching the girl.

"Mama," Nima cried, her face scrunched with fear and her arm outstretched to Ember. "I want Mama."

The leader of the assassins, Bastard Monk, jerked Nima to her back. He straddled her quivering body, crouched over her until he was nose to nose with her. "Your mother is already dead. I would know. I gave her the drug myself. Your father too, so shut your filthy mouth. There is no power on earth that can save you."

Nima's lip puckered and Ember went ballistic. "Leave her alone!" she screamed, struggling for just one inch of movement against the creep's boot that pinned her. "Don't you touch her!"

"You Americans." Bastard Monk sneered, an unforgiving glint in his eyes. "You think your freedom gives you the right to infect our nation with it? Watch while I offer the supreme sacrifice. Be prepared to learn of ways more ancient than yours. Tonight, you will see the evil pour out of this thing while I send her back to hell. And then it will be your turn. I will take your precious freedom and your lying tongue, once and for all."

He held the same kind of knife that Cold Eyes had threatened her and Rory with during the ambush. She could see it clearly now. Eight inch blade. Embellished handle with brass symbols. A dragon? A tiger? A snake? Maybe.

"Leave her alone," Ember demanded again, but Bastard Monk was no longer listening. He smiled while Nima sputtered and cried between his clenched knees. Ember offered a quick plea to the Tibetan goddess of war, the ferocious Palden Lhamo, if there really was such a being in the whole crazy universe of organized religions. *Now*, she ordered the mysterious divinity who scared the shit out of David. *Now would be a damned good time to show up and drink somebody's blood, Palden Lhamo! Start with him. That guy. That Bastard Monk.*

Bastard Monk turned as if he'd heard her mental prayer, his face twisted in a devilish smile and his eyes intercepting hers. "You are a very stupid woman to believe in myths and legends," he spat. "You would do better to believe in this."

With one quick flick of his wrist, he pressed the point of his blade beneath Nima's chin, nicking her. Ember would have kicked the shit out of him if she could've reached him. Nima squealed, and Ember arched her back, feeling the same pain. But she felt something else, too. Pure damned luck had offered one last chance. She intended to take it.

"And now you will return to Naraka," Bastard Monk chanted, his body swaying forward and backward over Nima's still form. He lifted the blade over his head, both hands wrapped around its grip. "I send you back to the deepest depths, back to the hell of uninterrupted suffering and eternal fire. Back to endless karma for all the evil you have wrought throughout your worthless existence."

"Return." The other assassins swayed along with their leader, their voices a rising crescendo. Even Creep Monk lifted his booted foot far enough up that Ember could draw in a lungful of air. She needed it.

"Return. Return," he chanted along with Bastard Monk.

Bastard Monk lifted the ceremonial blade higher. Ember raised her shoulders and head, enough that she was nearly on her side. Creep Monk's boot in her back offered almost no resistance. All the assassins seemed fixated on the ritualistic killing about to take place. Nima turned her head, her soft blue eyes radiating no fear. Peace flowed to Ember. The little girl stretched her tiny hand to Ember, her fingers beckoning. Was she ready to die? No way!

Ember eased her right hand up to her left shoulder. She'd only get one chance.

"Return!" Bastard Monk hissed, plunging the blade downward into—

BLAM!

Ember fired her trusty pistol, the one she'd laid out on the floor in advance. Once! Twice! Against all odds, she'd nailed both his hands before he could stab Nima. Before he even came close.

He looked so damned surprised. The blade vanished in a spray of red mist, ricocheting to who cared where. Dark red fountains spewed from the stumps at the ends of his arms.

As if in answer to her prayers, a battery of righteous thunder filled the small bedroom. Deafening, roaring thunder. Bastard Monk dissolved before her eyes. His body jerked with spasms. His neck began to bleed. His head. His eyes. All became blood and gore. Ember cringed, covering her ears at the noise. The assault was not coming from her hand. Her pistol didn't have that kind of capacity. Had Palden Lhamo finally shown up for the war? It sure felt like it.

Assassins stampeded in all directions, but Ember only had eyes for her little girl. She shouldered her way through the stomping forest of boots and legs until she could pull Nima into her arms and beneath her body. Squeezing her eyes shut, she clutched the child to her heart. Rory had already given his life. Now she would give hers. At least they'd die together.

"Shh," she soothed, even though she couldn't hear her own voice. Nima burrowed her face into Ember's breasts. "I'm here. I've got you now."

The thunder stilled. The smoke cleared. Ember lifted her head to understand what had just happened. There was no dragon, but one assassin still stood over her. Only this guy was different. He held a piercing light in his hand. The beam landed square in her eyes. A spike of adrenaline hammered at her last shred of logic. She still had her pistol. She didn't need to see him to kill him. No one was getting Nima. She lifted her piece, ready to blow this last demon back to—

"Hey, beautiful."

She squinted. Blinked. Wanted desperately to believe her eyes weren't lying. "Rory?" her disbelieving mouth croaked.

"Looks like you've got everything under control in here," he said easily, his hand outstretched to pull her up from the floor. No one ever looked better. Bloody, maybe. Scared, too. But never better.

She scrambled to her feet with Nima attached to her hip. "You're alive!"

"Coming through." Harley ducked around Rory. "Hey, Ember. Good to see you. Sorry I'm late. We kinda got hung up in a shootout."

"You got our girls?" Alex stepped through the hole in the wall behind her.

"I do now," Rory purred, pulling Ember under his arm.

Her knees threatened to collapse. She tucked her pistol into her belt and soaked up the strength flowing from him. "You're here," she whispered, tracing the angle of his brow with trembling fingers.

"Hey, Dennison. Not fair. I get one," Harley groused, gingerly lifting Nima from Ember's grip. "It's okay, little darlin'. Uncle Harley's got you now. Let's get you out of here and cleaned up. You want a chocolate bar?"

The blood-spattered child never batted an eye when she transferred from Ember's arms to her new protector. Harley had said the magic word—chocolate. And Nima could be bought. Off they went.

Rory caught Ember to him. Nose to nose and lips to lips, he was really there. And alive. And he looked like hell.

"I saw you die," she cried as the memory washed over her again, tracing the sharp corner of his jaw before she cupped it tenderly.

"You saw me get knocked out," he corrected, his breath warm in her face. Their eyes locked. There was no hesitation this time. He pulled her off her feet with one arm and kissed her, roughly, intimately, and thoroughly, his tongue entwined with hers.

Alex was out there somewhere, but she didn't care. Let him see. Let him know. She loved this man with her soul. Clenching her fingers into his hair, she kissed back with everything she had. The need to pour her heart into him consumed her. So she did. All her angst, all her sins, and all her love went into her kiss.

His lips were soft and willing, his tongue insistently branding her from the inside out. Nothing ever tasted so good. More. Wow, did she want more. Desperation took over. She'd nearly lost this guy. She couldn't kiss him hard enough or deep enough.

He came up for air. "Good heck. Do that again."

Sweeter words were never spoken. If not for the carnage around them, she'd have lain him flat, ripped his clothes off and—

Alex materialized out of the smoke in the hall behind Rory. "Will you guys knock it off and get the hell out of this mess?"

"Boss," Rory growled over his shoulder, his hands still full of Ember. "How many times do I have to tell you to watch your language? There's a little girl in the house and—"

"I know. I know. Harley's got her." Alex waved Rory's warning off as he turned and went back the way he'd come. "I cuss. Deal with it. Now move."

"Are you ready to hang up your six-shooter, Mrs. Dillon?" Rory asked as he turned out of the room with her still secure under his arm. She sagged against him, so thankful for the courage and strength of this particular man.

"I'd like to hold onto it for a little longer. You never know."

He branded a tender kiss to the side of her sweaty forehead. "Copy that. I'd like to hold onto you for a little longer, too. Hope you don't mind."

She melted against him, the words she'd longed to hear at last spoken out loud. The tears came as they stepped over bodies and pieces of the ruined home. Alex shot them a piercing look as they gathered with Harley.

Mayhem had come to D.C. By the looks of it, the assassins had been prepared to destroy anything and everyone in their path to get to Nima. Confiscated rocket-propelled grenade launchers lay alongside dozens of automatic rifles and various pistols on a tarp placed well away from the handcuffed surviving assassins. A heavy-duty truck rested across the curb, the tow strap still wrapped around the security door they'd pulled off the house.

An army of D.C. Metro police and FBI held several more black-clad men under armed guard. Emergency vehicles swarmed the streets. Medics carried stretchers filled with black-clad assassins strapped down tight. A news helicopter hovered overhead, its bright spotlight glaring back and forth over the scene.

"What happened to our FBI support?" she asked, shielding her eyes from the bright glare and dust kicked up from the chopper.

"Same as Maxwell and Fred," Rory whispered into the side of her head. "These assassins were ruthless. They killed everyone who got in their way. FBI has more than one crime scene on their hands tonight."

"But how did they know where everyone was?" Ember asked. "It's like they had ears and eyes everywhere."

"It's a scary new world," Rory muttered. "Look at our own NSA. With enough funding and the latest technology, anything is possible."

She shivered. *Wow* failed. *Holy shit* fit the evil of the day so much better.

"They almost killed you," she said.

"Mostly likely an RPG hit the Caddie," he filled in the missing pieces. "Too bad. I liked that car."

Alex motioned to the paramedics, and soon Rory and Ember were seated at the back of one of their vehicles getting treated; Rory for a bump and laceration on the back of his head and Ember for broken glass that pierced her bicep, but which she hadn't noticed. "Ouch." She winced as the medic probed a little too deep and pulled out another sliver of glass.

"You're officially an undercover operator, now." Rory smirked. "You've got the wounds to prove it."

"Ahem. Do you guys want to know what this little lady said to me?" Harley asked petulantly, still smiling that infectious little boy smile of his and holding Nima while the medics checked her over, too. She sported a colorful pink bandage on her chin and a big chocolate bar in her hand. One thing about Harley, he could make a dreary day brighter simply by showing up in the morning. And he knew his way around women of all ages.

"Sure, what?" Rory peered around Ember.

"You two were kinda busy." Harley arched an evil eyebrow. "When we cleared what's left of the house, she was fussing, so I gave her a little squeeze." He demonstrated and Nima willingly wrapped her arms around his neck. "She pats my cheek and, like right out of the blue she looks into my eyes and says, *'My two warrior sons wait at home.'* How crazy is that? Them are some pretty big words for a little gal, don't you think?"

Oh, no, Ember mouthed to Rory. Harley and his wife, Judy, had struggled to get pregnant since they'd married. He blamed his drug use in the past for their fertility problems, but if Nima told him that—

"Call Judy," Alex ordered calmly. "Let her know she's going to have twins." It would've sounded like a joke if he hadn't said it so seriously.

Harley cocked his head. "She did have a late doctor's appointment today. Guess I could."

"Tell her we're happy for you guys," Ember added before he handed Nima off to Alex and stepped away to make the call.

Nima rested her little head on Alex's shoulder and patted his arm like the comforting little angel she was. "Is your vision done giving yet?" he asked Ember.

"I sure hope so."

Despite the carnage and destruction, the armies of FBI SWAT and Metro police, Ember felt calm and peaceful. The vision had left out one very important detail—the moment when Rory came back to life.

Just then, Harley clapped Rory on the back. He wiped his eyes and turned away to regain his composure. At last able to choke out an explanation, he brushed a quick hand over his face. "Danged if little Miss Nima isn't right. Judy's pregnant. She just found out an hour ago. She's two months along and, umm...." The big sap had tears in his eyes. "I'm finally gonna be a dad. We're having twins."

"Good on you, man!" Rory added.

"Congratulations!" Ember jumped off the back bumper of the medics' truck. Harley snagged her up into a friendly hug while Alex and Rory both pounded his back.

"How in tarnation did that little tyke know before me and Judy?" he asked hoarsely.

Rory lifted both shoulders. "Nima has an incredible gift."

Ember held out her hands to Nima and the little girl traded places again, from Alex to her arms. The vision was finally complete. More ambulance sirens arrived with several news vans right behind them, The TEAM's signal to fade to black.

"Time to move," Alex ordered. "Come on, boys and girls. Peel out."

"Ah, Boss," Rory said as they walked away from the incoming press corps. "I've got to tell you. These houses of yours are not too safe."

"This one will be."

Ember looked twice. Alex looked too serious for the happy outcome of the operation. The silvery hint at his temples usually made him look distinguished, but tonight he looked older. Sadder.

The vision niggled at her, tapping like an impatient child with more to say whether you want to hear it or not. A game piece was still in play. The operation was not yet over. She could feel it. "Where are we going?" she asked.

He didn't even glance in her direction. "You'll see."

Twenty-One

Anxiety speared Ember's heart the minute the elevator opened. They were back at The TEAM's office in Alexandria. Mother welcomed them with open arms. Even she seemed a little sad around the edges.

When they cleared Mother's welcoming hugs, Alex waved them into the conference room. Kelsey was already there, as sad as Mother.

The door opened farther to reveal David, along with three elegant Tibetan monks dressed in their traditional red garb. He stood the moment he saw her. "Ember. Rory. I'd like you to meet the High Lamas of Tibet. They have been sent to collect Nima Dawa."

Oh, no. Ember pressed Nima into her arms against her. It was happening. The time to say goodbye was here and now. Her throat clenched tight. She couldn't swallow.

The elderly gentlemen stood and bowed to Ember and Nima. Ember expected the little girl to cower like she'd done earlier with the monks at Alex and Kelsey's place, but she clapped her hands in delight. And instead of stodgy old guys who might tolerate a child her age, these guys beamed to see her. Nima wiggled out of Ember's arms. As soon as Ember set her down, she ran to one of them and climbed onto his lap. Nima looked so—happy.

Alex shook hands with the monks, as did Rory, but Ember stood frozen at the door, unwilling to extend courtesy to the men about to destroy her life. She glared at David. He'd brought them here. Jerk!

Alex waved her into the room. "Come on in, Ember. Take your place."

So she sat between Rory and Kelsey while Nima played peek-a-boo with the monks.

"She looks like she knows these guys," Rory whispered out of the side of his mouth.

"Ah huh," Ember replied woodenly. That's exactly what it looked like. Nima acted like she'd forgotten who'd shared chocolate and baths and naps with her. She didn't look back once for Ember. Not even once.

When Kelsey's soft hand rested on Ember's arm, she turned away, sure if she looked into those gentle brown eyes, she'd fall apart.

Rory sat quietly at her other side, his fingers entwined with hers under the table. Did he know? Was he in on this? Was he a traitor like David and Alex? She glanced at him. No. He looked as stricken as she felt.

Alex didn't look any happier, but damn him. He'd done this behind her back. Everything was happening too quickly. She was supposed to have more time with Nima, but no. He'd assigned David and Mother to tie up all the loose ends while she and Rory were shuffled off to the safe house. *Damn you, Alex.*

"Mother has done a thorough job of authenticating these gentlemen's credentials," Alex said quietly. "They are precisely who they say they are. They've been sent by the Dalai Lama himself to take Nima Dawa back to her country tonight. They've also brought the woman with them who will act as nanny to Nima for the rest of her life. You are welcome to meet her, speak with her, and ask her or them anything you'd like."

"Is she the same nanny those other guys planned to use?" Rory asked. "Because that woman's a suspect as far as I'm concerned. She might be in league with the assassins."

"You are correct, Rory," David spoke up. "The Dalai Lama sent someone else, one of his most trusted women friends to take over care of Nima. You will probably understand when I tell you she left everything she owned behind in San Francisco and moved into an apartment in the area precisely one week ago in anticipation of this calling."

"Why?" Rory asked. "Are you saying... Do you mean to tell me that she moved before the Dalai Lama even contacted her? That she knew she'd be needed before Nima and her father had even set foot on U.S. soil?"

David nodded. "The truly faithful have been waiting a long time, Rory. Unlike most of us, they are in tune with the universe."

Alex interrupted with the introduction. "Ember and Rory, meet Kamalya. Mother spent the afternoon investigating her background. David is correct. Kamalya is as pure as the driven snow in the high Himalayas. She has the Dalia Lama's total confidence. " Tears brimmed in his eyes, too. That didn't help.

Ember choked. She didn't care about all the mumbo jumbo of miracles and ancient Tibetan folklore. Taking care of Nima was her job. A hole had opened up inside of her, a hole that was sucking the sweetest joy she'd ever known out of her life. The love of a child.

Mother ushered a young woman with long dark hair, dark eyes, and dusky skin into the conference room. The resemblance between her and Nima pierced Ember's heart. She could've passed for Nima's older sister—or mother. Dressed very conservatively in a long black skirt, a plain white blouse, and a multi-colored wool sweater draped nearly to her knees, she went immediately to Nima and bowed from the waist.

Once again, the girl chuckled with glee. Nima liked her, but Ember didn't. The strange woman exuded the spirit of a lamb. Who was going to teach Nima to be tough when the next army of assassins showed up? It was a mean world out there. No way could this woman teach Nima how to handle a concealed weapon or shoot straight. She was milk toast. Nima needed real skills in order to survive. By the looks of her, this woman might be able to teach her to knit and crochet when what she really needed was—Mrs. Dillon.

Rory's fingers locked together with hers didn't bring comfort. Her heart broke, wrenched out of her chest at the terrible position Nima would be consigned to for the rest of her life—a life without Mama Ember.

No. No. No! I don't want to do this!

"Is there anything you'd like to ask before they take their leave?" It was David who spoke. "They have a late flight to catch."

The calmness in his voice irked the hell out of Ember. This was nothing but a business transaction to him. She couldn't stand the sight of him. *Never, David. I'll never forgive you.*

Rory cleared his throat. "I think Ember and I are good as long as we're sure Nima will be well cared for and loved like she should be. Aren't we?"

She couldn't speak. Yes, goodbye was always coming. Yes, she was being emotional and unreasonable, but she'd fallen in love with Nima. There was no way she was okay or good with any of this.

David still acted kind and gentle, like he cared. "Ember? Speak up. Now is the time to ask questions. I don't want you to think we don't care about your feelings."

Kelsey shoved some tissues into her hand. Ember bit her lip and started shredding them. Like hell he cared about her feelings, but she said, "Umm, no. I understand."

"Let's get it over with then." Alex stood. "The sooner we're done here, the better."

Her heart climbed up her throat. Like it or not, the time to say goodbye had come. Alex took Nima into his arms first, blinking hard, his fingers splayed in a gentle cup at the back of her head as he hugged her to him. And Nima, in her wise little girl way, patted his shoulder at the same time. Comforting him.

And crack, Ember's heart broke. She shuddered. The pinch in her chest clamped tighter. Her whole world fell apart.

Alex wiped his face with one quick brush of his hand while Kelsey took Nima from him. Ember untangled from Rory's fingers and stood, unwilling to sit for her inevitable turn. The need to scream choked her. *I can't do it.*

Rory came to her rescue, his hand gently cupping her elbow to pull her into his side. Together they watched Kelsey kiss Nima's forehead and whisper, "You are such a beautiful child. Please live a long and happy life. Remember how to play. Come back to see us someday." Another motherly kiss, a hug and a pat, and Ember's turn had come.

But Harley stepped to her side. He must have known how hard this would be. Mercifully, he winked and took Nima first. "Hey, little darlin'," he murmured, his forehead to Nima's and nothing but love glistening in his handsome hazel eyes. "Me and my warrior boys are gonna come see you someday. Would you like that?"

She held her palms to the sides of his face, stretched her neck forward, and placed the softest kiss on the end of his nose. A big old tear dripped out of his eye, and Ember turned her back on the damned tragedy. *No! No! No!*

"Thank you for telling me they're on their way," he said hoarsely. "You've darned near made me and Judy the happiest folks on earth. Bye, darlin'."

Rory clapped his hands once, and Nima fell from Harley's arms into his with a big smile. Ember pressed her fist to her mouth, stifling the screams of her heart. There was no way she could tell her child of light goodbye.

Rory didn't seem to care that everyone watched while he wept openly. Tears dripped off his jaw. It was big girl Nima with her hands in his hair who patted his head to comfort him.

Ember melted. This was just as hard on him as it was her. She stepped to his side, her hand in the middle of his broad back so he'd know she was there for him.

He shuddered, struggling to speak. "You grow up to be big and strong, okay, little one? Don't be too mean or too powerful. Be a nice warrior goddess, okay?"

With two pudgy hands, Nima cradled his face until her nose touched his, and as sweetly as ever, she whispered her favorite word, "Yep."

He smothered her to him in one last fatherly embrace; his eyes squeezed shut and the pain of losing her laid bare for all to see. "I know you're not my daughter, but it sure feels like you are. I love you," he whispered. "I always will."

And Nima, for the first time in all their days together said, "Love you, ReeRee."

He turned to share the child they both loved, but Ember stepped back, afraid if she touched Nima again, she'd need to fight the world to keep her. *No.*

Nima reached for Ember, but she couldn't take her into her arms. No way. She shook her head in denial of the pain headed her way. Sad cornflower blues blinked in surprise.

"Take her, Ember. Come on, she needs you to tell her goodbye," Rory whispered gently.

"Umm, no." Ember shook her head. She bit her lip, reached over and patted Nima's cheek quickly with just two fingers. "Alex is right. Let's get this over with. Head 'em up and move 'em out, and all that jazz. Bye, little one. See you later."

"Mama?"

Ember willed herself not to shatter into a million pieces at that graciously bestowed title she hadn't earned or deserved. She never should've let Nima call her that. This was what happened when you fell in love. You always ended up with empty arms. It always hurt too damned much.

"Go on," she ground out, her heart clenched as tight as her jaw. "Be good. Bye."

"Ember," Rory pleaded. "Don't let her go like this."

I have to. God, it will kill me if I have to hold her only to give her up.

"Goodbye, Nima," Ember said more firmly. "See you… later. Yeah. See you later."

Reluctantly, he lowered Nima to the floor. Kamalya stepped forward, bowing to Rory as she took the little girl's hand. Together, they walked out of the Sit Room.

Ember stood numbly, watching her first and last operation come to an end. The conference room emptied around her. Alex and David thanked the monks for making the long journey and for being understanding of the delay. Ember listened to the buzz of courtesy and polite well wishes as everyone made their way to the elevator. Everyone but her and Rory.

He stood there at her side, probably not understanding why she was being unreasonable, but still there. Didn't he know? The pain of separation was always better handled like ripping a band-aid off—fast and quick. It had already dragged on for too long. She needed it finished before she had more time to think.

Alex called the elevator for the Tibetan entourage. David chatted quietly with the monks like they were best friends. He looked at Nima, which he hadn't done all day. She smiled up at him with those sweet, scary blue eyes. He patted her head. A telephone rang and Mother called to Rory from her desk to pick up the call. Ember felt the chill when he stepped away from her.

Nima turned around one last time. Her sad eyes pierced Ember's from across the work bay, and God. How much could a mother losing her one and only child endure?

Ember fell to her knees, her arms stretched wide, her heart crying out in one last, *'Please-come-hug-me, baby girl!'*

Nima fled the security of her new mother's grasp and ran as fast as she could, throwing her pudgy little self into Ember's open arms. She burst into sobs, burrowing her little body into Ember's arms and whimpering, "Mama. My Mama."

"I wish I were, baby girl," Ember sobbed, enfolding the child she loved with all her mind and soul, pressing her back into the gaping hole in her heart. She breathed in the smell of baby shampoo one last time. "I will never forget you. Never ever in a million years. I love you so much."

They rocked back and forth and Ember didn't care if the monks made their flight or not. Let them wait. They didn't count. Neither did David or Alex. Only Nima. Only this one last moment of pure unadulterated love, the precious thing she'd never once known in her life until this damned hard, bittersweet week with Nima. She breathed and breathed the scent of that perfect little girl into the depths of her soul and heart for the last time.

This was always the way the operation would end. She'd just never expected it would hurt so much, like every nerve-ending was being wrenched out of her body with needle-nose pliers. At last she gritted her teeth and smoothed Nima's hair out of her face. "You have to go, baby girl, and I have to stay, but someday I will come and visit you. I promise. Okay?" she asked, her compromise punctuated with gulps and sniffles.

"'Kay," Nima sniffled, her lips pursed together in the saddest pout.

"And Uncle Rory will come with me, and you can show us around your fancy temple up high in the clouds, or wherever you'll be living, okay?" Ember cupped her sweet baby's face in her hands, her heart broken beyond repair as she offered what little strength she had so Nima could leave in peace.

Nima's bottom lip quivered as she very seriously repeated, "'Kay."

Ember kissed her forehead fervently, instilling all of her love into the only child she'd ever loved. "Now, go be the best Dalai Lama the world has ever seen. Make your Mama Ember proud."

Nima threw her arms around Ember's neck and squeezed with all her might, grunting like any little girl who loved her mother with all her heart. She whispered the words Ember never thought could mean so much. "Love you, Mama."

Bravely, Ember loosened her grip. Nima ran to the waiting elevator. The doors closed. And just like that—the most perfect little girl in the world was gone.

Twenty-Two

It's always a bad sign when your child's caregiver cries the minute she sees you.

"It came on suddenly. Last night he sounded like he had a cold, and today he was tired. But then he started with a fever, and before I knew it...." Mrs. Godfrey blew her nose again.

Rory sat beside Tyler's bed, watching the little triangular patch of skin at the bottom of his neck suck in with every labored breath. Too congested to talk, Tyler's wide eyes above the oxygen mask betrayed his fear. He clutched his daddy's thumb tightly in one sweaty little hand.

"You're okay, Tyler. Daddy's here. I'm back and I'm not going anywhere."

Tyler inhaled a ragged wheeze, and Rory wanted to cry. He and Tyler had been in this same situation too many times in the last four years. His little guy seemed terribly frail in the big hospital bed.

"I'm so sorry," Mrs. Godfrey said for the hundredth time.

"It's not your fault, Gwen. Kids get sick. I'm glad you called my office," Rory said kindly, feeling his pockets for the cell phone he knew was no longer there.

"He's been such a good boy. He saved all of the cookies we made just for you. He said he wouldn't eat a single one until you came home."

"Well, we'll have a party when he gets out of here—a sugar cookie party. Would you like that?" Rory leaned in so Tyler could hear him better. But his son was very sick. He didn't care so much about sugar cookies right now.

Rory turned to poor Mrs. Godfrey. "Why don't you go home and get some rest? I'll call if anything changes."

The door no sooner shut behind her than Dr. Brown, Tyler's pediatrician, knocked lightly and let himself in. "My goodness, have you been in a war?"

"No, sir. Just a tough day on the job." Rory touched his fingers to the butterfly bandages across his forehead and cheek. He hadn't had a chance to clean up. The only reason he got Mrs. Godfrey's call at the office was because his cell phone didn't survive the blast that should've by all rights killed him. The TEAM was his second go-to emergency number. It was sheer luck he'd been there.

"It looks like you need to find yourself a different profession, young man. How's our little guy doing?"

"The medicine isn't working. He still can't breathe," Rory said bluntly. "Isn't there another course of action we can try?"

"Let me listen for a minute." Dr. Brown placed a stethoscope on the boy's chest. He moved the stethoscope again and again before he turned back to Rory. "This is my boy who was born early, huh?"

Rory nodded. Dr. Brown had been with him through those first dark days when he thought he'd end up at the cemetery instead of at home. Not once had the good doctor ever doubted his child would live. Ellie's obstetrician blasted Rory for allowing his ex-wife's drug use while he was deployed, but Dr. Brown only ever said Tyler was a fighter—like his dad.

"We both know his immune system is impaired, it will cause him trouble throughout his life. Pneumonia is a problem for youngsters like our Tyler here." Dr. Brown picked up Tyler's hand and checked his fingernails. "Give the medicine time to work. His oxygen saturation is much better. His nails aren't blue anymore. He's already had his flu shot, right?"

"Yes, sir. All immunizations are up to date."

"As I knew they would be," Dr. Brown said as he put a kind hand to Rory's shoulder. "Don't look so glum. We've been through worse, haven't we?"

Rory gulped. Yes. He recalled the days of honestly not knowing from one minute to the next if he should pray for Tyler to live or let the Lord take him. So he'd just thanked God over and over for every single second with his baby. His son.

"He's on a broad-spectrum antibiotic. All we can do right now is keep him hydrated and help him breathe. Listen. I'll make sure you get a cot in here. Go ahead. Get cleaned up. Feel free to take a shower if you want. I am assuming you're staying the night?"

"Yes, sir."

"As I knew you would be." Dr. Brown patted Rory's shoulder one more time. "I'll be back in a couple hours to check on him. It would do you good to get some rest, too."

Rory agreed, but didn't leave. Instead, he smoothed Tyler's sweaty face with a cool cloth and told every bedtime story ever written. He sang lullabies until his sad little boy fell asleep in his arms. And when Tyler slept, Rory dozed, but he never strayed farther than the restroom in his son's room. And when the nurses came in to check Tyler's stats and monitors, or when Dr. Brown returned for more blood work and x-rays, Rory was still there.

"I thought you'd be gone by now?" Ember scanned the empty work cubicles. She'd gone to the restroom to wipe her face and restore a shred of dignity. When she returned, Alex and Kelsey were on their way home. David had already left with the monks. Even Mother had closed up shop in a hurry. The only one remaining was Harley.

A tall, handsome man with hazel eyes that matched his hair, he stood leaning against the customer service counter at Mother's desk, waiting. Harley was one of The TEAM's nicest men. A goofy guy from upstate New York, he'd joined the Army, became a top-notch sniper and the best K-9 handler. He pulled a fake Texas drawl out of his bag of tricks whenever the moment required, and he was drawling plenty tonight. "Well, Miss Annie. I was admiring your shooting back at the ranch and I—"

"Harley, stop. I'm a nerd with a computer degree. I'm not Annie Oakley and I'm not Mrs. Dillon. What do you want?"

Of all the men she'd worked with, he was the one to watch out for. And it wasn't because he was fast with his hands, either. No. Harley had a tender heart and an inherent talent of knowing when one of his teammates was hurting. And sometimes he'd sit right down and cry with them. Other days it might have helped, but not tonight. She didn't need to feel any worse.

"I figured you'd need a ride home," he said softly, the phony drawl stored.

"Oh, yeah." She'd forgotten about that. She'd taken the metro to work the morning the operation started so her brother could change the brake pads on her car. Had he done what she'd asked? Probably not. Knowing her only sibling like she did, he'd most likely let that slide like everything else. "Go home. I'll call a cab. Judy's probably waiting up for you, what with the excitement of being pregnant and everything."

"No, ma'am. I'm escorting you to my Jeep, then I'm driving you home. Get your purse and come on." He offered his arm in a typical Harley-esque cavalier gesture. Native New Yorker or not, he was a southern gentleman through and through.

Ember relented. They walked to the elevator together and were soon on their way to her apartment off King Street in Alexandria. She'd chosen the apartment because it was close to work, close to D.C., and close to Reagan National Airport. But the real reason was the extra large bathroom complete with a tiled shower stall and an antique bathtub she adored. Any other night she'd be thrilled to be getting home early to soak the troubles of the day away. Not tonight.

"Alex is real proud of you," Harley said as he maneuvered through the late night traffic. "I could see it in his eyes."

"I don't care what he thinks. He's not my favorite person right now. David, either."

"It's hard saying goodbye, huh?"

She didn't answer. She didn't have anything nice to say and, *'No shit, Sherlock,'* seemed too harsh for gentle Harley.

"You need a drink?" he offered. "I got time."

Ember shook her head. "No, you don't, Judy's waiting. Besides, I wouldn't do that to you."

"Yeah, but I would for you." For some reason his voice got softer and softer.

"I wouldn't be much of a friend if I went drinking with a recovered alcoholic, now would I?"

"Recovering. Not recovered. We never recover, Ember," he said pensively.

She sighed. "Sorry. You know what I meant."

"I do, but I could always drink a soda. Coffee?"

"I know what you're trying to do, and thanks. I appreciate it, but I want to go home. I need to feed my... my cat and... and...." She choked. And what else? Maple Syrup was all that waited at home. The big fat neutered tomcat probably hadn't even missed her while she was gone. She might as well have a goldfish. Her lazy brother didn't count for beans. He was as bad as the cat—just another type of litter box to clean.

Nima's revelation drifted across time and space. *What do you really want?*

She bit her lip, hoping she could hold it all inside until she made it home. *I don't know.*

"I'm a good listener," Harley continued gallantly. "It's been a helluva day for you from beginning to end, and if you need a shoulder...."

Those warm hazels could tease the living daylights out of you one minute and just as quickly tear up the next. Harley was her friend, and yes, it had been a day she never wanted to repeat. "I don't want to work in the field anymore. I'm no good at it. I won't do it again no matter how much Alex pays."

He reached over for her hand. "It's a tough job, trust me, I know. Judy and I have discussed moving away from here and doing something else for a change, but honestly, I don't think I could find a better bunch of guys and gals to work with."

"You're good at what you do. Alex has a knack for hiring the best. We all know you're one of them."

"That's kind of you to say, but I look around our office some days and wonder what I'm doing in the middle of a bunch of geniuses like you and Mother. You gals are the smart ones. I only know how to shoot straight. Some days I wonder if I belong anywhere."

She knew the feeling. The lifelong feeling she shouldn't have been born argued with what she felt for Rory. He'd sure taken off in a hurry. She hid her insecurities from Harley. He didn't need to know how worthless she felt sometimes, like now. "You know better. That's your addict side talking. Are you still taking your meds and doing all those other things you're supposed to be doing?"

He arched a devilish brow. "Knock it off. I'm supposed to be cheering you up."

She sniffed. *I'm the one who doesn't belong.* Her apartment was only blocks away. *Please drive faster, Harley. I don't want to cry in front of you.*

In minutes, he pulled up to the curb in front of her apartment, still holding onto her hand. "Are you going to be okay?"

"I'm fine."

"No, you're not, but you will be." Want one or not, he pulled her into a big sideways hug. "Go on in and take a nice hot bubble bath, have yourself a good hard cry, and you'll feel better in no time."

"Does Judy do that when she's had a hard day?" Ember pulled out of his arms before she started crying ahead of the bubble bath he recommended.

"Heck no. Judy's tougher than me. That's what I do," he said in all seriousness.

She almost laughed out loud. Harley in a bubble bath would be a funny sight. She pushed out of his arms. "You're a good friend. Thanks."

"No problem, little lady. Like I said before, I'm a good listener. So is Judy. If you need anything, you let me know." He looked so serious. "We're here to help each other get through days like this. I mean it. Call me."

"I will. Thanks."

"I'll see you in the morning."

She turned at the doorway to her apartment building and waved to let him know she was home safe and sound. With a quick wave of acknowledgement, off he went in his bright, arrest-me-red Jeep, home to Judy and the wonderful news of his new happy family. And into the apartment building she went to—her cat, and possibly her deadbeat brother.

Ember unlocked her apartment door. Resting for a moment in friendly arms was what she'd needed, but the arms were wrong. They should've been Rory's, not Harley's. And she didn't have a clue what happened once Rory'd taken the phone call at the office. He'd disappeared without a single word when she needed him most, walked out like the mission was over. *Slam. Bam. Thank you, ma'am. Don't let the door hit you on the way out.*

When she snapped the light on, there sprawled Mr. Why-are-you-bothering-me Maple Syrup on the coffee table. His perturbed golden eyes narrowed like she'd disturbed the peace and quiet of his private lair.

"Hi," she said. Her silly greeting sounded hollow and loud in the otherwise empty room. The big cat rolled over on his back and promptly fell off the coffee table. Instead of coming to see her, he curled up under the table and went back to sleep without so much as a welcome home meow. Yeah, he missed her all right. As usual.

She turned on her music and let the sounds of ocean waves fill the place like they usually did. But tonight the soothing refrain irritated her. It resonated with the sound of too much—nothing. She snapped the contraption off. *What do you really want?*

Until this operation, she'd filled her heart and soul with things that now felt like absolutely nothing. At the end of an excruciating hard day at work, coming home to nothing was still—nothing. No matter how much she owned or how much she filled her apartment with peaceful, soothing music, it wasn't filling her soul at all, not the way her short time with Nima had.

What she used to think important was milk when she truly craved meat. It was a fat lazy cat when she desperately wanted a baby girl with soft blue eyes. It was Harley's hug of friendship when she yearned for the magnetic pull of Rory's strong arms holding her together. Anything less was just plain nothing.

Arghhh! My life sucks! Scrunching her fingers through her hair, she cried. Nima was gone, probably thirty-five thousand feet over the Atlantic by now. She was on her way to the Himalayas with a bunch of monks and a frumpy woman who didn't know the first thing about fashion, much less little girls.

And where was Rory? Maybe he'd had enough. Maybe she'd embarrassed him when she'd thrown herself at him when he'd rescued her. Of course, he probably couldn't wait to see Tyler. She didn't blame him, but he could have given her a goodbye kiss, or a handshake—or something.

What's wrong with me? Why am I falling apart? Is this emotional breakdown the result of all the adrenaline? Of killing all those guys? Of losing Nima?

She collapsed on the couch, more tired than she thought possible. But duty called. She wiped her face and cleaned the litter box, changed Maple Syrup's water bowl and refreshed his food. Next she tackled the clutter of dirty dishes in the sink and on the counter. *Wow, damn it. Gone for a week and Larry trashed the place.*

Moving from room to room, she stuffed empty pizza boxes, potato chip bags, beer cans and bottles into a large black garbage bag. Her second trip netted dirty clothes, socks, and underwear that never made it to the hamper. The pig.

Her home looked better, but her mood worsened by the time she peeled out of her filthy, blood-spattered clothes and stepped into the mounds of bubbles like Harley recommended.

The iron tub was her favorite feature of the apartment. Old-fashioned, with brass clawed feet, it had been restored with an elegant gold gooseneck faucet and handles. She sank lower into the steaming pool of relaxation. Her muscles relaxed. The blood dissolved off her skin. For a moment the hot water and bubbles felt good. It almost worked.

Maple Syrup stared at her, not willing to entertain the notion of coming too near the water.

"Come here, Kitty Kitty," she coaxed. "I could really use the company. Don't leave."

He twitched his whiskers and turned about face, his tail whipping from side to side.

"Don't go," she murmured. "I've been gone for days. You're usually happy to see me. What's wrong?"

Like he would answer. The haughty cat stalked out of the bathroom, his tail still twitching. *He's just mad because I've been gone a long time. He'll get over it. Just like I'll get over living without Nima. And Rory. And—* She melted into tears.

The memory of Rory beneath the shower spray at the first safe house intervened, and she wanted him there in the tub with her. Now. And Nima, too. She wanted that little girl with her, giggling in this tub, playing like they had at McCormack's before Rory barged in and saw them both naked. The look on his face....

Ember sank lower until the bubbles came up to her nose. That way her tears didn't have far to fall. The operation had been so damned hard, but she'd never felt so needed or so loved before in her life. What was she supposed to do now? Be happy she hadn't died? Was this all there was to living? An empty house and a cat with an attitude problem?

She blew the bubbles away from her face, and then she blew again. Before she knew it, every last annoying bubble had been blown, pushed, and kicked over the edge of the tub.

The floor ran with soapy water. The bath mat and towels were drenched. Her life sucked.

But then, because Mrs. Smoot in the apartment below would complain if water leaked through her ceiling; and because Ember lived with a lazy cat that hated water; and because there was no one else to do it, she climbed out of the tub and cleaned up the mess. And that's the problem when a person lives alone and decides to have a temper tantrum. No one cares.

When the bathroom floor was dry enough, she lugged the waterlogged towels to her washing machine, set it on spin, and let the machine do its thing. She wrapped herself up in her most comfortable bathrobe and put herself to bed, wet hair and all.

Just in case, she dialed Rory's cell phone and listened to it ring. He didn't answer. Oh, yeah. Caller ID. He could avoid her forever. She threw her cell phone at the wall. It would've shattered if Alex had thrown it. Hers bounced.

She couldn't even do that right.

Bereft is a good word.

So are miserable, devastated, inconsolable, and a bunch of other words in the thesaurus. Ember lugged them all with her as she stepped off the elevator the next morning. Like her waterlogged towels, they weighed her down. She hoped to see Rory, but his workspace was empty. Mother's wasn't. *Damn.*

"You have to tell me everything that happened while you and Junior Agent Dennison were running for your lives all over the country." Mother's bright blue eyes were as nosy as the rest of her. She read people a little too well and deduced how they felt long before they knew.

Ember's feelings were cloaked behind dark glasses and an intense need to get a grip. She'd known enough heartbreak and rejection before. Recovery was just a matter of time and the right makeup, hair-do, or clothes. "Not now. I need to get the debriefing done for Alex before I forget everything." She pulled her chair out and opened her computer for the day. As much as she enjoyed working with her cubicle partner, there were days when it was hard to get anything done.

"Come on, Ember. I've been sitting by myself for a week now waiting for you to get back. I bet you're glad I called the first night, huh? You didn't even know about those two cars at the first safe house, did you?" Mother was as determined as ever.

"Please. Not today. I'm busy." Ember didn't mean her words to come out nasty. She didn't want to talk about anything, especially not with the office gossipmonger.

Mother sniffed, her feelings hurt—or not. Also a master manipulator, she could use a tear here or an innocent look there to turn things her way.

Ember ignored her and pulled up the master debriefing template she'd have to complete as quickly as possible. *Wow. Who dreamed up these dumb questions?* Exact times. Precautions taken. Number of rounds fired. Windage. Elevation. Mileage. Location. The template looked more like a sniper's log than an operational report. And how would she know the elevation of every shot she'd taken, especially while they were running for their lives in the middle of a

Pennsylvania cornfield? She didn't have the luxury of a spotter or a Leupold rangefinder in the backseat, damn it.

She glanced over her monitor to Rory's desk. He said he'd help with this report. Where was he?

Means of transportation? *Sheesh! Let me think. Brand new Taurus. Brand new but slightly battered Taurus. Beat to hell Taurus, and, oh, yes, let's not forget the freaking train that nearly ripped my leg off. Then there was the smooth ride in a luxury sedan. Oh, wait. It blew up, too!*

Destruction of property. Provide exact details for insurance purposes. *Like the first safe house? McCormack's cute little mother-in-law bungalow? All my clothes?*

She closed the online debriefing form and browsed her email instead. Alex expected too damned much. She'd think about the stupid report later. "Anyone seen Dennison yet?" she asked without looking up.

"Nope," Mother replied huffily.

Be mad. I don't care. I am so not telling you anything about the op.

Ember snapped her computer shut and walked away, glancing at Rory's empty desk as she stalked to the women's restroom. Mother would come looking for her, but for a few minutes Ember had complete privacy. She hit redial on her cell phone and listened when no one answered on the other end. Rory was still avoiding her.

Splashing cold water on her face didn't do much to restore her disposition. When she returned to her desk, she found a bundle of folders and a note from David to come see him. She took the bundle and stalked over to his desk. "What's this, Tao?"

"Good morning, Ember. It's the background investigations into the High Lamas and Kamalya. Mother and I compiled it. We'd like your input before we send it into Alex. Is that a problem?"

"What could I possibly know about your investigation? I was in another safe house getting my ass shot off, or did you forget?"

David's eyes narrowed. He might not be able to read her through her dark glasses, but he got the drift. She was as sure of that as the fact she was making a fool of herself. Well, just damned great. Even Harley watched the drama from his workspace. Taylor Armstrong, one of the newest agents in the office, glanced in her direction before he swiveled his chair around to mind his own business. Junior Agent Steven Oakes, another rookie, did the same. Ember didn't care. David had undermined Rory and her every step of the way. He needed to back off.

"Ember. Listen—" He started to say something in his usual calm and extra gentle manner, but she cut him off, right at the knees.

"No, you listen, Tao. If you'd done a little more of your fancy investigating the first time around, we wouldn't have gotten our asses kicked at the last safe house, would we? And those old guys, those other monks, they'd still be alive, wouldn't they? Everything is your fault. You brought a murderer right into Alex and Kelsey's home because you didn't do your job. You should've known who those guys were, but you didn't, did you?" She glared down at him, making no attempt to lower her voice or hide her feelings.

"Ember, there was no way anyone could have known—"

"And there's no way I'm touching this, either." She tossed the folders on his desk. "Do it yourself."

His voice conciliatory, he stood and took a step toward her. "Come on, Emb—"

"Go to hell, Tao."

Twenty-Three

Little by little, the medicines worked. Little by little, Tyler smiled. And little by little, Rory knew everything was going to be okay. He stopped being the obsessive father. He even took a quick walk to the cafeteria and called Ember. Unfortunately, she was away from her desk, but no matter. He'd call her at home later. Calling her cell phone was out. It must've gotten damaged in the last firefight like his did.

"Knock, knock," Tyler croaked. Still plenty pale with dark circles under his eyes, at least his fever was down.

"Who's there?" Rory asked for the tenth or twelfth time.

"Boo." Tyler's brown eyes lit up with delighted anticipation.

"Boo, who?" He always was a sucker for a good knock-knock joke.

"Ha! Boo who! Whatcha... crying for... Daddy?" Tyler gasped and giggled. It took him a full minute before he could catch his breath, but soon enough the coughing attack ceased. He was officially off the oxygen mask and ready to go home. Today was the day. After five days in the pediatric ward, they were headed home for a sugar cookie party and a long daddy/son nap.

Rory bundled his son in an extra warm blanket and strapped him safely into the back seat of his mini-van. He didn't drive his Mercedes sports car much anymore, and he didn't care. The short drive home tired the boy out, so the first order of business was naptime. His apartment was not like those exclusive singles set-ups with pools and saunas and clubhouses nearby, but it was clean, fairly new, and the right size for a single father. They both had their own bedrooms, but Tyler was prone to show up in the middle of the night and schmooze his way into Rory's. He didn't care. It's not like anyone else was there.

He tucked Tyler into his own bed and set his antibiotics and inhaler on the kitchen counter. He made a pitcher of orange juice and checked the freezer for something to defrost for dinner. Mrs. Godfrey had fixed several frozen entrees. Her meatloaf was always good, but he opted for chicken noodle soup instead. Tyler was an easy customer as long as his meal came with noodles.

Resting the freezer bag of soup in a pan of cold water in the kitchen sink, he checked to see how his son was breathing before he tackled the stack of mail on the counter. Tyler was sound asleep and breathing easy. Rory sighed. So far, so good.

He delved into the litter of junk mail and bills Mrs. Godfrey had dutifully collected while he was gone. Between the paper shredder and the basket for incoming bills, he made short work of the nuisance mail. And in the monotony of letter sorting, the events at the final safe house flooded back to him. The explosion in the alley should've killed him. It was only by the grace of God that he'd come to with nothing more than a good laceration to his forehead and a knot on his head. He was proud of Ember. She'd fought tooth and nail to protect Nima.

His thoughts drifted. But darn. She'd nearly stopped his heart when she'd traipsed through McCormack's place in nothing but a black towel that barely hid her curves or her long legs. Catching her in the tub was surprise enough. There weren't nearly enough bubbles to cover that gorgeous body of hers, but the black towel escapade was another sight altogether.

He'd lost more than his last shred of common sense when she'd stalked back up the stairs. Of course he'd wanted to strip it off her. Her audaciously free spirit was hard to resist, and he was just a man, a very lonely man now he had time to think of it—of her.

She was right. For years he'd built a wall of secrecy, while her wall was built of black eyeliner, weird hair colors, and outrageous outfits. Nima's words flooded his heart. *If you hide, no one can find you.* Ember and he had both done a darned good job of hiding, but now he'd been found. So had she. It was time to move on and maybe make a move. On her.

Pictures of her transformation circled back around. She'd changed from the nut job in the local freak show to one of the most beautiful women he'd ever known. He picked up his house phone and dialed her office number.

Her voice mail message came on instantly. *"This is Junior Agent Ember Davis, genius and clairvoyant technician for Mr. Alexander Stewart. Please leave a name, number, and a message. I will call you when I get around to it. Maybe. Thank you!"*

Rory smiled. Yes, that was his girl through and through. He hesitated but hung up, leaving no message. That would be too impersonal. No. He wanted to hear her breath catch when he said, *'Hi there, beautiful.'* He wanted to sit back and listen to the silly, musical way she laughed. And he wanted to picture the sultry come hither look in her eyes when she whispered so Mother couldn't overhear their conversation.

He set the handset back in its charger. Tyler would sleep for a little while, then they'd eat dinner. Maybe once he was down for the night, there would be time to call Ember when he could have her all to himself.

But Tyler's first night home came with nightmares that Daddy was gone and a temperature Rory couldn't force down, not even with a cool bath. By 1 a.m., he was in the emergency room with Dr. Brown, and Tyler was back on oxygen.

Rory went home exhausted at 6 a.m., another antibiotic in his pocket and a still sick little boy in his arms. Pushing his apartment door open with his shoulder because his hands were full, he dropped his keys on the coffee table, and settled himself and Tyler on the living room couch.

And there they stayed for the next two days.

Alex could be so damned rude.

Ember re-worked her final debrief for the third freaking time. If he made one single red mark on this one, she was through. And that was another thing. Why couldn't a man who was smart enough to start a business and run it successfully learn to use the track changes feature on his computer? Why did she have to print every report, waste paper like it grew on trees, and, and....

"Do you need some help?" Mother asked in her usual solicitous way, hovering over Ember's shoulder like the patron saint of busybodies.

"No. Just tweaking it one last time so Alex will sign it," Ember replied with a restrained edge to her voice.

It had been a week since she'd come back to work and still no Rory in sight. She'd asked Alex, but he politely replied Rory was on personal leave. *Well, thank you very much, Mr. Boss Man. Who the hell didn't already figured that out?* He never divulged personal information, so she went back to her desk and waited and retyped and waited some more. Finally, he stood at her desk again, the same damned debriefing in his hand.

"What?" *Was it good enough or not? Did it pass muster?* She didn't know if she cared anymore.

"Do you have time to talk with me?" he asked, ignoring her nasty tone. He was difficult to read sometimes. Those icy blue eyes betrayed nothing, the problem with working with covert operators.

"Yes. I'll be right there."

He waited at his door. As soon as she entered, he shut it. "Please have a seat."

The only chairs in his office were the four around his small conference table and the one at the side of his desk, so she sat there. He took his usual chair behind his desk.

She liked looking at Alex. He was a handsome man for a boss; lean, athletic and extremely intelligent with dark hair and the barest hint of silver showing at his temples. Alex was a proud man and it showed. Today he wore a charcoal suit, with a crisply ironed white shirt and maroon tie.

Did Kelsey iron his shirts and dress him? Whoever did the actual buying and dressing at the Stewart home, it didn't matter. He was a fine sight every single day. And while he could be tough as nails, he could also be quite the opposite. She liked Alex as much as she liked anyone at the moment. Not so much.

"You're having a tough time with the debriefing report." He stated the obvious very well.

So? She waited, not sure what he wanted.

"I'd like you to talk with someone," he said gently, setting the report aside.

"Who? Murphy? Roy? What about?"

"No one here. I think you need to talk with someone else. I've got a couple suggestions, but it's entirely up to you."

She fidgeted in her chair. This might not be about the report at all. Alex was hinting at something else, and she didn't like the sound of it. He was about to get personal.

"About what?" she asked, her impatience showing.

"About the Lobsang op," he said softly.

He'd finally spit it out. *That wasn't so hard now, was it?*

Ember fidgeted again. Her temper tantrum knew no bounds. She'd become meaner with each passing day, crying in the women's rest room at the drop of a hat and snarky with everyone dumb enough to come within range. Harley was the only one still on her good side. She bit her lip, not willing to discuss anything beyond the facts of the operation. *Just the facts. Don't be nice to me and DO NOT mention Nima. Or Rory.*

"You miss her, don't you?"

Great! Stab me in the heart, why don't you? A kind touch was as good as a kick in the gut when you're already down.

And Ember was as down as she'd ever been. She couldn't answer if she wanted. Plus, her dark glasses were sitting by her computer instead of on her nose.

"Would you like to know what Nima said that morning at my house?"

Yeah, she wanted to know, but not now. Maybe when her heart wasn't so raw. Like never.

He didn't wait for an answer. "That sweet little girl of yours laid her head on my chest exactly the way Abby did when she was alive. All she said was, 'Daddy.'"

She didn't have to look at Alex to know he was emotional. When it came to children, and especially little girls, he was ten kinds of creampuffs all rolled into one. "It was exactly like I was holding Abby in my arms. I swear. For a second there, she even looked like Abby. I heard my daughter's voice again, but do you know what Nima did then?"

He was teary-eyed, and so was she. "What?" she asked softly, no longer needing to strike out at him. Alex had truly suffered in his life. She couldn't be mean to him, not anymore.

"She did this." Alex came around his desk, took her by the hand and lifted her off the chair. He pulled her close and leaned in to her face. Ember held her breath, afraid he might kiss her. He didn't. Very gently, he brushed his eyelashes across her cheek. In that instant, Nima's sweet smile sprang to her mind. She gasped, basking in Nima's unconditional love again.

"She gave me butterfly kisses, Ember," he said hoarsely. "That's all. It was nothing miraculous or out of the ordinary, but it was exactly what Abby used to do when she'd climb up on my lap after a hard day. She'd give me those kisses and make me believe I was a hero again. For a moment there with Nima, I totally believed I was holding Abby again."

Ember fell into those sad blue eyes and it all spilled out. "I miss her, Alex. Is that what you want to hear? I didn't think I'd ever miss anyone as much as I miss her. I mean," she coughed and sputtered. "It hurts. It physically hurts! God! It's like I've got a knife sticking through my heart. Every move I make, everything I do, it just goes in deeper and harder and... I miss her, damn it!"

"I know," he groaned. "God, I know, Ember. Honest. I really do." He pulled her into his arms and just held her.

Oh, freaking just great! This was as bad as Rory helping put her pants on. She couldn't stop crying so she didn't fight the kind embrace. Nima's infectious giggle echoed in her head, so did her bright smile in the bubble bath at McCormack's place; the cute way she'd wrestled with Rory the last day when he washed her face. And chocolate. Where in the high Himalayas would Nima ever get chocolate again, huh? And where the hell was Rory?

She cried. Alex gave her tissues. She was tired to her core, the laughing stock of the office and losing her grip. Todd's death had been hard enough to bounce back from, but this felt worse. Losing Nima ripped everything good out of her life by the deep dark roots. Her life had been one gut-wrenching loss after another. Enough!

Alex settled on the front edge of his desk composing himself while she mopped her face and tried to recover some semblance of pride. This was so not about the debriefing report.

"Kelsey would like to take you out for coffee, Ember. She knows what you're going through. She asked if you'd be interested. It's no big deal, just two mothers talking over coffee."

"I'm not a mother."

"Maybe not in the traditional sense, but you've lost a child. Kelsey understands."

"I can't. Not yet." *Probably never.*

"Don't worry. She just thinks you're one of the sweetest women she's known in a long time, and she knows you're hurting. She cares. That's the only reason she asked. But another person you might like to talk to is a friend of mine, Dr. Payne."

Ember about snorted. "Oh, that's rich. Dr. Payne? What kind of a doctor has a name like that?"

Alex didn't get the joke. "He's a behavioral psychologist and I'm simply offering. He helped Kelsey and me a few years back. I've got his number if you'd like someone to talk to."

"Why'd you and Kelsey go to him?"

"Before we got married, we'd both been through some hard times. I'm sure you remember. I had some anger issues. Kelsey'd just lost her boys. She was lost. I was an ass. Dr Payne helped us learn how to communicate a little better with each other. He's a good man. Jed recommended him to me and I'm recommending him to you."

"You don't think I know how to communicate?" she sniffed.

"I just think you might need someone to talk with. I'll give you his number and you decide. It's entirely up to you."

She sniffed again. She'd take the number. She could always toss it later.

"But the real reason I called you in here is to tell you how proud I am of what you did." He leaned over and placed his hand on her shoulder. Ember looked him in the eye. "You gave that little girl what she needed at the worst possible moment in her life. You went above and beyond the call of duty. You gave Nima safety, a measure of stability, and most important, you gave her love, Ember. She'd just seen her father assassinated, but you risked everything to save her life. You acted precisely like her mother."

That did it. Ember covered her face with her hands, leaned onto her knees and sobbed. "And it's killing me! Damn you, it's killing me! I've got... I've got a hole in my heart the size of freaking Texas. I don't know how you and Kelsey lived through this shit! I hurt every minute of every single day, and Nima wasn't even mine!"

"The second you begin to love them, they're yours," he said, his hand clamped onto her shoulder. He didn't let go. She sobbed into her knees and he placed several tissues into her wringing hands. Every part of her hurt until she wanted to throw up if only vomiting would expel the knives slicing her heart to ribbons. This loss felt more like being flayed alive. If only Rory were here, maybe she could cope; maybe he could help her understand. But he wasn't. *He's gone. Nima's gone. But I'm still here!*

Alex let her cry until the storm was spent. Nothing could be more embarrassing, but strangely, Alex holding onto her and letting her cry helped. Because he did know. He hurt for his little girl every single day and she got it. She wasn't alone like she thought she was. And maybe she was stronger than she thought she was, too. She didn't feel like it, but maybe.

"I wish tear ducts were on the bottom of our feet," she whimpered, the outburst over for the time being. Even that reminded her of Rory. "I, umm, need my dark glasses. I left them at my desk."

He was out the door and back in a minute with her sunglasses in hand. When she put them on, she swallowed what little dignity she had left and stood. "I'll think about your Dr. Payne," she said softly. "Thanks for talking with me."

"We've all been there, Ember. Every single one of those guys out there knows what you're going through, too. They're worried about you."

She stuffed the tissues into her sleeve and opened the door, her eyes forward and not looking at all those concerned guys and gals. At least Alex hadn't given her the debriefing report to do over, not that she'd have done it. She was tired. She was through.

There was only one thing left to do.

Morning came too early at the Dennison household.

Tyler still snored softly, his little body sprawled face down on Rory's chest. This was his idea of heaven on earth, his son sound asleep in his arms, breathing in and out like a healthy kid. No congestion. No rattle in his throat. Just his usual little boy snore. Rory dozed and let his son sleep as long as he needed. The latest antibiotic seemed to have done the trick. Tyler slept fitfully for the first time in days. So did his father.

When he woke again, he glanced around the apartment, thinking of the crazy scarf he'd made Ember buy in Ohio. She looked good in bright colors, but he'd lost track of it.

And now Thanksgiving was just around the corner. He needed to call his folks in Nebraska as much as he needed to call Ember. But she had yet to pick up her office phone when he called. It rang once and immediately went to her voice mail message. Her cell phone was the same so he'd stopped trying. Her home phone was no better. He was beginning to worry. Had something else happened while he was on leave?

Tyler stirred and coughed, stretched and yawned. "Hi, Daddy. Whatcha doing in my bed?"

Rory smoothed his hand over his son's shoulders and down his back. "Whose bed?"

Tyler chuckled. "Ha. I like sleeping on the couch."

"Are you hungry yet?"

Tyler's nose scrunched up as he thought really hard for all of two seconds. "Yep!"

The single word reminded Rory of another motherless soul. He brushed the pain-filled reminder of Nima away. "Come on, buddy. How about pancakes and eggs?"

"Kin you make 'em look like punkins?"

"How about turkeys? It's almost Thanksgiving." Rory had pancake molds for every season of the year and a couple others just for fun. Anything to make his little guy smile.

"Yeah! Turkeys! I yike turkeys, Daddy."

Rory ruffled his son's curly hair as they rolled off the couch together. They could practice enunciating those pesky

L words later. "I can make those pancakes fly if they'd make you happy."

"You can? Wow!" Tyler's eyes were as big as the pancakes would be, but the word brought a pinch to Rory's heart. On their way to the kitchen he dialed Ember's phone just to hear her say, '*Wow,*' again, too.

She didn't answer. Where was she? His heart hurt. He needed to know.

After breakfast, he stripped the sheets off their beds while Tyler played in the tub. When his house phone rang, he scrambled to get it. *Ember!*

"Hello, son. How are you doing?" His father's voice boomed through the phone.

"Hi, Dad. We're good," Rory answered, juggling the phone on his shoulder. He hoped he'd masked the disappointment in his voice while he helped Tyler out of the tub and into a towel.

"Glad to hear that because your mother and I are flying in for a visit tomorrow."

"Wow, tomorrow? Sure. Great." Rory ran a hand through his hair at the unexpected news.

"Anything wrong? You sound a little tired. Have you been sick?"

His father knew him well enough to know he was holding something back, so Rory spilled the beans. "Tyler has, but he's good now. When does your flight get in?"

Rory wrapped Tyler in a bath sheet while he jotted down the information and talked with his father for a while. He told him about the pneumonia and how sick Tyler had been. And of course, his father scolded him for not calling when Tyler first went into the hospital, but that's the way grandfathers were.

He didn't, however, tell his father about the Lobsang operation. That was his secret to keep. His parents had worried enough while he was deployed to Iraq. They didn't need to know the downside to his current job.

"You're sure we're not putting you two boys out?" his father asked.

"Heavens no. You and Mom never put us guys out. Tyler can room with me while you're here. Do you want to talk to him for a minute?"

Tyler took the phone and chatted with his Grandpa and Grandma. He was their only grandchild at the moment, and they visited as often as possible, but especially around the holidays. It would be good to see them again.

"Love you, Grampa." Tyler blew smacking kiss sounds into the phone and handed it back to Rory, his eyes lit with excitement instead of fever. "Grampa coming to see me!"

Rory ended the conversation with his father.

"How about we take our medicine to make sure you feel good while they're here?"

Tyler stuck both arms into his shirt as Rory pulled it over his head. "'Kay."

"And then let's have a sugar cookie party. We can frost them with orange and black and...." Rory thought of the silly scarf. "Maybe we'll go visit a special friend of mine."

Tyler wiggled his jeans up over his backside. "Be a robot!"

Rory immediately went into his jerky, robot dance routine. Tyler giggled and screamed at his daddy's scary automated sounding voice. Rory picked him up like an airplane and sailed him into the kitchen where his antibiotics were. Life was back to normal at the Dennison household. Almost.

Later that morning, father and son went for a quick ride. Rory picked up a bouquet of orange and bronze carnations on the way to Ember's apartment with a plate of orange and chocolate frosted sugar cookies. She shouldn't be working on Saturday, but if she were, he'd head to the office and surprise her there.

Tyler was excited to be out and about. It would be a quick visit. Then he'd get Tyler back home in time for his afternoon nap. But right now Rory needed to know how Ember was doing. He needed her. Warmth spilled out of his heart. The air seemed crisper. Oak and maple leaves appeared brighter and more radiant along with all those other colors she loved.

With an extra bounce in his step, he entered her apartment building. Instead of taking the elevator, he opted for the stairs, clearing them two at a time even with Tyler on his shoulders.

Tyler hung on tight, giggling with every bounce. "Again! Again!" he squealed when they reached the second level, urging Rory on like he was the racehorse and Tyler the jockey.

"We're already there," Rory announced when he spotted Ember's apartment number two doors to the right. "Number two eighteen. See?"

"Oh, goodie. Kin I knock?"

Rory tilted his son into the door until he could reach it enough to knock. It was time to share his son and life with this amazing woman. She had to be home. He could kiss her at her apartment, and he very much wanted to kiss her again.

Tyler gave three quiet knocks, while Rory pressed the doorbell. "How are you doing up there?"

"I good, Daddy!" Tyler thumped the top of his father's head in excitement. "I knocked!"

Rory smirked to himself. He was humming the theme song from, of all things, Tyler's favorite television show. He definitely needed to get out of his apartment more often. But no one answered. He sighed and rang the doorbell one last time. Dang it. She wasn't home.

As he turned to leave, the door cracked open. Some punk with a bright yellow Mohawk stuck his face out, squinting like a mole in the bright light of day. He smelled of bad breath and—pot. Rory's hackles lifted. What was this jerk doing in her home?

"Whatcha want, man? Whatcha selling?"

"Isn't this Ember Davis's apartment?" he asked as he pulled Tyler off his shoulders, shielding him from the fumes wafting out the open door and into the hall.

"She ain't here." The guy had yellow teeth and straggly hairs on his chin. He scratched his nose and other body parts while he talked.

"When will she be back?" Rory asked politely.

The punk belched. "Sorry. I kinda been sick and, umm, whatcha want again?" He scratched his shaved scalp alongside the Mohawk, like it might help his brain work.

"I asked when will Ember return."

"Uh, I don't know. She don't come home much anymore. You wanna leave her a message or something?" The guy scrunched up his face like it was hard to think rationally.

Rory took a tablet and pen out of his inner jacket pocket and scribbled a quick note to Ember that said, '*Call me.*

Rory.' He included his new cell phone number. "Tell her Rory Dennison came by to visit. Make sure she gets this." He handed his message along with the flowers and cookies to the guy at the door.

"Umm, yeah, man. Sure thing. Roy Dennis. Got it."

"No. The name is Rory Dennison. Rory. Not Roy."

"Whatever. I got it."

"Who are you?" Rory really wanted to ask, *'Who the hell are you?'*

The guy scrunched up his nose. It seemed to be his intelligent look for the day. He weaved back and forth like he might go down for the count. "I'm Larry, her main squeeze. It don't get no better than this, ya know what I mean?" he said, belching while he offered a Vanna White flourish down his scrawny body.

Rory stepped away, thoroughly disgusted. Tyler'd seen enough, but the punk at the door turned friendly.

"'S okay, man." He stepped out of the door and poor Tyler got a bigger eyeful than any little boy needed. Larry was dressed in black briefs—and nothing else. His scrawny chest and shoulder were inked with some bright red tribal tattoo. The punk looked like he was wearing tights. Ink covered his thighs and legs. For some reason, the idiot had pierced both hairy nipples. Not a pretty sight.

Rory turned his son away from the scene while Larry, the pothead, waved goodbye. "See you later, man. I'll be sure to give her the stuff, Roy."

And Rory wished Larry would shut up, go back inside and close the door.

"Wow, Daddy. He smelled icky," Tyler said as they walked to the car.

"He did, didn't he?" Rory belted Tyler into his booster seat, his mind a thousand miles away. He didn't know much about Ember's home life other than she had a cat, Maple Syrple, or some other off the wall name like that.

He was pretty sure she didn't have a man in her life right now, regardless what the doper, Larry, said. The punk said she wasn't home most of the time. Then where was she? Ember didn't do drugs, so what was some addict doing in her home? She could lose everything if anyone decided to call the police, yet Larry certainly hadn't hidden what he was doing.

"How are you feeling, Tyler?" Roy asked. "You ready to go home yet?"

"I fine," Tyler said, but Rory knew better. His son wasn't bouncing much anymore.

Instead of the impromptu visit to his office, they went straight home for lunch and naptime. Tyler went out like a light after that.

At last he dialed Ember's number. "Hey. This is Rory. I've been calling you for days now. We need to talk. Call me. I left something for you at your apartment today. Hope to hear from you soon. I love you, sweetheart."

There. That ought to get her attention.

Twenty-Four

Rory's parents adored Tyler. They'd all but moved to Virginia four years ago when he was born with complications. Rory's mother baked. His father built a walk-in closet in Rory's bedroom, and all because they were scared Baby Tyler wouldn't survive.

The news of this bout of pneumonia sent them into another tailspin. Rory's mother started baking and cooking the moment she arrived. His father decided the kitchen needed granite counter tops and immediately got in his wife's way. Rory smiled and stayed out of the kitchen. He knew when not to argue.

The news they'd decided to stay for Thanksgiving was welcome, too. Tyler was Grandpa's little helper and Grandma's best boy in the whole world. For once, Rory took a long nap on the couch without worry while Tyler got the daylight spoiled out of him. And all was right with the world.

The day after they arrived, Rory went back to work. It was a beautiful November day, chilly and bright with the definite hint of frost in the air. Autumn colors glowed everywhere. Red and orange oaks, sugar maples, golden aspen, it seemed the whole world was decked in the bright colors Ember loved. And because she loved them, Rory loved them.

For the first time in a long time, he drove his Mercedes to work. Instead of taking the elevator after he parked in The TEAM's underground secure lot, he ran up the stairs taking them two and three at a time. He arrived on the second floor without even breathing hard. It was a beautiful day—until he saw her.

He had to look twice. Ember? Where was the bright, vibrant blonde who loved little children and possibly him? Only a week had passed, but she'd changed. A lot. Dressed in black from head to toe, her gorgeous honey blonde hair was dyed black and twisted into shiny sharp spikes. Her feet and legs were encased in butt-high platform boots that made her look like an Amazon woman. She was a mix between steam punk, Goth maybe, and Rory didn't know what else. The spiked dog collar around her neck looked pretty damned sharp, too.

The rest of her clothing consisted of an extremely tight-fitting black leather jacket someone had taken a switchblade to for the sake of—fashion? Horizontal slashes marked it front and back, up and down the sleeves. A leather skirt completed the ensemble, or whatever she called it. Her pretty face concerned Rory the most. He stood there speechless. He'd never seen so much black eyeliner, lipstick, and mascara. It made her look cold. Hard. Sad.

"What are you looking at?" she snapped when he finally caught her eye.

This was not how he'd envisioned their reunion. "Umm, nothing."

Harley and David were at his desk in a minute with the latest sports highlights, all the operations in progress, which agent was where, and who'd just returned. But Rory couldn't take his eyes off Ember. After a few minutes of guy talk, Alex rounded Mother's counter. "Rory, it's about time you showed up. Good to have you back. How's everything at home?"

Rory shook his boss's hand. "Home is good. It's good to be back."

"Grab a cup of coffee and get settled. Then I need to see you and Ember in my office. Let me know when you're ready."

"Right now is fine with me. How about you, Ember?" Rory asked.

She didn't look up. "I'll be there."

He would've been more than happy to walk with her, but she bee-lined to Alex's office a step ahead of him. Alex sat at his conference table waiting, the debriefing report spread in front of him. "I have your final reports. Good job, you two. I'd like to clear up a couple discrepancies since you're both here."

"Sure. Anything you need, I'm sure we can help," Rory said, by now feeling the cold shoulder from Ember's direction. Or was it the rock solid ice cold shoulder? He glanced sideways at her. What on earth happened while he was off?

One by one Alex listed the few things he needed to understand better, like how Ember injured her leg.

"That was my fault," Rory answered immediately. "I underestimated the distance—"

"It was not," she snapped. "I hit a wall, exactly like I said in my report."

Alex glanced from her to Rory. "Anything to add?"

He stared Alex down. "I was agent in charge. That makes it my fault."

Alex wrote a few words in the margin of the report. "And the hospital stay in Chicago? Who do I send a check to?"

"I can get the address for—"

Ember jumped to her feet and stood over Alex's shoulder, pointing to her report with an ugly black fingernail. "Oh, for hell's sake, I put it right there. See? On this line."

He squinted at the report. "I see it now," he said softly.

Ember sat with a huff and crossed her long leather-covered legs. Rory sighed. Right now he didn't recognize the woman who sat beside him. At all.

"And I understand I owe David another car?" Alex peered over his readers.

"Yes, Boss." Rory and Ember answered at the same time. She seemed determined to have the last word, no matter what.

"Great. That will do it. Thanks for everything you did to make this a successful mission." Alex shook their hands.

Rory reached to open the door for Ember, but she brushed by him and stormed toward the restrooms. He glanced back to Alex. "Did something else happen while I was gone that I should know about?"

"She's not talking yet. Give her time."

"Copy that."

As perplexed as he was, Rory had plenty of work to do. Alex came back with a few minor changes. His boss was a stickler for accuracy and detail. All the agents joked the reporting process took longer than the actual operations, but Rory didn't mind. He checked his email, filled out the supply list for things he needed, and signed up for quarterly weapons certification. Everything almost seemed normal. When Ember returned from the restroom, he grabbed the opportunity to talk with her. Mother had just gone into Alex's office, so he figured he had time.

"Hey," he said softly. "How are you doing, honey?"

She shot him down with a huff. "What do you want, Dennison?"

"What's going on?" he asked quietly. "I thought—"

"Why don't we start with you? Where have you been?"

"Umm, home, with a—"

"Home? Ha. You expect me to believe that? You know what? I don't care." She slapped her desk drawer closed. "I've got work to do and not enough hours in the day to get it done. Leave me alone."

Mother came back and the opportunity was gone. Rory excused himself and went back to his desk, but he sat watching and wondering. Twice Ember glanced his way, only to jerk her eyes back to her monitor the minute he caught her looking. And she wasn't busy. He tried again, hoping she'd go out with him for coffee or something. But that set her off. She pushed her chair so hard it fell backward. "I don't need this bullshit."

He watched dumbfounded as she marched into Alex's office and slammed the door behind her. In two seconds flat she stormed out and straight to the elevator. The other agents watched in hushed silence. Even Mother sat stunned and quiet for a change.

Ember called the elevator. Without looking back, she stalked inside it, punched the keypad and was gone.

What just happened?

"Dennison!" Alex roared from his office. Harley was headed out of the office as Rory entered, shaking his head. Alex tossed a single sheet of paper across his desk.

Rory took the paper and sputtered. Ember's resignation? She'd quit? "What's going on?"

"There's a reason we have rules against fraternization on the job."

Rory shook his head, still trying to make sense of anything Ember-related. "But I—"

"I don't care what you two thought you were doing together on this op, but when it affects this team, it becomes my problem. I'm one techie short. I can't afford to lose her."

"But Boss, I—"

"Fix it!"

Rory shut his mouth, turned around and went back to his desk. He hadn't sat down for two minutes when Mother scooted her chair over to his workspace. "Did she do it?"

"Do what?"

"Did she quit?"

For the first time, he really looked at Mother. She'd been crying. Her eyes were red-rimmed and she looked devastated.

"What do you want?" he asked tiredly, not wanting to discuss the office drama.

"Just to do what I do best." She sniffed and wiped her eyes. "I want to help."

Rory wished she'd leave his workspace. He wasn't ready to trust her. "Leave it alone. I've got work to do."

"Okay," she said sadly, pushing to her own workspace.

In a few minutes, Alex was back with his usual belligerence. "Well?"

"Well, what?" Rory asked patiently. Right now he had a pain in his neck and another one leaning over his desk.

"I gave you an assignment to fix the problem you created."

"I created?" Rory jumped to his feet, once again toe to toe with his boss. "And how do you expect me to do that?"

"You were agent in charge. You're going to find out what's wrong with her. Do you hear me?"

Rory rolled his eyes at that ridiculous assignment.

"Fix it," Alex growled.

"Can I work any other miracles while I'm here?" Rory growled back.

Steely blue eyes said it for him. *Get it done.* Alex turned smartly back to his office.

In exasperation, Rory circled his workspace once before he pulled his chair back and finally settled. He did the only thing he could think of. He started a background investigation into one Junior Agent Ember Davis, the same as he'd do for any other person of interest. Glued to his computer monitor, he didn't hear Mother until she touched his elbow.

This time he wasn't so pleasant. "What?"

"Please talk with me," she pleaded.

Great. She'd been crying again. Not what he needed, another emotional woman. He tried to sound patient. "What do you want?"

"Let's go into the Sit Room. Please?"

Rory scowled, but relented. Once in the Sit Room, she shut the door and started to cry. He shoved both hands through his hair. Had the whole world gone bat-shit crazy while he was away? "I don't have time for this. What's so important you can't tell me at my desk?"

She composed herself enough to sit at the table. "I knew something was wrong the minute Ember came back from the Lobsang op. She wasn't herself. She was crying and wearing her sunglasses all day. I went to Alex, but he told me to mind my business. You know how he is, but I can tell. Something really bad is wrong with my Ember."

My Ember. Hmm. Still standing at the door and not wanting to engage in gossip, he knew what was wrong with Ember. Her heart was broken. She missed the little one she'd sworn to protect and ended up falling in love with. Heck, he'd fallen in love with both of them, and now they were gone.

"She went and got that awful tattoo. Did you see it? You probably didn't because of the obscene outfit she's wearing today, but Rory. It's a skull and crossbones right over her heart. It's like she thinks she's poison or something."

When Mother burst out crying again, he wanted to rip his hair out. No. He hadn't seen the tattoo, but it fit. Ember seemed determined to fight the world right now. Mother hadn't offered anything helpful until she slid an open folder across the table to Rory. "Take a look."

Reluctantly, he did, but if this was nothing more than her usual busybody interference, he was done. The top page in the file showed a police department mug shot and set of fingerprints of Ember. He sat. She looked to be maybe fourteen or fifteen years old with two lopsided ponytails. Her frightened face was covered with acne. His heart stuttered. *My poor Ember.*

"What is this?"

"Her juvie record," Mother whispered. "It was, umm, sealed, but I kinda—"

He waved her explanation off, studying the charges against the suspect. What? Murder? Ember? Now he was paying attention.

Mother kept talking. "Ember had an awful childhood. Her mother was an alcoholic and her father was never around. She told me once they really went after each other when they got together. Sometimes it got violent."

Rory scanned the rest of the file. Ember had been arrested all right, but only after she'd confessed to killing her mother. She was never charged, though. The police closed the case when they could find no evidence to support her wild claim. She was released into the custody of several different foster families until she turned eighteen, at which point she joined the Navy. The saddest footnote to her story was that her father was still alive at the time her mother died; he just didn't want her. He'd relinquished parental rights and let the state of Virginia keep her.

Mother rambled on. "I didn't believe it, so, umm, I got to checking around a little closer, and I, umm—"

"What?" Rory had no patience left for Mother's fake timidity.

"I checked the medical examiner's report. Ember wasn't home when her mother died. That's why they did an autopsy. It was an unattended death, so it didn't make sense she'd killed her mother when she wasn't even there. I checked her mother's physician's statements. I couldn't find anything hinting at foul play."

"Neither did the police," Rory said, tapping his fingertips on the juvie records beneath his hand. Mother was not gossiping. The detailed research made it obvious she cared about Ember. "Then how'd her mother die?"

"Official cause of death was myocardial infarction compounded by cirrhosis of the liver. The woman drank herself to death. Her body just gave out. There's no way a fourteen-year-old did that."

"But she blamed herself." He sighed. *She still does.* Things were beginning to line up.

Mother sniffled. "She told me her mother picked fights, blamed her all the time when things went wrong. You know how drunks are. They need someone to blame. Nothing is their fault. Their kids grow up with no self-esteem because they've never done anything right. No wonder Ember confessed. Her mother's death had to be her fault. She was the only one left."

"And she was a little girl," he said quietly. A little girl whose father had deserted her. No wonder she never wanted to be a mother. The teenage confession was mixed up with the dark change he'd witnessed. Having to give up Nima must have triggered it. Ember was an unwanted child who'd loved and lost a child. Did she feel as if she'd somehow deserted Nima? Did she think she was as bad as her mother? It made sense. Her maternal instincts were at war with her reality. She was hurt and locking the world out, protecting herself the only way she knew—by making herself untouchable. Unlovable. Poison.

"What next?" he asked gently.

Mother's eyes teared up. "I don't know. She won't talk to me anymore, and now she's quit. I'm afraid I'll never see her again."

Rory put his hand to her shoulder. For the first time, a twinge of compassion sprang to life for this annoying woman. Maybe she wasn't as bad as he'd thought. "Ember is hurting. That's why she's mad."

"I know. I just can't reach her anymore." Mother gulped back another sob. "She's mad when she comes to work, and she's mad when she goes home. Every day she gets darker.

She did the same thing when Todd was killed, but this is worse. I can't reach her, Rory. I'm afraid she might be thinking of killing herself."

"No." Rory knew Ember better than that. "She's mad at Alex and me. I'm not exactly sure why, maybe she blames us because Nima's gone. And she's probably mad at herself, too."

Mother shook her head. "I know she's mad at Alex and she had a knock-down drag out fight with David, but I get the feeling she's more than mad at you."

Rory sighed. He got the same feeling. *Poor Ember.* He wanted to hold her like he'd done after the altercation in the cornfield. She'd been mad at herself then, too, confused how taking life could sometimes be the right choice. Heck, he still struggled with it, and he'd been through sniper training and lived through one-on-one combat. Closing the folder, he pushed it back toward Mother.

"Burn it. No one else needs to see it, not even Alex. Do you understand?" He knew what he had to do and he knew where he had to go.

Mother went straight to the document shredder in the corner of the conference room and fed the file into the grinding teeth of the machine. In a few seconds she was back at the table waiting for further instructions.

"Would you please tell Alex I'll be out of the office for the rest of the day?" he asked. "Tell him I'm walking point for as long as I need to. I'll be back when the problem is fixed."

Mother nodded. Relief shimmered in her eyes. "Thanks, Rory. I knew I could tell you. You're Ember's friend."

Rory sighed. Friendship was not what he had in mind.

Twenty-Five

Ember heard the pounding on her front door all the way from the kitchen. She had no intention of answering it, which is why she ignored the doorbell. Unfortunately, Larry wasn't bright enough to figure it out.

The knife in her hand hit the crisp stalks of celery faster and harder. She'd stopped at the market on her way home for vegetables, potatoes, clams, oysters, and a pound of fresh shrimp. Today was a good day for seafood chowder, and she didn't care if Larry liked it or not. Little did he know, this was his last meal at her expense. One way or the other, her freeloading brother had to go.

Alex was right. She had done a good job on the Lobsang Op, but it was time to move on. Job turnover. Branching out. Aiming higher. Call it what you want, today was the day she took her life back and transformed into something besides a demented wack job. Assistant Techie Ember Davis was gone. She was moving on.

The blade pounded against the wooden cutting board. She almost didn't hear the angry male voices filling her front room until Larry yelled, "Some guy's at the door for ya!"

She didn't answer. Whoever it was, she wasn't interested. *Stupid salesmen!* She chopped harder and faster. Celery flew. Skewering an already peeled onion, she halved it with one hard slice. And then, because the smooth round shape of the onion resembled a bald head, she chopped the hell out of it until her eyes teared up. *Damn you, David.*

"Ember! Did you hear me or not?"

"I'm busy," she hollered right back.

"Door! Now, dumb ass!"

She grabbed a towel and wiped her hands. *Can't everyone just leave me alone?*

And there he was. Rory. Standing at her open door with a mad as hell look on his handsome, dark face. Her windpipe closed. She couldn't swallow much less speak up. Wow. He looked every bit as good as when she'd left the office—dark denim jeans, light blue polo that fit a little too tight across his chest. Long lean legs ending in leather cowboy boots instead of work boots. Her nose twitched against her better judgment, searching after the unique outdoorsy scent he always brought with him.

But there was no pleasant smile, no polite *'How are you doing today?'* No *'Hello beautiful.'* His jaw was tight, the cords in his neck sharp. With both hands braced against the doorjamb, he glowered as if waiting to be invited in. His knuckles whitened. No one stood in his way and yet he did not enter. What was he waiting for? An invitation? Well, he could stand there and wait 'til hell froze over for that to happen

Those damned alpha male blues radiated pure—what? Command? Dominance?

Not anymore, Dennison. Go away. I reject you first this time. Get the hell out of my life.

But wow. He looked good. Her gut clenched along with certain other muscles that seemed to have a will of their own. She hated the spell that his presence instantly held her in while she was trying to hate him. He was the dumb ass in her life. One of two. The other had already gone back to the couch he'd been sleeping on for days.

"What do you want?" she asked icily. She knew what she sounded like and she didn't care. He was old news. She'd moved on.

"I've come to talk." He had that tone of authority in his voice, that leadership thing he did so well. She recognized it for what it meant to her—absolutely nothing.

"I'm busy." To prove she meant what she said, she pivoted on the ball of her foot, marched back to the kitchen and left him standing there. He knew his way out. Suddenly, his hand was on her shoulder. She jerked out of his grip, but he turned her to face him, both hands tight on her biceps. There was no option but to look at him. "You think you can come into my apartment and—"

"I think I deserve to know why you walked out and quit without saying a word to me." His deep voice commanded her and she blinked.

"What the hell do you care? It's not like we meant anything to each other. One minute you're there, but the next you're… you're not."

"What are you talking about?" Latent anger welled behind those deep angry blues, but other emotions, too. Concern? Worry? "I was always there for you. Every step of the way."

He seemed to believe that line of bull. She didn't. "Like hell you were. You left the first chance you got. What? Couldn't wait to get it over with? One minute we're working together and all but playing house. The next you scrape me off your shoe like a… like a...."

Damn! She couldn't think with him standing so close. Every breath filled her with the scent her traitorous nose couldn't seem to get enough of—him.

"Mrs. Godfrey called. Tyler had pneumonia. I was at the hospital or on the couch with a sick little boy for a week." He pulled her closer, inch by inch invading her space.

She halted his embrace with a firm hand in the middle of his chest. Big mistake. His chest. Why did she think her puny little hand would stop that wall of muscle? And—wow. Those deep baritone vibrations coming out of his throat traveled right up her arm along with sizzling heat. Was he the one on fire? For a second there, she thought it was her, but now....

"Why haven't you answered my calls?" he asked. "I've been trying to reach you for days. What's wrong with your phones?"

"Tyler was sick?" Her heart stuttered along with her lips. Wow. Maybe he was telling the truth. *Maybe*—she gulped— *maybe I'm wrong.* "If you cared so much, w-why haven't you answered *my* calls?"

"Because I never received any. Here." He pulled his phone from his pants pocket, offering it to her. "Look. I never once got a message from you. Why didn't you call my home number if you couldn't reach me by cell? You could've left a message there."

For some stupid reason, she felt an urge to run her fingers over his head. *Damn! So he's got a cute little boy? He's still an ass—with really nice hair. And the cutest son, and—so what?*

She grabbed the cell phone out of his hand, impatiently scrolling through his missed calls and just as quickly, his incoming calls. The error of her stubbornness jumped out at her. She handed it back with a curt, "This isn't your phone."

"Yes, it is." He pocketed the phone and grabbed her arms again like he was afraid she'd bolt.

She stiffened. The only thing stopping him was her hand in the middle of his broad, rock solid chest. The man had wide shoulders. Her fingers absorbed the intensity radiating off him. The muscles of her throat constricted. Like dominoes, every downward muscle did the same. How on earth did that work?

"My last phone didn't survive the explosion at the safe house. Why do you always think I'm leaving you?"

Tenderness washed over her, but it didn't matter. He'd had his chance and he'd blown it. Big time.

"Because everyone leaves," she hissed, staring through the ghoulish eye makeup she'd slathered on. Even she could see the clumps on her lashes framing her view. Could this day get anymore bizarre? There he was, all-American handsome, and she'd purposefully turned herself into everything he hated.

Realization dawned. *I've been calling the wrong cell phone. No wonder he didn't answer. I should've answered his calls. I should've left a message. I should've called him at home. Wow. I suck.*

"Hey, hey, hey," Larry chuckled from some other planet—she wished. He must need another beer. She caught a peripheral of him leaning against the doorjamb in his usual stupor, obviously mesmerized by the semi-intelligent argument flying back and forth.

Rory shot him a scorching look over his shoulder, his hands still on her arms. "What do you want?"

Larry popped the top off his beer can, chugged, burped and kept on staring.

Rory ignored him and focused on Ember. "Listen. I'm sorry I had to leave that night without talking to you first. My babysitter called. She'd just taken Tyler to the emergency room with a bad case of pneumonia. He was in the hospital nearly a week. I'm sorry I didn't call you sooner but I was worried sick for Tyler. I couldn't think of anything else. When I finally took him home, he had a relapse. It's been a heck of a week, but he's doing better. We made cookies. We left you a big plateful along with some flowers and a note. Didn't you get them?"

Both she and he turned to glare at Larry. "Did I get any flowers or cookies?" she asked pointedly. It deflected a small fraction of Rory's intensity. Kind of.

Larry staggered back a step, pointing his beer around the room like it was a moving target. "Yeah, there's some stuff for you over there... somewhere. Hmm. That crap was here a minute ago."

"Who is that jerk?" Rory growled, but he didn't wait for an answer. She no more than opened her lips to explain when he cupped the back of her head, pulled her to his mouth and kissed her hard.

She protested (really, she did), but he didn't back off like a gentleman would've. The floor tilted beneath her feet. The room spun. Her resistance failed. She needed something, or someone, to hold onto. Besides, her lips were responding to that mouth of his, and that smell, that just bathed, clean Rory smell. Her nostrils flared, sucking it into her heart. Her soul. Her entire body leaned into him, her tongue to his mouth, her breasts to his chest, her thighs to his... *Oh wow. He's solid. Everywhere.*

Damn. She wanted him physically. Right now. Even in the middle of their first real fight. Make-up sex with this guy would be so incredible. The more his lips demanded, the weaker her knees became. Her fingers clutched his strong biceps for support and—

"Oh, man, do her!" Larry howled. "Go on! Do her! She needs a good screw! Let her have it. She's been a bitch since—"

In the blink of an eye, Rory knocked Larry into the next room and up against the front door. The beer can flew to who knew where. Rory's fist curled beneath Larry's chin, the promise of death in his voice. "You ever talk to my woman like that again, and so help me, I'll knock your dumb ass all the way to China. You hear me? You're not welcome here. Neither's your pot or whatever else you're using. I find it, I'm flushing it. Get the hell out of here before I call the police." Not waiting for an answer, he pushed Larry backward into the hall, slammed the door and locked it. Turning to her, he growled, "Who *is* that jerk?"

"Umm, my brother." But all she'd heard was—*my woman? Wow.*

"Your brother?" Immediately, both hands raked over his hair. "I'm sorry, but I—"

"I'm not. Thanks. I mean, really, I hate it when he's here. He smokes weed while I'm at work, and he won't leave when I tell him to, and—"

"He isn't welcome here, do you hear me? He's an addict. He stays away from you from now on." Demanding eyes challenged her to argue.

The reverberations of her out of control heartbeat had turned her brain to Nothing. But. Mush. *But it's my apartment. But he's my brother. But—you're right. I was going to kick him out today anyway. And you're so hot when you're angry.* "Okay," she softly acquiesced.

Rory strode across the floor and pushed her against the wall, or maybe it was the refrigerator, or whatever. It was solid, and she needed something solid behind her because she was falling into those dark eyes and.... *Black lipstick is so not his color.*

"Wait. Let me wipe your, mmm—"

He didn't wait. His mouth was on hers again, demanding more. His hips pinned her to whatever stood behind her, and the world fell away. All that existed was his mouth on hers, his hands moving purposefully down her body like he already owned everything he touched. The tactile assault left her weak. Compliant. Hungry.

When his fingers made it down far enough, he gripped a handful of her ass, and she forgot how to breathe. That was what she'd wanted for weeks. No, needed. No, craved. Every molecule in her system seemed starved for his touch. She was caught up in that hurricane again, and it was called Rory. *Yes, please. Oh, yes. Yes. Yes.*

"I'm only asking you one time." His breath hot and heavy in her face, all she saw was the stormiest eyes beneath elegant brows now narrowed to a demanding angry V. Could he get any more glorious? Even the black lipstick staining his mouth added to his ferocity. He was alpha. The dominant male. And he meant her to know it. "Neither of us is on a mission right now. We are not at work. The rules of our job do not dictate our decisions. You're just Ember, and I'm just me. Do I leave or do I stay?"

The sexiest smoldering gaze scorched her. His fingers and hands weren't doing too bad, either, not gripping her backside like they were. Waves of raw male energy disintegrated any notion of retreat or resistance. He couldn't possibly stand any closer unless their clothing disintegrated in the flames engulfing her. Her body arched, automatically sealing itself to him.

"Stay," she whispered meekly. *Wow, do I want you to stay.*

He relaxed and leaned in for another kiss. She raised her lips to meet his, but he stopped short, staring at the space beside her head. A bemused smile twitched the corners of his black lipstick-stained mouth. "You saved them?" he asked incredulously.

She glanced over her shoulder to see what held his attention. *Arghhh! Linoleum, just swallow me up!*

Now he knew for sure what an idiot she was. Stuck on the refrigerator with cute little ladybug magnets was the paper doll family she and Nima had cut out of newspaper. There for all the world to see stood the dark-haired Rory paper doll holding hands with the blonde-haired Ember doll and a blue-eyed little Nima doll between them. And dangling off a piece of red ribbon was the damned pinecone he'd given her.

"It's all I had left and I... I couldn't throw them away. I couldn't lose that, too," she squeaked out the pitiful explanation.

The tender look on his face melted her heart. He leaned in to kiss her.

"But wait!" In a fleeting half-second of clarity, she ducked out from his arms, grabbed his hand and pulled him into the bathroom. He eyed her extra-large and comfortable bathtub, his brows arched in a roguish devil-may-care smirk. And there he was, the playful man she knew.

A smile tugged her lips for the first time in days. "Sit," she commanded in her most I'm-in-charge voice. It sounded more like milk toast than authority, but he sat obediently on the edge of the tub nonetheless. "Tip your head back."

"My goodness, you're bossy," he said, his voice husky, deep, and so-o-o messing with her head.

She shivered as she gathered cotton pads and makeup remover from her cabinet. *You're so dumb, Ember. He never left you. Ever. He's not the leaving kind of guy, remember?*

"Head back," she ordered again, trying desperately to maintain what little composure she had left. He complied, leaning backward so she could remove the lipstick from his mouth. But in doing so he pulled her between his knees, his hands comfortably secure on her hips. Like that helped.

The more he complied, the more that alpha male thing seemed to be in control. She could so not concentrate in this position. Everything she loved about him came back into brilliant clarity. His clean-shaven chin and freshly trimmed hairline. Masculine Adam's apple. Long, black eyelashes that amplified his dark eyes, more black than blue right now. All of her senses itched to touch, smell and drink him in. To taste.

With trembling fingers, she soaked the cotton balls in the gentle astringent and wiped the black lipstick from his mouth and— *Oh, those lips.* The moment her fingertips made contact, her pulse quickened at the gentle act of service that felt a lot like foreplay. Rory pursed them to the right, then to the left. She concentrated as hard as she could. Shivering from head to toe, she gently cleaned and—oh, hell! The moment his lips were clean, she wanted to mess them up again in the worst way.

Very carefully, so as not to spill the makeup remover on his shirt or jeans, she dabbed more lotion onto another clean cotton ball and wiped his mouth a second time. Like there was any lipstick left by then. Every muscle yearned toward him, drawn by a fierce magnetic pull claiming her right down to her toes. His hands rested achingly warm on her hips, his thumbs rubbing the intimate intersection where thigh joined with abdomen. Heated pools of the steamiest obsidian measured her every move. Every glance into those pools left her wanton.

"Are you done with me yet?" he asked, his voice rumbling all the way to the pit of her stomach. Her body clenched. *I've only just begun, Agent Dennison.*

"Yes. I mean, no. I mean...." She gulped. *Spit it out!*

He stood. With one deft turn, she was the one on the edge of the tub. He took the lotion and cotton out of her hand. "Your turn. Sit still. Head back."

Now he commanded her—and she liked it. When he eased his knees between hers, she had to hoist her tight leather skirt up to make room for him. It was impossible to sit still, much less breathe with him where he was. She wiggled on the edge of her tub, but it brought no relief to that raging fire in her belly.

"Close your eyes."

She did, but not being able to see only heightened her other senses. Her nose twitched like an addict needing his scent to live. The temperature of her skin elevated to flash fire.

With two fingers beneath her chin, he tilted her face up. "These are the black lines from your vision," he said quietly. With the lightest touch he cleansed the oily black from her eyes and lashes. "And these are the prison bars of your vision." Just as gently he removed the lipstick from her lips, and like an idiot she sat there breathing him in. Basking. Wanting. And oh, so needing.

Ember couldn't take it anymore. She had to look.

"There will be no more defacing yourself, do you hear me?" His gaze drifted to her neck. "Do I see another mark defiling the body I cherish?"

"Uh, huh," some sap replied. *Wait. That's me.*

"How can you treat yourself like poison when you are light and life to me?" he asked sadly.

He tenderly touched the fresh and still sore skull and crossbones inked at the top of her left breast with the pad of his thumb. Bending, he pressed a gentle kiss to the tattoo, chilling her with the moist heat of his breath. Shivers raced up her neck, causing another bout of butt-tingling wiggles.

"You and I are very much alike, Ember," he whispered. "You've built walls to keep me out, and I've built force fields to keep you out. We've created avatars; people we're not so no one can see who we really are. I did it to protect Tyler and my ego. You wanted to scare the world away. We might've thought we were keeping ourselves safe from being hurt again, but we were doing something else, too. We weren't living. Let's not be afraid to live, Ember. Let's not lie to each other anymore."

He pressed his forehead to hers until they were nose to nose, his hands on her shoulders and the saddest light in his eyes. There was no sense trying to talk. She was putty in his hands. Silly Putty.

"I like the amazing, strong woman I see now." He kissed her forehead while his fingers trailed fire along her neck, but then he tweaked one of the spikes on her head. "But these things could put a man's eye out."

She pulled the spiked cap of hair off. Soft blonde layers fell where shiny black had been.

Warm surprise flashed in his eyes. "A wig? Cool. So that's how you change your hair color all the time. I've always wondered how you could change hair color so fast."

He pulled her up off the tub in one swift armful and turned her to face the mirror above her sink. He stood behind her with one arm around her waist, his other hand combing gently over her head and through her hair. Soft moist nibbles caressed her neck and ear.

Shivering, she closed her eyes at his touch, every nerve in her body electrified at the delightful sensation of his hands. Her toes had surely curled in her leather boots. The rest of her had.

"Open your eyes," he ordered. Tracing the edge of her ear with his tongue, he softly touched each ring and stud anchored there while he watched her in the mirror. "Hmm. What else do we need to remove?"

No sooner asked than done. As quick as a wink, the gold and silver studs were off her ears and in a jumbled pile next to the sink. Nestling back into his arms, she faced the mirror and his mischievous smile. *No more earrings or studs. I'm good with that.*

He traced her lips with the tip of his index finger. "Open wide."

She did as he commanded; content to play the game if it got her what she wanted.

He leaned into her neck, his breath hot and moist on her already sensory-overloaded skin. If he kept this up, she'd explode. His dark eyes didn't blink from her gaze as he traced her wide-open mouth with just the tip of his finger. "The tongue stud, too, or whatever you call it. I don't want anything in your mouth but me the next time I kiss you."

She obediently removed the metal barbell, and without waiting to be asked, she also took the diamond stud from her nostril. Her hands shook. She almost dropped it. When it was on the counter, she backed into him and once more pulled his arms around her. *These are small things, Dennison. I can live without all this stuff, but I can't live without you.* The realization hit true. *I don't want to live without you, Rory. Not ever again.*

His hands moved slowly over her shoulders and down her arms before coming to rest at her waist. *Arghhh.* She had to close her eyes just to think straight. His hard body pressing against her backside had already melted all logical connections in her once analytical brain. How could he be so calm when she was ready to scream? She stood overloaded, all circuits charged to the hilt, amped up and ready to pop.

Opening her eyes, she caught his smirking reflection in the mirror again, his arms comfortable around her like he owned her body and soul. Her feet couldn't seem to hold still, but then, neither could the rest of her. Impatience tinged with a hint of anxiety tiptoed across her shoulders and down her spine. She'd never been treated so tantalizingly kind before.

He'd stimulated every last nerve ending in her body, and they were both still dressed. What would happen when she got him out of those jeans? Her toes curled. *Hurry it up, Dennison. Body and soul and whatever else—it's yours—just kiss me.*

"Is there anything else I should know about?" he asked seductively.

Oh. My. Gosh. Yes!

She grasped the zipper pull on her cute little hacked-up leather jacket. Before she had a chance to yank it down, he intercepted her hand. "Here. Let me help you."

She blinked up at him like a total dope. In oh, so slow motion, he pulled the zipper of her very cute leather jacket down tooth-by-tooth, centimeter-by-deliciously seductive centimeter. The man definitely knew how to tease her feminine libido. His eyes locked on hers in the mirror for the next mind-blowing reveal.

At last, her overly endowed cleavage came in to a much fuller view, then the cups of her lacy black bra, and finally, her clenching abdomen. Any fool could see the embossed imprint of her hardened nipples through the thin silk of her bra. Smoldering heat reflected back from the mirror. His frank admiration swept over her reflection, taking in the view of the intimate apparel he'd bought in Chicago. She was wearing the panties, too, only he hadn't gotten that far yet.

A deep rumble thrummed from right inside him when the diamond stud in her quivering navel sparkled into view. With his heated breath heavy on her neck and his eyes scorching all the way into her soul, it was all she could do to not combust on the spot. Leaning her head back against his shoulder, she nuzzled his cheek and took another deep breath.

Kiss. Me. Damn it.

He shook his head sternly. With just his index finger, he traced a burning ring of fire around her navel. Every muscle clenched all the way to that other, deeper place, now drenched with need and craving to devour him. "This, too, little girl. Take it off. Now."

Desire seized her core. Somehow, every piece of her anatomy seemed connected by an invisible string he had only to tug to make her comply. She couldn't get the belly button ring off fast enough. But then she couldn't play the game anymore. In a heated rush she turned into him and planted her mouth on his, hungry and demanding at the same time. "Rory!" she mumbled around his lips, frantic to be skin to skin after all this mind-blowing game playing.

The fire stoked hot and out of control. Kissing him only added to the need to be one with this man. This alpha. This incredible sexy lover.

Unzipping her leather skirt without breaking contact with his mouth, she wiggled out of it and the jacket, too, letting them fall to the floor while she maintained the lip lock. He wasn't the leaving kind of guy. She got that now. Well, that was a damned good thing, because she had plans for every inch of him, plans that couldn't wait.

So what if she stood there in nothing but bra, panties, and butt-high boots? Judging by his heavily hooded eyes, he didn't mind. They strayed to the mirror behind her. The blue had left his eyes. Only darkest black remained. Knowing exactly what he was looking at, that she was nearly stripped naked and he approved, created another firestorm of wanton need.

With no patience left for any more foreplay, she latched her fingers to the sides of his head and poured her heart and soul into her kiss. Gripping her backside, he pulled her off the floor and onto his hips. With the sure, swift strides of a man who knew what he wanted and where he was going, he carried her out of the bathroom and down the hall into her bedroom.

Talking was done. Finally!

Twenty-Six

Afterglow is such a beautiful word.

Rory sighed as he covered his gorgeous lady with her zany pink, black, and lime-green patchwork quilt, pulling the soft, warm blanket up to her chin. Ember lay exhausted and very satisfied in his arms, her back to his chest. He was tired, too, but profoundly content.

They'd barely made it to her bed before the passion they'd both been holding back during the operation burst out with a life of its own. He honestly didn't know how her bra made it all the way up to the framed picture of Paris on the wall, now hanging askew on its hook with the lacy embellishment draped at one corner.

She'd changed from a raging woman in emotional pain to a very docile lady in love. Even now she snuggled his hand between her bare breasts, needing him to cup and fondle, like he needed persuasion. It crossed his mind he should let Alex know the problem was fixed, and, oh, by the way, he would need two more weeks off to take Ember to Paris, France, or maybe his place for the rest of her life.

She pushed her butt against him. "I like making love better than war."

"Me, too." He smoothed his hand over her hip until it came to rest on her thigh. "I'm sorry I kicked your brother out."

"I'm not. Larry only shows up when he needs a place to flop. He'll find one of his druggie friends and sponge off them for a while. That's all he's good for. Absolutely nothing."

"He did look kind of shocked when he found himself out in the hall, though."

She chuckled, her eyes closed in near slumber. "Good. You saved me the trouble."

He buried his face in her hair and closed his eyes, content for the first time in a long time. They woke later and made love until late afternoon. The workday that had begun so wretchedly turned into a day of discovery and play.

He brought two cups of coffee to her bed, but they didn't get around to it. She'd finished her seafood chowder for lunch. To go with it, they built chicken and avocado sandwiches that might as well have been oysters on the half-shell. Everything seemed to feed their insatiable hunger for each other's bodies and souls. They came to rest momentarily in her living room in front of the fireplace. Her zany quilt was all that covered them for now.

With his arms full of Ember, Rory called home and chatted with his mother, then Tyler. Yes, he'd be home in time for dinner, and he was bringing a surprise. Tyler tried to find out what the surprise might be, but in the end, Rory just hugged Ember tightly on his lap and said, "It's a very good surprise. You'll like it. Bye, son. Now go tell Grandma I'll be home soon."

He hung up the phone. Ember's arms were still around his neck and his arms around her waist. Given the chance, he'd haul her off to her bed again, but a morning and afternoon of hot steamy sex was enough for one day. And to think he was getting paid to do this, too.

She was pretty worn out. Apparently it was exhausting being a bitch twenty-four-seven. All the sex hadn't hurt her, either. "What are you smiling about?"

"Alex chewed my ass pretty good when you left this morning."

"Why?" She leaned back to see his expression.

"Guess he thought we'd been up to something. It stands to reason. He did catch us kissing."

"Ha!" She giggled in that deliciously rich voice of hers. "I wish we'd been up to something a whole lot sooner. You made me mad in Chicago when you wouldn't kiss me."

"I'm sorry." He smoothed his hand through her hair. "I'm a serious kind of a guy and we were on a mission and.... Do you forgive me?"

She kissed his cheek. "You should be the one forgiving me. I was out of line."

"Nah. The op wasn't supposed to get as exciting as it did." He traced the swell of her full breast beneath the quilt, rubbing the pad of his thumb over the tip of her nipple, bringing it to a peak.

He liked her naked and in his arms. She was the most luscious woman he'd ever known. Her body responded to his like they were meant to be together. How could a woman with the sizzling looks of Marilyn Monroe contain the sweet spirit of Dorothy from *The Wizard of Oz*? Ember was the epitome of innocence in a sex symbol's body. Everything about her stoked the fires of protectiveness. He pulled her close, needing to mate with every last piece of her.

"I was thinking of starting my own business," she said wistfully.

That came out of the blue.

"You were?" He pushed a stubborn strand of her hair off her face. "Why?"

"I quit, remember? Besides, it's time to do something different."

He hadn't seen that one coming, so he kept his mouth shut. Flames flickered across the gas log for a few quiet minutes.

"Can I tell you something, Agent Dennison?" she asked quietly.

"After everything we've just done together, I'm only Agent Dennison?"

"No, but I'm not good at relationship stuff, and I don't want to scare you away."

He arched an eyebrow. "Trust me. I'm not scared of you. What's up? Just say it."

"I love you."

Zing! His breath caught. He honestly didn't see it coming so soon. And yet, his heart told him true. He'd been thinking the very same thing.

"And now you can leave if you want."

Again with the leaving! What the heck?

"But no matter what you think, you're a good man and a great father and—"

He shushed her with his lips to hers in a gentle crush. Finally ready to love again, he turned her on his lap to face him. "Why, oh, why do you think I'm going to leave you? I've got news. I'm not the leaving kind of guy. Think about it. Your father was the biggest ass in the world for deserting you like he did. I don't know what kind of guys you dated before Todd, but look at me." He tipped her chin up to see into those soft green pools of Ember. "Look at me."

She obeyed.

"I am not leaving you. Not now. Not tomorrow. Not ever. Do you hear me?"

She sat up straighter on his lap, the quilt pulled up to her chin even as she wiggled her backside on his thighs. "What does that mean? Exactly."

He shrugged like it was no big deal. "Just that if you decide to start your new business on the east coast, you and I will be able to spend more time together. You'll get to know Tyler. I'll learn to like your cat. Speaking of which, where is that fur ball?"

"I don't care." She cupped his chin and directed his gaze toward her. "And I was only thinking about starting a new business. I might not. Tell me more."

And he fell into the purest pools of emerald. No, he dived in. Heart first.

"It means you'll sit by my side at my Thanksgiving table. You'll get to meet my mom and dad tonight. And you and I are going take Tyler up to Vermont to get our Christmas tree. Then we all might head west to the family farm in Nebraska for Christmas."

Without a doubt this was the right time and the right woman. His body ached to prove the depth of his love again. He cradled her in his arms. "Do you want to know the very best part?"

"Yes?" she asked breathlessly.

"I love you, Ember Davis. I'm going to love you every single day for the rest of my life and every night, too. I will never leave you, little girl."

A tear trickled out of the corner of her eye. For some reason his choice of words, *little girl*, or *that's my girl*, or *good girl*, hit a tender spot. It was just something his father always said to his mom. Here Ember was all grown up with a hot body that screamed sex appeal, but the little girl Ember still peeked around the edges, still waiting to be seen, noticed and loved.

She crashed into him, her mouth on his lips, her hands in his hair. Those luscious breasts were uncovered and pressed against his chest. The quilt slipped away, and talking was way overrated.

Easing her to the floor with him, he poured his heart into every kiss, every nibble and every taste of the woman who would be the rest of his life. The quilt became mattress as the need to couple with her took control. The glimmer of orange glow cast by the fire on her bare skin only enhanced the heat between them. There was no stopping.

Never before had he felt such a strong compulsion to shelter her physically and emotionally, to strengthen and restore what damage others had done. The purest love shone up from her eyes as he settled into a near push-up stance above her, his weight supported on one elbow and forearm. The deep emerald of her gaze glimmered with sparks not cast by the fireplace. Lowering his body onto and into hers, he watched the green turn dark, then misty, then brim until her heart spilled over.

When she sighed and closed her eyes, they came together in shuddering tenderness. More of melting than of mating, his heart exploded at the sensation of her body accepting his, filling him even as he poured all he had to give into her. There was no way to contain the act of giving and taking. They shared until he collapsed with his face in her neck, sure there was no better way to die. Her hand cupping the back of his head held him steady, but it was her next words that sealed his heart to hers forever.

"Rory Dennison," she breathed.

It was just his name, but it was *his* name. Soon to be hers. Soon to be theirs. He rolled to the side of her, cocooning her in the shelter of his arm where she belonged. Now she owned all of him and it was good.

They still lay bound together and pleasantly spent when the phone rang. He stretched to reach it on the end table while Ember giggled beneath him, gently brushing her hands over his chest.

"Hi, Mom," he muttered. Mothers. They seemed to have impeccable timing. She needed him to pick up a pint of heavy cream for dessert. "Sure thing. We're on our way."

He tossed the phone onto the couch. "Have you had enough lovemaking for one day?" he asked even as his body responded again to the lovely naked lady beneath him. At the rate they were going, they'd miss dinner. Maybe breakfast.

She wrapped her arms around his neck and pulled him down to her lips for one quick peck. "I have now."

"Then let's go to my place. Tyler's waiting and I understand we're having pot roast with all the fixings." He set her on her feet and stood next to her. "Let's get dressed."

The glitter in her eye took his breath. "Shower first?"

Hell, yeah.

"Hey! I know you," Tyler squealed when he pulled the door open. "You had pink hair. Where is it?"

"I left it in my drawer," Ember answered. She and Rory had finally made their debut as a couple, but she'd not expected the ecstatic welcome from Tyler when Rory unlocked his apartment door. Tyler must've heard the key in the lock. He recognized her right off, but he was not the picture of robust health she remembered. Dark circles shadowed his blue eyes. He'd lost weight.

"You keep hair in a drawer?" His eyes widened. "Me and daddy don't."

"Where do you keep your hair?" she teased.

He pointed to the top of his head. "Whatcha think? On our heads. You wanna hear a joke? Knock-knock."

"Tyler," Rory cautioned his precocious son. "How do we greet adults?"

The same wide-open smile Ember remembered lit Tyler's drawn face as he stuck his hand out for a handshake. He cocked his head and said, "We say I glad to meetcha! So knock-knock."

Kneeling, she played along. "Who's there?"

He beamed. "I Tyler."

"I Tyler who?"

"I, umm, I, umm." He shifted his feet, wiggling and glancing sideways to his dad. "Oh, yeah. You not Tyler. I Tyler. I Tyler-rific!"

"That's a funny joke!" Ember giggled. This little guy was downright adorable. She opened her arms for a hug and mini-

Rory responded with gusto, charging into her like a linebacker.

"Tyler, take it easy," Rory scolded when she had to put her hand to the floor behind her to keep from being knocked to her butt.

"No, he's fine." This was what she wanted, a welcome home by the person most important to the man she loved.

"He's been practicing that joke on me all afternoon," Rory's father said, rolling his eyes. "I'm glad he got to try it out on someone else for a change."

Tyler twisted in her arms to face his dad. "Where my surprise? Bemember? You was bringin' me a surprise."

"You're hugging her," Rory said with a big grin.

Tyler looked back at Ember, the same adorable thick lashes as his dad's fluttering on his cheeks while he digested the news. Rory's parents hovered nearby. His mother wiped her hands on a kitchen towel, a knowing smile tugging at her mouth. His father looked mildly pleased, but not as keenly interested as his mother.

"But, Daddy," Tyler said, his brows furrowed and the cutest puzzled look on his face. "Kin we keep her?"

That was all she needed to hear.

"Yes, we are going to keep her," Rory said with a throaty chuckle. He tugged Ember and Tyler up off the floor and presented her to his parents. "Mom and Dad, I'd like you to meet my fiancée, Ember Davis. Ember, my parents, Sawyer and Ruth Dennison."

Fiancée. Wow. When did that happen?

"It's about time," Ruth declared, her eyes scrolling over Ember in one quick assessment that didn't betray anything other than the happy welcome Tyler had already declared.

Rory and Tyler shared Sawyer's good looks. It was easy to see where they got their strong profile and even their cleft chins. But their eyes? The deep blue belonged to Ruth, and right now that beautiful color was washing over Ember in a warm wave of acceptance. She scolded her husband. "You see what I mean, Sawyer? We need to visit this boy of ours more often. First Tyler gets sick. Now Rory's getting married. My heavens, we're missing his whole life."

"It looks to me like he's doing okay, Ruthie. He's got his old man's eye for a good-looking woman." Sawyer winked at Ember. "Come here, little girl. Let me give you a proper Dennison welcome." He hugged her in one arm while he shook Rory's hand. "Congratulations, son. Your mother's right. It's time you and Tyler had a good woman in your life."

Now it was Rory's turn to blush. "Thanks, Dad. We're getting married before you two head back home. Hope you've got the time, umm, that is, if it's good with you?" he asked Ember, his brows lifted with his question. "Sorry. I should have asked you first. I kind of got ahead of myself."

And wow. Did good things really happen that fast? To her? But then he made it worse. Rory dropped to one knee, his eyes brimmed and glistening. He reached for her hand, interlocking their fingers. "I love you, Ember. I don't have a ring to put on your finger yet, but I don't want our mission to end. Will you marry me?"

The room hushed. Even Tyler stopped bouncing on the balls of his feet and spun around to watch.

"Wow. I mean, yes. I really will." She had to blink to keep the tears from falling.

Ruth didn't seem to have the same problem. "Oh, for the love of God, come here." She grabbed Ember's hands, her eyes glimmering "I've always wanted a daughter. Now, I finally have one."

Ember hesitated. She let Ruth pull her into a hug.

Tyler broke the emotional moment with a boisterous, "C'mon guys. I wanna eat."

Sawyer scooped him onto his shoulder for a quick ride into the dining room.

Rory hung back with Ember.

"I guess this means I'm not starting my own business," she murmured.

His hand slid down to her hip while he planted a kiss into the side of her head. "Do what you want. The studs and wigs, too. I don't know what got into me earlier. They don't matter, you do. If they make you happy, wear 'em. Be whoever you want to be. Just let me love you while you do it."

She circled his waist with her hand, sliding her fingertips beneath his belt. With his shirt tucked in like it was she wasn't touching skin, but the intimate gesture sent goose bumps shivering up her spine. She knew exactly what had gotten into him earlier because it had gotten into her as well. As old as life itself, it was the animal within, the need to claim her mate. Only this time it came with a promise. It came with love.

"I'll talk with Alex in the morning," she whispered. "Maybe he'll take me back."

"You know he will, but make sure it's what you want."

"I am pretty spoiled. I have you, Tyler, and Maple Syrup. What else is there?"

He stopped short of the dining room doorway, his hands on her hips and his lips in her ear. "The rest of our lives, Mrs. Dennison. And after that, there's always forever."

Her heart caught. *Forever. Wow.*

Epilogue

Weddings have a way of taking on a life of their own, but what did Rory expect? He'd asked Ember to marry him, and with Ember came energy, bright colors, and one very strong woman with a definite opinion. Of course there'd be life, only with her it would be extraordinary.

He should've known everything had already changed the moment he saw the white doves rise up from the chapel steps when he and his parents arrived. Tyler couldn't chase them away fast enough, and somehow that was fitting, too. The doves were an unexpected wedding present from a little girl a world away and the last of Ember's vision.

The Lobsang Operation might have ended on a bittersweet note, but Tyler's happy giggle when the birds lifted heavenward was Ember's future. Her life was just beginning. Rory's too. There'd be toasts and cheers aplenty, but by the end of the day, the right Mrs. Dennison would finally be at his side and in his bed.

His best man? Connor Maher. Who else? Her bridesmaid? Mother, of course. The audience was filled with family from Nebraska as well as everyone from The TEAM. She'd invited Larry. He had yet to show, but everyone else did. The chapel was full.

Tyler preceded Ember, taking giant steps instead of the much shorter ones they'd practiced. Halfway up the aisle he started counting. It was one of the self-calming skills he'd learned. Other people might think he was just being obnoxious, but this little guy was learning how to control his ADD. Out loud.

"One. Two. Free. Seven. Nine. Ten. Twelb. Fip-teen. One hundred!" he proclaimed loudly and proudly, beaming up at his proud father and his best man. "I did good, huh, Unca Connor?"

Uncle Connor Maher replied just as loudly, "Yes, you did. Good job, Tyler!"

And Rory thought, *oh, those pesky Fs and Ths.* He winked at his son and Tyler squeezed both eyes shut in the cutest double wink. If that little guy smiled any wider, his face would split.

The audience chuckled. Rory's gaze shifted over the head of his precocious son. The *Wedding March* began and there she was, the woman he'd literally lived through and fought hell for. All of his past mistakes came down to this one defining moment. There was a world of truth to thanking God for unanswered prayers because there she was, the perfect answer to all of his.

His dad winked at him, too, but honestly, Rory only had eyes for that stunning woman on Sawyer Dennison's arm, the one dressed in a simple strapless gown from some crazy expensive boutique. The smooth satin bodice accentuated her lovely figure without revealing too much more than the exquisite angel wings tattooed across her bare shoulder blades. The skirt tiered from the waist to the floor in rows of taffeta. Her natural colored locks hung loose and casual to her shoulders, nearly a perfect match to the honey-color of the dress.

But it was the orange and black scarf circling her neck that proved she was still the woman he loved. She wore no veil. A single white rose, a gift from Tyler, adorned her hair. Rory's eyes glistened, remembering. It was supposed to have been a surprise, but Tyler didn't understand the nuances of keeping a proper surprise. Just because he'd whispered, *"Guess what? You gonna be my mom and me and Daddy got you a purdy flower,"* in her ear did not qualify as keeping the secret.

Ember was nervous. Rory knew all of her tells. She might look overconfident to everyone else but this traditional marriage ceremony was a huge step out of her comfort zone. She'd surprised him when she'd asked to meet with a priest. But her neck was stiff, just like it was when she'd turned into Mrs. Dillon in the cornfield. And if she kept biting her lip the way she was, there'd be none of it left for him to nibble on. She hadn't looked up yet. Her lips were moving. It looked like she was—

Oh, my heck, she's counting.

Sure enough. Just before his father handed her over, Ember turned to Connor Maher and asked in the same incredibly loud voice that Tyler had just used, "One hundred! I did good, huh, Uncle Connor?"

Tyler enthusiastically answered before Connor could stop chuckling into his fist. "You did real good, Mama! I proud of you!"

The audience wiped tears of laughter while the priest took control of the ceremony. Ember finally looked up. The most glorious emerald greens lit up the chapel and Rory was a smitten man again.

He secured Ember's hand over his arm, his heart bursting with pride for the connection between this daring brave woman and the little guy grinning up at her like she was his very own fairy godmother come to life.

After the priest finished his few opening remarks, Rory turned to Ember to declare his wedding vows. He grasped her slender fingers. The audience hushed.

"Oh, Ember," he said hoarsely, his tender heart stuck in his throat.

The smile dropped off her face. And there was that scared little girl again—still thinking she was unlovable and that this was just a dream. She tugged her fingertips nearly out of his hand before he snagged them tightly, pulling her closer until they stood nose-to-nose and eye-to-eye.

"Oh, no you don't, Agent Davis. You're not getting away from me. Not this time. You and me are not the leaving kind of people, remember?"

She had an adorable way of trying not to cry. Ember blinked those thick full eyelashes extra hard like they were supposed to be windshield wipers or something. No luck. One crystal tear wended its way alongside her nose. He watched it drip off her jaw, bounce once off the edge of her scarf and drop smack dab into that extra warm valley between her extra lovely breasts.

When he lifted his gaze back to hers, she gave him the military two fingers to her eyes hand signal to look at her eyes, not her boobs. A wave of heat flamed his whole body. He would've laughed if they'd been anywhere else. Leave it to Ember to bring spontaneity into what could've been a stuffy marriage ceremony.

The time had come and he knew what he wanted to say.

"Hey there, little girl." He pressed his forehead to hers; his eyes brimmed. "You have made me the happiest man in the universe. From this moment on, I pledge to you all my days and all my nights for as long as we both shall live. I promise to hear you when you speak, to listen to you when you whisper, to wait for you when you ask."

He took a deep breath, filling his chest and letting it out slowly. "And if you will have me, I vow to care for you when you're sick, to pray with you when you pray, and to cry with you when your heart is broken. I give you my hands to use as yours, my heart to keep as yours, and my life—just to be yours. And if forever is not enough, I swear to you, my darling wife, my only lover, and the perfect mother of my son, I will not leave you even then. I pledge to you, Mrs. Rory Dennison, and you alone, my undying fealty, my whole heart and my soul. Amen."

He pressed a tender, chaste kiss onto her forehead and took one step back. Now it was her turn. She took a deep breath, and he made sure to keep his eyes on her face despite the way her breasts heaved when she took that deep breath.

"Wow. Oh, wow," she whispered.

The chapel stilled and once more, Ember refused to look at him. She cleared her throat, gave her head a little shake, and took another deep breath. This had to be hard. Her whole life was changing right down to her name.

She kept blinking and biting her bottom lip. The pink tip of her tongue slipped out more than once to run a lap over top and bottom lips, but still she didn't lift her chin. She wouldn't meet his eyes. For the life of him, he didn't know what was wrong. They'd written their vows together. All she had to do was say them out loud for all to hear.

She grabbed his hand and finally met his gaze, her fingers cold and clammy. "I'm sorry, but I... I can't do this."

His heart dropped to the floor. He held onto her hand tighter.

"I mean, I really thought I could, but I can't. I really tried, honest, Rory, but I just can't. The words just won't come, and I can't... I just can't make them."

"But Ember... But...." His stomach pitched a fastball up his throat. *You're leaving me at the altar?* "But I love you," he breathed.

"Wow. Rory. Me too." She reached between those luscious breasts of hers and pulled out a tightly wound scroll of paper. "I stayed up all last night memorizing this thing, but I'm sorry. I just can't think straight right now. Is it okay if I read my vows to you?"

The prettiest teardrops lined her lashes and he nodded, weak with relief. *Oh, God yes. Read the darn thing. Just don't ever scare me like that again.*

She cleared her throat again. "Okay, so here goes. I, Ember Esmeralda Davis, do solemnly vow to love you every day and to honor you in all I say for the rest of my life." That seemed to be all she needed the scroll for, just to get started. Her gaze shifted off the paper in her hand. She stepped into him, pressing her body to his, the written vows forgotten. "And I promise to love you faithfully, Rory Dennison, to live with you playfully every single day for the rest of our life. I promise to support your dreams and to always have your back no matter if we're in the middle of cornfields or in our office or wherever. I vow to be the best wife and friend for you, the absolutely best mother to Tyler. But most of all, I promise to breathe and breathe and breathe you into my soul until there is no more you, and no more me—until there is only us."

Wow. She'd stabbed him clean clear through.

"I love you, Rory," she whispered, her lips just a few centimeters away. "I want you more than I've ever wanted anyone."

He leaned in for a taste of heaven, but—

"Ahem." The priest intervened.

Ember huffed through her nostrils and rolled those dazzling greens. "What now?"

"Do you have the rings?" Father O'Connell asked.

Connor prompted Tyler to join the wedding couple at the altar. Rory carefully untied the two silver bands from the pillow that Tyler clutched under his arm like a football. *Yes, there's my boy, a future Cornhuskers quarterback if ever there was one.*

Rory placed one of the wedding bands on Ember's left hand, the one with the full carat diamond, raised her fingers to his lips and kissed them without taking his eyes off her. There was no way this enchanting woman was leaving or getting away. She'd just infused a heady shot of relief and a heaping dose of gratitude into his heart. One more scare like that, and he'd have to throw her over his shoulder and haul her off for another round of hot and heavy.

She placed the other ring on his ring finger, a titanium band with three inset diamonds signifying their new family, one for Rory, Ember, and Tyler. It was she who leaned in this time, and Rory had to suppress a grin.

"Ahem."

"Excuse me," she whispered impatiently to the priest, "but isn't this the part where you tell the groom to kiss the bride?"

"Well, uh, yes, but first—"

"Well, am I or am I not the bride?"

A benevolent smirk tugged the corner of Father O'Connell's mouth. "You are."

Enough said.

Ember pushed her bridal bouquet into Mother's hands. In one step, she was in Rory's arms and love took over. Before he knew it, his hands were on her butt while her fingers clenched his head in place. Like he was going anywhere else but where all that breathing into each other's souls could begin. How was he going to get through the rest of the day? His fingers ached to undress her. His gut growled with the need to consume her. And every other organ seemed darned intent on her, too.

Someone clapped, giggling with glee. Tyler. All other sounds faded into the tender heat of this first wedded kiss. The priest's voice droned on, bringing Rory back to reality just in time to hear Father O'Connell pronounce them to be man and wife. Rory shifted his hands off her backside, aware he had family in the audience and a son who didn't need to see his father pawing his new mother.

With a sly smile and a wink, Father O'Connell turned them to face the audience. "While I still have the chance, may I present Mr. and Mrs. Rory Dennison?"

Rory raised his blushing bride's hand with his in victory. The audience clapped.

A mighty "Oorah!" filled the chapel. Marines. You've got to love 'em.

Ruth wiped her happy face while Sawyer did the same. Kelsey mopped her eyes. Alex beamed. Harley gave Rory and Ember the thumbs-up sign and a wicked smile. Zack just winked, the dog.

And just like that, Rory Dennison took a wife. A real wife. One who loved him enough to die for him. A woman brave enough to stay.

THE END

Sneak Preview of TAYLOR

Book 7

In the Company of Snipers

An arrow!

Taylor Armstrong bowed his chin to his chest and shuddered. Waves of red hot pain slapped over him from the arrow nestled like a living thing snug in his pectoral muscle above his right nipple. It was master. Satan incarnate. And coming to in this dank, dark place wherever he'd been dumped was Hell.

The morning that began with routine arms certification at the shooting range had morphed into a nightmarish struggle for survival. Glimmering light at the bottom of his prison door told him day was nearly done. So was he.

Stabbing pain was definitely the mother of invention. Every tug of his cotton shirt against the arrow enhanced his misery. It had to go. He tore it very carefully and tossed it to the shadows. Every movement hurt. Every breath. Even the feathers at the end of the shaft caught even the slightest intention to move, offering continuous jolts of razor-sharp reminders to, *Hold still. Leave it the hell alone!*

God Almighty, he wanted to, but the arrowhead had gone too far into his body to be pulled out the way it entered. He would know. The pain beneath his right shoulder blade evoked instant compliance in the one split second he'd mistakenly leaned against the wall behind him, thinking he could use it for support.

What couldn't be reversed had to go forward and through because that's what arrowheads did. Like stupid bone-headed Marines, they weren't designed to retreat, only to advance.

But once the arrowhead was completely through, and its wicked tip sticking out of his back, he could snap it off and pull the remaining slick shaft from his chest. At least that was the plan. If he lived long enough.

It would be no simple feat. Getting back onto his feet would be a chore in itself. But if some guy in Utah could hack his arm off to escape the boulder that tried to kill him, Taylor could surely do this. The arrow was made of wood and Taylor knew wood. The polished hardwood shaft would follow wherever the vicious tip led.

Blood ran down his chest. It didn't gush, just trickled in a steady stream like it had all the time in the world to get where it was going. The trail of hair down his belly funneled the red stream to the dimpled bowl of his navel. An innee, a bizarre and silly sight on such a desperate day. Funny the things a man notices when Death draws near, how some things become clear while others fade.

Like Three Star USMC Lieutenant General Michael Armstrong, his father, the last image Taylor needed here at the hour of what very well might be his death. He forced his mind from the cold-hearted man who'd raised him, and upward to the only One who'd truly heard him. It had taken eighteen years to learn to pray and from a USMC chaplain no less, but prayer brought comfort. It brought hope. Even here in this darkest of dark places.

"God Almighty. I don't want to die," he whispered. "I wear your patron saint on my neck. Think you could send him to me now? I could sure use his help."

Saint Michael the Archangel. Patron saint of soldiers and warriors. The tough looking guy on the medal Taylor'd worn around his neck for as long as he could remember. Funny. Never once did he relate the archangel on the medal to his father even though their names were the same. The guy decked out in an armor breastplate, his spear stuck in the top of the serpent, Lucifer's head, always seemed more of a friend, someone he might be able to rely on. Was it asking too much to get a special appearance now? Isn't that what patron saints did, showed up in a guys' darkest hour?

Taylor's prayer would have disgusted his father, but so many things did. It didn't take much for a son to disappoint a Two Star as driven as his father.

Real men don't cry. Only sissies pray.

"Screw you, General!" Taylor bellowed into the dearth of silence in this god-forsaken place, jolting to life the beast burrowed into his chest. *Never Father. Never Dad. Just yes, sir, General, sir.* Anger surged along with the pain.

His father railed on. *Quitters never win and winners never quit.*

The chant nagged, its paternal lesson ever taught. A thousand times he'd heard it in rain, in snow, in defeat and in tears, and a thousand times he'd cringed at the lack of empathy it invoked. Sheer desperation drove Taylor not to give in to despair. That's what got a man killed—what went on in his mind. More than anything he needed his father out of his head.

Shut the hell up, General!

Taylor sucked in another breath before he chickened out, before his weary mind came up with another one of his father's stupid pearls of wisdom. Just that fast, another tough man sprang to life in the darkness. Of all the unlikely guardian angels God could've sent, he'd sent Taylor's boss. Alex Stewart. And along with him came his single favorite admonition. *Think.*

"Easy for you to say, Boss," Taylor murmured, thankful for the steady advice but worried he might be losing his mind here at the end of his time. This damned small shed was getting crowded. "Guess I'd better get my sorry ass moving, huh?"

Without a doubt, Alex wouldn't have answered had he really been there. Instead, he would've spiked an impatient brow, offered a hand up, and pulled the sonofabitchin' arrow out with his bare hands.

If Alex could do it....

Taylor pushed sideways from the ground, a task all by itself when a guy's trying damned hard not to bump the three-foot arrow he's been impaled with. Sweat trickled into his eyes. Sucking in a careful breath, he pushed up from the dirt floor. And so it began. The final dance with Death.

"No-o-o," he growled at the shadows lapping up his legs and at the side of his peripheral. He refused to go down in the first round. Hell, no. Getting to his feet was just the beginning.

God Almighty, don't let me faint like some damn sissy girl. Not when I've come this far.

He faced the wall. The problem was the shaft extending in front of him was almost an arm's length and Taylor was weak. Only his fingertips and the feathered fletching at the farthest end of the shaft touched concrete. It would have to do. He steadied his weight, one foot forward, one back. He'd only get one chance.

Summoning the stern image of his father, the arrogant prick who right now would be taunting him and calling names if he were there, Taylor roared, letting loose the torment of years. "You. Son. Of. A. Bitch!"

He rammed the shaft into the wall, striving for the most direct frontal attack he could muster. Resistance vibrated up the wooden cylinder, but Taylor would not quit. He growled. He grunted. At last the arrow plunged deeper into his tortured body. It parted strands of muscle on its way through, layers of skin until—the tip pierced his back. And still he pushed his weight forward. The tip was not enough. The entire arrowhead had to follow, and with it, several inches of the shaft. The plan wouldn't work unless there was a considerable length of the shaft at his back.

Shifting his stance for added leverage, he eyeballed what was left of the shaft in front of him. A couple more inches ought to do it. He groaned at the sheer torture of the act and pushed his body closer to the wall. Finally. It was done. A good portion of the shaft now extended out his back, its evil twin wedged firmly between the concrete and his bloody heaving chest.

He brushed the sweat and tears off his face. Adrenaline roared over him, an avalanche and him the weakest twig in its ferocious path. He blinked in shock. Waves of unconsciousness surged hard and fierce against the physical torture of his accomplishment and the fear—because Taylor was very afraid.

The dance of death began in earnest. His life flashed through his mind, a lightning strike he couldn't control. With startling clarity his past unwound—his lonely childhood, all those angry awkward school years of never belonging. Always looking over his shoulder for someone to be there for him. Someone who wanted to be there for him. Like her.

A childhood friend he hadn't thought of in years smiled through the murky mist; a dark-haired girl with sparkling stars in her eyes. She seemed the only bright spot in the endurance test that had been his life. But what was her name? Was she even real? Reality eluded him, not that it mattered. She was just a ghost of things not meant to be. He'd given up on happiness so long ago. Why wonder now?

He flattened his palms to the wall and refocused. He needed to rest. Round two might end him. Bowing his head, he let the ways of a good sniper wash over him, let it wash the agony away. His breathing slowed. His heart rate decreased just a fraction, but enough. The chant of a steady man began anew. *Think calm. Think center. Think peace. You're a proven warrior. A winner. A fighter. It's just an arrow. It's just wood. Think calm. Think center. Think peace. You can do this.*

But could he? All strength had fled his legs. He sank to his knees. Then his butt, paying strict homage to the devil lodged in his chest. This next part he could do sitting down, so he settled, facing away from the wall. If nothing else, it would give him a shorter distance to fall.

He leaned into the wall just enough to know when the tip of the arrowhead behind him met concrete. That was important. Simply ramming the wall wouldn't achieve an end to the torture. The arrowhead had to hit the concrete at the perfect angle. With enough impact. Once ought to do it.

With an excruciating quarter turn of his torso to the right, he gripped his right elbow with his left hand, drew his right arm across his chest—and cried, because every last piece of him hurt like hell to move. The arrow never let up, never gave him one second of relief. Hopelessness choked his last ounce of courage, but it was now or never.

Almighty God, help me finish the race. Don't forsake me now.

He sucked in one last breath, squeezed his eyes shut, and leaned as far forward as he could. With all of his heart and soul, Taylor slammed his back to the cold concrete wall behind him.

SNAP! The arrow tip broke off behind him and—*Sonofabitch! It hurt!*

Sucking in more air, he wanted desperately to rest. To cry! But all he could do was shudder and rely on the wall to hold him upright. Shadows loomed over and around, taunting him to give up. To lie down and die. No way. Not yet. He was still breathing, wasn't he? There was still hope.

"Thank you, Father," he murmured weakly. In no way did he mean General Armstrong. Those days were gone. Dead and gone. But the instant connection to a greater Being sustained him. A good thing because this next step would take all he had left to give.

He ran his index finger along the arrow shaft in front of him to the fletching, igniting a burning vibration resounding in his chest. Pain was an unwelcome friend, but a friend nonetheless. Somehow, causing a small level of his own agony told him he had more control than he thought. And that newfound knowledge was all he needed.

He could endure. He would live. The arrow was broken. Half of it lay behind him in the dirt, the other half slick with blood before him. And waiting. But he could do it.

You're no son of mine, the General taunted yet again.

God, I wish, Taylor thought.

Right on cue, Alex showed up with another, *Think. Damn it. Think!*

"I am, Boss. Honest. I'm trying."

It did not escape Taylor that he was caught between two strong bullies, one who inspired men to follow while the other badgered, belittled, and denigrated those he was not strong enough to lead. And therein lay the reason Taylor left the Corps to follow Alex. With him there could be no try. There would be no fail. Only do. Only live. Only honor.

Taylor dusted his fingers and palms to the ground beside him. The stump of the arrow still embedded in his chest had become the rudder that would now determine his course. It all came down to this defining moment. He gritted his teeth, let out a mighty, "Oo-rah!" and wrenched the evil thing clean. Clear. Out!

Quaking with the mighty victory, he lifted the bloody shaft over his head like a winner—for all of one second. The damned arrow's departure brought as much pain as its arrival. His arm fell weak and useless to his side.

Somewhere in the far off world of shadows and ghosts, his father's bitter voice faded to black, gone again, like this fight against all odds was no big deal after all, especially since his son had done it. Of course. Daddy Dearest at his best. Show up. Sound off. And leave.

Alex growled a departing, *Well done, son.*

Taylor dropped the broken shaft and let the darkness swallow him whole.

Winning felt like shit.

Thank you for reading Rory!

Be sure to check out the rest of the guys and gals of Irish Winters' series: *In the Company of Snipers*

Other Irish Winters' books:

King of Hearts, Deuces Wild Series, *#1*

Joker Joker, Deuces Wild Series, #2

Smoke, Hearts and Ashes Series, *#1*

Ash, Hearts and Ashes Series, *#2*

Coming soon!

Seth, In the Company of Snipers, #17

One-Eyed Jack, Deuces Wild Series, #3

YOU are the key to this book's success!

Please tell other readers why you liked Rory and Ember's story by leaving an honest review at the retail site where you purchased it. Recommend it to your friends. Lend it. Most of all, enjoy it!

The best way to keep up with my new releases, giveaways, and actionable intel is to sign up for my spam-free newsletter at IrishWinters.com.

About the Author

Irish Winters is an award winning, Amazon best-selling author who, when she isn't writing, dabbles in poetry, grandchildren, and rarely (as in extremely rarely) the kitchen. More prone to be outdoors than in, she grew up the quintessential tomboy on a dairy farm in rural Wisconsin, spent her teenage years in the Pacific Northwest, but calls the Wasatch Mountains of Northern Utah home. For now.

She believes in making every day count for something, and follows the wise admonition of her mother to, "Look out the window and see something!"

Connect with Irish!
On Facebook: https://www.facebook.com/author.irishwinters
On Twitter: https://twitter.com/irishwinters1
Or at www. IrishWinters.com

www.ingramcontent.com/pod-product-compliance
Lightning Source LLC
Chambersburg PA
CBHW061039190726
48286CB00006B/1531